A Note on the Author

ALEX REEVE lives in Buckinghamshire and is a university lecturer, working on a PhD. *The House on Half Moon Street* is his debut, and the first in a series of books featuring Leo Stanhope.

@storyjoy

THE
HOUSE
ON HALF
MOON
STREET

ALEX REEVE

RAVEN BOOKS

LONDON · OXFORD · NEW YORK · NEW DELHI · SYDNEY

RAVEN BOOKS
Bloomsbury Publishing Plc
50 Bedford Square, London, WC1B 3DP, UK

BLOOMSBURY, RAVEN BOOKS and the Raven Books logo are trademarks of
Bloomsbury Publishing Plc

First published in Great Britain 2018
This edition published 2018

A catalogue record for this book is available from the British Library

ISBN: HB: 978-1-4088-9269-5; TPB: 978-1-4088-9270-1;
PB: 978-1-4088-9271-8; EBOOK: 978-1-4088-9268-8

2 4 6 8 10 9 7 5 3 1

Typeset by [insert typesetter name]
Printed and bound in Great Britain by CPI Group (UK) Ltd, Croydon CR0 4YY

To find out more about our authors and books visit www.bloomsbury.com
and sign up for our newsletters

For Michelle, for everything

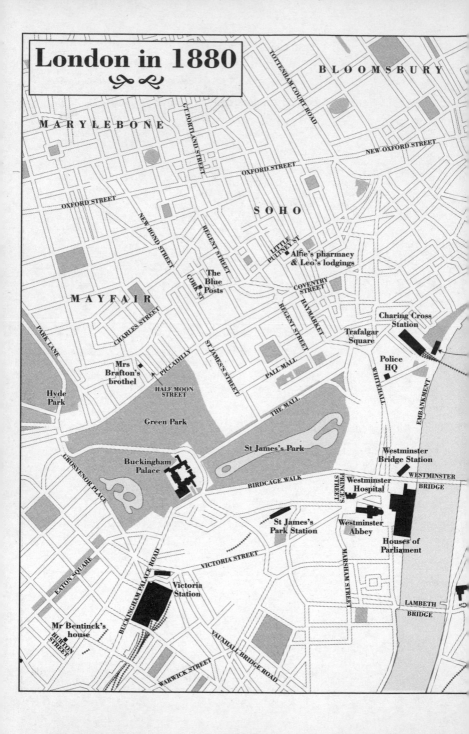

London in 1880

MARYLEBONE

BLOOMSBURY

TOTTENHAM COURT ROAD

GT PORTLAND STREET

NEW OXFORD STREET

OXFORD STREET

SOHO

OXFORD STREET

NEW BOND STREET

REGENT STREET

CORK ST

LITTLE PULTNEY ST

● Alfie's pharmacy & Leo's lodgings

The Blue Posts

COVENTRY STREET

MAYFAIR

CHARLES STREET

HAYMARKET

REGENT STREET

Charing Cross Station

Trafalgar Square

Mrs Brafton's brothel

● PICCADILLY

ST JAMES'S STREET

PALL MALL

Police HQ

PARK LANE

HALF MOON STREET

WHITEHALL

EMBANKMENT

Hyde Park

THE MALL

Green Park

St James's Park

Westminster Bridge Station

Buckingham Palace

BIRDCAGE WALK

PRINCE'S STREET

Westminster Hospital

WESTMINSTER

WESTMINSTER BRIDGE

St James's Park Station

Westminster Abbey

GROSVENOR PLACE

Houses of Parliament

VICTORIA STREET

MARSHAM STREET

EATON SQUARE

BUCKINGHAM PALACE ROAD

Victoria Station

LAMBETH BRIDGE

Mr Bentinck's house

BURTON STREET

VAUXHALL BRIDGE ROAD

WARWICK STREET

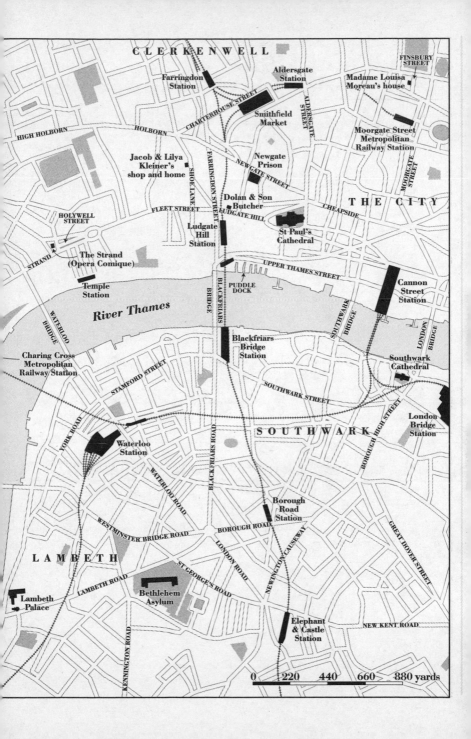

MR HURST WASHED THE blood from his hands in the
sink, and dried them, leaving pink smears on the towel.

It was a bone-cold January day and I had nowhere soft to
get any warmth. The examination room was in the bowels
of the hospital and tiled on all four walls, the only natural
light coming from high, frosted windows level with the
pavement outside. Mr Hurst didn't notice the chill, having
greater mass than me and doubtless retaining heat, much
like a chimneybreast, and being further warmed by the
inner glow of his renown. He was the best surgeon in his
field, acknowledged by everyone whose opinion counted,
although his patients were less likely to complain than
most, being already dead. His specialism was the washed-up,
pushed-off, dug-up and poisoned of London, all the poor
wretches whose cause of death was considered suspicious.
He cut them open and studied their innards, and I sewed
them up as good as new, more or less, and wrote down his
findings for the police.

'Drowned. River water in the lungs. Bloated. No signs
of a struggle. No bruising, stabbing or ligatures. This wasn't
foul play. Do you have all that?' I nodded, shivering, huddled
down in my chair by the foldaway desk. 'No doubt he was
drunken and fell off a bridge. One less fool in the world.'

He checked his pocket watch. 'Finish up, will you? I have a dinner.' He pulled on his coat, and was gone.

The dead fellow's name was Jack Flowers, formerly of Ludgate Hill, only twenty-six years old – my age or thereabouts. He'd been married six years. For a second I felt a pang of jealousy.

He was naked now, but had been found fully clothed floating off the quay at Limehouse with a bottle of Barclay's light ale in his jacket pocket, still stoppered. His wallet was saturated. I counted five pennies and a farthing, making the bargee who hauled him out unusually honest. There was a postcard as well, faded and damply translucent. No handwriting, but I could make out the picture of a beach and two ladies paddling under an ornate pier, with the words 'Southend-on-Sea' printed above. Poor bastard, dreaming of a day out in the sunshine, and ending up on a metal slab with his chest unfolding like the last bloom before autumn.

I wondered if he'd known what was happening in those final moments: the stink of the silt in his nostrils, the slap of the Thames chop against his face, the soot-black wharfs and distant people, out of reach, out of earshot, his arms growing weak as the cold embraced him.

'I hope you *were* bloody drunk,' I said.

My voice echoed off the walls and my breath fogged. Jack Flowers had no breath. Mr Hurst had taken out his lungs and weighed them – thirty ounces for the right and twenty-six for the left – and then stuffed them back into his corpse.

He reminded me of a bear, this Jack Flowers. He had sturdy knees, thick arms and curly black hair on his head that extended unbroken from his face down to his chest, gathering densely around his cock and swarming over his legs and feet. Even his toes sprouted little outcrops of hair.

I wrote down 'Male' on my folio.

I washed the retractor in the sink and hung it on the wall. I'd labelled each hook so everything had its place: callipers, bone saws, ruler, trocar, scissors, pliers, a row of scalpels of all different sizes. The water was freezing and my hands were puffy and sore as I dried them. I wished I had some gloves and a thicker waistcoat and a scarf I could wrap around my neck and tie a knot in.

I put his wallet and keys on one side to give to the widow. Everything else I piled in the basket to be burned or given to the poor, all except that bottle of ale, which one of the porters would probably have, not minding it had been in the pocket of a dead man bobbing around in the Thames. I rinsed it off in the sink, and noticed something written on the label. I squinted closer, and could make out a single word: *MERCY*. It seemed like an odd thing to write. The bottle was still full, so perhaps it was a plea to the demon drink, a final attempt at abstinence, or maybe an offering to God, a prayer for forgiveness. Either way, it hadn't been answered.

'Almost over now, Jack.'

The needle pushed easily through the pelt of his chest as I made the first stitch.

When I was finished I wheeled him back to the mortuary and went to find Pallett, the lad the police had sent for their copy of the report. In the early evening, the hospital was subdued. This was my favourite time, when most of the doctors and surgeons had gone home and the nurses could relax, with no one barking at them to fetch more splints or shine a light just there, no, not there, *there*.

I could hear voices from the men's ward, a low babble broken by an occasional whoop when three of a kind beat two pairs. They were waiting for their supper. Later on, when they'd had their fill, they would get livelier. Disagreements could turn nasty. It wasn't unknown for someone to die of something other than what they came in with, and end up in one of my reports.

I found Pallett at the nurses' station, which was a desk, a blackboard and a collection of cupboards behind the main entrance. Nurse Coften looked up and smiled. She had a calm gentility, as if she was a lost duchess from some faraway land.

'Is it him you want?' She pointed with her pen at Pallett, who was slouching against the wall looking uncomfortable. 'He's been mooning about waiting for Cecilia, Nurse Rasmussen that is.'

Pallett went red, right to his ears. 'I'm not,' he said. 'I have to wait somewhere, don't I?'

'He's got a uniform now,' she continued, angling her pen up and down to sum it up. 'He thinks she'll be impressed.'

It was new to him, but not new. His helmet perched atop his head like a cherry on a cake, and that jacket had been worn by a good many men. It was too small for his substantial frame, with mismatched buttons and a stain that might have been blood. But still, it marked his ascension from trainee to the ranks of Her Majesty's Constabulary at the third attempt, a day I'd begun to doubt would ever arrive. He was an honest lad but no prodigy. They didn't send their best men to fetch reports on drowned drunks from the likes of me.

I read it to him, which took all of one minute.

'The family's in the chapel.' Nurse Coften pointed with her pen again, studying us over the bridge of her spectacles. 'The widow will be wanting to know.'

'Isn't it the hospital's job to tell her?' Pallett protested. 'This wasn't a crime.'

'No. He was examined at the request of the coroner. He's your responsibility, not ours. What would Miss Rasmussen think?'

He wilted. 'But I don't know what to say.'

'Say it was an accident. Say he fell in the river and there was no crime. He wasn't clubbed on the head or robbed. That's what they'll want to know.'

'And give them these,' I said. 'Keys and wallet. And tell them he didn't suffer any pain.'

'Is that true?'

'Probably not, but they'll be comforted.'

He nodded and stroked his moustache. For all his size it was a feeble wisp of a thing. I could have done better myself. 'Drowned, not clubbed on the head, no crime, no pain.'

'That's it. Good man.'

He still didn't move. Nurse Coften and I exchanged a glance. 'I have paperwork,' she said.

I sighed and turned to Pallett. 'All right, I'll come with you, *Constable*, but you're doing all the talking. And take off that bloody helmet, for goodness' sake.'

Pallett did so, clutching it to his chest. 'Much obliged, Mr Stanhope,' he said. 'You're a proper gentleman.'

The chapel was at the back of the hospital, a white-walled room with a painted cross and pews that were creaky and prone to collapse, cast-offs from the Abbey across the road. A little boy was hurtling around, chased by his sister, and a younger lad was asleep, despite the din, curled up next to his mother. She was about my age, plump around the perimeter, wearing a shawl, spectacles and an expression of despair as she watched her offspring. She stood up as we arrived but still only reached my shoulder. We introduced ourselves and she thanked us for taking the trouble.

'He drowned,' Pallett announced. 'It was an accident. He wasn't clubbed on the head or nothing.'

She closed her eyes, and I could see she had a bruise on her cheekbone. 'So you're saying he just *fell in*?'

'Exactly,' said Pallett. 'He had these on him when they fished him out.'

He handed her the keys and wallet. She didn't even look at them. 'What about his satchel? He always had his satchel. Took it with him every day.'

'I'm sorry, no,' I said. 'It most probably sank.'

She nodded, watching her children racing between the pews. 'So that's it, is it? Nothing more to be done?'

'Were you expecting something else?'

She smiled thinly. 'He knew some bad people, that's all.'

'I assure you Mr Hurst found no sign of foul play. I wrote the report myself.'

'Then it must be true, mustn't it?'

I was a little shocked by her attitude. Relatives of the deceased normally just nodded mutely and escaped as quickly as they could. One or two had even called me *sir*, though I doubted that was part of Mrs Flowers's vocabulary.

'It was a tragic accident,' Pallett added, and for a moment I thought he'd exhausted his reserves of cheer, but then he remembered. 'He didn't suffer any pain, neither.'

She took a deep breath, and picked up her smallest child, still fast asleep. 'Jack was a lovely lad when I first met him, always joking, making me laugh. He worked at Smithfield's and I was in my father's butchers, so I saw plenty of him. In the summer we used to go over to Hackney with his brothers, and they'd go swimming in the ponds.'

'That sounds very pleasant,' I said, hoping it wouldn't continue for long. I was already thinking about the evening to come, and was too excited to be patient.

'It was. All afternoon, hours at a time.' She looked at me sharply. 'That's the thing. He could swim like a fish, could Jack.'

———

At the end of my shift, I left by the staff door on Princes Street, gathering my coat around me. When I had first started at Westminster Hospital I always used the main entrance, gazing in awe at the Abbey and the Houses of Parliament, feeling special to be standing in such a spot. But the route was longer and the pavement busier, and I soon fell out of the habit.

Even the stench was stifled by the cold. It wasn't far, a mile at most, and I almost ran, keen to get home and get ready, rehearsing in my head how the evening would unfold. I weaved through the crowds in Trafalgar Square, past poor Admiral Lord Nelson, stuck for ever on his column without even a stony-faced Lady Hamilton for company, and up Haymarket, dodging between the carriages at Charles Street, whose houses were glorious, with shiny black doors, pale stone pillars and hanging baskets of ivy.

Above Coventry Street, the townhouses decayed into crooked tenements abutting the pavement, with bars over the windows and heavy locks on the doors. Some workmen were tearing down a building to widen the road, sledge-hammering the walls and blowing great clouds of dust into the air. They were shirtless despite the weather, their britches held up by braces over their bare shoulders or pieces of rope tied around their waists. I had never taken off my shirt in public even as a child. My mother had suggested it once when we were playing in the garden on a hot and humid day, but my father put a stop to it. One of his parishioners might turn up and then what would they think? The Reverend Ivor Pritchard believed we should cover our nakedness. It was one of the few things we agreed on.

My room was above a careworn pharmacy on Little Pulteney Street in Soho, an area that almost succeeded in not being a slum. It was run by Alfie Smith, an ex-army man and widower, and his daughter of eleven, Constance, a sharp-eyed little thing, all skin and bone and too clever by half.

The shop was empty but for Constance, spinning on her stool, pushing off the counter with her hands and then brushing the dusty carboys of coloured water with her feet, leaving glossy trails on the glass. As soon as she saw me she leapt up, staggered dizzily and shouted: 'Powdered Coleoptera beetles!'

'Powdered what?'

'Coleoptera beetles. What's your guess, Mr Stanhope?'

'I don't know. Let me think.' I scanned the shelves. They were crammed floor to ceiling with pots and potions, but there was nothing to give me a hint. 'Heart palpitations?'

'Wrong.' She bounced up and down on her toes, grinning impishly. 'Do you surrender?'

'No, I still have two more guesses.' I narrowed my eyes at her, but she was unmoved. 'Could it be skin rash? No, no, that doesn't count. It wasn't a proper guess.'

'Yes it was. One left.'

'One? You're an inconsiderate girl. Some people have more respect for their elders. Some people are generous and give clues.'

'Stupid people, not me. One left.'

'All right. Is it ulcers?'

'No!' She clapped her hands together. 'It's blisters! It cures blisters. I win again. That's eight for me, five for you.'

'Don't gloat too soon,' I said, but without much conviction.

By my reckoning I would very soon owe her a cream pastry of her choice from the French tea shop on Regent's Street. I had won the first four straight while she was working from her own knowledge, especially as she leaned towards the morbid and infamous, like phosphorus, which cures bellyaches but also destroys the bones, and arsenic, which aids sufferers with malaria but is also a deadly poison. The pharmacy stocked both and I guessed them easily, but then she started consulting her father's pharmaceutical books for obscure remedies and soon overtook me. Powdered beetles? Good grief.

I climbed the stairs, thinking I would have to go to the laundry on Saturday morning. If I'd won she would've had to wash all my shirts, which seemed a decent wager when I made it.

My little room overlooked the yard. I had a chair by the window so I could read in the light, a wooden bed with a sunken mattress, a chest of drawers supporting an almost-complete Staunton chess set (the white queen having long since been deposed by her jealous subjects and replaced by a wine cork in a satirical act of rebellion) and a too-large mahogany wardrobe that had been adored by Alfie's late wife but he couldn't bear to look at any more.

I hung up my jacket and bowler hat, and tossed my shirt in the bottom of the wardrobe. This was the part of my day I hated most: peeling off the two yards of bandage that was wrapped around my chest. The material was spotted with old bloodstains where it had rubbed against the skin under my arms. Every day I tried to find a clean part of the fabric, and every day two new stains formed. My cilice, I called it, after the horsehair shirts monks wore as a penance for their sins, although it seemed to me I wasn't the sinner but the victim of God's cruel trick, and He should wear the dratted thing instead of me.

That man today, the corpse, Jack Flowers, probably woke up yesterday morning, got dressed and went out to work, or to look for work, and in the evening drank himself into a stupor, and never once had to consider his body; its hair, its skin, the size of its nose and the thickness of its fingers. He had no idea how fortunate he was. No such luxury for me. I had to think about my body all the time.

I dabbed myself with balm and winced at the sting of it, and then lay back on my bed, savouring the coolness. The gooseflesh was worth it.

After ten minutes of bliss, I dug out another cilice from the drawer and bound myself up, flattening my breasts from their God-given shape. Wearing only my underclothes, I was boyishly spare, lacking any noticeable contours. When I closed my eyes I could sense the way I should have been: the breadth of my shoulders, the length of my feet, the heft of my thighs, the weight of the *thing* hanging down between my legs. But when I opened them again I was still the same, a child's stick-drawing of a man, absent shape, absent strength, absent the very parts of a man that make him a man.

I pulled on my trousers, settling the roll of cloth I'd sewn into the crotch into place. I'd grown used to it there, the bulge as I sat down, the pressure of it against my thigh. In my early days I hadn't known how to position it, having almost no experience of the male physique. I'd seen my older brother Oliver naked just once as a boy, bursting in on him in the bath, standing in the doorway transfixed by the little fish swimming between his legs. I knew they got bigger as boys became men, but I didn't know how big, so I experimented with the length and breadth of the roll of cloth, resulting in some strange looks from passers-by and one offer of temporary employment from an unsavoury photographer.

I would wear a clean shirt tonight, pure white cotton, discovered by lucky chance the previous summer in a shop on Carnaby Street. On the most important night of my life I'd be wearing a shirt with the legend 'J. Kingsmill, Fourth Form' sewn into the collar.

Having rushed home, I now realised I was early. There was nothing to do but wait. I perused my little shelf of books, Dickens and Meredith mainly, but also Thackeray, Trollope and Butler, settling for my most comforting, my most familiar, a stiff, stained copy of *Barnaby Rudge*, situated at the end, easiest to hand.

Books were my education. At eleven years of age my father had looked me up and down, his gaze pausing disapprovingly on my small yet ineluctable chest, and declared that my studies were over. I was top of my class, even called upon to instruct the others when the teacher was away, yet I was evicted, forced to rely on the library we had at home, snatching time between learning to play the cacophonous violin and condemning seedlings to death in the flower beds. My father read widely and quickly on a range of topics, Hardy, Homer, Browning and Carlyle, Darwin and John Stuart Mill, as well as books on anatomy and ornithology – his other principal passion besides dogs and God, in that order – so I could tell a sparrow from a wren by the age of eight, but never mastered my mother's delights of music, planting and pruning. That I took so much after him was a source of sadness for her and bewilderment for me, but I don't think he noticed at all.

Finally, the hour struck seven, and it was time to leave the house. As I was opening the back door I heard Constance call out: 'Are you going to learn some more remedies, Mr Stanhope?'

'No, Miss Smith. I'm going to play chess. A game I can win at.'

But that was a lie. I did go west towards my chess club, hunched against the cold and spitting rain, but I carried on walking, just like every Wednesday, onwards into the tangled mews above Piccadilly.

The pavement was empty and the lamps were broken again. A dog overtook me on my way, trotting with an easy, muscular gait, tongue lolling. On his hind legs he would have been as tall as me. He seemed to know where he was going, and I followed him into the gloom, unable to keep myself from smiling. At that moment everything seemed possible. If I just keep putting one foot in front of the other, I thought, I will reach my heart's desire.

———————

Elizabeth Brafton's brothel was on Half Moon Street, which ran between the lofty affluence of Mayfair and the ceaseless noise and bustle of Piccadilly. The house was set back from the pavement behind an iron railing, squashed between grander buildings like a thin book on a shelf of fatter volumes. It didn't advertise itself. I had tried more commonplace dolly-houses before finding Mrs Brafton's, and they were uniformly appalling. The girls did what they were paid to do, but they didn't understand. Most attempted to treat me as a woman or just lay there in dumb confusion. One or two made an effort, working doggedly through their repertoire and crying out with pleasure rather as a news-seller cries out the title of his paper, with worthy intention but so much repetition it loses all meaning.

It was my friend Jacob from the chess club, a wise old Jew with special tastes of his own and a wasteful way with pawns, who suggested I should try Mrs Brafton's. Since then I'd been coming every week for nearly two years. Weekly was all I could afford, but if I'd been richer, if I'd had all the money in the world, I would've come here every day, every hour, just to be with my Maria.

Mrs Brafton was in the drawing room, richly dressed, one arm resting on the mantelpiece. She was a widow, perhaps forty-five years old, upright and unyielding, with russet hair pulled into a schoolmistress bun to hide her wisps of grey. Outside of this place you'd never guess what she was. She treated the girls like her children and liked to pretend that her customers were friends, come round to pay a visit. We all played along.

'Good evening, Mr Stanhope,' she said. 'How are you? Very well, I trust?' Her voice was melodic and refined. Sometime in her past, long before she became what she was now, she'd received an education.

'Yes, thank you.'

The Colonel was slumped and shrunken in a chair, little more than a pile of clothes and a bald pate, as smooth and pink as the meat of an uncooked fish. I doubted he'd ever been a real colonel, but she always called him that. He was the only customer she ever personally entertained, out of habit or pity. The girls, chattering starlings that they were, told me he was too old to perform these days and paid for nothing more than her womanly company. They said you could hear her knitting needles click-clacking through the bedroom door.

'Miss Milanes is waiting for you in the first-floor room,' she said, and smiled. She had a girlish mouth and a banker's eyes. I dropped two half-crowns into the willow-pattern bowl on the dresser.

On the stairs, little Audrey winked as she passed me with a customer in tow. He was out of breath, paunchy and reeking of sweat. His wife probably doted on him, this dank-browed shopkeeper in worn-out shoes, but she wouldn't do for him what Audrey would do. I'd been with Audrey once, on an early visit before Maria. The walls of her room were mounted with manacles, and there were ropes and buckles and canes with wickerwork handles on the shelves. Lithe and tiny as she was, she would cheerfully beat you raw for a florin, and for six shillings you could beat her in return. But that wasn't my preference. I was a traditionalist.

And I was in love. Today was the day I would prove it.

There were faint sounds from the other rooms: footsteps and low voices, a woman's laugh rippling into a lascivious giggle. I paused at Maria's door. I would soon be in her arms, and wanted to savour these final seconds. I had waited all week. *Maria Milanes.* Just the sight of her name in my diary was enough to make my stomach lurch, and the taste of it in my mouth was like plums in honey: *Maria Milanes.*

Her grandmother had been Italian, she'd once told me, and had pronounced their surname in three syllables, the last rhyming with 'tease'. But her late mother had thought this too foreign and reduced the syllables to two, the last rhyming with 'drains' or (and Maria hesitated at the word, as if I might not know the meaning of it) 'mundanes'. When I laughed and told her that 'mundane' has no plural, she pouted and turned away, only relenting when I insisted, nuzzling at the nape of her neck, that she could never be mundane, and was quite the most singular person I had ever met.

I knocked on her door, wondering if knocking was the wrong thing to do, or if my rat-a-tat-tat was too frivolous, too silly. It didn't matter. She opened the door and threw her arms around my neck.

'Leo,' she breathed into my ear. 'I love you, my Leo.' And then she kissed me.

2

'I'M GLAD YOU'VE COME,' she said. 'I worried all day you mightn't.'

'Of course I've come. I always do.'

'One time you didn't. I waited and waited.'

'I was unwell. I told you.' The monthly blood had come sooner than I'd expected, and I'd stayed at home, in physical and mental anguish. 'Is something wrong, my love?'

She sat on the edge of the bed kicking her bare heels against the frame: thump, thump, thump. Her room was quite different from Audrey's; no horrors here, just frilly lace on the curtains and bedspread, a gilded clock on the mantel and a dressing table with an oval mirror and a million bottles and jars. It was a pretty room for a pretty girl.

She was all curves, my Maria. Not one part of her was hard or bony, and her softness was always moving, in her cheeks when she smiled, in her breasts when she inhaled, in her calves as she kicked. Even her hair was forever alive, bouncing when she moved her head or tickling my face as she lay in my arms.

Her only imperfection, in her eyes though not in mine, was her stain. It spread from her nose down her cheek and across her chin like a spill of blackberry juice on white linen. She covered it with powder and the ribbons of her bonnet, and sometimes with her hands or even a fan, which was all the more endearing for being such a ridiculous affectation.

She shrugged, a little sorrowfully. 'It's just that I look forward to you coming. I miss you in between. The week seems so long, and I get worried if you're late. I know it's silly.'

'I'm not late.' The clock stood at seven-thirty precisely.

'How long do I have you for?'

'For ever.'

'No, really. How long?'

'Two hours, for tonight.'

I took her chin in my hand and kissed her mouth chastely, just a soft pressure, but she responded more strongly, with warm, wet lips and tongue. I pulled back, knowing the moment would soon arrive, relishing the anticipation.

'Not yet.'

There was a jug of ale on the dressing table. She poured two glasses and held one out to me. 'To Leo and Maria,' she said. 'For ever and always.'

We clinked and drank, sitting side by side on the bed. Over the past few months we'd spent hours in that spot while she talked and I listened, absorbed in her every word, flattered by her confidence, until I felt I wasn't with another person at all but was continuing an internal train of thought barely interrupted by the time we spent apart. She always chose the same side, with her stain away from me, though I told her endlessly it was delightful and she had nothing whatever to be ashamed of.

'There's something I want to tell you,' I said. 'An idea for the two of us.'

'What sort of thing? You mean for us now?'

I laughed and shook my head, and she seemed a little relieved. 'Nothing like that. More of a gift. We'll talk about it later.'

She touched my cheek and I could resist no longer. I kissed her again, running my hand down her back, and she stood up to undo the hooks on her bodice, half a smile on her face. Finally, she stepped out of her petticoats and was naked in front of me, leaning against me with her lips on my forehead. The hollow between her breasts smelled of sweat and ginger mint. She kissed me fiercely, and I felt her tongue touching mine and her teeth nipping my lips. Her hands were on my arms and then my shoulders, pulling urgently at my jacket and unbuttoning my shirt, and then she knelt at my feet to tug off my shoes, staring up at me with wide eyes, part invitation and part challenge.

She laughed at my avid expression, and stood up to unwrap my cilice.

'Oh Leo, you're bleeding.'

I flinched as she touched my sores with the end of her finger and then her tongue.

'Oh darling, it hurts you so.'

She went to her dressing table, bending over it in a way that made me want to burst, and sorted through her perfumes and ointments, searching for something. The jars were arranged around a doll I hadn't seen before, with staring, ceramic eyes and a red, kiss-shaped mouth. I'd always detested dolls; cold, counterfeit babies foisted on me by my aunts. Why would she have such a thing here, in plain sight?

She returned with a pot of balm, and dabbed my sores. I stroked her hair and she guided me backwards on to the bed and unbuttoned my trousers, so I was naked, a skeletal gargoyle next to her loveliness. I covered myself with my hands.

'Don't,' she said, and touched the hair between my legs.

On the pillow was my instrument, a baton of soft leather that could be fastened with straps around my waist and between my thighs. Maria loved to see me putting it on. She would grip it in place or sometimes put it into her mouth, and even though I couldn't feel it I was excited beyond endurance. She smeared some more balm on her hands and massaged it in, rubbing up and down.

'Maybe I should try wearing it one day?' she whispered.

The thought was too horrid to contemplate. 'I wouldn't want to see you like that.'

'But you might find it nice.'

'I would not.'

She grinned, and I sensed she was going to tease me some more, but when she spoke it was in a serious tone. 'Why do you love my body, but not your own?'

I pulled her gently towards me. 'Because your body's perfect.'

'No, really, why?'

I looked down at my anatomy, which was not something I generally chose to do. It was too skinny and angular to be a woman's body, the result of starving myself to avoid gaining a feminine shape. But it wasn't a man's body either. So what was it? Something detached from me, I supposed, a vessel for my brain and soul, needing maintenance and sustenance but having no greater value. I couldn't imagine anyone *loving* it.

'This isn't me,' I said. 'Not as I should have been.'

She took my cheeks in her hands and looked into my eyes. 'Leo, I wish …' She stopped and pondered, and then very softly kissed me. 'I wish you everything good in the world.'

But I had the feeling that wasn't what she had started to say.

———

When we were fully spent, I unstrapped my instrument and dropped it on the floor, out of sight. We lay together on the sheet, chests heaving, skin shining, listening to the heedless clatter of the carts and carriages outside. She shifted towards me and laid her head on my shoulder, one knee slung over my leg. I could feel her breath and the tiny brush of her eyelashes when she blinked. She smelled of us.

After a few minutes, she sat up and pulled the sheet around herself, her hair falling over her shoulders. 'Have you ever wanted to just run away, Leo? I mean, completely.'

'Many times. Why do you ask?'

'When was the first time?'

'The first time was … well, it was premature. I didn't succeed.' My fingers itched. I could almost feel the steadfast cloth of my brother's jackets and trousers hanging in his wardrobe.

'What happened? Tell me.'

'I was twelve. Mummy had taken Oliver and Jane out to lunch. I was being punished for something or other, made to stay at home and take dictation for my father's sermon. When it was all finished, he went out into the garden to practise and I was left alone in the vicarage.'

I hesitated. There were things I couldn't bear to explain, even to her.

On that day, my father had been outside, preaching in his loud baritone, exhorting the magpies and thrushes against their sins. There was no one else in the house. I just wanted to pretend for a little while, like dressing up. I knew it was wrong, but I couldn't resist.

I slipped one of Oliver's shirts off its hanger and put it on over my chemise, hugging it around myself. It was far too large and delightfully shapeless. Without stopping to think I threw off my skirts and pulled on a pair of grey flannel trousers and a blue blazer with black buttons. I rolled up the sleeves, shortened the braces and pushed my hair up under his tweed cap.

In the mirror, a boy with my long face and small eyes considered me. I'd never been pretty, but he looked *right*. When I smiled, he smiled, and when I shoved my hands into my pockets as I'd seen boys do, he did the same. His shoulders were straight and his chin lifted. He tipped his cap. He placed his feet wide apart and inhaled from an imaginary cigar, carelessly blowing smoke into the room. He looked into my eyes, and when I winked and he winked back, I realised that it wasn't me who was real and him a reflection, it was the other way around.

'I decided to leave the house,' I said to Maria. 'It was a new feeling. I could go anywhere, just jump on a train and become someone new.'

I would never have been brave enough. I would have been terrified of being caught, of what my parents would do, of the shame. I would never have dared.

But he did.

He was the same as any other lad, swinging his arms as he strolled along the pavement. He even tried to whistle. It was a revelation: no skirts to pick up, no bonnet to fiddle with, no harsh undergarments to pinch and scratch. On that short walk, something changed. I didn't have the words to describe it even to myself, but somewhere inside I knew that this unnamed boy, in his stolen trousers and gaping blazer, was me; me as I was meant to be.

I didn't have long to enjoy it.

'It turned out that Oliver had left Mummy and Jane to their lunch and met some friends. They came around the corner and saw me. They made me go back to the vicarage. It was a long time before I tried again.'

They chased me down the street, hooting as my hair spilled out. My brother just stood there with an expression of disgust on his face. When they got bored and left me, I ran home and got changed again, and wept for an hour on my bed until Mummy and Jane returned and made me watch them practising piano.

'Poor Leo,' Maria said, and took my hand in hers.

'We could run away, together, you and me, if you want to. I'll leave my job in the hospital and go wherever you like.'

'What a lovely thought.' She squeezed my hand, but showed no sign of taking me up on the offer. I would have done it in an instant. I would've left with her right there and then, out into the evening with only the clothes I had with me and no clue where our footsteps might carry us.

She got out of bed and pulled on her drawers. Normally, we would lie naked together in the half-dark and I would tell her about my week, the people I'd seen and spoken to. It was my favourite time, almost better than what came before. And we still had more than an hour.

'I wonder how you do it,' she said, perching on the edge of the mattress. 'You spend all day with dead things, touching them. It must be awful. They used to be people and now they're nothing.'

I sat up and put my arm around her, breathing her in as she rested her head on my shoulder. Her mother had died the previous year, and her grief still bubbled up from time to time.

'They're not nothing. I take care of them. We have to know what happened, how they died. We owe it to them and their family.'

'Was there a family today?'

'There was a widow and some children. They were too small to understand.'

I felt a clutch of pity for them, more now than I had that afternoon. Sitting there in the comforting cool, the loss of their father seemed oddly sharper. Even so, I couldn't shake off the suspicion that this sudden tenderness was one more betrayal by my ovaries.

'What was her name?'

I confess I struggled to recall. 'Um… Flowers. Her husband was Jack. He drowned. What is it?'

I thought I knew all her expressions, from helpless laughter to wrenching grief, but this one was new to me. Her face was blank, as if her thoughts were elsewhere, and she wasn't seeing the room or the bed or anything.

She shook herself, and was my playful Maria again.

'Jack Flowers. What a sweet name.'

'Maybe. Mr Hurst thought he was a drunkard. He had a bottle of ale in his pocket.'

'In his pocket? So they have clothes on when you get them? I didn't know.'

'Only when they arrive. The mortuary assistant undresses them, or I do.'

She widened her eyes. 'Ladies, too? You must see all their small-clothes and everything. Is that what my gift is, a dead lady's petticoat? That's not a good sort of gift.'

'How many sorts are there?'

'Ones I like, ones I don't. Ones that are really for the gentleman who's giving it to me. I get those a lot.'

She grinned, teasing me again, but I disliked mention of her customers, even by implication. I didn't count myself one of them.

'Better than that, much better. I thought we could go to the theatre together. It's a musical production called *HMS Pinafore*. I have tickets.' I got out of bed still naked in my excitement, and fetched them from my coat pocket. 'It's supposed to be wonderful. I'd be honoured to take you. Will you come?'

'Oh Leo, you can't mean it. You know how Mrs Brafton is, with her rules. She doesn't like me as it is.'

'Then we won't tell her. It's on Saturday, a matinee performance, two o'clock.' I put one of the tickets into her hand and closed her fingers over it. 'The theatre, nothing more.'

She examined the ticket. 'Leo …'

'There are songs. You love to sing. I hear you sometimes.'

'You know why. I was born under a stage. It's in my blood.'

'Exactly. You sing well enough to be on the stage your-self. One day you could be.'

She laughed and pointed at her stain. 'Silly! How can I, with this?'

'No one would care about that. They'd hear you and… well, anyway, please say you will. We'll wear our best clothes. We'll be just like other people.'

She sighed. 'Oh, Leo.'

'Please.'

'Very well. I'll go with you. Thank you.'

She kissed me, and it meant more than anything else we could have done together, being the simplest of things: the kiss of a woman for her lover. She crawled into my arms again, and I was aware of nothing else until she was shaking me awake.

'Leo! It's almost ten! You have to go.'

I was bleary, struggling to surface from my dream; we had been together in our own home in the early morning, the light slanting against the angles of the walls, with nothing to do all day except sleep and read and make love.

She shook me again. 'Mrs Brafton will be angry with me.'

I yawned. 'She might not have noticed the time.'

Maria held my face in her hands. 'She will have. I have another customer, Leo. Please don't be cross. You know what I am.'

'Yes, you're the loveliest girl in the world.' But it was a hollow compliment, and she didn't smile.

I got out of bed and pulled on my trousers, struggling to bind my cilice and hopping around the room with my shoes. I kissed her as I left. 'You'll meet me there? The Opera Comique on the Strand. Saturday at two.'

'I will.'

'Say it. Please.'

'Opera Comique. Saturday at two.'

'You're perfect. Remember I love you.'

Downstairs, Mrs Brafton was seated in an armchair reading a pamphlet, spectacles balanced on the end of her nose. The Colonel had gone and three other men were waiting. One of them, tall and well-dressed with a neatly trimmed beard, glowered at me.

Mrs Brafton pursed her lips. 'You're late, Mr Stanhope. It's not good enough, of you or Miss Milanes.'

'Please, don't chastise her. It was my fault. I fell asleep.'

'Asleep?' She looked at me as if I was mad, and one of the gentlemen rolled his eyes.

'I can compensate you.'

She waved the suggestion away. 'It's not a question of that.' She softened, just a little. 'But it mustn't happen again. Do you understand?'

She glanced at the tall gentleman, who nodded curtly and started up the stairs.

I watched him go with a rising hatred. I heard Maria open the door to him, and the low murmur of their voices. I wanted her to spit in his face and tell him she would never, ever be with anyone but me. I wanted her to scream so I could run up and pull him away from her, and throw him down the stairs. I wanted to beat him bloody until he crept from the house and shrivelled in the gutter with the horse piss. I wanted to take her hand and run away with her to a new life in some far-off town where no one would know anything about us, and we would be together.

Mrs Brafton cleared her throat. 'The same time next week, Mr Stanhope?' She had her black leather appointment book open.

'That gentleman –'

'Is her next customer, Mr Stanhope.'

If I didn't leave she would call Hugo, the doorman and general custodian, who was three decades older than me but still as strong and fierce as a rhino. He loved to stand among his hives in the garden wearing a vest, rain or shine, and lift dumb-bells, one in each hand, while bees crawled across his formidable forearms.

'Yes, of course. Same time next week.'

Out on the pavement, I kept my face down. Sometimes Maria would tap on the window and blow kisses to me as I walked away, but not today. I couldn't bear to look back and see some dreadful silhouette. I pulled my coat tight and strode into the darkness.

When I got home, I realised I didn't have my keys. In my rush to get dressed they must have dropped out of my pocket in Maria's room. But I couldn't go back for them. I couldn't face Mrs Brafton again.

I threw pebbles up at Alfie's window and begged him to come downstairs and let me in, which he did, eventually, muttering about drunk lodgers who didn't give a damn about other people's sleep. But he didn't really mean it, and patted me on the shoulder and wished me goodnight before he crept back up the stairs.

I sat at the table in the back room surrounded by the usual boxes of pharmacy stock, and rested my head on my arms. I hated what she did for a living, but without it I would never have met her. I told myself it was just her body I had to share, just her body, nothing more. It was me she was meeting at the Opera Comique on Saturday at two o'clock. It was me she would be eating toffees with in the stalls. And afterwards, it would be me who took her home and talked to her of this and that, perhaps brushing fingers as we walked.

It was me she loved.

3

ON THURSDAY EVENING I went to my chess club. This was my manly life: I had squeezed out of the acute-angled range of a girl's existence for the embracing obtuseness of masculinity, only to find much of it still out of bounds. I would have loved to try kicking a ball to a team-mate or wrestling an opponent to the ground, but I could not. I would be exposed instantly. But I could play chess.

The club was above the Blue Posts on Cork Street, popular with rag-trade men and printers who spilled out on to the pavement with hands cupped around their pipes and tankards lined up along the windowsill. I arrived at the same time as another member whose name I didn't know, and he pushed through the crowd ahead of me.

Upstairs, the smoke stung my eyes and caught in my throat, a miasma hanging over the players as they hunched by their boards, plotting. Jacob was already engrossed in a game with Berman, a student with slick hair and an annoying habit of moving a piece and holding on to it, examining the board from every angle before letting go. Jacob yawned and flicked his cigar, scattering ash on to the jacket he wore every day without fail, regardless of rain or sunshine, until it was indistinguishable from him, stinking of smoke, beer, whisky and the metallic tang of his jewellery shop.

Berman was an average player at best and got flustered with me standing there, quickly throwing away his knight on an ill-advised quest to capture Jacob's rook. What game he had deserted him after that, and Jacob took his other knight and a bishop in quick succession, poring over the board like a pampered old bulldog with a juicy bone. Within ten minutes Berman had retired sulkily to the bar.

Jacob ordered two pints from the lad whose job it was to run up and down the stairs, laid out the board and made a fuss relighting his cigar and noisily sucking on it. He loved to keep me waiting, but I wasn't concerned. All this was a prologue to his favourite game, which wasn't chess, although we often played that at the same time.

It was my turn to be white. I moved my pawn to king four, and Jacob made a hissing sound between his teeth. 'Always so conventional, Leo.'

I waved a hand at his side of the board. 'You can move out your knight first if you want. Go ahead, challenge my convention.'

He mumbled something and then moved out his pawn in a Sicilian defence. When I rolled my eyes he shrugged: 'You're white. I had to follow your lead.'

I moved my queen's knight and he moved another pawn and sat back in his chair. 'So?' he said. 'What's the news?'

'It was wonderful. Maria said yes.' I couldn't help but smirk at him.

'And you'll take her to see the Gilbert and Sullivan, will you? All that singing and prancing. My Lilya loves it, for some reason.'

I moved my other knight and we played in silence for a while, exchanging swift, familiar moves. The game was still finely poised when the boy arrived with our drinks on a tray. Before I'd even taken a sip, Jacob ordered two whiskies and another ale for himself.

He sat forward and spoke in what he thought was a whisper. 'And she understands? About you?' Aside from Maria, Mrs Brafton and her girls, there was only him – and one other – who knew I wasn't born a man.

'Of course. How could she not?'

He shrugged. 'I don't know what you do with her, how it works, what goes where. I've been married twenty years. More. How much *novelty* do you suppose there still is? It's like putting on old socks.'

'Lilya's a fine woman.'

'Yes, yes, of course, a fine woman, a fine wife. She suffers me, for the most part.'

'She's a saint.'

'Ha! You see? The child of a minister and still you know nothing. We don't have *saints*.' He drained his tankard and picked up mine. This would be his fourth at least. 'But if we did,' he continued, 'then you're right, she would be one. Lilya, patron saint of tolerance.'

'Check,' I said. This was often the way. While sober he was methodical and cautious, but later in the evening he would become reckless, rampaging forward and allowing me to pick off his pieces.

He blocked with a pawn, protected by his queen, and I moved up my knight. He castled his king but I had expected that and put him in check again with my bishop. He stared sourly at the board. 'You're a better player these days. I used to be able to win sometimes, but not now. How long has it been? A month at least.'

'Last time you were sober.'

'It's no fun playing sober. Anyway, this girl, this … Maria.' He licked his lips. 'You think she cares about you?'

'Is it so unbelievable?'

'Ha! Well, there's a question.' He was starting to slur his words. 'You're not what girls dream of, my friend. Not even a whore. I'm sorry, but there it is. And there's no need to look like that, you know it's true.'

I set out the board again in silence. I would be black this time. He moved his king's rook pawn and I responded with my queen's pawn, sipping my whisky. If he wanted to make such silly moves, this would be over all the more quickly.

He ordered two more whiskies and a bowl of nuts.

'She does care about me,' I said.

He grimaced. 'Maybe. Who knows what goes on in a woman's mind?'

He started to laugh, guffawing harder and harder until he was beating the arm of his chair with his palm. He glanced at me and laughed harder still, almost silently, going red, until finally drawing in a huge gasp.

'Who knows what goes on in a woman's mind?' he repeated. 'Not you, strangely enough.' He started chuck-ling again, re-amused by his own joke.

'Very funny.'

'I'm sorry.' He wiped his eyes with his sleeve. 'I'm an old man and you are a young *romantic*, in love with a girl. What could be more natural or more foolhardy?'

'We love each other.' ·

'And you want to rescue her, yes? Take her away from that wicked life.'

He was right, but I wasn't going to admit it. 'We're only going to the theatre.'

'Yes, a *matinee*. Bah! It'll be full of children.' He waved a hand. 'No chance of a hand on her knee at a *matinee*. How much are the tickets?'

'What does that matter?'

'Ten shillings each, yes? You're overpaying. For a quarter of that you can love her whenever you want and never have to buy her dinner, or marry her, or sit through Gilbert and bloody Sullivan.' He laughed again.

I was close to just getting up and leaving, or tipping over the board. If he'd been younger I might even have hit him, which I'd never done to anyone. 'You're obnoxious when you're drunk.'

'I will save you the trouble,' he declared, ignoring me. 'I will buy the tickets from you and take the sainted Lilya. Lucky for you I'm not strict about the Shabbat. I will suffer the awful *Pinafore* for your sake.'

'Just play, will you?'

I won that game too, with a kind of cold anger, tearing through his pawns and trapping his queen, taking two of his bishops as she struggled, and ending it with two long thrusts of my rooks.

He stood up, unsteadily. 'Piss,' he said, and stumbled towards the door.

I laid out the board again and waited. Portas-Meyer, a better player than me, invited me for a game, but I declined, expecting Jacob to come back at any minute. I wanted to beat him again. When he didn't reappear I reluctantly went down to the privy to find him, just to check he was still breathing. I wasn't certain which outcome I would prefer.

I found him in a cubicle with his trousers around his ankles and his chin on his chest, snoring gently. I slapped his face, harder than was strictly necessary, and he opened his eyes.

'You should go home,' I said.

He stood up, swaying, and I thought he might vomit on me, but he swallowed hard and seemed to get his stomach under control.

'You're right,' he mumbled, and tried to walk, but his trousers were still down and he fell against the wall, banging his forehead on the corner. He touched the graze with his fingers, staring at the smear of blood as if it belonged to someone else.

Outside, the bitter cold made me light-headed. I'd drunk more than I'd intended and eaten almost nothing. Jacob's house on Shoe Lane was well over a mile away.

He was attempting, unsuccessfully, to pick up his hat from the pavement.

'You mustn't be offended,' he said with deliberation. 'I can be inconsiderate sometimes. I want what's best for you, you know.'

'I know.'

He waggled his finger at me. 'Don't lie to me. You're upset.'

Upset; such a feminine word. I wasn't upset, I was *angry*.

'I'll walk home with you.'

He shook his head. 'Not necessary. I'm quite capable.'

'You're old and drunk.'

'Well, I can't stop you, can I? And I do have responsibilities. Seven children.'

'Four of them have already left home.'

And so we walked through the pools of lamplight, me with my hat pulled low, hands deep in my pockets, and Jacob veering from side to side with his shirt untucked, one brace lolling around his knees.

'I've nothing against whores,' he said after a while.

'Obviously.' It was Jacob who'd recommended me to Mrs Brafton.

He jabbed a finger at me. 'Now who's judging who?'

'Not at all. Keep walking.' I could feel the flicking of rain on my face and, more urgently, was starting to need the privy myself. I should've gone back at the club, but had been preoccupied and, unlike Jacob, I couldn't just stop and piss up against a wall.

'What else could I do? Seven children already and Lilya as she is. It was all for her sake. Anyway, it's in the past. She's too old now, so we can rut like foxes and never get an eighth.'

I walked a little faster, forcing him to scamper.

We were passing the flower market, all closed up, but it smelled heady even in winter. Some boys were playing a game between the columns, skittering stones across the paving. They paused and watched us, almost invisible against the grey.

'It's just that you can't trust a whore. I'm not condemning them, it's what they do. They deceive for a living. They whore with their mouths as well, you know.' He stopped and chuckled, leering at me, his beard glistening in the rain. 'You know what I mean. They tell you what you want to hear.'

'You don't understand how it is with us.'

'I'm sure you're right.' He took my hand in his. He was slurring and bilious but, even so, it was a strangely sweet gesture. 'You've given your heart to this girl, Leo, but she may not be what you think. And you don't take it well, my friend. Old men are always trying to charm ladies and they treat us with contempt. We come to expect it. We're grateful if the truth was told. But you're not made that way.'

I let go of his hand, a little sharply. 'How am I made?'

He shook his head. 'I don't mean that. Not *physically*. You've done it before, that's all I'm saying. You have a history of stupidity.' I walked on and he hurried to catch up. It was properly pouring now, and umbrellas were sprouting in people's hands. I was getting soaked, and my need for the privy was increasingly pressing. 'I hope it's different this time. I pray.' He opened his arms and shouted up into the rain. 'Let it be different for Leo this time! He deserves to be happy!'

'Be *quiet*, Jacob.'

'Well, why not? It's possible. Whores can't be whores for ever, can they? What do they do afterwards, eh? They settle down with some idiot like you, and no one's any the wiser. Half the women in London were probably whores at one time.' A gentleman passing by with his wife stared at Jacob, but he was oblivious. 'Only, hold something back, will you, Leo my friend? Just in case there isn't a wedding and a bower of roses.'

'You don't understand. She's … damn you, Jacob.' How could I possibly explain to him what Maria and I meant to each other? I stopped walking, feeling a sob rise in my throat. I swallowed it down, breathing through my nose. My head was throbbing, my armpits were aching from the cilice and my bladder was bursting. I couldn't abide the thought of losing control. 'You can find your own way from here.'

'Leo? What's wrong? Where are you going?'

I didn't answer him. I was desperate for home.

When I finally lay down on my mattress to go to sleep, my last thought was this: thirty-eight hours to go, and we will be together.

4

THE ENTRANCE TO THE Opera Comique wasn't near as swish as the Savoy or the Olympic, being little more than a wood-framed canopy and a propped-up hoarding of a jolly admiral holding a telescope to his eye. I had passed it two dozen times before, but had never been inside. Now, standing there half an hour early in my best trousers and shirt, with clean hair, freshly polished shoes and a box of toffees in my hand, it was more down-at-heel than I had remembered, and I wondered if it was good enough for Maria.

I was planning to invite her for a stroll down to St James's Park afterwards. There was a bird house by the lake filled with exotic waders and brightly coloured ducks, and for a farthing we could buy a bag of grain to feed them. I hoped there would be time. I hoped it might become a regular arrangement. I couldn't afford the theatre every week, but a walk in the park was free, and we could touch and talk and shelter under the trees when it rained, and occasionally steal a kiss when no one was watching.

I paced up and down, too excited to stay still. This was my first time. Never before had I enjoyed the simple pleasure of courting a girl.

And if I could do this, who knew what else was possible?

The crowds started to gather on the pavement. Jacob had been right; there were lots of children with their parents, but also some couples and a large group of women, chattering at high speed. One of them had seen the play before and was trilling a chorus to the others, waving her arms and acting out the different parts. I searched among the faces. I wanted to see her eyes and her smile as she arrived.

At a quarter to the hour a young flash in a waistcoat opened the door and started ushering everyone inside.

'You coming in, mate?'

'I'm waiting for someone.'

'Your lady's not shown up? It happens.'

I took a dislike to the man, and decided my time would be better spent searching for Maria.

I hurried down Holywell Street. The pavement was scanty and crowded with men gazing into the windows of lewd bookshops, shaded by the overhang of buildings tilted so far forward they seemed about to spill their licentious contents on to the street below. There was no sign of Maria.

By the time I got back to the Opera Comique, the usher was about to shut the door. She might have gone in while I was searching for her, so I handed him my ticket and rushed along the passage and down the steps.

The curtain was just rising. The stage showed a merry dockside scene crammed with coiled ropes and wooden barrels, and behind them the sun in the sky and sails on the horizon. The actors came on and started singing, but I wasn't listening. I pushed through the shrubbery of knees to my seat, ignoring the sighs and tuts, searching every face for Maria.

The song finished and the sailors started up a cheery conversation. The audience was laughing. I looked back at the door, supposing she might be about to arrive, flustered and apologetic. I would forgive her, of course.

The woman sitting on the other side of the empty seat offered me a pitying half-smile, and the space between us took on a vast scale, a flagrant cavity in the otherwise packed theatre. I slumped down and watched the play, and even started to feel sympathy for the downtrodden Ralph, willing to fight for his beloved but kept from her by petty rules and conventions. It was a feeble comparison and I despised myself for snivelling.

When the lights came on for the intermission, everyone stood up. There was no room to breathe. All these people had someone to talk to, someone to share their opinions with. But after only half the performance I was already confident that true love would prevail through some unexpected turn of events, and Ralph and whatever-her-name-was would be wedded, and there would be a lot more rip-roaring songs. I couldn't bear it.

I escaped down the hill to the Embankment and sat on a bench staring out at the Thames, which was as black and cold as wrought iron. It was nothing like the play; gulls picking at shellfish, boat engines hacking, the stench of tar in my nostrils, crowds of people with dour faces, and everything covered with the soot and grime of London.

My times with Maria were brief glimpses into a life I could almost have, crueller for being so tantalisingly close. And I was foolish enough to hope. Not a plan or even an intention, but a *hope* that Maria and I might one day live together as normal people. I didn't yearn for greatness or wealth, just the kind of homely mundanity that every other man takes for granted: socks to hang by the fire, a book to read, a dog to walk and the sound of Maria's laughter every day of our lives. Was that too much to ask?

Perhaps I was deceiving myself. Over the years I'd learned to pass as a man, keeping my voice deep, sitting with my knees apart and my elbows out, never putting my hands on my hips. But a natural man had a cock that wasn't attached with buckles, and a bellowing laugh. He didn't have to flatten his chest with a cilice or pad out his shoes with newspaper.

The Thames grew even darker as the sun dipped, and mist lingered on the water. I could almost feel the weight of my clothing pulling me down between gasps, the biting cold of it, the sweep of the current tugging me. I could taste the engine oil shimmering on the surface like tarnished copper.

But these thoughts weren't mine, not now. They were just echoes from years ago. I toyed with them, holding them up for scrutiny and then putting them back, feeling hysterical and foolish. After all, if every fellow whose girl broke a promise threw himself into the Thames, Mr Hurst would be a very busy man indeed.

While I had still been a porter, a patient in the women's ward had been found to possess male parts despite having long hair and wearing a silk dress and a boned corset. We were all shocked, even me. I went to visit this pale and desolate boy, and he introduced himself as Eliza. I held out my hand, but he couldn't shake it because he was tied by his wrists to the bedstead.

'I'm not really frightened,' he said. 'I'm a butterfly, and we're not meant to live for long. Better to be a butterfly for a day than a caterpillar for ever.' It sounded like something he'd practised in his head.

It was the first time I'd met anyone with anything like my affliction, or indeed known that such a person could exist. I had the urge to tell him about myself. I wanted to know if he felt the same, if he spent all his time watching every movement, listening to every tone of his voice. I wanted to know if he sometimes grew melancholy too, exhausted by such unceasing vigilance.

But the risk was too great, and anyway I never got the chance. The police came for him and put him into a men's prison and later into a mental asylum, according to the *Pall Mall Gazette*, where the doctors ran electricity through his skull and might have drilled into it as well if he hadn't declared himself gratefully and for ever healed.

That would be my future too, if I was caught.

I was fifteen when I became the male I should have been all along. A wealthy family had recently arrived in Enfield, and everyone was talking about them. The gentleman had taken a share in the jute factory at Ponder's End, and was apt to drop pound notes on to the collection plate with a kind of casual flourish. My father did everything he could to impress the man, delivering sermons on the value of industry and the importance of an orderly society, and my mother invited them round for tea, including the son, who was a year or two older than me. She made the two of us sit together on the sofa, and kept throwing us sidelong glances while the men discussed the shortcomings of the Liberal government. The son was narrow-faced and ungainly, but had an amusing way of rolling his eyes when his father wasn't looking. I quite liked him, and would gladly have spent more time with him, but the idea of *kissing* or *marriage* was abhorrent. Pure madness.

It was clear I had to start my new life as a man as soon as I could.

I'd been helping some local children with their times tables for threepence each, and when I'd saved enough, I walked down to the market and bought myself a cap, a pair of britches, a white shirt and a sturdy pair of lace-up shoes, all in good condition. I couldn't afford a decent coat, but I found a tatty one with torn lining and two buttons missing, and haggled the price down to sixpence.

Now, all my family were out. I sat at the bathroom mirror and cut my hair with scissors, and then crept downstairs with my little bag in my hands. I'd packed five books and a silver rose brooch my mother had given me. Everything else I left behind. It would be hard, but I was sure I could do it, and there was work in London, so I'd been told, for young men of intellect and fortitude. This was the beginning of everything.

It was a freezing-cold November day and there was frost on the windows. I thought of my buttonless coat, which I wouldn't even be able to do up. My father had bought himself a Sunday-best one a few weeks before, with big black buttons, and I considered stealing it, but he was over six feet tall and broad around the belly, and I wanted nothing of his. Nothing except those big, black, beautiful buttons.

I took the scissors and cut two of them off, leaving ragged tufts of cotton sticking out. I sewed them on to my own coat with thread from Mummy's sewing box, and they looked very fine indeed.

There was a noise at the front door, people coming into the hall, taking off their shoes. I slipped into the kitchen, easing the back door open just as Mummy came in. At first, she didn't recognise this slim young man with his cap in his hand. Her mouth hung open, on the brink of shouting for someone to come, until realisation descended.

She reached out to my shorn head. 'Lottie … my darling. Who did this to you? What happened?'

I hadn't wanted her to see me. I knew I would be tempted to stay, for her sake.

'I cut off my hair.'

She half-smiled and examined me again, as if I was tricking her and had a ponytail tucked under my collar. 'I don't understand.'

'I'm sorry, Mummy. I have to go.'

She frowned, still lacking any comprehension. 'Lottie, you contrary girl. Go and get changed this minute. Quickly, upstairs before your father comes home.'

She was already in motion towards the door, as if she could return everything to normal just by wishing fervently for it to be so; my hair would grow back, these clothes could be thrown away, my momentary silliness forgotten, if only I would just *do as she told me*.

But I couldn't.

I put my hands in my pockets in a deliberately masculine gesture, and to hide that they were shaking. 'This is who I am.'

'Upstairs, *quickly*. He'll be home any minute.'

'I know. I have to leave before that.'

'Leave? What are you talking about? Where are you going?' Her fingers were twitching as if she might unpick my clothes right there in the kitchen before this insanity went any further.

'Anywhere. I can't live here.'

I was almost weeping, but not quite. If I wept, I would have to embrace her and then I wouldn't be able to go. I had to be resolute, even though it was unspeakably cruel, leaving her here with my father, who had so little to say to her, and Jane, whose attention was already far away, planning a family of her own.

'You can't leave. You're just a girl.'

Just a girl. I smiled at that, aware of how callous it must seem. She was more of a child than I was, an innocent, married to my father at seventeen, passed to him by her own father like a sickly foal that wasn't expected to last. She'd defied expectations by surviving, and had somehow managed to remain untouched by it all, determinedly unaware of her husband's indifference.

She implored me. She told me to stop being so selfish, and that I was upsetting her even though I knew full well how delicate she was. How could I be so unkind, and on a Saturday as well, when we should all be together as a family? And when I told her that I had always been male underneath my skin, she sat down on a chair with her hands over her face and told me that God had made us all and we couldn't *choose*. Even to think about such things was lunacy, idiocy, *blasphemy*. Why was I hurting her this way?

I almost stayed. It would have been so easy; she could have snicked off those buttons and got to sewing while I

46

dashed upstairs to change and find a bonnet to hide my shame. In half an hour we could have been doing a jigsaw puzzle together in the parlour.

And then what? I would never be anything other than what I was. If I didn't leave now, I would be leaving in a week, or a month. I had no choice.

I put on my cap and picked up my bag.

Jane had come into the room, and was glaring at me with her arms folded. 'I never thought you'd actually do it,' she said.

Mummy was barely able to speak through her tears. 'Tell her, Jane. She'll listen to you. Tell her she can't leave.'

'I have to,' I said, sounding more calm than I felt.

'Wait one minute,' said Jane.

'What for?'

'One damn minute.' I'd never heard her swear in front of Mummy before.

Jane left, and Mummy and I stared at one another. When Jane came back she pressed something into my hand. 'From the collection plate.'

'You mustn't,' I said. 'This is five pounds. He'll be livid. And I stole his buttons for my coat.'

Instinctively, Mummy inspected my stitching.

'You see?' I said, taking her hand in mine. 'I did learn something after all.'

'Keep the money,' said Jane. 'If you're truly going, then go now.'

She was furious with me. But she was still my sister.

And she was right, it was best not to meet our father. Any fear I'd ever had of him was long since scabbed over and peeled back and scabbed over again, until it was no more than scar tissue, but Mummy would never be able to withstand him. I didn't know what he would do if she put herself between us.

At the last, I couldn't stop myself from drawing Mummy to me, but it wasn't the embrace we would normally have shared. It was a brief and narrow-elbowed thing.

'You know you've always been …' *My favourite* she had been going to say.

'I'll write to you as soon as I get there. I promise.'

But I never did. At first I didn't know what to say, and then the weeks turned into months and it seemed too late, and then it really was. She died four years later, her typhoid-weakened chest finally giving way to pneumonia. Jane told me that my father had barely visited his wife in her last few weeks, preferring to spend his time doing good works in the town, and Mummy gave up asking for him. But she never stopped weeping for her little Lottie, her darling, difficult daughter, and begged them to find me, even right up to the end. But they hadn't known where I was at the time, and maybe hadn't tried as hard as they might.

For a while after that, I was not myself.

Ever since that day I had known that no matter how lost I became, no matter how desperate, I could always locate my North Star, my guiding light, in my absolute hatred of the Reverend Ivor Pritchard. He was living in Hampstead now. I could picture him settling down in his armchair with a Young's Concordance and a briar pipe, facing the fireplace, a dog lying loyally at his feet. Perhaps a cold-meat supper, if one of his parishioners had been so kind.

And somehow that settled it. I wiped my eyes. Nothing was ever achieved by giving up at the first obstacle. I would persist with Maria. I would ask her again and again until she was ready to come to the theatre with me.

And one day, who knows?

We were meant to be together. I was certain of it.

5

ON MONDAY MORNING, THE clock hadn't yet struck six when I came downstairs. Alfie was in his dressing gown adding up his takings at the counter, his flickering candle casting peek-a-boo shadows behind the packages and bottles on the shelves. Constance was awake too, polishing the floor on her hands and knees with her own invented emulsion of beeswax and turpentine, which smelled as foul as my mood.

'Pyrogallic acid!' she shouted as soon as she saw me.

'Later.'

'Later won't help you,' she replied in a mock-serious voice. 'You're doomed, Mr Stanhope.'

'I know.'

'And you're not to cheat and look it up. I have dozens of remedies I can ask you.'

'Leave the poor man alone,' muttered Alfie with his nose in his account book. 'I'm sorry, Leo.'

'That's all right. You're up early.'

'Seeing the bank this morning.' He gestured glumly at the notes and coins in front of him. 'Just when you need a bank, you can least afford to pay them back.'

Now that I looked more closely, the pile was mainly coins: pennies and halfpennies. 'I could pay the rent early if you want. A month in advance.'

'No, it's all right, thanks. I've had an idea. It'll change our fortunes, I'm sure of it.'

'Oh?'

'You'll see.' He went back to his counting and I thought he looked tired and somehow older, his dark beard streaked with grey like a hearth in need of a good sweep.

I set off for work, walking briskly. Mr Hurst was both punctual and punitive. He'd fired his last assistant for lateness after employing him for twelve years. He still called me Nicholson from time to time.

In the early morning, with dawn still more than an hour away and the sky glowing red along the horizon, the overnight snow had partially melted, leaving a sediment at the edge of the pavement as if the world had started to rust.

Ted Boyd, who ran the grocery next door, was setting up for the day, putting out crates of cauliflower, spinach and rhubarb. His shop was expansive and colourful, making Alfie's pharmacy seem small and drab by comparison. He clapped me on the back.

'Early start, Mr Stanhope?'

I bought a dry and tasteless apple from him and forced it down my throat as I walked to the hospital.

Mr Hurst was outside his office talking to a policeman. There was nothing unusual about that in our line of work, but I didn't recognise the man. He was older than most, with cropped, receding ginger hair and hard eyes.

'Ah, Stanhope. This is …'

'Sergeant Cloake,' said the policeman, without putting out a hand for me to shake. 'There's been a burglary in the mortuary.'

'Oh?'

'A break-in,' said Mr Hurst, correcting him. 'Nothing was actually taken.'

'But things were broken,' said Cloake. 'Destruction of property. He smashed a window and a bottle of ale.'

I remembered the one. I had left it on the shelf for the porters. 'Who was it?'

'We don't know.' He turned to me, jaw jutting. 'Do you have access?'

'No,' interrupted Mr Hurst, before I could reply. 'He's just my secretary. Only the mortuary assistant and I have a key.'

'Is Flossie all right?' I asked.

'It was at night, we believe,' said Mr Hurst. 'She wasn't there. And the window wasn't *smashed*, Sergeant, it was forced. Cleverly done too. It's not easy to open a window from the outside, and no one even noticed it until this morning.'

Cloake scowled. 'Most likely body snatchers. Ghoulish is what it is.'

'Don't be ridiculous. The bodies are all still there. None were *snatched*.' Mr Hurst checked his pocket watch. 'We'll leave you to continue your expert investigation into the crime. We have work to do.'

His office was opposite the examination room, a mass of journals and books covering a desk so large I fancied the room must've been built around it. I spent the rest of the morning taking dictation while he marched up and down declaiming his latest article on crush injuries. Through long years of practice, I was able to correct his factual inconsistencies and grammar while thinking about something else entirely, about how next time I would bring Maria a pastry, or a box of honeyed plums from the market for us to share, our fingers sticky with the juice. She adored plums more than anything.

As the clock struck three, Mr Hurst put on his apron and I knew it was time for some proper work.

The mortuary was chilly. Underneath the window at the far end, a workman was positioning a ladder, with a screw-driver and a wrench tucked into his belt. It occurred to me that the intruder must have been quite agile; the drop from the window to the cold, stone floor was eight feet at least. Why risk a broken ankle and not steal anything?

'Vandals,' muttered Flossie, peering up at me. She was a twinkly-eyed woman, quite at odds with the nature of her position. She'd been a nurse and had retired to the less strenuous role of logging the deceased in and out, prepar-ing the forms and suffering the stench of decay without complaint. She had a bent back, and laboured in the half-dark like a cheerful goblin.

The room was long and narrow, a bigger sister to the examination room, lined with trolleys and tables. Two years before, a pleasure craft had collided with a collier ship and the corpses had overflowed into the hallway, stinking the place with silt and sewage. But most of the time there were few bodies here, and today only six, laid out on the trolleys and covered with sheets.

'Anyone for Mr Hurst?' I asked.

'Oh yes.' She pointed to the nearest trolley. 'Never ends, does it?'

She pulled back a sheet to reveal a small man with a head as bald as an egg. He was thinner than I was, with skin pulled tight over his bones, and a great gash across his neck, brown and congealed.

'His wife cut his throat in his sleep, apparently. She'd had enough of him. I s'pose we've all been tempted.'

'And how is Mr Liddle?'

'Much the same I'm afraid, thanks for asking.'

It didn't take long. We were a well-oiled machine, Mr Hurst and me, sawing and sewing. I wrote down the notes without him having to say a word. He read them over and briskly signed underneath.

'Let's get on with it. I have a meeting.'

I wheeled the trolley back to Flossie and she had another one all ready to go.

'A lady,' she said, looking mournfully at the physical terrain under the sheet. 'Bludgeoned, washed up at London Bridge by the wharfs. I go past there every day on my way here. Makes you think, doesn't it?'

I wheeled the gurney into the examination room and Mr Hurst groaned. He hated doing women.

I pulled back the sheet from the face of the deceased, and it was Maria. It was Maria. Three words that do nothing to sum up that moment. It was Maria lying there, dead. *It was my Maria.*

Even now, I can still see her. She's not lost to me, not entirely. I can reach out, and there she is.

———

Her head drops to one side as if she's just resting. I think that she might open her eyes, so I touch her cheek, and it's cold. Her hair falls across her face, covering her stain. It must tickle, I think, her hair on her skin like that, why doesn't she brush it away? I do it for her, but it falls back.

Any second now, she'll open her eyes and jump up and laugh, telling me it's all just a game and I'm so *silly* for being scared. She's like a child when she laughs, open-mouthed and unconstrained. But she just lies there, still. I reach out and feel where her heart should be beating.

'What are you doing?' says Mr Hurst, and he looks at me sharply.

'I'm … I don't know. I'm sorry.'

I fetch my folio and pen, dropping the pen on the floor. My palms start to sting and the balls of my fingers ache. I'm aware of every part of me, of my skin beneath my clothes.

Mr Hurst is reading the form. 'Found on Saturday afternoon by London Bridge, north side.' He pushes at her cheeks with his forefinger. She doesn't move. 'Port-wine stain. Some ante-mortem lividity too, very minor.' He pulls open one of her eyelids and peers underneath. 'Rigor mortis has passed. Conjunctiva inflamed, probably by the water. Are you getting all this?'

I make my notes: rigor mortis passed, port-wine stain, conjunctiva inflamed, minor lividity, not the cause of death.

He pulls the sheet away completely, and she doesn't cover herself up. She's unashamed. Her arms lie along her sides, and the curves of her thighs are squashed out against the metal.

Her legs are covered with dried mud. Her feet are caked in it, and spattered with beads of inky-black tar. I peel off a piece of soft river-weed that's stuck to her.

'Damn it,' he says. 'Look at this.' He sighs, blowing out his cheeks, and checks his pocket watch. 'It's not good enough. I can't examine her in this state.'

'I'll wash her,' I say quietly.

'Good. Be quick, and let me know when it's done. I'll be in my office.'

I fill a bowl in the sink. The water is icy, but Maria doesn't flinch. She doesn't shiver. She lies still while I sponge away the mud and tar from her calves and thighs, from the dimples in her knees. It's even in her hair. I clean between her fingers, along her wrists. She accepts it. I take her hand just as I've done a thousand times before, sitting on her bed while she kicks her heels against the frame, thump, thump thump, and talks and talks and talks. I love her voice. I love that she talks so I don't have to.

Her fingernails are purple with livor mortis. She always keeps them so exact; neat little rounds. I find myself shaking. I can't stop. My breaths are coming too quickly and I can't suppress them. I hold on to her hand for fear of falling over, for fear of going berserk and destroying everything in this place; smashing my desk to pieces, breaking the chairs, ranting and screaming and never stopping until they drag me away.

But it passes. I can breathe again.

The water is dirty now so I empty it and refill the bowl, watching the level rise to the brim and overflow into the sink. I plunge in my hands and it numbs my skin, creeping up my arms.

I return to Maria, and bend down to kiss her mouth, and she kisses me back, just a little bit, her dry lips sticking to mine.

She's cold. Not just her hands, which are always cold – little blocks of ice on my warm stomach, making me shudder and laugh – all of her is cold: her shoulders, her chin, her chest. She's as cold as the room. I turn her on to her side. She's heavier than I expect, hard to move. Her arm flops on to the metal and the sound of it echoes off the walls. And that's when I see the wound.

The back of her head is crushed. It is concave, pummelled by something the size of a man's fist, but harder. Much harder.

I see it all. She would be unaware. It would be sudden. She would hear something behind her and it would happen before she could even turn round. The soft footsteps, the pause, the sudden savagery, the twisting fall into shallow water, drawing her blood away as she lies there.

I see it again, and again, until it's all I can see, and the room and the world are gone.

———

I awoke lying on a sofa. For a second I was giddy, and then the truth closed in over me.

'Come on now,' someone said, a woman's voice. 'What's wrong? What's up with you?'

I was in the nurses' room. It was their sofa I was lying on, pushed up against the wall between the lockers and the cabinets. Nurse Coften was the only other person in there, looking down at me with an expression of concern, her black hair framing her face and blotting out the lamplight.

'You passed out,' she said. 'Are you sick? Have you been getting enough to eat? You're very thin, you know. There's nothing to you.'

She was a wasp buzzing round my head. I could barely bother to open my mouth to reply. I wondered if I had dreamt it all, but then I saw Maria's lifeless face again in my mind.

I sat up and vomited on to the floor.

Nurse Coften sighed and fetched a cloth. She knelt at my feet and cleaned it up, sponging it off my shoes. The room reeked of it.

I wanted to touch Maria, one last time, but by now Mr Hurst would be performing his examination and I couldn't bear to see her like that. I couldn't contemplate it.

'You should let me look at you,' she said. 'Or one of the doctors. You're obviously poorly. It won't take long.'

'No.'

My throat was hoarse from the sick. I climbed off the bed and stumbled out into the corridor, with Nurse Coften following behind. 'Mr Stanhope, please ...'

'Leave me alone.'

I somehow made it to the front entrance, where I was sick again on the steps. A gentleman was just getting out of a cab, and I almost threw myself inside.

———

I lay on my bed staring at a money spider making its way across the ceiling. I wasn't aware of sleeping, but I must have, because I awoke, sweating and breathless, and the spider had moved to a different spot.

Once, I thought I was in Maria's room again, and she was sprawling languorously beside me, but when I tried to touch her, searching furiously among the rucked-up blankets, she wasn't there.

Finally, I wept. It wasn't the memory of her face, or her injury, it was the fleeting thought of that damp strand of weed clinging to her foot. I wondered if it had happened quickly, over in an instant, or whether she'd lain there for a time being stroked into sleep by the river.

Once I started to weep, I couldn't stop.

Hours passed, I supposed. The sun fell, and rose and fell again. Outside, voices were raised, horses' hooves clattered in the street and rain hissed against the window. I took no notice of any of it. I would never have left my bed again, but for the need from time to time to squat over my chamber pot.

It was early morning. My window was a plus sign against a slab of white light, and the spider was slowly traversing the wall towards me. I wondered if its movements around the room were planned, part of a fixed route, or if it just meandered aimlessly in the hope of coming across a smaller insect to eat. This kept happening; for a moment I would forget and think of something else, and then the memory would return and I had to twist my fists in the bedclothes or stuff them into my mouth for fear of screaming.

There was a gentle knock at my door. I ignored it. The knock came again, this time with Constance's voice.

'Mr Stanhope? How are you feeling?' If it had been anyone else, I wouldn't have answered. But she was so young and so tremulous. And she was Constance. 'When will you be getting up? It's been two days.'

I had thought it had been longer, but it wasn't important. 'I'm unwell. I need to rest. Please leave me alone.' All my body was hurting. My skin itched, my muscles ached and my chest was sore from weeping.

'I've made you some mint tea. Shall I leave it here?' She was standing right outside my door. I could see her shadow underneath it. She wouldn't come into a man's bedroom of course, but even so I slid further under the blankets.

'Thank you, Constance.'

'It's here. Do you want me to pour it for you?'

'No, I can manage.'

There was a pause, and I could hear that she hadn't moved. 'I'm pouring it for you. I'll pass it in.' The door opened a crack, and her hand appeared holding a cup and saucer. 'It's there,' she said. 'Don't trip over it.'

'I won't. Thank you.'

There was another pause, and the sound of her leaning against my door and sliding down until she was sitting on the floor of the landing. 'I have a cup too,' she said. 'I'll keep you company if you like.'

I realised I was thirsty. The smell of the mint was over-powering. I crawled across the carpet and took a sip of the tea, and she must have heard the chink of the china because she said 'that's it', as if I was an infant being given medicine.

I sat against the door too, so we were back-to-back on either side. I could feel her weight when she moved.

'Isn't that better?' she said. 'You do like a cup of tea.'

'It's delicious, thank you.'

'Welcome.'

She said nothing for a while, and then: 'Do you want to play guess the remedy? We never finished the last one. It was pyrogallic acid.'

I sighed. I didn't want to guess. This silly thing, this game we played, was something I'd done *before*.

'I'm tired, Constance.'

'Go on,' she said. 'What's your first guess?'

'All right. Pyrogallic acid. Does it bring the dead back to life?'

'No! Don't be horrid.'

'You're right. I'm sorry. Headaches?'

'No. One left.' She was muting her usual triumphant tone.

'Ulcers?'

'No again. Why do you always guess ulcers? It's never ulcers. Pyrogallic acid prevents infection.'

'Truly? Well, now I know. Congratulations, you win. Thank you for the tea. I need to sleep now.'

'All right. Call down later if you want something on a tray. And Mr Stanhope?'

'Yes, Constance?'

'That's nine to me, and five to you.'

She left, and I went back to bed and slept for three hours, dreamlessly, until another knock woke me, this one rapid, loud and insistent.

'Leo!' It was Alfie's voice. 'Two policemen are here, and they want to speak to you.'

They were standing in the shop with that stance that said they were here on business, and impatient to be getting on with it. I'd kept them waiting while I got dressed. Alfie was standing behind the counter while Constance spun on the stool and watched with open fascination. It took me a bleary second to realise one of them was young Pallett, still bulging out of his ill-fitting uniform.

'I'm Sergeant Cloake,' said the other one, apparently not recognising me, although we'd met at the hospital after the break-in at the mortuary. I didn't mind a bit. I hadn't liked him then and I didn't now. 'And this is … what's your name again, son?'

'Pallett,' said Pallett.

'Right. This is Constable Hallett. We have some questions for you.'

'Concerning what?' demanded Alfie, and I was reminded that he'd once been a sergeant in the army.

'A girl was murdered.'

'What's that got to do with Mr Stanhope?'

'We don't rightly know,' said Pallett. 'We was told to fetch him. We don't know what for.'

Cloake was annoyed. He hadn't wanted us to know they were just errand boys. 'Don't make us arrest you,' he said.

'On what grounds?' asked Alfie, but I put my hand on his arm.

'It's all right.' I turned to Pallett. 'I just have to use the privy.'

I went out before they could argue, and into the yard. The privy was a shabby thing of misaligned bricks and a clamorous iron roof. I tugged the door shut behind me and sat down to do my business, looking back at the house through a crack in the wall. I was shaking, and not just from the ice-cold seat against my backside.

If I went with them, I would be uncovered. I was certain of it.

Over the past ten years I had avoided unfamiliar places and was rarely drunk, never out of reach of my cilice, my sanitary cloths, a privy cubicle. I kept a map in my head and always knew what came next. But I'd been to the police station many times in the course of my work, and I'd seen the lines of men shuffling forward to be admitted and then herded off towards the cells. There, I would have no control. Sooner or later I would be searched, or required to change my clothes, or need to piss. And, after all, I truly was a criminal. Every time I called myself Leo and put on trousers I was breaking the law. My crime wasn't something I'd *done*, out of greed or ill-temper, it was something I *was*, every minute of every day, flouting the will of God who'd created me as a woman.

I had to get away. It didn't matter where. I'd done it before.

I exited as quietly as I could, easing the yard gate open and slipping out into the alleyway behind the shops and houses, unseen. As I reached the junction to go right towards the street, I heard a sound behind me and then a voice.

'Sir?' It was Pallett.

I almost fled. Up ahead, the alleyway formed a tunnel between the houses, an oblong of pale light and the outline of a broken-down gate: the servants' entrance to heaven.

'You have to come with us, Mr Stanhope.' Pallett was half a foot taller than me even without his helmet, and broad enough to fill the alleyway. 'You must've got lost, sir. Sometimes folk see a policeman and they get confused.'

'Yes, that must be it.'

'Never mind, eh? We won't mention it to Sergeant Cloake. He's not very understanding about such things. Probably best not to let it happen again, though.'

And I'd always assumed he had the brains of a billy club.

He stood aside for me to squeeze past him, and followed me back to the shop. Constance was still on her stool, wide-eyed, and Alfie was standing with my coat over his arm, his mouth set grimly. 'It'll be all right, Leo.'

I walked out between the two policemen. I wasn't handcuffed, but there was an unmistakeable sense of being guarded. I ducked to get into the carriage.

6

PALLETT GUIDED ME THROUGH the heavy wooden doors of the police headquarters on Whitehall, his hand firmly on my shoulder. I felt myself trembling. I followed him into the guts of the place, a long corridor of smoke-stained windows lined with policemen behind desks, writing on forms or typing on machines; the deafening racket of a thousand tiny hammers. We went down a flight of stairs to another corridor, underground now, lamp-lit and stinking of mould, finally stopping at a plain office dominated by a hulking desk, with empty shelves and a discoloured square on the back wall where a picture had once hung. I put a hand on the chair and it was damp. The whole room was damp, probably the whole basement. Condensation was rusting the shelves and the pipes over-head, glistening on the metal like the brow of a guilty man. I gathered my coat around me and fumbled in my pocket for a cigarette, just to feel the warmth and dryness of the smoke in my throat.

'Why am I here?'

'Someone'll come soon,' Pallett said, as if I was an imbecile. 'Detective Ripley. I don't know him well, but I hear he's a good man. Don't worry, Mr Stanhope.'

The degradation of pity from Pallett. I reasserted myself. 'So how goes it with that nurse of yours? What's her name?'

He reddened. 'Miss Rasmussen. I'm meeting her for tea with her parents on Sunday.'

'That's very promising. Good for you!'

'Thank you, sir. Very kind.'

He left me alone, but didn't lock the door.

Minutes passed as I tried to piece everything together, pacing around the little room, circling the chair and rapping my knuckles on the desk with every pass. They had already discovered I knew Maria, or why else would I be here? Most likely they had talked to Mrs Brafton. I wondered what she had told them. She was normally so protective of her customers' privacy – discretion above all else, she always said – but this was not a normal situation. And I was not a normal customer.

I folded my arms, reaching to the sore spots where my cilice rubbed against my skin, and dug my nails in on both sides. It didn't help.

My cigarette was no more than an ember by the time he came in. He was a big man in an ill-fitting suit that looked as if he wore it every day and possibly every night, with the glossy albumen of his breakfast smeared down his waistcoat. He didn't shake my hand but pulled out a folder, licked his finger and started leafing through the papers. I sat down, feeling dainty and dandified by comparison, perching upright in my chair while he sprawled opposite me.

He had a paper bag with him, and he opened it and unwrapped a pasty. I suddenly felt hungry.

Eventually he looked up and fixed me with faded blue eyes, one lazy lid giving him a half-asleep expression. There was something calculated about his slow manner, and it made me uncomfortable.

'I'm Detective Sergeant Ripley,' he said, and I recognised a northern accent, reminding me of my sister making me snigger with her voicing of poor Jane Eyre's travails. 'You seem anxious, Mr Stanhope.'

Mister Stanhope. So no one had told him what I was, at least not yet. Still, he would probably find out soon enough. I am the Cockless Man, the only one of my kind. Put me in a zoo with the panda bears and giant tortoises. I'll wear my bowler hat and growl at passers-by.

'I'm just a little unsettled by this place, Detective.'

'It can have that effect.' He tore his pasty in two and handed me half. 'Chicken and potato. My treat.'

'Thank you.' Politeness is never wasted.

'Good teeth you have. Not like mine.' He showed me his, grimacing, and they were black and chipped. 'Too much drink and football. Too many fights. I grew out of it, one way or another. You're not the fighting type, are you, with those teeth?'

'No.'

'Well-bred. Educated.' He pulled out a piece of paper, and I recognised Mr Hurst's report from the hospital. 'Do you understand why you're here?'

'Not really.'

He spoke through a mouthful of food. 'You knew the murdered girl, didn't you? Don't bother, I know you did. You were a customer of the brothel on …' He checked his notes. 'On Half Moon Street. When did you last see her?' When I didn't respond he sat back in his chair and sniffed. 'This'll be easier if you're straight with me. I don't care about your morals, I'm not your vicar. Your name was in the appointment book. You were a regular customer, weren't you?'

'I suppose so. I last saw Maria a week ago today, in the evening.'

'Good. The first answer's always the hardest. You were with the same girl every week for more than two years. You must have got to know her.'

'Yes. We were close.'

'I see.' He was expressionless but for his half-closed eye, which made him seem as if he was about to wink at me. 'So it was more than just the usual. You cared about her.'

'What's that got to do with anything?'

He smiled. It was disconcerting. 'You'd be surprised how common it is.'

'I don't know what you mean.'

'Maybe you saw her with some other johnny and couldn't bear it. Next thing you know, you're stood over her with blood on your hands, wondering what you did. You wouldn't be the first.'

I stared at him. What he was saying was ridiculous. 'You don't understand … I would never harm her.'

'Not intentionally. You just lost your temper and before you knew it –'

'No! We were always kind to each other.' Once, she had winced when I touched a graze on the nape of her neck, and I had insisted we stop and put ointment on the spot. I had rubbed it in myself while she held her hair to one side and told me over and over again how gentle I was.

'Do you own a weapon, Mr Stanhope? A club or a cudgel?'

'No! You can't think I would hurt Maria.'

'Can't I? Why not?'

'Because …' There were so many reasons that I couldn't single one out: because I loved her, because I wanted to spend my life with her, because she was the only person I'd ever met who knew what I was and didn't care. In the end, I came up with the stupidest possible answer. 'I would never do something like that.'

'Well someone did. If it wasn't you, then who was it?'

I opened my mouth to speak but nothing came out. It hadn't occurred to me that she might have been killed by someone she knew, *someone I might know*. People were stabbed, bottled and throttled all the time. I saw them almost daily in the hospital, and most were victims of petty thievery for a wallet or a ring. They were a tithe the city demanded. Men had turned up on the slab minus nothing but a pair of shoes. I hadn't considered for a second that Maria was murdered by an actual *person*. I felt as if I'd betrayed her by not wondering before. I'd just lain in bed, thinking of myself.

'I don't know. I can't believe it, truly I can't. Everyone adored her.' I heard my own use of the past tense and reached for the sore at my right armpit, giving it a brief, fierce pinch.

'Yes, I'm sure she was sweet as treacle,' said Ripley. 'But I need facts.'

Facts? How could *facts* sum up everything she was? But if that's what he wanted, I'd done it dozens of times before for policemen too lazy or illiterate to read my reports.

'Very well. Occupation, prostitute. Aged twenty. Father unknown, mother deceased. Port-wine stain on face, left side.' I could hear my voice trembling, and took a breath. 'Blunt instrument to the head. Minor lividity on back, bruising that is, ante-mortem by a few days. Conjunctiva inflamed ...'

'What?'

'The surface of the eye,' I said, pointing to my own. 'Is that enough facts? It's all in there, I'm sure, if you can make sense of Mr Hurst's grammar and handwriting. Plus the lengths of her fingernails, the weight of her lungs, the contents of her stomach.'

He looked at the front of the report, frowning, and then turned it over. 'Nothing about her innards in here.'

I remembered that Mr Hurst had been in a hurry, and even though he coveted the parts, loved to measure them and cut off little pieces to study under his microscope, he hated sewing up the corpses afterwards. When he had first discovered I had nimble fingers – almost like a woman's, he said – he started delegating the task to me, considering it a rudimentary exercise beneath his attention: *I'm not a bloody undertaker.*

Ripley started writing scratchily in his notebook, but his pencil lead snapped off and he cursed, tugging open the desk drawer and searching through it. I sat in silence listening to the pipes overhead bumping and gurgling as air pockets formed and broke. Eventually he found a sharpener and solemnly sharpened his pencil, dropping little curls of wood on to the floor. When he was finished he held it up to check the point.

'We spoke to your Mr Hurst. He said you fell ill and didn't go in for two days. You seem well enough to me.'

'It was unexpected to see her like that. I was upset, naturally.'

70

'*Naturally*,' he repeated, mocking my use of the word. 'He's a sack of wind if you want my opinion, but he was keen to be of assistance. He said you were a good employee, very thorough. Never normally late to work.'

'So?'

'He said you know a lot about bodies. Causes of death and the like.'

'She was clubbed on the head. You don't need to know much about causes of death to do that.'

The words were out before I'd truly considered them. How callous I was. This wasn't chess, this was Maria's last minute of life.

Ripley surveyed me, rubbing his chin. He didn't have a beard, just an untidy moustache in the manner of almost every policeman in London. 'Crime of passion, then. Spur of the moment. Where were you on Saturday?'

I thought back, and realised, with a cramping not unlike stomach ache, exactly where I'd been. 'I was at the theatre. The Opera Comique.'

'Who with?'

'Alone. A woman in the next seat might remember me. And I spoke with the doorman as well.'

'What was the play?'

'*HMS Pinafore*.' I didn't mention that I'd only seen the first half.

Ripley rolled his eyes. 'You went to that bunk on your own? What on earth for?'

'I bought two tickets, one for me and one for Maria. She didn't arrive. Now I know why.' And I'd been so resentful, so self-absorbed. I hadn't considered that she might have been injured, let alone *this*.

'And you didn't think it was a bit odd? You didn't wonder where she was.'

'Yes, but, well, I was never certain she'd come. I hoped she would, but I'd only ever met her at Mrs Brafton's before.' I felt my cheeks go guiltily red. From his viewpoint, I must have seemed pitiful.

He pulled out a metal case from his pocket, and removed a cigarette and a match from it. He didn't offer me one, but lit his own and closed his eyes, inhaling deeply and then blowing a smoke ring. It floated between us. 'Not cheap, the theatre, is it? Five bob at least. What did you think would come of it, eh? Did you plan to rescue her and take her off to a cottage in the countryside? Is that what you wanted?'

'It wasn't like that.'

I had never actually hoped for a house of our own with an arch of wisteria over the porch and a square of garden where Maria could tend the roses. That was my father's dream, not mine. I knew ours would be a life of hard graft, with no collection plate or, for that matter, willow-pattern bowl to support us. In the minutes before I went to sleep each night I pictured us in a shop together in some little town far from here, and one day opening a place of our own, perhaps a bookshop, and living in the rooms above it. And we would be happy. Or, we would have been.

'Then how was it? Why didn't you court a normal girl?'

Because no normal girl would have me. 'She didn't choose that life. Her mother was a dancer on the stage – you know the kind, a drunk. She sold Maria when she was eleven years old. Can you imagine that? I wanted to give her a better life. Are you married, Detective?'

'Aye, I am, and if any bastard laid a hand on my missus I'd kill him, I make no bones about it. But you fell for a girl anyone could have, anyone at all, for a few pennies. Must've bothered you, didn't it?'

I knew he was trying to make me angry. He was an ignorant man, lacking imagination.

'When I met her she was eighteen. She'd already been living that life for four years. If you assume three customers a day for three hundred days a year, that's almost four thousand times before I even met her. Possibly more.'

Ripley sat back in his chair and surveyed me. I'd clearly surprised him, but I didn't know whether it was because I'd done that calculation or because the number was so high.

'That's a very ... rational way to think about it.'

'Factual. And yes, I did want to rescue her from that, of course I did. But I still admired her for surviving it. Any normal person would be hardened or destroyed, but she was gentle, kind and beautiful. Do you know, she wept over her mother's death, even after everything she'd done to her?'

I was tired. I wanted to go back to bed for ever. But Ripley wasn't finished. He scratched his head and started sorting through his papers again, though I sensed he wasn't really reading them.

'What aren't you telling me, Mr Stanhope?'

'Nothing.'

'I could wring it out of you.'

'Probably, if you wanted to, but it wouldn't be the truth.' My palms prickled at the sight of his fists on the desk, but I wasn't afraid. *Detached* was more the word.

'Again, very rational.'

'Factual.'

'Factual then. You're a factual man.' He took a long pull on his cigarette and then dropped it on to the floor without treading on it, so it lay there slowly smouldering, a thin wisp of smoke curling and dissipating in the air. 'Fair enough, we'll have to do this the hard way then. Come with me.'

'Are you letting me go?'

He laughed, but there was no humour in it. 'No, Mr Stanhope, I'm not. You're my best suspect, and there's something not right about all this. An educated young man like yourself, good job, nice manners, pretty teeth, falling for a girl like that. It doesn't add up. But I'll get to the bottom of it in the end, I usually do.'

I followed him up the stairs and into the light. He barged through the double doors and along the corridor without waiting, so I had to hurry to keep up. It was madness. I was running to my own incarceration while whoever had really killed her was walking around as free as a bird.

———

Ripley led me almost back to the entrance, but before we got there we turned away through a metal door guarded by a heavyset constable with a pistol in a holster. On the other side there was a shit-smelling room, cold as death, divided into a pair of cells with bars running from floor to ceiling and a single, high window. The right-hand cell had a group of men in it, and I hoped he would put me in the other one. He didn't.

'Move back,' he said to an older inmate who was holding on to the bars, staring at me as the door was unlocked. I didn't meet his eyes. Another man was lying on the floor, unmoving, in some kind of stupor, and two others were seated on the bench, arms around their knees. The pail in the corner was the source of the foul odour, pervading everything.

Ripley pulled out another cigarette and stuck it between his lips, taking an age to light a match. He seemed never to hurry anything. 'Any valuables on you?' he asked. 'Money, pocket watch, pen, anything? Best hand 'em over to me now or you'll be handing them over to this lot later.'

I gave him my wallet. 'I want it back afterwards.'

He hesitated, and I realised with a shiver he didn't think there would be an *afterwards*. 'All right. You'll be here until you're charged, and then the court cells. Then Newgate, more than likely, which'll make this seem like paradise.'

The door swung shut behind him, and I was left alone with the prisoners, and that pail.

The older man went back to gazing at the wall through the bars and tugging hairs out of his nose between a thumb and forefinger. The two men on the bench, who seemed to be brothers, were muttering in low voices. One of them had a diagonal cut and bruises across his face. He was having trouble talking, and kept fingering the half-inch stitches that were keeping his wound from parting. The fellow on the floor just lay there. I sat on the floor next to him with my back to the wall, taking the lowest-status position in the cell.

I was afraid. I couldn't stay here long with these men, let alone Newgate Prison. I would be discovered for certain.

How could this have happened? It was only Wednesday, wasn't it? Only four days since I'd been waiting for Maria outside the theatre, believing that my new life was about to start, and a week since I had last seen her.

I would never see her again. I knew it was true, and yet it seemed impossible. Somehow, I still believed that if I went to her room and knocked on her door, I would hear her footsteps as she rushed to throw it open. I would feel her arms around my neck and her hair against my cheek, and I would breathe her in. She smelled of ginger mint.

And then I remembered her face in the hospital, pallid and still. I had no right to be afraid. What did my well-being matter beside her suffering?

'Shut up, will ye?' The older man by the bars was scowling at me. His voice sounded like a coal scuttle being dragged across a concrete floor. 'Ye keep *sighing*.'

'I'm sorry.'

'Are ye ill?'

'No, I'm just … nervous about all this.'

'Then piss yourself in silence.'

I nodded, and rested my forehead on my arms. But he wasn't wrong. I really did need to piss.

As darkness descended a young policeman came in and lit the lamp at the far end, creating a dim light, barely enough to see. He sat in the chair and within a few minutes his chin had sunk down to his chest. It was obvious I would be here for the night. I lay on the hard floor, wondering why I had ever complained about my saggy mattress – truly I was a pampered and self-indulgent man. I closed my eyes, desperate for sleep, just so I could leave this horror behind for a few hours.

But I still needed to piss. A couple of times one of the others had released a fulsome stream into the pail, more or less, and then gone back to his place without a word. I crossed my legs and squeezed my thighs together.

Once all was quiet, and my cell-mates seemed to be asleep, I stood up by the pail and started to remove my trousers. I got as far as pulling them down and turning to sit.

'You'll no shit in here or I'll make ye eat it.'

The older man was just a silhouette, but I could see his jutting chin. I pulled my trousers back up and lay down again, praying I could hold on.

I woke with a jolt when the man with the cut face started whimpering, and his brother shouted out in a thick voice: 'Hey, coppers! He's bleeding again!'

'Excuse me,' I said, wishing I could mimic his way of speaking instead of sounding like a character in a play, the overeducated fop who never ends up with the girl. 'I have some experience of surgical sewing. May I take a look at him?'

I had in my mind some idea of removing a thorn from the lion's paw and making him a loyal friend for life, but his brother spat on the floor at my feet.

'Touch him and I'll break all your fingers.'

And that was that, until the two men finally slept, snoring and snorting.

When a dreary dawn was seeping into the room and I was certain they were all asleep, I crept to the pail and eased myself silently on to it, clenching my bladder and trickling out the merest drops. Even that seemed too loud, echoing off the brick walls, so I tipped the pail on to one edge, allowing my stream to slide silently down the inner side. It was ecstasy! I was almost done when I unbalanced slightly, and moved my foot back an inch to steady myself. The base of the pail slid away and fell with a crash, slopping a tide across the floor to where the older man was lying. For a moment I thought he might remain asleep, but as he felt the surge of wetness he leapt up, staring at the arm of his jacket, now soaked, and then at me, with my trousers round my ankles.

'I apologise,' I said hastily. 'I can pay for any …'

'Look what ye did, you bloody meater.'

He shoved me against the wall, his face right against mine, and then stepped back. I thought it would be all right, but he slammed his foot against my knee and the pain shot up my leg as I fell sideways. He kicked me in the stomach and I couldn't breathe. I was dimly aware that I was rolling in the piss, but all that mattered was taking another breath. When it finally came, it hurt like hell.

He crouched down and raised his fist. I tried to squirm away, but to where? Where could I go, in this place? One thing would lead to another, and I would be found out and violated before the police could intervene. I didn't think I would survive it and wasn't sure I wanted to.

But the blow never landed.

There was a noise outside and a constable came in carrying a bucket and some bowls. I'd never been so glad to see anyone in my life.

'Porridge!' he called out.

The older man stepped back, his fists clenched and eyes narrowed to cracks. I was able to stand, wet and sore, and pull up my trousers.

'Excuse me,' I said to the young policeman. 'I need to see Detective Sergeant Ripley.'

'He ain't come in yet,' he replied, with a tinge of disapproval.

I straightened my soaking jacket and squared my shoulders. I only had one option left. 'I want to confess.'

Not to murder, but to gender. Better to tell Ripley now than let these bastards have their sport with me, and end up being cut up and weighed by Mr Hurst. Even so, I knew what it meant: prosecution and humiliation, and Ripley would have even more reason to think I was guilty of the bigger crime. The lovelorn deviant was an obvious suspect.

Worst of all, someone out there would be laughing at their ridiculous luck.

At that moment the door opened and Ripley himself strode into the room. Judging by his face, he'd been woken early and wasn't happy about it.

'Stanhope,' he said. 'You're free to go.'

'What?'

Was this some trick he was playing? I wanted very much to leave, but I couldn't understand why he was letting me. I expected him to slam the door in my face or grab me and throw me back inside, but he didn't. He handed me my wallet without a word.

I followed him outside to the yard in a daze, gasping as the frigid air met my piss-sodden clothes.

A horse had collapsed on the cobblestones, and a group of policemen and stable hands were gathered round where it was panting. Ripley contemplated the scene. 'They'll have to shoot that, poor thing.'

'Did you find Maria's killer?'

'They'll be serving horse stew tomorrow. And no, as it happens, I still think you did it.'

'Then why …?'

He drew deeply on the last stub of his cigarette. 'I was told to let you go. The higher-ups have decided you're not a suspect. Apparently they know better than I do.'

'I don't understand.'

'You've got some powerful friends, it seems, Mr Stanhope. Don't worry, you'll be back here soon enough. I'll get you in the end.' He dropped his cigarette and fished in his metal case for another, but it was empty. He patted his pockets and frowned. 'Damn it, left my ciggies on my desk. They'll be nicked for sure. Bunch of bloody thieves, policemen.'

I walked away just as the horse started to squeal.

I couldn't understand it. What powerful friends could I possibly have? My few friends hadn't even known I was incarcerated, and none of them could be described as powerful. The only remotely powerful person I knew was Mr Hurst, but the police would never release a prisoner on his say-so, and in any case he wouldn't be bothered with me. I was a nobody.

Why had they let me go?

———

I awoke the next day at eleven o'clock with a griping pain in my guts, and realised the curse had come in the night. All those words for the monthly blood – the *visit*, the *time*, even the *blessing*, God help us – but the curse is what it was, at least for me. I always felt surprised by its arrival, every time, as if, by deliberately not anticipating it, I might fool it into overlooking me. And yet it came. For some reason I would never understand, God had put me into a female body with female secretions. Perhaps it was His idea of comedy, but like any joke it palled through repetition.

I cleaned myself and scrubbed my underclothes until the water was red. I hung them over a loop of string in the wardrobe to dry, and settled a clean flannel into place in my trousers. I told myself this was simply maintenance I had to perform, nothing more. My hands were red too, stained by my own blood, and yet it didn't feel like mine.

I knew I should go back to work, but I'd missed three days already, and what was one extra? It didn't seem to matter. As I left the shop and walked down towards Piccadilly, I could feel the moist, warm flannel commencing its customary abrasion of my skin.

The horses were stamping their hooves and whickering at the cab rank, irritated by the haze of brick dust floating over from the workings on the Quadrant.

'London Bridge,' I called up to the driver. 'North side, near the wharfs. I need to get down to the river.'

We set off just as raindrops started tapping on the tarp roof, taking a crooked route eastwards towards the Strand. As we went by the Opera Comique, I looked away, afraid I wouldn't be able to stop myself from searching for her face among the people waiting to go in. We drove on, passing within sight of St Paul's Cathedral as it stared down at the busy streets like the stern schoolteacher of an unruly class, and then bore right and lurched off the road, pulling up at the entrance to a rutted track that led down between the wharfs. I'd only ever seen them from a distance before, shrouded in fog, lined up like mourners at a funeral. Up close they were vast and dark, eight storeys or more high, and sheer, with lofty windows shuttered against the weather. The rain was easing, but water was still pouring from the gutters, and I sloshed down to the dockside through a brook.

There was a set of stairs built into the stonework of London Bridge. I climbed down, taking care on the slippery steps, clinging to the metal rail. The wind was swirling and my coat flapped against my legs. The smell got stronger as I went down, and I could see the green slime and flickering reflection on the arches. Water was being blown off the surface of the river, mixing with the rain, seeping into my collar and dripping down my neck.

At the bottom, a low-tide beach of heavy stones was exposed, slick with engine oil and littered with driftwood, tar and tangled fishing lines. We were below the level of the city, and the rattle of traffic was swamped by the rush of the wind and slap of the waves against the stanchions of the bridge. The river seemed wider from this low down. Clinker dinghies were being rowed just a few yards out, and in the deeper water there were barges and great ships with flags flying on their masts.

I picked my way across the stones, arms out for balance. The curve of the Thames and eddies from the bridge had caused a lagoon to form, shallow and rank, and the water was calmer there, sheltered and green with river-weed.

Such a beautiful person, lying here, dying here, in the margin of the Thames.

I crouched down, collecting a frond in my palm and letting it fall back. I didn't know what I had expected to feel: some remembrance of her in the stones, some sense of her soul still lingering. I touched my finger to my lips and it tasted salty.

A seagull dropped down and started pulling at something, a crab or a barnacle, and then another joined it. They glared at me indignantly, and didn't leave even when I stood up. She can't have lain here long, I thought. She hadn't been pecked.

I took off my bowler and slapped it against my coat a couple of times, shaking off the water and scaring the gulls back into flight.

I had believed I would want to stay longer. I had thought that being here would mean more. But there was nothing of Maria in this place. It was bleak and hard, fallen off the edge of the city, and she had been warm and gentle, and the kindest person I'd ever known.

The rain was getting stronger, splashing and glittering in the puddles. There were no cabs so I started walking home, winding between the quarrelling wharfs. The way was dark and convoluted, and I lost my bearings more than once, but I wasn't afraid. I even enjoyed it. There was a freedom in not caring what happened next.

I remembered what Jacob had once told me, late at night over a glass of whisky, when Lilya and the children had long since gone to bed. Angling forward and waggling his finger with that wry expression he wore when about to say something he thought was clever, he said: 'As long as you're still on the board, Leo, you can still win the game. Even a pawn can become a queen in the end.' And then he'd laughed, and I'd laughed along with him.

7

I DISCOVERED THAT MY grief was inconstant. One minute it was engulfing me, closing over my head, vast and cold, and the next it was a dense core in my stomach, an unreachable certitude. Sometimes I laughed and even sang, and at other times I knew I couldn't live without her, and had to pinch the skin on my wrists to keep myself from weeping.

I did not receive an invitation to the funeral. This was not unexpected; her profession hardly encouraged the circulation of black-bordered cards to every fellow who'd known her. For a little while I felt relieved; I was frightened of the casket and the knowledge that she was sealed up inside it. I couldn't keep from my mind what she had become: the parts, the skin and bone and muscle and brain, all well on the downward slope of decay by now. I'd seen it before: nails rotting in their sockets, teeth falling from their gums, intestines turned to liquid, oozing and fetid. That was what was in the box, just the parts. Not Maria. All of what she really was, was gone.

I could guess what Jacob would have said, could hear his gruff voice in my ear: Bah! You don't go to a whore's funeral. It's like eating a steak and then mourning the cow.

And yet I knew that if I stayed away I would never forgive myself. So I sent a note to little Audrey, including

84

half a crown, and received a reply by return, written in a round, careful hand, providing the details. Maria's remains would not be displayed at the house on Half Moon Street but would go directly to the West London cemetery.

I tossed the paper on the fire.

Constance had cooked breakfast with more zeal than skill, but I barely tasted it, which I might once have called a blessing. Alfie had risen early and was crawling around with a tape measure, making chalk crosses on the floor of the shop.

'How did it go with the bank?' I asked.

His expression darkened. 'Bit of a setback. You know how it is.'

'My offer still stands, you know.'

'Thank you, Leo, but we'll be all right. I have a plan.' He pointed at my smart clothes. 'What's the occasion?'

'I'm going to a funeral. Just an acquaintance.'

The little betrayal snatched at me, but I couldn't face a more complete explanation. I gave him my best sad–but–there-we-are smile and set out, feeling as if every soft part of me had been removed, like one of the bodies on Mr Hurst's slab, and I was nothing but a skeleton covered with skin.

The cab made slow progress. I would have preferred the journey to take for ever, but eventually we arrived. The cemetery sprawled along the Old Brompton Road, with great shoulders of limestone and a grim, gated entrance that loomed over the pavement with a frowning lintel, jawbone columns and a gaping, voracious arch.

A small group was huddled on the pavement. Mrs Brafton was resplendent in her black funeral weeds: a bombazine gown constructed around her formidable frame, and a huge bonnet mounted on her head like a cannon. She was standing with the Colonel, who was sporting a dress uniform far too big for him. Behind them, the girls were clustered together, but I only knew Audrey by name.

Is this everyone? I thought. Is this all she's worth?

Mrs Brafton turned to me with a blank expression. 'Mr Stanhope. I wasn't expecting *you*.'

'I know I don't have an invitation, but I had to come.'

'I thought you were with the police.'

'They talked to me, yes.'

'Why did they let you go?' She pursed her lips and I realised she didn't want me there.

'You can't think ... it had nothing to do with me. Maria and I loved each other.'

'That's absurd.'

I was in no mood for scorn. 'I cared for her more than you did. You wouldn't even have her casket displayed at the house.'

'Out of respect for our customers.'

'Out of respect for their money.'

She raised herself to reply, but before she got the chance, the Colonel piped up. 'Now listen here, young man, you keep a civil tongue or I'll make sure you do.'

It was an empty threat: the only thing keeping him upright was the stiffness of his uniform, and I was far more frightened of Mrs Brafton, who was twice his size. But it had the effect of breaking the tension, and she turned away.

It seemed that I would be admitted.

I stood on my own for a while, eyes stinging, until I felt a touch at my elbow, and there was Audrey. She was truly tiny, and could easily be mistaken for a twelve-year-old. She was neither pretty nor plain, but had an odd self-possession, perhaps necessary for her regular employment.

'You mustn't blame Mrs Brafton,' she said. 'She feels the burden if any of us comes to harm.'

'What she said isn't true –'

'It's all right, I know it weren't you. This weren't a woman's crime. Takes a man to do something like that, and you're a woman underneath.'

I sighed. It was hardly worth correcting her, and at least there was one person in the world who didn't suspect me, even if her logic was flawed.

Up the road, a carriage was approaching, rocking its way over the cobbles. It pulled up beside us, and half a dozen ladies disembarked, staring up at the wintry sunshine and raising parasols or shielding their eyes. After them, a reverend emerged. He was clearly as deaf as a stump, and held up an ear trumpet quizzically whenever they spoke to him.

'Who are they?' I whispered to Audrey.

'Church people. It brings out all sorts, a bit of murder. They only care about girls like us when we're dead. Before that we're the devil's work. Quakers, Baptists, Methodists, Catholics, Jesuits, all the same. Even the Sally Army once with placards and singing songs right outside our door. And often as not the gentlemen come back after dark.'

An older woman lurched out in faded weeds, a toothless smile on her face. I realised from her delirious expression that she was simple, not really aware of what was happening. She had watery eyes and the ruddy, veiny skin of a heavy drinker, but her lips were full and red. I was sure I had seen her somewhere before.

'Who's she?'

'Maria's mother, or what's left of her.'

This was foolishness. 'Maria's mother is dead.'

Audrey shook her head. 'No, that's her all right. Maria took her to church most Sundays. She used to set off at dawn and walk all the way to Bow, and half the time she'd get there and Mrs Mills would be too sickly. She still enjoys a drink or two, or five or six, even now.' Audrey confided the last words in a whisper. 'She's more mould than bread these days, is the truth.'

'Are you sure that's her mother? Not an aunt or a friend?'

'Course. It's tragic really. Who'll take her to church now?'

I couldn't believe what she was saying. I'd spent hours comforting Maria about her mother's death. I tried to make sense of it.

'Did you say her name is Mills?'

'Yes, Maria's name was Mills. Maria Mills. Milanes was just her stage name, if you like. She was a proper actress, that one. Brought up that way, she said, and I think she really might've been. Not like me, I never had the knack. Too honest, I s'pose. But Maria came in one day, rabbiting on about this shop she'd been in called Milanes, selling purses and shoes and such, and how *exotic* it sounded.' She smiled sadly, clasping her hands together. 'She called herself Milanes ever afterwards, and the gentlemen seemed to like it. I could never bring myself to do the same. Plain old Audrey Kerry, me.'

'But she told me her mother was dead.'

'Don't think too ill of her.' Audrey wiped her eyes with her sleeve, as Mummy used to tell me off for doing when I was seven. 'She couldn't help what she was.'

I edged closer to Mrs Mills. Now I had a good look at her, the family resemblance was striking – the same triangular face and curly hair, the same sharp nose and small hands, just transposed to an older and considerably more florid form. She was all that was left of Maria, a link to her past and a ghastly warning about her future, if she'd had one.

I felt churlish, being angry with Maria at her own funeral, but I couldn't help it. Why had she lied, to me of all people? She knew I wasn't born with the name Leo Stanhope. She knew everything about me.

The carriage with the pall-bearers arrived; six young men dressed identically in funeral garb. They were cheerful, whispering and smirking behind their hands. The driver spoke sternly to them, but they continued to grin apishly as soon as his back was turned.

And finally, the hearse, a glass box on wheels pulled by two horses. It was progressing slowly, and our little group had grown quite restless by the time it reached us. The casket was so small I couldn't believe she could be within it. Even having seen her in death myself, I was still wishing there had been some terrible mix-up, and she was sitting at home in her room wondering where everyone had gone.

Some passers-by on the pavement stopped and removed their hats, and the driver of a carriage slowed respectfully. I could see shadowy faces pressed up against the windows, fascinated by it all: the solemnity, the ceremony, the weeping, the death.

The lads slid out the casket and hefted it clumsily on to their shoulders. For a second I feared she would be hurt.

The hearse driver and the reverend led the way into the cemetery, followed at a stately pace by Mrs Brafton, the Colonel and Mrs Mills, the latter tottering uncertainly, and then the girls and the ladies. I was last, on my own.

Elm trees lined the pathway on either side, and beyond them lay little beds of purple shrubs and patchy lawns awaiting the dead. In the distance, the chapel's domed roof stood out against a cloudless sky.

This is it, I told myself. They're going to bury her now. Maria will be put into the ground in this place. What am I to do then?

After perhaps five minutes of walking, the grass on either side became punctuated by tombstones, statues and crosses, clean and stark, casting shadows over one another. The further we went, the denser and more weathered they became, a memorial forest with green lichen and moss creeping up from the roots, shrouding the names and dates of the deceased.

We turned left at the crossroads towards an empty area, damp in the shade of the trees, where an oblong hole was already sliced out of the ground. The lads placed the casket on a wooden bier on the further side. Mrs Brafton and Mrs Mills took up prime positions at the head of the grave, next to the reverend. I was shoved down towards the other end.

The reverend cleared his throat, but at that moment there was a sound behind us. A gentleman and a lady were approaching from the chapel. He was finely dressed, in a top hat and fashionable frock-coat, carrying a rolled-up umbrella which he was twirling in his hand. As he came closer I could see he was broad and plump, with a ruddy face and a well-groomed beard, scattered with grey.

Beside him, or just a step behind, she was a dainty miniature, listening attentively as he spoke. Her dress was black and made of the finest silk, far outshining even Mrs Brafton's, and soft enough to show the outline of her legs as she walked. It was lacy at the neck and pinched in at the waist, sweeping up behind her in a confection of folds and layers that seemed to float in the air. Her mouth was broad and her skin was pale with just enough years to have fostered smile lines. I couldn't help but stare at her, even here, even now. Any man would.

'Good afternoon everyone! What a turnout, eh?' the gentleman called to us, in the sort of tone you might hear any day in the better parts of Mayfair. And yet there was something in how he pronounced the 'r' in 'turnout' that echoed rolling fields and bubbling brooks rather than England's better public schools. Jane, far more attuned to social dissonances than I, could doubtless have placed his accent to a specific county, but even I knew it was a long way west of here.

I had never seen Mrs Brafton look so gratified. 'Mr Bentinck,' she said, shuffling the girls and Mrs Mills along to make room for the gentleman by her side, leaving no gap for the lady. 'How wonderful that you've come.'

'Oh no, *you* should stand at the head, Mrs Brafton,' said Mr Bentinck, indicating the spot with his umbrella. 'Miss Gainsford and I will do quite well over here.'

Mrs Brafton edged uncomfortably back towards the reverend, half-turned away from him as if to deny it was any longer her proper place, while Miss Gainsford moved between the group, kissing the girls on each cheek in the Continental style, and even allowing the Colonel to raise her hand to his dry lips. When she reached me she gazed into my eyes and I kissed her hand also, amazed at the softness of her glove and the lightness of her touch.

'Nancy Gainsford,' she said, and even through her air of bookishness there was a hint of the docks. The whiff of cockles never quite washes out. 'And you are?'

'Leo Stanhope,' I replied, feeling awkward that I didn't have a formal invitation. She frowned slightly, as if trying to remember something.

When she'd greeted everyone, she took her place among the ladies, who fidgeted like mallards next to a sleek, white tern.

'Carry on, my dear chap,' Bentinck said to the reverend, who began to speak, or rather, deaf as he was, he began to shout.

He explained to us that Maria was a good, Christian woman and had lived a decent life. A couple of the girls – I counted seven of them, although it seemed like more – exchanged glances at this. He continued, yelling that Maria had been cruelly taken from us in an act of violence that could only come from the devil, and that the perpetrator – at which point he paused and, I thought, might have glanced at me – would come to judgement, probably in this world and certainly the next. Then he leafed through his Bible while I dug my nails into my palms. He found his place and started up again, raising the pigeons from the trees above us. I had heard the reading many times before – it was a favourite of my father's – and I could easily have recited it alongside him, but I barely heard the parts about a time to heal, to embrace and to laugh, and fixated instead on the time to kill, to rend, to hate and make war. That was where old Solomon really struck a chord.

The girls and Mrs Brafton were openly weeping, and even Miss Gainsford was dabbing her eyes. Only Mrs Mills seemed unaffected, grinning like an imbecile and humming to herself.

The pall-bearers started threading ropes into the handles of the casket. The corners of my mouth twitched downwards and my chin start to tremble. I clamped my teeth together hard. Of course, I knew men were capable of tears – I'd watched husbands identify their wife's remains, and had once had to lend a tactful handkerchief to Alfie when he reached the final chapters of *The Old Curiosity Shop* – but not me. Never me. I mustn't draw attention.

The pall-bearers paid out the ropes hand over hand, lowering the casket into the ground, and I noticed something out of the corner of my eye. A woman was standing aside from the rest of us, eighty or more yards away. She wasn't wearing black, and was hesitant, pacing up and down as if she wanted to join us but didn't know whether she'd be welcome. She found a bench and sat down to watch from a distance.

Mrs Brafton noticed her too, and whispered loudly to Mr Bentinck, and then pointed at her. He nodded and strode off, but the woman hurried away towards the chapel before he could reach her.

The reverend closed with a blessing, and then announced there would be beer, sandwiches and cake served in the Station Tavern on Lillie Road, kindly paid for by the estimable Mr Bentinck.

I stayed at the graveside. I didn't want to be first into the pub, although I would've had to run full pelt to overtake a couple of the pall-bearers, who had shot off in that direction as though launched from catapults. The laggards waited gallantly for the girls, offering comforting arms around their shoulders.

I looked down into the hole, and had a fleeting fear of falling in. There were brush marks on the lid of the casket. I had thought it was made of mahogany or teak, but in fact it was a soft, pallid wood dyed darker to appear more expensive. I felt a sudden fury – with Mrs Brafton for not buying something befitting Maria, and with Maria herself for lying, for dying, for being in that box instead of here with me.

There was a sound behind me. An old fellow was standing there, propped up by his shovel.

'I'll be wanting to fill that in,' he said, indicating the pile of earth on the grass.

'Just give me a few minutes, please.'

'Aye, I'll give you five, but no more.' He put his shovel on his shoulder and wandered off to fill in some other hole, or dig one, or have a cup of tea in his shed. I didn't give a damn as long as he left me alone.

I sat down on the grass under a tree, remembering Maria's voice, and her laugh, when I noticed the woman who'd been there earlier, who'd watched us from the bench. She was walking towards the grave, the sun behind her forming a saintly halo. As she came closer, I saw she was perhaps fifty years old, with a moon-shaped face and hair that might once have been black, but was faded now, white-streaked and flamboyantly swept underneath her hat. Her clothes were plain, but not fraying or patched.

She lowered her head at the graveside, and crossed herself in the manner of Roman Catholics. As I stood up, she startled, not having noticed me before.

'I shan't be staying,' she said hastily. 'I just wanted to pay my respects.'

'It's quite all right. How did you know Maria?'

'Why do you ask?' There was a keen intelligence in her gaze, which rested for an instant on my chest and hips, and then my eyes. I felt as if she was totting me up like a column of figures, and I'd been found slightly short.

'I just want to know more about her. It turns out … I didn't know her as well as I thought. Are you a friend of her mother?'

'Like I said, I'm not staying.' She squinted in the direction the others had gone. 'I'm not welcome.'

'Why not?' I'd had enough of mysteries. 'I'm curious to know, if you don't mind.'

She rolled her eyes and fished into her purse. 'Not here. Come to my house, if you must.'

She handed me a card and stalked away towards the entrance without waiting for a reply. The card was thin and messily hand-stamped:

Madame Louisa Moreau
3 Finsbury Street
Midwife

Suddenly I didn't feel like staying. I wiped my eyes and took a fistful of the soil piled up on the grass, mixing my tears with it so part of me would always be with her. I let it pour into the grave and watched it skittering across the lid.

***

The pub was packed. The hearse driver turned out to be the funeral director as well, a Mr Atkins, the *younger* Mr Atkins he proudly announced, having been given this task by his father as an act of trust, so he'd be obliged for any appreciative comments we might have, preferably in writing.

He'd arranged for the wake to take place in the back bar of the Station Tavern for just the price of the victuals, and the landlord had lined up sandwiches and half-pint glasses of porter on the counter. I took one and sipped from it, relishing the sourness in my throat. There was a cake too, which the landlord was cutting with a long, bone-handled knife. I drained my glass and took another. Blessed numbness; it was the only way I could stop myself from running off down the street.

All around, the noise was rising and falling like waves at the seashore. Audrey was on the far side of the room with Mrs Brafton, who spoke closely into her ear. Audrey nodded, and they broke off their conversation as one of the other girls joined them.

I didn't know why I was there. I should have gone home. The burial was over, and no one wanted to talk to me; word seemed to have got round, and I kept getting strange glances, as though I might suddenly turn rabid and butcher everyone.

I decided to finish my drink and leave, but one of the ladies, who was showing her respects by eating a plate of sandwiches and quaffing a third glass of porter, cornered me to ask, with a leering expression and wet lips, whether I'd ever spent any time in a mental asylum. I was about to tell her that I had not, but I did sometimes feel a strange madness upon me, finding myself grovelling on all fours, snatching and growling like a wild animal, when someone tapped on a bottle several times. Gradually, the talking ceased until only the Colonel and the reverend were still going, as deaf as one another. They were prodded and nudged into baffled silence.

Mr Bentinck gazed around the room with a sort of benign smile, as if he was about to bless us. He seemed like a kindly uncle who spends his spare time building model ships out of matchsticks.

'A tragedy,' he said. 'A loss to us all. Let's raise a glass to Maria.'

He sat down abruptly and there was a smattering of polite clapping. He had already recommenced talking to Mrs Brafton, gesturing with the stem of his pipe, when Miss Gainsford stood up and clinked a fork against her glass.

'Thank you, James,' she began, so quietly I had to strain to hear. 'So very kind, but I feel more needs to be said. Maria was such a special person. We all loved her.' For a second her voice cracked and she took a sip of porter. 'I knew Maria for such a brief time. Just a few short years. She was a light in our lives though, wasn't she? A light that has gone out, but I know we won't ever forget her. She was a kind person, and as pretty as a picture.' Her hand went to her cheek, as if involuntarily recalling Maria's stain. 'She came from nothing, you know. It was one of the things we had in common. She grew up penniless and did what she had to do to survive, for herself and her mother.' She nodded towards Mrs Mills, who was perched by the bar with her back to us. 'And she never complained, which is unusual in this modern age, isn't it?' She surveyed the room, her eyes resting longest on Mrs Brafton. 'She was the best of us, I think. And now we have to carry on without her, though I don't know how we shall.'

She sat down and sipped her drink, white-faced. Mrs Brafton exited in the direction of the privy.

The cake was just yellow crumbs now, but the knife was still on the plate. I picked it up, and it weighed nicely; not too big, not too small. I could see my face reflected in the steel, fogged by a smear of sponge. I thought about its sharpness, the ease of a scalpel parting the flesh. I thought about deep water, the weightless sensation of sinking down into it. I wasn't afraid of these thoughts. They gave me a kind of relief. I could leave at any time. I could leave and be with Maria.

'Mr Stanhope?' I turned and there was Miss Gainsford. She was standing very close, disconcertingly so, so that I could have seen down the front of her dress if I'd chosen to, which I didn't, quite. I put down the knife. 'I was very sorry to hear you were inconvenienced before, by the police. They really don't have a clue about anything, do they?'

'No indeed.'

'We live in a topsy-turvy world, don't you think?' She seemed to have a practice of phrasing everything as a question, forcing me to agree with whatever she said. I wondered what she would do if I didn't. 'You were fond of Maria, weren't you?'

'We were fond of each other.'

'Of course. She was special, and I adored her. I always used to give her first choice of things, dresses and jewellery and the like, although I couldn't be too open about it because you don't want to cause jealousies, and girls can be so petty.' She wiped her eyes and stared at the floor, gathering herself. 'The dress she's in now was one of mine. Silk and lace. I had it made for a trip to the Continent and only wore it twice. I never guessed it would end up being used for this. Well you don't, do you?'

'It's a kind thing to have done.'

'It's the least I could do, the very least. Not just as her employer, but as her friend.'

'Oh, I thought —'

'What?' She angled herself even further forward. I could smell her hair.

'I thought Mrs Brafton was her employer.'

'Well, yes, of course.' She appeared surprised that I didn't know. 'Elizabeth runs the place on Half Moon Street, but Mr Bentinck owns it. That place and some others as well, although it's the … let's say it's the ruby in the crown of our empire. I help him with this and that, ledgers and accounts and so forth.'

'So Mrs Brafton's just a kind of manager?'

'You might say that, I suppose.' She placed her hand on my shoulder and whispered into my ear. 'She's just staff really, more of a housekeeper. She's a fearful snob and acts like the lady of the manor, but it's a place of *business* at the end of the day, and businesses have to make a *profit*, don't they?' She flashed me a brief smile. I inhaled her perfume and watched her lips. The way she angled her head and looked straight into my eyes almost invited a kiss. 'Did Maria never mention me?'

It struck me as an odd question, and a little uncomfortable. The truth was I'd never heard of her until that day, yet she was clearly hoping Maria had chattered on to me about their great friendship.

'We didn't really talk about other people very much.'

More specifically, I thought, *she* didn't talk about other people very much. I talked about them all the time.

Mr Bentinck appeared at Miss Gainsford's elbow. She introduced us and he shook my hand in an uninterested manner, leaning in close to speak to her in what he seemed to think was a quiet voice.

'I'm leaving now. Let them have a few more drinks and then settle up, will you? I don't want this going on all afternoon, especially in the circumstances.'

'Of course, James,' she said. 'They have to work tonight.'

I could see his growler carriage through the window. It was black and sleek, with shiny brass lamps.

As soon as he'd gone, she turned back to me. 'It's been such a *pleasure* to meet you, Mr Stanhope. I wish it had been under better circumstances. Poor Maria, she really was an angel, wasn't she?'

I watched her go, which was a pleasure in more than one way. Audrey sidled over with two glasses and handed one to me.

'Well I never,' she said. 'Miss Gainsford don't talk to just anyone, you know. We didn't expect her here, let alone Mr Bentinck. Quite an honour for Maria, him coming.'

'Is it?'

'Oh yes. He's an important man. Related to the Cavendish Bentincks, you know.'

'Really?'

'Yes,' she said firmly, irritated by my sceptical tone.

I thought it unlikely. George Cavendish Bentinck was a Member of Parliament and his family had wealth going back generations. James Bentinck didn't seem like the blossom of such a tree. Even its most distant twigs surely didn't reach as far as a West Country boy running a London brothel.

'And Miss Gainsford is his bookkeeper?'

'Mr Bentinck makes all the money and she counts it for him.'

'A lot of money?'

'He's got a house in Belgravia and a cottage in the country. Cookham, by the river. Beautiful it is. He has an art collection and –'

'And how about Miss Gainsford?'

Audrey shrugged. 'Don't know. Never been to her place, only his.'

'Oh. Oh, I see.'

'You're shocked.' She smiled and cocked her head to one side. It was amazing how innocent she could appear. She could've been one of my mother's maids. 'Nancy Gainsford's worked for him for years. The two of 'em used to do everything in them days, I heard, until they got Hugo as well, to sort out any trouble. He was a boxer when I was a little girl, you know, and well known around these parts. He had posters.'

'Would Hugo sort out one of the girls too, if needs be?'

'Oh no, he dotes on us when he's not with his bees.' Her chin was quivering. She was doing everything she could not to cry. 'I don't s'pose they'll ever find out what happened. Nobody cares about us, especially the police.

And the worst of it is, I keep thinking, if I hadn't agreed to swap with her, she might still be alive.'

'Swap with her?'

'She wanted that Thursday off, and said she'd do my next two Tuesdays.' She gave a sad little shrug. 'Never will now though, will she?'

'Do you know why she wanted to swap?'

'No, she didn't confide in me, not like that. We weren't close or nothing.' She took a gulp of her ale, and I realised she was a little drunk. 'It's just ... two deaths in a few days. Makes you think about things, that's all.'

'Two deaths? Who was the other one?'

'Jack Flowers, one of Mr Bentinck's men.'

It took me a moment to remember how I knew the name. 'The man who drowned? But that was an accident.'

'So they say, but I don't know. Two of 'em in such a short time.'

I couldn't make sense of it. The death of Jack Flowers had been so *commonplace*. It was part of my ordinary life, working at the hospital and going home, living from one Wednesday evening to the next. How could he possibly be connected to Maria? And yet, it was, undeniably, an odd coincidence.

'I didn't know he worked for Mr Bentinck.'

'Oh yes. Nasty piece of work too, was Jack. If he hadn't been dead already he's the first one I'd have thought did for Maria.' She finished the rest of her drink in one large swig, slamming her empty glass down on the bar. 'But I'll tell you this: if I ever find out who did kill her, I'll rip off his balls and stuff 'em down his throat.'

8

ON MONDAY MORNING, I went back to work, though I would much rather have stayed in bed.

Everything was normal. At the staff entrance, the doorman greeted me with a nod and went back to his puzzle. The hospital looked the same and smelled the same, but still felt unreal to me, as if someone had rebuilt the whole thing for my benefit.

I found Mr Hurst in his office. He looked up briefly from his desk, and went back to reading *The Lancet*, pointing at the chair to indicate I should sit. He kept me waiting several more minutes before putting down his journal and removing his spectacles.

'Well?'

'I'm sorry, sir,' I said, sitting up straight. 'I knew the girl who died and I was very shocked to see her. I was sick and needed time to recover and then there was a funeral. I wasn't myself. I promise it will never happen again.'

I'd honed this little speech in my room before dawn. I'd experimented with a longer version too, explaining how we'd loved each other and even including an exhortation to his charitable nature, before remembering that no such thing existed. He only cared about things he could dissect.

'Reliability!' he bellowed abruptly, making me jump. 'Reliability above all things! That's what I ask. The dead don't take days off.' It struck me that arguably the dead took the rest of time off, but he wasn't in the mood to be nit-picked. 'What is a man if he can't keep his word, if he can't be relied upon? He's no better than a savage.'

'Sir, I'm sorry I let you down. I promise –'

'You've been a fine secretary: polite, hard-working, good handwriting and stitching. You've learned a lot. And you've been punctual, or so I thought. But I've no place for people who faint about and take a week off without so much as a by-your-leave. It's not good enough, do you hear?'

'I do.'

He sighed, and put his spectacles on. I could feel him relenting, just a little. He went back to his journal, turning over two pages in quick succession, unread, and then looked up at the ceiling in exasperation, as though it was its fault. He took his spectacles off again and wiped his forehead.

'What happened, Stanhope? The police were here, one of those detective fellows, asking me about *you*. And that dead girl. Do you know what she was?'

'Yes, sir.'

He puffed out his cheeks. 'Damn it all! Can you tell me she was a relative, a neighbour, a childhood friend?'

'No.'

'Damn and blast!' He put his spectacles back on with the air of a judge putting on the black cap. 'You leave me no choice, none at all. I spoke with the bursar and will be taking on a new secretary. He said we should let you go completely, but I argued on your behalf. Lord knows why.'

'Thank you, sir.'

'If you wish to be further employed at this hospital you should report to the chappie in charge of the porters. What's his name?'

'Greatorex.'

'That's him. Report to him this morning and he'll assign your duties. For what it's worth, Stanhope, I'm sorry to see you go.'

―――――

If I was honest, despite the demotion and commensurate reduction in salary, it was a relief not to be working for Mr Hurst any longer. I didn't think I could watch another body being cut up after Maria, and I welcomed the routine of being a porter again. There was an irresistible detachment to it. No one took any notice of the porters.

Lloyd Greatorex was a fastidious fellow, twice my age and as much a fixture in the hospital as the walls and windows. I sometimes had the impression he could be in more than one place at once. I would notice him in the men's ward, checking the splints and bandages, and the next minute he would be coming towards me along the corridor, and the next showing some junior porter how to manoeuvre a trolley down a step. Everyone took him for granted, but if he ever left the place it would collapse around our ears and no one would have a clue why.

We'd shared a glass or two in our time, in the Lamb and Flag. I had the feeling he'd been grooming me as his protégé at one point, and had been disappointed when I became a secretary. Even so, I knew he was secretly proud that one of his own had scaled such heights. I still had his card wishing me good luck.

His office was in the basement, more remote than even the examination room. It was packed floor to ceiling with files and books, in part to keep out the malodorous fumes from the patients' baths next door. He looked up from the schedule that he kept with him every minute of every day, strips of paper filled with names and shifts, separated by sheets of pink blotter.

'Stanhope,' he said. 'The prodigal prince returns.'

'Couldn't stay away.'

'Not what I heard. I heard you stayed away too long, and that's why you're back with us riff-raff.'

'I'm grateful for your concern.'

I hadn't meant it to sound sarcastic. I really was grateful; he had probably been given the choice about whether to take me back. But somehow we'd always spoken to each other this way, a mixture of apparent distrust and grudging esteem. It was hard to break the habit.

'Fallen from heaven?' he said. 'Must be quite a bump. I suppose you think you'll be getting the best shift, do you?'

'I hadn't given it any thought.'

'Well, Torbin's retired now and Watson's taken his place.'

'So I get Watson's old position in the men's ward?'

'No, Roper's been sent there.'

'You mean I'm in the stores?' It wasn't so bad as long as you kept a close count of what the other porters took out, and they already hated me anyway.

'Not so lucky. Young Perch has taken over there. He can carry more than Roper ever did, and he farts a good deal less and all.'

'Poor old Roper. Too much suet.'

Greatorex nodded grimly. 'The exercise'll do him good, and his gas is better spread around the place than building up in the stores, especially in the winter when the fire's lit.'

'So there are no positions at all?'

'I didn't say that.'

He made a play of examining his schedule, his lips moving a little. It pleased him to make me wait. I noticed his hair was thinner and more salt than pepper these days, and his finger was shaking. But he still had to hand the same foul concoction he claimed kept him regular – a cold, thin soup of mushed vegetables in water that made the room smell comfortingly of compost. When he smiled I could see the dregs of it on his teeth.

'Nights is all I've got. Not the wards either, the Other Departments.'

The Other Departments shift was the worst one; administration, mail room, reception, records, kitchens, corridors, offices and toilets. It was upstairs and downstairs, stretched throughout the hospital with no simple route or regulation, and wherever you were, you could be sure you should've been somewhere else. Most people, when they first became a porter, dreaded the diseases, excrement and stink of bile, but you soon got used to those. It was the *walking* that really got to you.

'All right.'

'You'll find things have changed, mind. The rear stairs are down only now and it's eight rounds instead of seven. New layout in the stores, but young Perch can show you. He'll have some overalls for you too.' He paused, stroking his chin. 'This is your last chance, you know. Any difficulties and you'll be out. Nothing I can do.'

'I know.'

'We're covered tonight so you can start tomorrow. Be here at six. Welcome back.'

I reached home at lunchtime. I still didn't have a replacement key, so I went in through the front door, nodding to Constance, who was minding the shop, rushing through too quickly for her to delay me with some obscure remedy she'd found.

Soon I would have to be awake every night. I lay on my bed and tried to sleep, but it wouldn't come, so I read *Barnaby Rudge* until dinner, and then left the house for chess club. I usually only went on a Thursday, but made an exception as I knew I wouldn't be able to go again for some time. I was surprised to find Jacob there.

In the end I surrendered to his wheedling and told him about the funeral, the speeches, and the peculiar midwife, Madame Moreau, and what she'd said to me at the graveside. He was as helpful as ever.

'Bah! Who knows? Who cares?'

He took my knight and lined him up alongside my bishop, rook and three pawns, turning him to face me accusingly.

'Do you think I should tell the police about her?'

'Them?'

He wasn't an admirer of the profession after two boys had broken into his shop and stolen a gold bracelet. He'd come downstairs with a hammer, and would have split their heads, so he said, if he hadn't made the mistake of roaring first and alerting them. The police did little with his description of two quick-footed urchins with demons' faces, so he was left frustrated and out of pocket, and had blamed them ever since.

He puffed on his cigar and grimaced at me. 'The police just ask damn-fool questions. As if I'm too old to lock up my own shop.'

On the other side of the room a little cheer went up as a close game was resolved, and the two players shook hands. Jacob looked over his shoulder at them and rolled his eyes. 'Such good losers, you English. So much easier to be polite in defeat than victory.' He watched me take one of his pawns, stroking his beard. 'Who do *you* think killed Maria?'

'I have no idea.'

'Think! If you had to say, then who?'

He moved his bishop and I almost took it, before realising I would be leaving my queen exposed to his rook, which was sneaking up on the left side of the board. I was uncomfortable and quite unable to concentrate. I moved my queen to a safe place and he moved his bishop immediately, threatening both my remaining bishop and the squares around my king.

'Wouldn't you like another drink?' I said.

He snorted. 'No more alcohol! You've grown arrogant, my friend. You resent me my one win in, what is it, weeks? Months? What's wrong with you?'

'You're distracting me. I don't know who killed her. One of her customers maybe.'

He narrowed his eyes. 'Don't you *want* to know?'

'Yes, but …'

I couldn't tell him about Maria's little shams: her name and her mother. I'd already reached the conclusion they weren't lies. Not exactly. She had simply composed the world as she wanted it to be to survive the life she led. It almost made me love her more. Jacob wouldn't understand, and it would confirm all his prejudices about her, about the two of us. But I knew he wouldn't let it go until I said *something*. He was intolerable that way.

'Perhaps Mr Bentinck? He seemed less than trustworthy.'

Jacob relit his cigar and pointed it at me through a billow of smoke. 'James Bentinck. Do you know about him?' I shook my head, suddenly aware I'd placed my other knight in danger. He grunted and took it. 'The rumour is he used to have a respectable position, and a wife. She died, and not long afterwards he opened his first place. Back in the sixties. Not the one you know, much smaller, out east. Stepney. Poor area. Too many Jews.' He sniggered at his own joke, his beard waggling. 'He'd been in the civil service or something like that. He came into a bit of money and that woman, what's her name, the pretty one?'

'Nancy Gainsford?'

'Yes, her. She does stick in the mind, does she not? She had the *expertise*. There were other places around, long-standing, and they didn't like this upstart stealing their customers. It's a rough trade, but he learned it fast. A *natural*. There were a few battles, and people got hurt. Burnings, beatings and stabbings. Even a drowning. Bad times. Bad for business. So Bentinck negotiated a truce, and after a few years they found they were all working for him. Or gone. So there you have it; that's the kind of man he is.'

'Madame Moreau certainly seemed wary of him.'

'Sensible woman.'

'I wonder how she even knew Maria.'

He shrugged, spilling ash on to his sleeve. 'I would have thought that was obvious. An occupational hazard. Why do you care? Unless you think it was yours, in which case you're even more deluded than I thought. Your move.'

'If she was pregnant, then someone must be the father.'

'Brilliant. You've grasped that much at least.'

'Thank you, Jacob, I'm finding your sarcasm invaluable.' I moved my bishop to the only square it could go to. 'What I mean is, that could be why she was killed.'

'My friend, you loved her, and you think she was pure, but still, she was a whore. Don't look like that, it's a fact. Why would any man care if she was pregnant?'

'I don't know. But someone killed her for something.'

I took one of his pawns and he took mine. 'An eye for an eye,' he said. 'And a pawn for a pawn. You're running out of pieces.'

'I shouldn't have come. I can't concentrate. There's so much I don't understand.'

'Bah!' He pointed my pawn at me. 'These girls, they're so sweet, so cooperative, telling you how *handsome* you are and what a wonderful gentleman. You want to be their hero because you know no better. But it's all fake. They lead a different life from you, and you know nothing about them. Pray you never do.'

'I can't.'

'Then my advice is worthless and we should go back to playing chess, especially as I'm winning. As ever, you will do exactly what you want.'

———

I was at the hospital by five-thirty in the afternoon the next day, getting my overalls and itinerary from young Perch and learning the new layout of the store room – office supplies at the back, medical disposables at the front, and otherwise the same as before.

My first task was to collect the mail. This involved carrying a basket around the offices and emptying the trays of outgoing letters into it, before lugging the whole thing down to the mail room. I wasn't even halfway through my round when the basket was already full, so I went down and waited at the stable door of the mail room as if hoping to be petted.

On the wall there was a map, peeling at the edges. I put my finger where the hospital was, on the curve of the river as it wriggled through London. I traced it east, through Barking, Dagenham and Basildon, places I'd never been to, and then past Canvey Island, which wasn't really an island at all, to Southend-on-Sea, a minor town on the estuary where the Thames sucked the filth of London out into the English Channel.

I had found a postcard from Southend-on-Sea in Jack Flowers's wallet. According to Audrey, he had worked for Bentinck, and I wondered whether Maria had known him.

I was preoccupied through the rest of my shift, such that I didn't even hear Nurse Coften when she hailed me.

'Someone's calling you. Are you deaf?' asked the old goat in the wheelchair I was pushing, which was fine coming from him after I'd just wiped his shit off the corridor floor.

She looked tired – the nurses rotated shifts – but happy to see me. 'Mr Stanhope!' she said. 'I'm glad you've recovered.' She glanced down at my overalls with the unspoken message: *even though you're so diminished.*

'I'm sorry I was rude to you before. I know you were trying to help me.'

'Yes, well, you weren't yourself I'm sure.'

After she'd gone, the old fellow twisted round and gave me a curious look.

'I'm always myself these days,' I said to him, by way of explanation. 'But I used to pretend to be someone else.'

He laughed so hard he coughed up blood into his hand.

By the end of my shift I was almost falling down with exhaustion, counting the minutes on every clock I passed. My muscles and bones were aching to get horizontal and stay that way for at least eight hours. I'm not a man who can do without sleep.

My last task was the post again, this time delivering the new morning's letters and parcels from the mail room to all the wards and offices. It was as interesting as it sounds.

My travels took me past the children's wards, the last of which was a small room filled with cots all lined up, as if the babies were displayed for sale. You heard it before you saw it, squalling infants protesting on the shoulders of the nurses, whose patience and calm were a thing to witness. The nearest girl smiled at me as she stroked the back of the baby she was soothing, singing in a low voice and rocking to and fro, almost dancing.

I thought of the strange woman I had met, the midwife. How had she known Maria? Was it no more than the obvious reason? In all my time with Maria, I had never really considered the possibility of her becoming pregnant, but Jacob was right, it was a natural consequence of what she did. She must have believed she was facing it alone, but she wasn't. I would have raised a child with her. I would have done anything she wanted.

When I got home I fell asleep instantly, fully dressed and still wearing my coat. I woke up not even an hour later covered in sweat from a bad dream, my fear still hanging in the room even though I couldn't remember what I'd been afraid of.

It was two weeks since I'd last seen her alive.

I was determined not to rush. Something of Ripley's ponderous manner must've rubbed off on me. I got dressed and brushed my hair, waiting for my better judgement to tell me not to be such a fool, but it didn't, so I pocketed Alfie's spare key, put on my bowler hat and left the house.

I just couldn't believe the police would ever find Maria's killer. Audrey was right: Ripley wasn't interested, not really. A girl like Maria, he thought she'd brought death upon herself. He'd arrested me because I was the most obvious person, and then he'd let me go because someone higher up had told him to. I still couldn't fathom who or why. Why would anyone be interested in *me*?

It was that more than anything. I couldn't make sense of what had happened: her death, my imprisonment and unexpected release, the mysterious midwife. But if I told Ripley about it, he'd jump to the most perfunctory conclusion: that Maria had been pregnant and was killed because of it, by a jealous wife or an angry customer or *someone*. He wouldn't really care who.

On the Embankment I followed the crowds to the Metropolitan Railway Station, a squat building with arched windows, mock-columns and a curious stepped roof. It was small yet grandiose, like the gatehouse of a minor country estate. I bought my ticket and descended the steep stairs, underground. The walls were plastered with advertisements for all sorts of things: shampoos, chocolate, Three Castles cigarettes and Steedman's Soothing Powders. The air was dense with smoke, swirling in shafts lit by the skylights overhead.

It was full of people, and more were arriving all the time. I wove between them to the end of the platform, and stood under a sign saying 'Third Class'.

In just a few minutes there was an explosion of light and noise as the train burst out of the tunnel, propelled on a billowing surge of steam. As it pulled to a halt, the doors flapped open and dozens of passengers were disgorged.

The train had seemed huge from the outside, but inside it was barely high enough to stand, with a curved ceiling so it could slip through the tunnels like an earwig. I had travelled this way a few times before, when I first got my position at the hospital and was living in Camden Town, but my unease had never completely worn off. Not so for the fellow opposite, who was fast asleep, nodding in agreement with the urgings of the engine.

As we accelerated, I opened a window to let the wind rush on to my face, stinging my eyes. It was exactly how I imagined it would feel to fall from a great height.

A minute later the train slowed down again, brakes screeching. At the platform an attendant in uniform shouted: 'Westminster Bridge!'

After an hour, and more than a dozen stops, we reached the morose-sounding Moorgate Street, where I exited the station, blinking in the sunshine.

I set off, following the map Alfie had lent me, watched by two old men smoking bacca pipes on a doorstep. Most of the buildings I passed were derelict, and even those that weren't were hunched and creaking, their foreheads almost touching across the alleyways.

Cripplegate was an apt name.

Between the meagre curtains I could see people sleeping, eight or ten to a room, huddled close together like baby mice. The alleyways were murky, but there was movement in the shadows. I passed an old woman all in black, dipping and slipping like a wounded crow, carrying a sack on her back that probably contained everything she owned. A little girl ran away from me, hurtling through the doorway of a tenement on bare feet, a cadaver of a place with dark, impenetrable windows like eye sockets long since excavated.

Finsbury Street sloped upwards, unlit and unmade, bitten deep by gutters full of rancid water and excrement. There was a pub just in view at the end, and a number of young men were drinking outside. Men don't usually stare at other men for long, but these did, unbothered by the potential for conflict, perhaps even welcoming it. I was scared but also slightly thrilled. What more masculine experience could there be than to face up to another man and look him in the eyes, knowing that one of you will be defeated?

Her house wasn't hard to find. The second door on the right had a brass plaque on the wall reading: *Madame Moreau, Midwife.*

She opened the door wearing an apron, with her sleeves rolled up. 'What do you want?'

'I've come like you said. My name's Leo Stanhope. We met at the cemetery.'

She blinked three times in quick succession and opened the door wider, looking out along the road both ways. 'I see. Well, you'd better come in then.'

9

I FOLLOWED HER INTO the parlour and immediately recoiled. On one wall there was a rack of implements that looked like household tools: pliers, tongs, a serving spoon with a sharpened edge and a whole row of metal crochet hooks. In the middle stood a large table, six feet or more in length and at least three feet wide, with a butcher's-block groove around the edge. A black bloodstain spread out from the centre and down the sides, and at each corner a strap hung down to the straw-covered floor.

Madame Moreau beckoned me through a further door and into the back room. It was difficult to believe they were parts of the same house. There was a dining table and four upholstered chairs, a piano against one wall and a finch in a cage hanging above it, fluttering and angling its head at me. On the opposite wall, Jesus hung from a cross bleeding cracked red paint down his hands and feet.

She sat at the table. 'It'll be three shillings, in advance.'

'Pardon me?'

'Three shillings. More if it's the later months, but you're not far gone from the look of you. Guaranteed, otherwise your money back.'

'Money back for what?'

She folded her arms. 'Are you pregnant or not?'

'No! I'm a …' but I trailed off. It was ludicrous to insist that I was a man after that question. And she knew my name. I glanced back at the door.

She smiled thinly and patted my hand. 'Don't worry. What you are means nothing to me. I've seen it all: women who dress up in suits and ties, gentlemen who wear dresses and grow their hair, and wealthy ladies who are best friends, inseparable day and night, more in love with each other than their husbands. I have an eye for it. And an ear. Are you sure you're not pregnant? One little slip, easily done.'

'No,' I replied, realising my mistake. This wasn't a place where women came to give birth, this was something else altogether. No one would come here unless they had to, unless they were desperate. Women were sometimes brought into the hospital after such procedures, and the nurses would whisper the word to each other in the corridors, eyes alight at the wickedness of it: *abortion*. The destruction of a life not yet started.

She produced a little bottle with a colourful label from her apron pocket. 'If you don't want the hook there's Widow Welch's, but it don't always suffice. No money back for that.'

'I'm not pregnant.'

'The clap then?'

'No!'

She raised her eyebrows and blinked several times. 'Then why in heaven's name are you here?'

'You gave me your card at the funeral of Maria Milanes, remember? Maria *Mills*, I suppose. I just wanted to speak to you.'

'Oh, I see. I assumed … well, that you were in trouble. It don't do to discuss these things in public.' She stood up and tapped the cage, arousing the little bird to a frenzy of excitement. She poked a nut through the bars, holding it there and making kissing noises while the finch scratched at it with its beak.

'Androgyne,' she said. 'That's the word for your type. You're an androgyne. A person who thinks they're the opposite of what they are.'

I shouldn't have cared, but it was irritating to be so patronised, so reduced, by someone who did what she did. 'Not that it's any of your business, but I don't *think* I'm a man. I *am* a man.'

'Is that a fact?' She didn't seem at all bothered by my sharpness. 'There was a man here this morning as it happens. I don't get them often, which is why I mention it. Sitting right where you are now, drinking my tea, leaving his mucky boot-prints all over my floor. He came in with a girl, not married or nothing, and put his hand in his pocket, no quibbling over the odd farthing like some of 'em.'

She paused, as if she expected me to say that at least the fellow had done the decent thing, but what was decent about it? Paying for that wasn't *decent*, it was an abomination.

When I didn't reply, she continued: 'So I chatted to her while it was going on, giving her something else to think about, you know. She told me how he'd tried to worm his way out of it until her two brothers caught up with him. One of 'em has a bit of a reputation. Anyway, after that, she said, her lad had begged to be allowed to take her straight down to me, and pay for it and everything. Don't know what she saw in him. She was a pretty thing and he wasn't a looker in any light and had the manners of a hog. Do you know what she told me?'

'How could I?' I was becoming impatient. Would she ever get to the point?

'Well I'll tell you.' She interlaced her fingers, reminding me bizarrely of my father, who would rather have slit his own wrists than sit here and listen to this woman. 'The girl said, "If I'm not with him, then I'll have no one." And there you have it. She'd rather be with that gormless waste of skin than be on her own.'

'Not all men are the same.'

'No, not all. Some are worse. He didn't beat her or rape her as far as I know, though of course she had them brothers, so maybe it was fear of them rather than any forbearance on his part.'

I folded my arms. 'You've made your point. You don't like men.'

'It's not a question of *liking*. I see what I see. And what I don't see is why any woman would pretend to be one. Do you want to be Prime Minister? Or a priest? Or stand outside the pub making suggestions to every woman passing, is that it? You can act like a man if you want but you can't win a pissing contest or grow a beard worthy of the name. You still bleed. Men fight and drink and plant their seeds in any woman who's willing, and some who ain't. Why would you want to be like that? Is it to get work?'

My position at the hospital had nothing to do with why I was a man, though it was true no woman would ever be offered it. I was a man because, underneath my skin, I had a man's beating heart. Nothing more, nothing less.

Sometimes I wondered whether I might go to sleep one night and wake up the next morning the way I should have been. And if that miracle were to happen, nothing would change, and everything would change. I would have the same lodging, the same life, the same love for Maria, but I would be whole. I would be one person through and through.

But no one else would ever understand that.

'I'm just here to ask a question, that's all. I'm trying to find out about Maria. There are things she wasn't altogether truthful about.'

Madame Moreau shrugged. 'Well, that was her choice, wasn't it? Not your business. You should go home. I only deal with females as a rule.'

I stood up, frustrated. The finch chirruped, still pecking at the nut on the floor of its cage. Its plumage was a perfect bright yellow with black on its wings and head, but its eyes were mismatched. One of them was glossy black but the other was milky. Half-blind. I could still remember one hazy summer day, peering through binoculars while my father whispered in a state of high excitement: 'Look, Lottie. It's a siskin! In our garden! A siskin!' But it flew away before I could get a proper look.

'Did Maria come here for ... to see you on a professional basis?'

She creased her whiskery top lip into dark, vertical lines. 'Did you hear what I said? Go home.'

'Please. I need to know. It can't make any difference now. Was she pregnant? And if so, can you tell me who was the father? Does the name Jack Flowers mean anything to you?'

'No, and don't be idiotic. She was a whore, so how would she tell? Elizabeth Brafton likes to believe she's running a high-class establishment, but it's still a dolly-house, isn't it? There are still consequences, though she doesn't want to think about them.'

'You mean pregnancy?'

'I mean *abortion*. I'm an abortionist, and not ashamed of it. And a seller of remedies for various ailments, including the clap, which you haven't got, apparently. No one wants me around unless they need me.'

'I see.'

'No you don't,' she said with another thin smile. 'Perhaps you are a man after all.'

'I work in a hospital. I see women come in bleeding from such things. Some of them die of it.'

'Not my doing. That's what happens when ladies are too proud or too scared to come to me and get it done proper. Too afraid of being found out. But we're all sinners, aren't we, *Mister* Androgyne?'

'Stanhope.'

'If you say so.'

She ushered me towards the door and I caught sight of a photograph on her wall. It was a group portrait of men and women in uniform. The woman at the front, with eager eyes and a pointed cap, was certainly Madame Moreau, perhaps fifteen or more years before. They were posed of course, looking ahead, backs straight, soldiers and doctors and nurses, pushed together for this moment, but still they were delightfully animate. They seemed on the verge of breaking into laughter and ruining the whole thing. They were barely holding it back. I wondered where the photograph had been taken and who these people were. Other people's lives, I thought. Some far-off place, some far-off war.

'Goodbye, Madame Moreau.'

I hadn't yet reached the corner of the street when four men stepped out of an alleyway in front of me.

'Hand over your wallet.'

Their leader was cocky, not even twenty years old. In the gloom he seemed entirely grey: face, hair and jacket. The others were of a similar age but were more restless, shifting their weight from foot to foot. I backed up as they spread out on either side. No matter which way I turned, one of them was behind me.

My skin was tingling. I was no longer excited by the idea of fighting – now I was shaking and couldn't stop. People were killed this way, for a few pennies or an item of clothing. The span of my male life wouldn't even exceed my female one. My body would end up naked on Mr Hurst's table: *female, roughly 25, multiple wounds, death from blood loss, no culprits identified*. He wouldn't recognise me.

'Go on, Micky, have him,' said one of them, mimicking a punch with his fist, full of acts of violence another man should commit. 'Look at him! He's a weakling. Have him, Micky.'

Micky didn't need any encouragement. He lunged at me with his left hand and punched me in the mouth with his right, a short jab, almost a flick, and I staggered backwards, the pain welling up. I could taste blood. Before I could respond he punched me in the stomach and I doubled over. I managed to take a short gasping breath and force my eyes open, but all I could see were his shoes, too small for his feet, toes poking out where he'd cut off the ends. I thought, well, at least he won't kick me, but then he brought up his knee into my cheek and I heard a crack. There was something hard in my mouth and I spat it into my hand. When I opened my palm, it was my tooth, wet with blood and saliva.

He pulled me upright, his fist gripping my shirt, reaching for the wallet inside my jacket pocket. I heard a ripping sound as my shirt seam tore. Instinctively I covered myself and twisted away.

Footsteps were coming down the road – here to watch the fun.

'What are you doing?' Madame Moreau was standing in the street holding a metal poker, pointing it at Micky. 'You know better than to harass people who come to my door.'

She raised the poker, but he quickly put up his hands and almost wailed: 'Didn't know he was one of yours, Madame. It's always ladies, ain't it?'

'It don't matter who it is. No guest at my house is to be interfered with. Do you understand? *Do you understand?*'

'Yes. I'm sorry, Madame.'

'I pulled you out your mother's cunny, and don't you forget it. Now get home.' His friends sniggered, but she wasn't finished. 'And take these vermin with you.'

They nodded dumbly and hurried down the hill, just slowly enough to tell themselves they weren't fleeing.

'Thank you,' I said, thickly, my lip starting to swell. Rescued by a woman. I was truly the feeblest man alive.

She indicated my shirt where I was holding it closed across the rip.

'Do up your coat, you fool. And get home.'

'I will.'

She took a deep breath. 'There was one gentleman Maria mentioned a couple of times. A soldier, she said. An officer. They used to go for walks in the park. I don't know his name.'

'A soldier?' I couldn't remember many soldiers visiting the brothel. It wasn't all that near the barracks. 'Are you sure?'

She stalked back to her house without replying, or even a backward glance.

———

'What happened to your face?' Greatorex was peering at me with a disgusted expression. I knew I must look a sight, and I felt silly too, and craven. A *weakling* was about right. I'd been shaking all the way home, and had jumped like a rabbit when a beggar stood up suddenly from a bench in Holborn.

'I'm all right.'

'Have you been fighting?'

Not really. 'Don't you ever go home?'

His wife had died soon after I came to the hospital and he hadn't missed a day; I wondered if anyone was looking after him now.

'I have to keep an eye on things.'

I smiled lopsidedly. 'I don't need supervision.'

'Really? Turning up looking like that? Maybe I should join you on this shift.'

'I'll be fine, thank you.'

I set off on my round. I should have started with the offices, collecting the letters and parcels from their trays, but I had another destination in mind. Once I was sure Greatorex wasn't following me – which wouldn't have surprised me in the least – I made a beeline for the records office.

It was, of course, locked. Welsh Morgan ran the place and knocked off at six o'clock sharp even if there was a queue of people waiting. But I'd been down here at least daily for two years, and I knew their routine. I knew Welsh Morgan drank too much most lunchtimes and his assistant had to do the afternoons on his own, and I knew his assistant fed the stray cats that came to the back window. He said it was to keep down the rats, but that was no reason to stroke them and give them names. And I knew Welsh Morgan and his assistant possessed only one key between them, and at night it was tucked under the door with just a sliver of blue ribbon poking out.

It took me ten seconds to get in and shut the door behind me.

The cabinets were arranged around the edge of the room, with the patient records along the back wall in alphabetical order. 'F' was for Flowers. There was a whole garden full of Flowers in there and I had to hold each file under the window to make out the writing. The ones supplied by Mr Hurst – supplied by me – were pale blue instead of manila, with a small black cross at the top left to indicate that the person had not left the hospital alive.

I could feel something soft against my leg: a cat. He was a big fellow, bulkily muscular with thick, golden fur and a flat, doleful face. I stroked him, feeling ridges of scar tissue around his ears and neck. He mewed and put his front legs up on the filing cabinet as if he meant to scale it. On the top there was a jar full of meat bones, and I dropped one on to the floor. The bruiser set upon it hungrily.

'Did you get locked in?' I said to him, and then heard another noise.

It was a snuffle, half a snore in the back of the throat, the sound of a man sleeping. Or waking. I could just make out a figure curled up under a table, wrapped in some kind of blanket. I couldn't tell whether it was Welsh Morgan, sleeping off another session at the pub, or his assistant, so attached to the cats he couldn't face being parted from them. Whoever it was snored again and stirred, but then settled, and was silent.

I dropped another bone for the cat; he wouldn't mew while he was eating. I pulled out the next Flowers file, and thanked goodness it was the right one. I held the paper up to the dim light and tried to make out my own handwriting.

God, I was good: neat, legible and to the point, not a word wasted.

Jack Flowers. 26 years of age. Deceased 19th of January 1880. Drowned in the river. Water found in both lungs, weighing 30 oz (right) and 26 oz (left). Bloating. No signs of a struggle. No other markings. Death by misadventure, not considered suspicious.

The last thing I saw in the room was the cat's shining eyes reflecting the light from the corridor – the only waking witness to my crime.

But I had found what I was looking for: the widow's address.

EXCEPT MRS FLOWERS WASN'T at home.

Late the next morning, after spending three and a half hours cursing the transparency of my curtain and a further half hour trying to hang up a blanket to block the light, I set out eastwards.

Ludgate Hill was a dull thoroughfare leading from Fleet Street towards St Paul's. There was a small shop on one corner, little more than a narrow window and a door painted with the legend *Dolan and Son, Butcher*. A woman I didn't recognise was unlocking it. She looked as if she'd spent her entire life facing a gale at sea, and could have been aged anywhere from forty to sixty, such was her leathern face and sparse hair.

'Good morning.'

She jumped and turned with her back to the door.

'What do you want?'

'Is this the right address for Mrs Flowers?'

'She ain't here. Who are you?' She seemed suspicious, and was fumbling for something in her apron pocket.

'My name's Leo Stanhope. I met Mrs Flowers at the hospital after her husband's death. I gave her the police report.'

'Oh Lord, no.' She put her hand across her mouth and seemed about to sink down on to the step. 'You're from the infirmary. Is she … is it bad news?'

'I'm not from the infirmary.' She was on the very brink of tears. 'Is that where Mrs Flowers is?'

Finally, she found what she was searching for: a folding pocket knife. But she didn't threaten me with it, she just turned it over in her hands. 'Blasted hooligans took her away right in front of her little ones. They was terrified. Not safe in our own beds any more, are we? I thought you was one of 'em before I got a proper look at you.'

'You mean she was kidnapped? Is she all right?'

'No. They bludged her on the head, the cowards. She's lucky to be alive.'

———

It was raining heavily when the cabbie left me on Cleveland Street, just south of the Euston Road, standing outside a building four storeys high, set among a hotchpotch of factories and commercial premises. Above the door a single word had been carved into the lintel: *Workhouse*.

I knocked and waited. Eventually a face poked out, a woman of perhaps thirty-five, slim and earnest with her hair tied back.

'Yes?'

'Is this the workhouse infirmary?'

'The workhouse has closed, now it's just the infirmary. I'm the matron here.' She wiped her hands down her cotton pinny, for the thousandth time that day by the look of it.

'I've come to visit a patient of yours. Mrs Flowers.'

'Visiting day is Tuesday.'

'My name's Stanhope. I'm with the police.' It was a lie, but an easy one. 'It's an urgent matter, relating to a crime, a serious crime. I have to speak with her today.'

She narrowed her eyes. 'You should get some ice on that.'

I'd forgotten how I must look. 'It's just a bruise. I got it in the course of my duties.' I stood up a little straighter, feeling genuinely proud for an instant, before I remembered it was a complete fabrication.

'You'd better come with me.'

I followed her through a gloomy atrium and onwards to a hall full of boys in beds shoved together so tightly that for most there was no way out without clambering over other boys. Some of them were lying on top of their blankets and others underneath, dozing or cataleptic. Just a few were engaged in games of cards or pebbles, resting on their elbows or sitting cross-legged on the floor. Even so, there was no laughter, no clamour or commotion from so large a group of boys. They barely looked at us as we passed.

Beyond that was a further hall, similar to the first, full of men and stinking of vomit. I could feel the density of it in the back of my throat like a lump, and had to swallow hard to avoid gagging. Most of them were old, or looked old. The wretch nearest the door was writhing to and fro in his bed, twisting his jacket around himself. The next was lying with his mouth open, his skin the colour of dishwater. Both his sleeves were empty.

Westminster Hospital was a palace by comparison, but it was for those who could pay. This was for everyone else.

The matron led me to a nurses' room containing a table, four mismatched chairs and a cupboard covered with piles of paper.

'You'd better take a seat. I'll fetch her.'

Five minutes later, she returned. I'd quite forgotten what Jack Flowers's widow looked like, and would never have recognised her with that huge bandage around her head. But then she scowled at me, and the memory came flooding back.

'You again?' she said.

We sat face to face across the table. The matron left us to speak alone, interrupted only by the clattering of a moth trapped in one of the lamps, its wings beating against the glass.

'How have you been?' I asked.

She sipped a glass of water and wiped her mouth. 'Dandy.'

'A lady at the butcher's shop told me you were here. She said you'd been attacked.'

'So have you from the look of you.'

I essayed a smile, conscious of its malformed quality. 'I wanted to ask you about your husband.'

A flicker crossed her face. It didn't seem quite like grief. More like fear. 'Why? What's he to you?'

'Someone else has died. I'm wondering if there's a connection between the two deaths.'

'What connection?'

I found myself leaning forward across the table. 'Her name was Maria Milanes. Or Mills. Does that mean anything to you?'

'How could there be a connection if Jack died by *accident*?' She narrowed her eyes. 'That was what you said, wasn't it?'

'Yes, but –'

'Did this woman drown?'

'No.'

'And you think it was Jack that did for her?'

'Certainly not. Your husband died before she did.'

She looked away, out of the window, at the rain and the backs of other buildings. 'You're not making any sense.'

The matron returned carrying a dripping-wet muslin bag. 'Put this against your face.' When I hesitated she pursed her lips. 'We don't have much ice left and I've taken the trouble.'

I did as she instructed, though it was barely ice any longer, even in this cold, and the water trickled down my neck, making me shiver.

The matron turned to Mrs Flowers. 'You can go home now, Rosie, if this gentleman will see you back safely. It's all right, he's with the police.'

'I'll be quite well on my own,' she said. 'It's broad daylight.'

'Better to travel with someone,' insisted the matron. 'You've suffered a serious injury.'

'I'm happy to accompany you,' I said. 'You can trust me completely.' I was thinking she might be afraid of me, after her recent injury, but she just sniggered in response.

The matron turned to me. 'Promise you'll take her all the way home.'

And so we found ourselves side by side outside the infirmary, her with a bandage around her head and me with an ice pack held to my chin. At least the rain was easing.

'You can clear off now,' she said. 'You've no need to stay.'

'I made a promise. We can walk up to the Euston Road and get a cab.'

'Good idea,' she said, but as I set off up the road she went the other way, south, and I had to run to catch her up again.

'I thought you were getting a cab,' she said, adjusting her bandage. It was discoloured, with a brownish blotch where she'd bled into the fabric, or someone had, perhaps its previous incumbent. My scalp itched just looking at it.

'We'll walk if you prefer,' I said, as she quickened her pace. 'So, did your husband know anyone named Maria?'

'His aunt's named Maria. Or it might be Marion. She lives in Norwich and has six children and two grandchildren. All boys, more's the pity.'

I sighed. 'This Maria was young. She lived locally.'

Mrs Flowers looked up at me. In fact, she looked up at almost everyone; she was less than five feet tall and seemed to be built wholly of cushions, aside from her face, which was narrow, with no softness at all, and predisposed to asperity. 'You men,' she sneered, apparently summing up her life's wisdom in two words.

'Pardon me?'

'Pretty girl was she, this Maria? Seems to me you're more willing to chase around asking questions about her than you were about my Jack. Didn't want to know about him, did you? Just told me he fell in the river and that was that. Seems to me you're choosy about who you help and who you don't.'

She was taking a zigzag route through the side streets, practically running as we turned the corner past the Princess Louise. I wondered how much more time I'd be forced to spend with her, surely the most recalcitrant woman on earth.

'Mrs Flowers,' I said. 'Or, it's Rosie, isn't it? May I call you Rosie?' *Rosie Flowers?* Good grief. As if her life wasn't hard enough.

'You can call me Mrs Flowers, or better still nothing at all, which is what I shall be calling you.'

'Mrs Flowers, when we last met I told you in all good faith what the surgeon had told me, which was that there were no suspicious circumstances. Now I'm not so sure.'

She walked on in fierce silence and crossed over Oxford Street between two stationary carts. The rain had backed up the traffic, and the toll man had left his booth and was walking up the line with his hat pulled over his ears, collecting coins and abuse from the drivers.

Finally, she shook her head. 'I don't know any Maria. That doesn't mean he didn't, though.'

There was a whole tome in that one sentence. I let it go.

'How were you hurt, Mrs Flowers? The lady at the shop said you were accosted. Was it something to do with Jack, do you think?'

'She says things she shouldn't.'

'Did you go to the police?'

She just snorted.

By the time we reached her address on Ludgate Hill, my feet were aching.

She turned to me. 'This is my home, so you've kept your promise. Goodbye.'

I looked at the name: *Dolan and Son, Butcher.* 'Is this your shop?'

She nodded, and swelled with pride so she came almost up to my chin. Her eyes were apple green. 'I was Rosie Dolan and my father's the son in the name. Should be called *Dolan and Daughter* now, but he's given up mostly and I'll not be naming it *Flowers the Butcher*. Anyway it's not a butcher's any more.'

She pushed open the door and I was assailed by a great whoosh of heat and the most delicious smell. It was like Sunday lunch in the vicarage, a leg of lamb or topside of beef with apple tart to follow, and Bridget, our maid, bustling from hob to oven and smacking our fingers with a spoon whenever we stole a knuckle of dough.

I followed Mrs Flowers inside, eyes wide with admiration. She had three children and her own shop, and yet she was only about my age, maybe even younger.

The leather-faced woman rushed out from behind the counter and swamped her in a bear hug. 'Thank goodness! I was so worried.'

The room was stuffy, dimly lit by a wall lamp and the orange glow from an oven against the back wall. Arrayed along the counter were tray after tray of pies, golden brown, each the size of a boxer's fist. It was heavenly.

Mrs Flowers went around the counter into the back and I heard the sounds of joyous, childish yelling. Their mother was home again.

The leather-faced woman blew out her cheeks and smiled at me. 'Thank you for bringing her back, sir. We was so worried, me and my Bert.'

'Where did they take her?' I asked, all innocence.

'They stuck her on some boat down at Puddle Dock, the bastards. Pardon my language, but that's what they are. As if she don't have enough on her plate.'

I knew of Puddle Dock vaguely, one of a hundred little docks and quays along the Thames. Almost everything went in and out through them: goods, raw materials, live-stock, gold from Africa, wine from France, flowers from Holland. They were the mouth and anus of the city.

'And no husband now.'

She rolled her eyes, and leaned towards me. 'Jack weren't never any use. He never lifted a finger, except to carry his beer from the table to his mouth. He was charming enough when he wanted to be, I'll give him that. He used to stand right where you are now and sweet-talk the ladies into buying twice what they needed. Some for a rainy day, he used to say, though why you'd need more pies because it's raining is a mystery to anyone. But once that door was shut he was different. Used to break my heart, what she had to put up with. Don't do to say so, and I wouldn't normally, but it weren't the worst thing that could've happened, him drowning like that. Let's just say, none of us'll miss him.'

Mrs Flowers returned with the youngest of her children on her hip, a boy of perhaps two years. He had his arms around her neck and his slimy face pushed up against her bandage.

I fumbled in my pocket for some coins. I had a trick: I could balance ten pennies on the back of my forefinger and, with a flick, catch them all in the same hand. Children loved it. I didn't have ten pennies, but I had some odd change, a few farthings and halfpennies, and I showed him. As I snatched the coins from out of the air, his eyes widened, and when I revealed them to him in the palm of my hand, he laughed as if it was the best thing he'd ever seen.

'Very amusing,' said Mrs Flowers drily. 'But if you're not buying then you'd best be going. We've a lot to do.'

She put on an apron and started repositioning the pies in the trays just so, as if their exact alignment was important – all of this while holding the child, a skill verging on witchcraft.

'If you'll answer a question I'll buy three; one for me, one for my landlord and one for his daughter. She'd do well to learn what a pie is supposed to taste like.'

She shrugged. 'You can ask.' I picked out a mutton, a kidney and a sweet apple one for Constance. 'Two shillings and threepence,' she said. It was extortion no matter how fine the product, but I paid willingly.

'Now, here's my question. Have you or Jack ever been to Southend-on-Sea?'

'That's it? Southend-on-Sea, that's your question?' She raised her eyebrows, with a twitch of a smile that lit up her face. 'Very well, yes, Jack and me went away for a weekend there once, before my first was born.'

'Nine months before,' muttered the leather-faced woman, and Mrs Flowers shot her a look.

'And he kept a postcard of it on his person?'

She stroked her child's hair and he rubbed his face on her shoulder, leaving a trail of mucus. 'That's more than one question.'

'I bought more than one pie.'

I was shifting the terms of the deal, but she didn't seem bothered. 'All right, for all the good it'll do you. He liked looking at the picture. He said Southend-on-Sea was the best place he'd ever been, but he was brought up at Smithfield Market so anywhere else must've seemed pretty special. Then we had Robbie and never went away again. Why do you care, anyway?'

'I just want to know the truth. Does the word "mercy" mean anything to you, aside from its usual meaning? He had written it on a bottle of ale. Perhaps he was becoming interested in religion, or temperance?'

She rolled her eyes. 'No. He was the opposite of those things, and anyway, he never learned to read or write more than his own name. And "mercy" means nothing to me, beyond that I could do with some. Now go about your business, and stop cluttering up the place.'

I wrote out my name and address, but I wasn't certain she could read either. It would probably go straight on the fire. 'Please take this, in case you think of anything else. Will you be safe now, or will they return, do you think?'

She produced a short, heavy-handled axe from under the counter and pointed it at me. 'And I've got a cudgel upstairs I'm going to bring down too. I'm fully prepared.'

I didn't doubt it; she was four feet eleven inches of fully prepared.

I munched the mutton pie on my way down to Puddle Dock. The pastry was crisp, the gravy rich and sweet, and the meat fell apart. I was tempted to eat the sweet apple one as well.

The sun had come out, and I saw smiles and even laughter as I passed St Paul's Cathedral. It always seemed so pale and pure from a distance but, as with so many things, it was a good deal grubbier close up.

I yawned, not having adjusted to working nights. I didn't mind particularly; there was something delicious about heading off to the hospital when most of the world was finishing for the day, and a peacefulness in crawling under the covers while everyone else was hard at work.

The smell of the river grew stronger at the bottom of the hill. The wharfs were packed together and it was difficult to know which was which, so I wandered along Upper Thames Street towards Blackfriars Bridge until I found the sign, high up on a wall, almost invisible under layers of dirt. The road between the buildings was unmade and worn into grooves by cartwheels, sloping down into the water and effectively forming the dock. Puddle was right: it was small and shallow. And empty.

The dock-master was reading a newspaper in his office. He was a lifer, comfortable behind his desk but retaining that wary twitch from an itinerant career on the docks. I'd seen plenty of stevedores, mostly with crushed heads or split sides, one squashed flat by a two-ton crate. Witnesses always swore it was a terrible accident, and mostly they were truthful, no doubt, but none of them minded one less man at the morning call.

My experience so far suggested that no one would tell me anything voluntarily, so I opted for a ruse.

'Good afternoon,' I said, in a brusque, do-what-I-say tone. 'My name's Detective Sergeant Ripley from the Metropolitan Police.'

He put down his paper and brushed his hands over his few remaining strands of hair. 'You ain't police,' he said. 'Where's your uniform?'

'I'm a detective. We don't wear uniforms.' I was doing my best to sound like a real policeman, combining arrogance with apathy.

'One of them detectors, is it? I heard about you. What do you want, then?'

I lit a cigarette and failed to blow a smoke ring. 'Someone was brought here against her will a few days ago. There was a boat in the dock at the time. Do you know anything about that?'

'Don't know nothing.' He glanced shiftily from left to right. He couldn't have looked guiltier if his hands had been covered in blood.

'Tell me now and I'll be on my way. Otherwise I'll be forced to have a look through all your paperwork, just in case there's anything suspicious. I'm sure you don't want that.'

He wiped his nose with his sleeve, and sagged. 'There might've been a lighter here, thirty foot or thereupon. Four nights, no more. But there weren't no crime.'

'How do you know?'

'They never loaded nothing. No cargo.' Like all dockers he assumed the only crime was smuggling or, strictly speaking, smuggling without him getting his cut.

'Whose boat was it?'

'Scraggy bloke. Sometimes a bigger bloke with 'im. They paid cash.'

'Did you get their names, or the boat's name?' I was sure there must be some kind of register of shipping on the Thames.

He shrugged. 'Paid cash, like I said. But I'll tell you one thing that wasn't normal. They had coffins onboard.'

'Coffins?'

'Strange, isn't it?' He frowned queasily. 'At first I thought maybe they was bringing them in from overseas, but why would anyone do that? Didn't seem right to me, coffins on a boat.'

———

On my way out of the dock-master's office, I passed a man leaning against a wall. He was dressed scruffily in the manner of a merchant seaman, but quite lacked the bulk most of them develop over a lifetime of lifting cargo and hauling ropes. He was scrawny and furtive with a thin moustache and a long nose that immediately made me think of a weasel. I tried not to catch his eye, and hurried homewards.

Dusk was falling and I was looking forward to perhaps an hour of sleep before I had to go to work. The streets were deserted, and I watched my shadow overtake me as I passed each streetlamp. My footsteps sounded hollow, and for a moment I thought I could hear a matching set behind me. Probably they were no more than an echo. I pulled my hat lower over my brow and walked faster, but the echo continued.

By the time I reached Little Pulteney Street it wasn't an echo any more. I could hear breathing. There were no lights on in the pharmacy so I would have to use the back door, which meant going via the alleyway. I spun round before I got to it. Part of me expected some innocent fellow to just carry on past, and part of me feared that it would be another thug trying to steal my wallet.

It was neither. It was the weasel-man from the dock.

He scratched his cheek and looked up at the top window. 'Didn't know this place was still going. My old man's gaff was on Bridle Lane and we used to come here for poult-ices when his leg went gammy. You live here, do you? Got a room?'

The road was empty but for the two of us.

'Are you following me?' My voice was higher-pitched than I'd intended.

'I knew you weren't a real detective.'

He seemed entirely relaxed, picking at the peeling paint on the pharmacy window frame.

'What of it?'

'Friendly warning is all. Stay out of other people's business.'

I straightened my shoulders, thinking about Constance, probably making dinner while Alfie did his accounts for the day. I wasn't going to be threatened here, outside our home.

'I'll do whatever I like.'

'Now you see, that's the wrong answer. I came here with a *friendly* warning.'

He took a step towards me and I moved sideways, trying to give myself room to dodge around him and escape towards the crowds on Piccadilly. I feinted left and went right, ducking under his reaching arm, feeling his fingers brush my collar, not quite gripping. I didn't fall – credit those unwanted ballet lessons for that – but I stumbled and felt his hand on my shoulder, pulling me backwards. I swung round and punched him across the mouth. It hurt like hell. I thought my hand would fall off. He staggered back, touching his lip and staring at the blood on his fingers.

'That was a mistake. I know where you live.'

'Who are you?'

'Just a messenger. Mind your own business from now on, if you know what's good for you. There are important people who don't want you nosing around. You've been warned.'

He left me standing alone, my heart pounding in my chest.

11

'YOU MUST BE MAD,' replied Detective Ripley at my suggestion that he should interrogate the dock-master.

It was mid-morning the next day, and we were sitting in the stagnant lobby at the police headquarters on Whitehall, surrounded by complainants, relatives of criminals, drunks sobering up and poor folks just getting inside out of the cold. Only the first group cared about how long things took, and from time to time went up to remind the desk sergeant of their existence, the identifying marks of their stolen property and their disgust at the rising level of crime in the city.

Detective Ripley had met me here as a mark of disrespect; whatever I had to say wasn't worth a trip to his dank office. He was wearing the same suit as always, still in need of a good flatiron, and his shirt was scattered with the flotsam of his last meal. The costermonger sitting next to him on the bench, stinking of whelks and vinegar, was the better dressed of the two.

'Go home, Mr Stanhope. And what on earth did you do to your face? Someone finally given in to the urge and punched you, have they?'

I ignored his question. 'The boat must have something to do with this. An unpleasant fellow followed me from the dock. He told me to stop asking questions.'

'Should've taken his advice.' Ripley shook his head. 'You said the boat was gone. So there's no evidence.' He stood up and stretched his back, wincing. 'Too much sitting, not enough walking. The wife says I have bad posture, but I think it's all this sitting around. I used to walk all the time, miles every day. Now I just fill in forms. Should've started a decorating business in Doncaster like my sister said.'

'Doncaster? Is that where you're from?'

I don't know why I asked; I just wanted to know more about this man who thought I was guilty of murder.

He frowned and sucked on his teeth. 'Originally. Then Nottingham and then here. Three years in this filth.'

'Is it so bad?'

'Murder's murder wherever you are. You're still dead. The difference is at home we always knew who did it and where they lived. Even if they wouldn't admit it, we *knew*. Here it's everywhere. You never know a damn thing. And whatever you want to do, you need permission from the higher-ups, *gentlemen* who've never once worn through the soles of their shoes.'

'Of course,' I said quickly. 'The same gentlemen who told you to let me go.'

'Yes, very good, Mr Stanhope, you're a sly one. Yes, those gentlemen. Someone told them it wasn't you, so I got the instruction to let you go.'

'Then let's find who really committed the crime! Let's walk down to the docks and talk to the dock-master. No forms, no sitting. Let's go right now.'

He shook his head. 'Tempting, but we already have a suspect in the cells.'

'What suspect?' He smiled, showing me his broken teeth, but didn't reply. 'You can't keep locking people up until they confess. You need evidence.'

'We have evidence enough of her depravity, believe me.'

'Depravity?' I couldn't think who he could be talking about. The brothel business was illegal, of course, but he must walk past dozens of them every day. It was hardly *depraved*. Then the answer came to me. 'Madame Moreau.'

'*Louisa* Moreau, yes. That Brafton woman, the brothel-keeper, told us all about her. We went to her house, me and Cloake, and searched the whole place thoroughly. It's like a bloody abattoir.'

I thought back to that warm room in Cripplegate. 'What did you find?'

Ripley gave me a slow look. I could see him wondering whether to tell me it was none of my business. Eventually, he sniffed and stretched his back again. 'Plenty that could've killed the girl. A poker, a billy club, a rolling pin the size of your arm.'

'All households have those. And anyway, *why* would she have killed Maria?'

'The girl got ploughed and Moreau tried to fix her, and it ended bloody. Or something like that. Doing what they do, what can they expect? It's a bad life and a short one.'

'Has she confessed?'

'She told us she was the last to see the girl. Mostly she just sits there in silence. She'll get a bad back, you mark my words, all that sitting. Though her neck'll probably give her more trouble soon enough, come to think of it.'

After he'd gone, I sat on the bench for a while, thinking. Could the murderer truly be Madame Moreau? I tried to imagine it, that moment, those long fingers grasping a billy club and bringing it down on Maria's skull. And that face, hard and lined, clenched with the effort. Is that how it was? Perhaps she was capable, but why? Why would she kill Maria?

Even as I shuddered at the thought of it, the image wouldn't hold still in my mind. I couldn't keep it fixed.

On my way to the exit, I passed the door into the cells where I'd been kept. The grim-faced police guard was just coming out, and I could see the bars of the cells and the high window. I wondered if Madame Moreau was in there.

On an impulse, I stopped the door just as it was about to shut, and slipped inside.

Maybe she was involved in Maria's murder and maybe she wasn't, but either way I wanted to talk to her.

———

The first cell contained two men, neither of them my former fellow inmates who, I supposed, had been shipped off to prison. These two were sullen, glaring at me from under their brows.

The ladies' cell was separated from the men's by a brick wall, presumably to protect their privacy, at least on a visual level, though it wouldn't help with the stink or stop men yelling out improper suggestions. Still, there was something about Madame Moreau, an intrinsic austereness, that discouraged such carnality.

She was seated on the floor with her arms wrapped around her knees and her face lowered. Her black and white hair, so dramatic when I'd last seen her, hung down loosely outside her bonnet. I realised she was praying, so for a while I stood silently with what little reverence I could muster, until I grew uneasy, trespassing as I was, and cleared my throat.

'Madame?'

She looked up, and I took a step back. Her face was bruised and puffy, purple and green across her cheekbones, with one eye half-shut and lips bloody and broken. Her skirt was ripped at the hem, revealing bare, white feet, and she was holding a rosary, spinning the beads in her fingers.

'I don't know anything,' she muttered. 'Why won't you leave me alone?'

'We met at your house, do you remember? I'm Leo Stanhope. What happened to you?'

When she didn't reply I waited, listening intently for sounds outside, any sign of someone coming in. But there were only the low tones of the men in the next cell.

'Madame,' I tried again, 'I don't mean you any harm. I just want to ask you a couple of things.'

'It weren't me,' she said, her voice barely above a whisper. 'I keep telling you. I don't know who it was, but it weren't me. Why won't you believe me?'

'I'm not working with the police. Was it them that did this to you?'

She touched her cheek with her fingertips and looked around the cell as if there might be a mirror. When I'd last seen her she'd been magnificent, the queen of her own domain, raising a poker to those thugs in the street and scaring them away. But here, in this place, she was frail and desperately small.

'I won't confess. I'd never hurt anyone.' She held up her rosary. 'And I won't hang myself neither, whatever they're hoping. It's only strung with cotton. You can tell 'em that.'

'I'm not supposed to be here. The police don't know. It's just you and me.'

'Please go away.'

She went back to her praying, though I doubted God was listening. It occurred to me how rash I was being, talking to a woman who knew what I was and had an excellent motive to direct attention away from herself. She could easily betray me. But somehow, I didn't believe she would.

'Madame,' I said. 'If I uncover the truth, you could be freed. Assuming you're innocent, of course.'

'But I'm not innocent.' She toyed with her rosary, tugging on it, testing its strength. 'They know what I do. They say I've killed loads. All those little ones never born who'd have grown up and made more babies, and so on and so on, thousands and thousands, never living because of me. They say I deserve this whether I did for Maria or not.'

'And do you believe that?'

'Sometimes. But where else can they go? Girls of twelve whose fathers would've thrown them out of the house, even if it was him that did it to her. Women not married, and rich ladies whose husbands never touch 'em, and girls like Maria, who'd lose their livelihoods and maybe more. Will it balance, do you think, the babies never born and the ladies I've saved?' She raised her chin, braced for the answer, and in the light from the high window her face took on a sickly, viridian sheen.

'I just want to know about Maria.'

'I keep telling them, I'm not a murderer.' She looked me in the eyes for the first time, with a spark of her old self. 'Though if I get my hands on the copper who did this to me, I might have a change of heart.'

'If it wasn't you, Madame Moreau, it must have been someone else. Maybe the soldier you mentioned before? You said they used to go for walks in the park together.'

'It makes no difference. I already told the police about him, and they weren't interested. Didn't even write it down.' She almost smiled, though the attempt looked painful. 'It's too late now. They'll hang me for this even though I would never hurt her. I knew Maria when she could shin up a drainpipe and be in and out in a trice, her pockets full of whatever she could grab. And even before that, when she was just a babe, she used to play in the straw beneath my table, more than once, more than a few times. Her old lady had a taste for gin and didn't mix in nice company, though those days are behind her now, of course, poor thing.' She looked at me solemnly, brushing her hair back under her bonnet, mustering some of her previous hauteur. 'That's the truth, but it isn't what they want to hear, nor you neither, I daresay. I mean, you're not the truth yourself, are you? You're a falsehood, a walking, talking lie. Was it you that told them I did it?'

'No. The detective said it was Elizabeth Brafton who accused you.'

She raised her eyebrows. 'Elizabeth? Well, ain't that something. She was nothing but a washerwoman in the brothel when I first met her. She has those airs and graces, but back then her job was cleaning men's seed off the sheets and girls' blood off their smalls. Hard to believe, isn't it, a person of her type, educated, much like yourself, but she was widowed and fallen on hard times and I suppose it was better than starving. She and I were friendly back then. I told her that place was a goldmine, being where it is. We was going to be partners, you know, and make it into something. She took the idea to Mr Bentinck for the both of us, and they cut me out. He put her in charge. We haven't been friendly since then.'

There was a noise from outside, the scraping of a chair against the floor, and I remembered I wasn't supposed to be there. I had to be quick.

'Do you own a boat, Madame Moreau? Or have access to one?'

'A boat? Like on the river?'

'About thirty feet long, moored for a while at Puddle Dock.'

'What would I want with a boat? I don't have that kind of money. I've only been on a boat twice and I was sick both times, over to France and back again. I even married one of 'em, but he was weak in the chest. Bullet wound. He was very poorly.'

'You were a nurse.'

'A wife, a nurse and a widow. A woman's life in a nutshell.'

'What about the soldier, the one Maria knew? Can you tell me anything about him?' She looked away and started fiddling with her rosary again, and I banged the bars in frustration. The noise rang around the room. 'Surely you would rather tell me than be hanged!'

She climbed to her feet and steadied herself, holding on to the bars, our hands almost touching. 'I saw her before she died.'

'What day was that?'

She thought for a few seconds. 'Friday afternoon. I was at home, knitting with Berthe from up the road and I thought it might've been one of her girls at the door. But it was Maria.'

Friday was two days after I'd last seen her.

'Why did she come to you?'

'I'd helped her in the past. She'd left it a little late this time, and it wasn't so straightforward. I told her she could doss down if she wanted, which I don't normally, but like I say, I knew her mother when she still had all her marbles.'

'So she stayed at your house? When did she leave?'

'In the morning. Early. She said she was coming back at lunchtime. I got us some fried fish and carrots, but she never came. Then I found out that ... well, you know what happened.'

'And you're sure she intended to return?'

'Oh yes. She had plans, she said, and had some nice clothes with her in a bag.'

'Like for the theatre?'

'She never said. I thought she was going to meet her soldier, which is why I mentioned him. Those girls, they can't live that life for ever, you know. They're like apples, lovely when they're ripe, but before you know it they get wrinkly and then go off altogether. No one wants a mouldy apple. So the clever ones find some nice gentleman to fall in love with them.' She was sounding uncomfortably like Jacob. 'He writ her a letter. She kept looking at it, sort of sad. Girls keep letters, they're sentimental that way.'

'Do you know what it said?'

'No, she didn't show it to me. But I knew something wasn't right.'

I was aware I was gripping the bars tightly. 'What do you mean?'

'I get a feeling sometimes, an ache in my bones. And I had that feeling. I had it and I didn't take any notice. If I'd stopped her from leaving that morning, she'd still be alive.' She paused and put her fists to her mouth. I realised she was weeping. 'I was busy with another lady who'd just come in, and Maria was gone off before I could say anything. I never thought … I should've run after her. Next thing I knew, she was dead.'

'And the letter from the soldier? Where is it now?'

'Still in the house, I suppose, in her bag. I told the police the same thing. That's all I know, truly.'

I had to read that letter.

There were voices outside the door, and someone's hand on the handle. I looked around, but there was no other way out and nowhere to hide. I'll just push past them as they come in, I thought. I'll be gone before they can stop me. But Madame Moreau reached out through the bars of the cell and grabbed hold of my sleeve.

'Promise me, if you find anything, you'll tell the truth, the real truth. I don't want to hang.'

'Of course. If I find anything to exonerate you, I'll make it known, but if I find you *are* guilty of this, I'll watch your execution with a smile.'

She let go, and I was almost at the door when Sergeant Cloake came in.

———

As soon as she saw him, Madame Moreau backed away from the bars and sat down in the corner of her cell, as small as she could make herself.

Cloake ran his hand pointlessly across his short-cropped ginger hair. His eyes were pale and blue, like the sky on a cloudless winter morning. I felt a shiver run up my spine.

'What are you doing?' he barked at me. 'Who said you could be in here?'

'Detective Ripley,' I lied, moving smoothly past him towards the door.

I felt his hand on my arm, and the slightest of squeezes that could so easily become a clench. 'Ripley didn't say anything to me about that.'

I turned, and decided to go on the offensive. 'Why is her face bruised like that, Sergeant? Who did it to her?'

'She resisted.'

'You're supposed to uphold justice.'

He sneered. 'She'll get justice all right.'

'But what if she didn't do the murder? It would mean you'd beaten her for no reason, and the real culprit is still at large.'

He interlaced his fingers and cracked his knuckles with a sound like pencils snapping in two. 'The same thing could still happen to you, if you get my meaning.'

An imbecile would have got his meaning. Subtlety wasn't a feature of his otherwise delightful nature. But I was angry and reckless, and the portcullis had lowered on my wiser thoughts.

'You should be ashamed.'

He turned towards Madame Moreau and rapped his knuckles on the bars. 'Look at me, woman. You'll get a fair trial all right. Shouldn't take long. Then it's the noose.'

12

ON SUNDAY, MY DAY off, I slept through the afternoon and only awoke when Constance called me down for dinner at six, which was breakfast for me. She claimed it was mutton pie, but the soggy pastry and stringy meat bore little resemblance to one of Mrs Flowers's masterpieces.

My mouth was still bruised and I was having trouble eating. Judging from Constance's frown, I wasn't a pleasant sight. She dissolved some salicin in a cup of water and handed it to me. 'Drink this,' she said, and wouldn't take no for an answer. Someday, I thought, she will make someone a truly terrifying wife.

Afterwards, I set out into the dark-brown evening with a flat cap on my head and my coat pulled around me. I missed my bowler, but I needed the anonymity. Tonight I would commit my first crime – or, more accurately, my first crime since leaving the house wearing trousers.

Burglary was not something I'd ever contemplated before. How did one even go about such a thing? Burglars in plays were always the rogues; slothful and vicious, bested by the hero in the final scene. Should I wear a scarf around my face and carry a crowbar under my jacket? It didn't seem a good idea. Surely the art of being a good burglar was not to be noticed, and I could think of few things more conspicuous than blundering about with a crowbar jammed into my armpit. And where would I even get one?

In the end I settled for a candle, some matches and a foot-long poker from the fireplace. I wrapped it up in a towel for reasons I couldn't really explain – it just felt peculiar to walk around London carrying a metal stick. I realised I wasn't cut out for a life of crime.

I walked briskly from Moorgate Street Station, shying at every alleyway and open door, keeping my face lowered. At Finsbury Street, the only people in sight were a gaggle of children playing in the dried mud. A girl was hopping and jumping along the pebble squares, her hair bouncing as she counted out the steps: hop, hop, jump, hop, hop, turn. That was me, I thought, fifteen years ago. I was so good at those games. No one could ever beat me.

Madame Moreau's windows were dark and empty. Three doors up, there was an alleyway between the houses, dimly lit by the glow from the city. I took a deep breath and a tight hold on the poker, and went inside.

As I reached a T-junction at the end, where the alley-way met the path along the back of the houses, there was a bovine sound from the yard on my left: a groan. I froze, and silently extracted my poker from the towel, just in case. There was another groan, and a plop of release, a fart and a stream of liquid, followed by more releases, erratic and aerated like the output of a faulty bilge-pump. The instiga-tor of the noise sighed loudly and blew his or her nose, and then there was some rustling and the sound of clothing being reassembled. The privy door banged open and in a few seconds I was alone again.

Madame Moreau's fence was high and the gate was bolted from the inside. I reached over as far as my arm would allow, but the bolt was out of reach. I put my eye to a knot-hole in the wood, and could see a dingy yard no bigger than Alfie's back room. There was a pile of logs propped against a lean-to, and a brick privy with a wooden slat roof.

I put my hands on the top of the fence and tried to pull myself up, but couldn't even get my nose level with my knuckles. My arms weren't strong enough. They should've had that piston power that men born men find so easy to call upon, the way I can call upon a memory or the next move in a game of chess. They should've been thick and dark, and covered with hair. But they were feeble things, and would never hoist me over that fence without more leverage.

I searched along the alley until I found an unlocked gate. Inside the yard was an old bath, upside down, perished with holes. I dragged it back with me, wincing as it scraped and clattered along the ground, and climbed on top of it, heaving to get my weight as far over the fence as I could. My feet dangled briefly in the air and I fell head first, landing in a heap on the other side.

I picked myself up gingerly, checking for anything broken. My clothes were covered in dirt and my palms were grazed, but I was in one piece.

I cupped my hands against the window. At first it seemed completely dark inside, but gradually shapes started to emerge: a stove, some plates and a saucepan still covered with the remains of her meal. The police had taken her away before she'd had time to wash up. She was such a fastidious person in her own way, and seeing her room like that was almost more shocking than her battered face at the police station.

I prepared myself, poker in hand and towel wrapped around my arm to provide some measure of protection. I swung back, but then paused.

If she'd left in so much of a hurry, was it possible the back door was still unlocked?

I tried it, and it opened.

I was surprised at how much relief I felt. An unlocked door was almost an invitation, and meant I could leave her house just as I'd found it, minus only Maria's bag. And if this soldier was, in fact, the killer, I was doing Madame Moreau a favour. She would thank me, if she ever got the chance.

The room smelled of old food and dead plants. The grate was white with ash. I lighted my candle, a fat, stubby thing, more smoke than light. It hissed and spat like a theatre audience when the villain creeps on to the stage.

The finch's cage was on its side on the floor, and the little yellow bird was jumping and flapping furiously. I hung up the cage again, and pushed a couple of nuts through the bars. He set upon one immediately, pecking and scratching at it with the edges of his beak. I considered liberating him rather than letting him starve, but he would probably fall victim to the first cat he came across, so I gave him some water from the jug and four more nuts.

'Don't eat them all at once,' I whispered. 'And don't tell anyone I was here.'

The front room was a mess. Ripley told me the police had searched the place thoroughly, and they certainly had, with no care or consideration. The drawers had been emptied out and tossed on to the floor, and the hulking treatment table was covered with old newspapers, strips of unfinished knitting, empty picture frames, a broken pot, rusted blades and other metal implements I couldn't identify and didn't want to, and a whole box of tallow candles burned down almost to nubs. Did the woman throw nothing away? I never kept anything, save my chess set, a few books and a silver rose brooch my mother had given me. What was the point of possessions when, at any moment, you might have to up sticks and leave them behind?

Maria must have lain on that table, looking up at the ceiling plaster, distracting herself from Madame Moreau's attentions. I couldn't imagine how invasive that must have felt. For all my times in bed with Maria and others, my own body remained unsullied. I was the most experienced virgin in history.

I wondered if it had been painful. I wondered whether she'd wept, without me there to comfort her.

There was no sign of any bag. I was hopeless at finding things, and had once spent ten minutes searching my room for my bowler hat when it was on my head all along. What kind of bag would it be, anyway? In my mind's eye it was like the beaded one I used to carry my books to school in, but it could be anything. Any colour. It was even possible the police had taken it, although that seemed unlikely; they'd been looking for the weapon Maria was killed with, not a bag of lady's clothing.

The stairs rose steeply from a small hallway between the front and back rooms, and the view to the top was obscured in shadow. I felt my fingers prickle.

'What's up there?' I whispered to the finch, but he was too busy with his nut to answer.

I took the steps one at a time, testing for creaks as I went, with no idea why I was being so cautious. It wasn't as if there was anyone to hear me. At the very top, on the tiny landing, I stood, controlling my breathing, with a door on either side leading to the front and back bedrooms. I decided to try the front bedroom first.

It was like stepping into the chancel of a run-down church. The walls were red and blue, and Jesus was hanging on a cross, suffering for my sins just as I suffered for His. Faded velvet drapes shrouded the window, matching the coverlet on her four-posted bed, and an oak-framed painting of exotic fruit hung on the opposite wall. The dressing table in the corner was crammed with bottles and jars, but all the drawers had been emptied out on to the floor: her small-clothes and chemises, all exposed and inspected by the police. They hadn't cared a jot about her privacy, but then, I reflected, neither did I.

Outside, the game was continuing. I could hear clapping: hop, hop, jump, hop, hop, turn, faster and faster, until you miss one or you stumble.

A mahogany wardrobe hulked in one corner, the knots in the wood glowering suspiciously at me. I could see myself in the mirror. I looked scared. Inside, three dresses were hanging, including the one Madame Moreau had been wearing at the cemetery. Beneath them, tucked away behind a pair of lumpy shoes, was an embroidered carpet bag with handles. I pulled it out and stared at it, remembering that I'd actually seen it before, in Maria's room, dangling from a hook on her door.

I was about to open it when I heard a sound from downstairs.

I blew out the candle and waited in silence, sitting on the bed, hugging Maria's bag to my chest.

For a while I almost thought I'd imagined it, but then there was the unmistakeable clank of a window being shut, and the whir of the finch's wings in its cage. Someone was making a poor job of creeping about.

All my senses became heightened. The traffic on the City Road was rumbling like an approaching army, and my breath was deafening. I gripped the poker and eked myself on to the floor, slithering underneath the bed and lying flat against the rug.

Footsteps sounded on the stairs. The door opened and a pair of shoes appeared – small shoes for small feet. It was just a child, a little girl, perhaps one of the ones who'd been playing outside. She walked around the room, pulling open the cupboard and burrowing in the wardrobe, humming a little song.

The silhouette of a face appeared, upside down, curly hair trailing on to the rug. She squinted, trying to determine if I was really a person; there wasn't much light under there. I kept still, but she kept looking.

'What are you doing, mister?' she said.

'Hiding.'

'Who from?'

You seemed to be a ridiculous answer in the circumstances, so I changed tack. 'This isn't your house.'

'Not yours, neither.' Irrefutable logic.

I slid out from under the bed. She was about six years old with a bony, scrunched-up face like a knuckle, straggly red hair and a frank, analytical gaze. She eyed the bag and took a step backwards towards the doorway, ready to run if she had to.

'The gentleman give me threepence,' she said. 'Another if I find it.'

The only people who knew about the bag and the letter were me and Madame Moreau … and the police.

I peeked between the curtains. There was a man standing in the alleyway opposite. He was dressed in dark clothes and keeping quite still, seeming to want to remain unobtrusive, although his attempt was impaired by his glossy top hat. He stepped out of the shadows to look up at the window, and in the dim light I could see a broad face decorated with a beard and lavish moustache. He was no policeman.

'Did he tell you to find a bag, like this one?'

She nodded. Part of me wanted to give it to her, otherwise she'd have to return empty-handed, and what would he do to her then?

But I couldn't.

'I'll give you a shilling if you just run away,' I said, thanking goodness he was such a cheapskate. 'Sixpence now, and another when he's gone. Is that a deal?'

I held out a coin and she looked from it to me and back again, assessing her options. She could run downstairs and call out to that man, but then she wouldn't get that extra sixpence.

'The back door's unlocked,' I said.

Greed won over risk. She grabbed the coin and scampered away. I heard a faint click downstairs as the door closed.

I peeked through the window again, and the fellow was pacing around, impatiently working his jaw. I didn't know whether to leave or not; if I did, he might hear me, but if I stayed he might come in himself, and I'd be trapped.

I waited five minutes, straining to hear every sound, almost jumping out of my skin when a cart rattled up the street. When I dared to look out again I was mightily relieved; he was striding away down the hill towards the city.

At the entrance to the alleyway I paused, looking both ways for the little girl. I was just about to give up when she appeared, staying just outside my reach in case I demanded my first instalment back.

I found a sixpence in my pocket and held it up to the sky. At arm's length it was the size of the moon and just eclipsed it, a black disc with an eerie glow. I produced another sixpence and balanced both on the back of my finger, and then did my trick, flicking them up and snatching them out of the air in one movement. She didn't so much as crack a smile, but glared at me with open suspicion, until I handed her one of the coins. When I gave her the other as well, she positively grinned.

'For never telling anyone I was here. Agreed? Not a soul.'

'Yes. Thank you, sir.' I was *sir* now, apparently.

'Are you …?' I didn't know what I wanted to ask. Are you safe? Are you healthy? I had the urge to take her back to Alfie's and feed her a square meal, but she hurtled away with her profit before I could suggest it.

On the underground train, I opened the bag and sorted through the contents: Maria's clothes and underclothes. I was overcome with the smell of her, transported to her room, watching from the bed while she hung up her frock and straightened the hem. I had to bury my face. The woman seated opposite me looked away.

I could feel something cold and metal in there too: a pair of keys. I held them up, and almost laughed. They were my keys. They had fallen out of my pocket in her room on that last evening, the last time I'd seen her. She must have been bringing them to me. She *had* meant to meet me at the theatre. She was a sweet, sweet girl.

At the bottom of the bag I could feel something else, a solid weight that wasn't clothes. I pulled it out and almost gasped with shock; it was that hideous doll that had been sitting on her dressing table amidst all her perfumes and ointments when I was last with her, a loathsome thing, a parody of a baby, stillborn and grotesque. I'd been surprised then – she'd never seemed so sentimental. But this was no dog-eared keepsake; it was new, and expensive.

Jane had collected dolls in the room we used to share. Some of them had been gifts to me, but I had no use for them so they soon migrated towards her embrace, where they were named and posed and placed into the rigid hierarchy of her affections, in which only the finest few, the prettiest and most compliant, ever progressed to the hallowed sanctum of her pillow. None of my cast-offs ever made it that far, being tainted by orphandom, and they had to be content with lesser positions on the dresser and cupboards, but at least that was better than being trampled into the carpet on my side of the room with the books and puzzle pieces and sad, solitary chess men.

I rubbed the doll's hair between my finger and thumb where it emerged through pinholes in its scalp, framing the doll's bulbous face. I supposed it was made of a horse's mane, heated and twisted into curls to encourage little girls to brush it.

An unwilling logic put the parts together in my mind. Maria had been pregnant and people give dolls to babies. Either she'd purchased it herself in expectation, or she'd received it from someone who knew about her condition. Either way, she'd honoured it in pride of place on her dressing table, her equivalent, I deemed, of Jane's sacred pillow. And if that was true, then at some point, for some reason, she had been content to be pregnant. No one who was unhappy about it would tolerate a doll in their bedroom. I wondered what had changed. Why had she subsequently visited Madame Moreau?

But I had a more urgent concern: the letter from the soldier. That was why I'd gone into Madame Moreau's house and expended all that energy, not to mention three sixpences. I needed to know who that soldier was.

I rifled through the rest of the bag, searching among her clothes. When I'd finished, and was sure I'd been thorough, I did it again.

But there was no letter.

13

IN MY ROOM, I combed through every pocket and crevice of Maria's dress, petticoats and undergarments. I spread them out and lay amongst them, first with my arms wide and then curled up, gathering her to me, hiding my face and sobbing.

Afterwards, I sat on the bed with the doll in my hands. I didn't like it looking at me so I faced it to the floor, but that seemed unkind, so I shoved it into a drawer, which seemed crueller still; a punishment. It struck me that perhaps I had *wanted* Jane to adopt those dolls of mine all those years ago, so they could receive rationed love from her rather than none at all from me.

Maria had never given me a gift. I would have adored a lock of her hair, wrapped in a ribbon, tucked into a little box that I would carry with me always. I half-wished I'd snipped some while she lay on Mr Hurst's table, but that would've been a pretence. It wouldn't have been a real gift.

But then, what of Maria *was* real? She had hidden things from me, and, worse, had told untruths. And they weren't just wishful fantasies, as I had thought, they were substantial: a pregnancy and a soldier. Had she ever been truthful about anything? Perhaps she was no more real than the doll.

And yet I loved her anyway. Even if it was no more than infatuation, or worse, *gratitude*, I loved her, because she was the only person who knew what I was and didn't care. In her eyes, I was as male as any other man. I may never have known the real Maria, but there was one thing I was certain of: she had known me.

Enough snivelling. I scooped the doll back into the carpet bag and made a decision. It was everything I had of Maria, but I still couldn't abide it. Better it was loved by somebody else.

———————

Late the following morning, after another shift at the hospital and four hours of sleep, I stumbled downstairs to the shop where Alfie was fiddling with some mechanical equipment, a drill of some kind. In his shirtsleeves, his forearms were hard and sinewy; no one would treat him lightly.

'Have you seen anyone suspicious around here?' I asked him. 'A furtive, weaselly fellow.'

'No.' He frowned at me, running his fingers, shiny with grease, through his hair. 'Why do you ask?'

'He was hanging about outside. I didn't like the look of him.'

'I'll keep an eye out.'

Constance came in when she heard my voice. 'Nitrate of sodium,' she barked, and Alfie grinned. He knew the answer, but I didn't. My mind was slurry.

'Shouldn't you be at school?'

'I'm helping Father with his machine.' She gave me a monkey grin. 'But I can still find time for tea and cake at your expense ...'

'Only if I get it wrong. All right then. Fever?'

She cackled at the suggestion. 'Not even close.'

'Indigestion?' But I knew that was wrong. It was just the mention of cake that had made me think of it. 'I think I should have more guesses for the last one. It's only fair.'

'You should've thought of that when you made the rules.'

She knew I wouldn't get it. She actually licked her lips in anticipation, the wretch, and I couldn't help but think of the urchin I'd met in Madame Moreau's house. She'd been half Constance's age and a quarter of her weight, a rat in the slums, breaking into houses and risking the workhouse or worse, and for what? That man would most likely have stolen back his money and beaten her too for good measure.

'Well?' demanded Constance.

I sighed, tired of the game. Tired of everything.

'Ulcers!' I declared with a kind of grim brio. 'It has to be ulcers sometime.'

'No it doesn't,' she beamed. 'Nitrate of sodium is for heart disease!'

'Very well, you win, young Miss Smith.' I shook her hand formally. 'If your father can spare you, we'll head to the bakery forthwith so you can drain my resources with cake and cream and jam!'

In all my life I'd never seen anyone so thoroughly delighted.

Constance admired a high-class place on Regent Street with the name 'Celine's' inscribed in exotic writing across the window. It was warm and cosy, with zinc-topped tables and a strong smell of coffee. She ordered a small selection of cakes, peering over the menu at me to be sure I didn't mind such extravagance.

I ordered a pot of tea and felt my shoulders relax. I realised I'd been hunching them ever since I left Cripplegate.

Constance was enthralled, staring at the gilded mirrors and neat, efficient serving girls as if she'd fallen into a fairy tale.

'I'm going to Paris one day,' she declared.

'Why? Is it so different from here?'

'I don't know. That's why I want to go there.'

I glanced around at the room – at the staff dressed in the French style, a picture of the Parisian skyline pasted on to one wall, English people drinking Indian tea and crunching on Italian biscuits.

'I don't suppose it's very much like this.'

'Exactly!'

She sat back, her mood drooping as we waited for the cakes.

'Father's very worried,' she said eventually.

'What makes you think that?'

'He's at his ledgers all the time.' She wound her fingers into the tablecloth. 'I know we're running out of money.'

Alfie had told me that the pharmacy had thrived when Helena, his wife, was alive, but since then it had diminished despite all his efforts. I had never met her – she died six years previously – but he said she was quite a lady, a former schoolteacher, intelligent and forthright. He also said that Constance was the image of her, which always made Constance blush, although she confessed to me once that she could scarcely remember her mother, and there were no pictures of Helena in the house.

'I offered him the rent early.'

'But you can't afford it either. You should try to get your old position back. It's no good being glum all the time. Have you even tried?'

'Of course,' I lied.

But she was wise, even at eleven. 'You must, and soon.'

'You needn't be concerned about money.' I gave her what I hoped was a reassuring smile. 'Your father has a new venture that he's confident will be a success.'

'I know. He gets these ideas. Last time, he decided to become a photographer and sent away for the parts to make a camera. They're still outside in the box they came in. And the time before that he took an interest in glass-blowing.'

'You mustn't worry about it. He's doing his best to take care of you.'

'Someone has to do the worrying, Mr Stanhope.'

She was a little shame-faced, but I hadn't meant to admonish her. And perhaps she was right to be worried. If the pharmacy failed, Alfie would have to find a position working for someone else and wouldn't be able to afford Constance's education. The ragged schools wouldn't take her at eleven, so she would have to find work too, most likely in a factory. It wasn't a pleasant prospect. I had hoped she might one day become a governess, but then remembered it was the future my father had intended for me, having little faith I would attract a husband. I vowed to make certain Constance could pursue any path she chose.

The girl arrived with a tray, and unloaded a flowery teapot, two china cups and saucers and a fluted plate of iced fairy cakes. Constance's eyes were as wide as the saucers. I could tell she was trying to be polite, so I nudged a pastry fork in her direction.

'Go ahead.'

I tried to drink my tea but it was too hot against my bruised mouth, so I sat in thirsty silence and watched her eat. She was meticulous, making the most of every forkful, holding the plate beneath her chin to catch any crumbs, and then prodding around it with the end of a licked finger.

'I have something for you,' I said. 'It's not new, but I thought you might enjoy it.' I produced the doll and waggled it at her, making its head wobble morbidly from side to side.

'Oh,' she said, her mouth still full from the last cake. 'Thank you. She's beautiful.'

Something in her manner seemed less than excited. 'Are you too old for such things now?'

'I still have my dolls from when I was little.' She was trying to appear grateful, cradling it and examining its clothing. 'I shall call her ... wait.' She was searching under the neck of the dress. 'There's something here.'

She withdrew a piece of paper, folded into an inch square, which had been tucked inside the doll's clothing. She opened it out and it was a sheet of blue writing paper, translucent at the creases as if it had been read and refolded many times.

'Let me see,' I said, but she moved it out of reach.

'It's a letter. To someone named Maria. Was the doll hers before?'

'Yes. Can I have it now, please?'

'From Major Augustus Thorpe. An officer!' Her eyes were scanning down the page. 'Oh poor Maria. He's broken her heart. Who is she?'

'Someone I … I knew. It's not your business.'

'But it's so sad. Were they in love?'

'No. Can I see it now please?'

'Did she move away?'

'No.'

'Then why doesn't she want the doll any more?'

'For goodness' sake, just give me the letter, Constance!'

She placed it on the table between us, making clear how offended she was.

I didn't know why I was so cross. I should've just let her read the letter in peace; she'd found it after all, and it wasn't mine any more than it was hers. I'd intended this to be a treat for her, and I'd ruined it. We sat in silence for a while, as I poked my tongue into the gap between my teeth, feeling the sore strands of flesh in the socket.

'I need to read it,' I said.

'Very well,' she replied, icily polite.

I picked the damn thing up.

The handwriting was upright and elegant, and it was on well-cut bond paper; an educated gentleman.

Augustus Thorpe (Major), St George's Barracks, London
   January 16th 1880
   My dear Maria,

It pains me to write this, and yet I must. It is my duty to my family and my regiment.

I have no desire to cause you anguish, but in all conscience I cannot continue to meet with you as we have these past months. Your circumstances make it impossible. I'm sure you understand why this is.

I wish you well, now and always.

Augustus

That was it; terse and to the point.

Major Augustus Thorpe. I'd never heard of him. I'd met customers at the brothel occasionally in passing, hateful men, entirely mercantile, sorting through their pockets for change as if they were paying to have their shoes shined. I'd sometimes heard them too, grunting like foraging pigs or murmuring about their wife who nagged them or their mother who'd never loved them.

I had written many letters to Maria, two dozen at least, on cheaper paper but with longer sentences, and adjectives, so many adjectives, like *joyous* and *beautiful* and, my most common, my all-time favourite: *eternal*. Oh, joyous, beautiful, eternal love! When I fell in love with Maria it wasn't a tentative step, I flung myself from the precipice. Who was this Augustus Thorpe, with his stiff formality, citing her *circumstances* as if they were an accident of fate, a thing he couldn't have anticipated? The only adjective he seemed to know was *impossible*.

I felt as if I had swallowed a lump of clay. I had told Maria everything about myself, and yet she hadn't even told me her real name. And now here was this soldier, who she had met for *these past months* for intimate walks in the park. Perhaps he was the one she loved. After all, it was his letter, not mine, tucked inside that doll's dress, worn down by overuse, treasured.

Where were my letters, my passionate, florid, adjective-filled letters?

They were nowhere.

———————

I worked that night in a distracted and irritable fashion, only realising on my way home that I'd delivered Doctor Anderton's mail to Doctor Anderson. But there was nought I could do about it now, and it was their own fault for having such similar names.

After a terrible morning of sleep, three hours at most, I sat alone in the back room. Constance was at her school on Dean Street, and Alfie was minding the shop and finishing the assembly of the contraption he'd acquired, which had taken four men to deliver.

I liked the back room. It was always changing: boxes of stock piled up and slowly emptying, jars of chemicals spilling over in dusty swirls, and our footprints criss-crossing on the floor, a diary of our day.

That morning it also housed the tin bathtub that was generally kept in the yard. Alfie loved to bathe, invisible in the steam but for the beacon of his cigar, telling ribald stories of his army days and laughing until he couldn't speak. I envied him that bathtub; my washing was limited to a flannel and a bowl in my room. As a child I'd loved the sound of water being poured in, the smell of soap, the ceremony of the kettle, my mother towelling Jane so vigorously you'd think she was trying to rub off her skin. I'd lie there for hours, my head poking out of the grey water or sink-ing below the surface into that misty, silent world, my hair floating in front of my eyes. I was at home underwater. No one could be cross with me there. No one could tell me to take care of my fingernails or keep my knees together or sit with my back straight.

But I wasn't a child any longer, and I had no Mummy to tell me to scrub the mud off my knees. I was a man now, and had to choose my own path.

Madame Moreau might be guilty of the crime. I didn't know for sure that she wasn't. And yet, deep down, I didn't believe it. She seemed to care about Maria, and there was something else — she could've told the police about me at any time to deflect attention away from herself. It would have been easy. But she hadn't. That counted in her favour.

Still, there was a very good chance she would be hanged. The police had extended their meagre imaginations no further than a woman with a French name whose profes-sion fairly guaranteed no public sympathy. They'd rather hang her and be done with it than face the toil of finding out what had actually happened. They certainly wouldn't be interrogating a major in the British Army.

I poured out a cup of tea, wrapping my hands around the pot until the heat was too much, and then just a little longer, eyes closed, feeling my skin begin to burn.

Could Thorpe have been the father of Maria's preg-nancy? It made me feel sick just thinking about it. If so, his letter of rejection was probably why she'd gone to Madame Moreau. She would be worthless to Elizabeth Brafton large with child.

I had to speak to Thorpe. But how?

I could imagine the letter I might write: *Dear Major Thorpe, the prostitute you were visiting has been murdered, and I suspect you're guilty of the crime. Could we meet to discuss it please? Yours sincerely, someone you've never heard of.*

I sipped my tea. Try as I might, I could only think of one other approach, and truly, it was the most abhorrent idea I'd ever had. Anything but that. Please, God, if you ever thought of me as more than a plaything for Your cruel amusement, find me any other way than that.

14

MY SISTER JANE LIVED in a three-storey townhouse on Maida Vale, less than an hour's walk north-east from the pharmacy. It wasn't a journey I made often. She was the one person I still knew who had known me before I was Leo, and I didn't like being reminded of it. Neither did she.

Her door was opened by a Negress in a mob cap.

'I'm here to see Mrs Hemmings.'

'No salesmen,' she said in a thick accent, starting to close the door.

'She's my sister.'

She looked me up and down, visibly unconvinced. 'You'd better wait here.'

She shut the door, and I peered in through the stained-glass window at the hall. There was a pedestal table in the corner that I was sure had been in our childhood house in Enfield. It was always so easy for Jane. She wanted for herself exactly what our parents had wanted for her, and they had loved her for it: a nice house with bay windows and a covered porch, and a nice husband with a suitable position. And most importantly of all, as many offspring as a single womb could gestate.

Needless to say, I had never been gifted any furniture. She was their beloved daughter, and I was nobody's son.

After a few moments, Jane opened the door and the smile died on her lips. 'Oh, it's you,' she said. 'I thought it was Ollie.'

'Can I come in?'

'Howard isn't here.' She was a respectable woman, and wouldn't want the neighbours seeing a man enter the house while her husband was out. I'd never met the fellow, a banker in the City apparently. 'What do you want? I told you before, I won't give you any more money.'

'It's not that.'

How typical of her to remind me. I had needed some funds at twenty-one years old, in debt and with some delinquent habits, having recently discovered my mother had died. Who else should I have turned to but my sister? She acted now as if I was almost a stranger, but we'd shared a bedroom for fifteen years, out of preference. We'd lain awake at night talking in the pitch black until all there was in the world was her voice, so close it could have been inside my head. I had curled up beside her when I suffered nightmares, fought like a feral cat over the encroachment of her clothes on to my side of the wardrobe, applauded while she practised her pliés and woken her up almost every morning by throwing open the curtains, upholding a younger sibling's right to be infuriating. She was the first person I had told I was really a boy, and the first to berate me for being so stupid.

In the house, a baby started to cry. Jane stepped back into the hall. 'Cecily!' I could hear the maid making soothing noises.

'Another one?'

It showed how long it was since I'd last seen my sister. Almost a year, I thought.

'Yes. A girl. Two of each now.'

The immutability of her children's genders hung between us.

'You look well,' I said. This much was true. She was almost as tall as me, clean, well-fed and pleasantly dressed. But I knew her secret, just as she knew mine.

'I can't say the same for you. Have you taken up *boxing* now?'

'No, it's just a bruise.' I had hoped it had started to fade.

'Are you still at the hospital?' This, again, was a laden question, a reminder of her previous generosity. After she'd lent me the money, she'd told me about the cousin of a friend of hers who had recently left the post of junior porter, creating a vacancy. That was all she'd done, but the way she acted you'd think she'd secured the position for me personally. I always suspected she did it not out of any sisterly affection, but so I'd have the means to repay her, even though she certainly didn't need the money.

'Yes, I'm still assistant to a surgeon,' I lied. 'I have a home and friends. I have a good life.' *In for a penny, in for a pound.*

'Do they know what you are, Lottie?'

'They know I'm a man, and my name is Leo.'

The wailing continued. I would've liked to meet my new niece, but that offer wasn't made.

'There was a pope called Leo who turned back Attila the Hun from Rome, did you know that?'

'I didn't.'

'He unified the Catholic Church.' I wasn't clear whether she regarded this as a good thing or not, but anyway, she continued. 'You were christened Charlotte, but you don't call yourself Charles now. Why is that?'

'I wanted a new name. Besides, I was always Lottie, never Charlotte.'

She knew this well enough. She resembled my mother physically, uncannily so, but she thought like my father. And me, if the truth was told. We didn't agree on much, but we operated the same way; identical looms turning out different cloths.

'Have you ever considered how similar Leo is to Lottie?' she asked. 'L and E and O, three letters the same. And three missing, T and I and another T. Interesting, isn't it? You've half the name you had, and only a tit missing.'

I wasn't so easily shocked or provoked. All she'd done was reveal a tiny fraction of her secret: she was, quite simply, the most intelligent person I'd ever known. I'd met doctors, lawyers and priests, and not one of them was fit to stand in her light. As a child I'd been obsessive about chess for a while, playing every minute I could, against my mother, my neighbours, the verger and various members of my father's congregation, and I could defeat them all. I could beat Oliver too, or at least get ahead before he swept a fist across the board and stormed away, but I couldn't compete with Jane. She could win without trying, reading a book at the same time, while I sat opposite her, fixated on the board, fuming and grinding my teeth.

I wondered whether she ever demonstrated that intellect to Howard, the banker. Somehow, I doubted it. What a waste. Both of us had changed, but I had become what I should always have been, and she had buried her true self.

'How many books do you own?' I asked abruptly.

'We have a whole library,' she replied, with the merest glint of amusement showing through her defences. This was an old lark between the two of us, to count the books in a household. Fewer than twenty and we despised the family as ignorant dullards. We were charmless children.

'Are you allowed to read them?'

'When time permits.' Meaning when Howard wasn't there, I presumed. 'Are you here to discuss my reading habits?'

'No. I need your help. I need to find a gentleman named Augustus Thorpe.'

She shrugged. 'Is that it? Well that's simple, I've never heard of him. Truly, Lottie, did you come all this way on the off-chance I might know this one fellow in the whole of London? What an idiotic excuse.'

'I didn't think *you* would know him. I thought *Oliver* would know him. Augustus Thorpe is a major at St George's Barracks. Oliver's still stationed there, isn't he? It's urgent I speak with Thorpe, so please ask him.'

She raised her eyebrows and didn't say anything. The avenue was quiet aside from the wind in the trees lining the pavement and the distant clip-clopping of horses on the Edgware Road. Inside the house, my niece's cries had been replaced by the whistling of a kettle.

A boy appeared in the doorway. At first I didn't recognise him, but then realised this must be Walter, her eldest, who I still thought of as chubby and pink, barely able to talk. But here he was, at – goodness – eight or nine years old, with brushed hair, a long chin and blue eyes that showed no recognition of me.

'Hello,' I said.

'Go inside,' Jane told him, giving me a look straight from our childhood: *don't give away who you are*. I wondered what her children and husband knew about me. I was sure the name Leo never came up, but what about Lottie? Was Auntie Lottie dead, or had she never existed at all?

I fumbled in my pocket for the note I'd brought with me. I'd lost too many games of chess to my sister not to prepare thoroughly. 'Here's my address,' I said. 'And my name: Stanhope, in case you'd forgotten. He should ask for me. And this is the name of the gentleman: Major Augustus Thorpe.'

She didn't take the piece of paper. 'It's not me you need a favour from, it's Ollie.'

'You know he won't talk to me.'

I had tried, a long time ago, but my letters were returned unopened.

She sighed. 'What's this all about anyway? Why do you need to speak to this gentleman?'

'A young lady was murdered, and he knew her. The police already have someone in custody, so he's not a suspect. But I'd like to ask him some questions.'

'Murdered? What on earth have you got involved with?' She was backing into the hallway, her hand reaching for the door.

'Please, Jane. I would never put you in any danger, I just need Oliver to ask this man to get in touch with me. For the sake of the young lady who was killed, please be persuasive.'

Still, she didn't take the paper. 'Why should I? This has nothing to do with us.'

It was my turn to shrug. 'I can come back tonight and ask again. And tomorrow if needs be.'

She knew what I meant: my nieces and nephews would meet their uncle for the first time, and I could introduce myself to Howard as well. I was sure he'd be interested to meet the brother-in-law he didn't know he had.

The truth is, I wouldn't have done it; the cost of her embarrassment might be my own imprisonment. But in my experience, threats were the only way to deal with her.

Finally, she took the paper. Checkmate, for once. 'I'll ask Ollie, but I can't promise he'll say yes.'

'But you can promise you'll try.'

'I can and I do. But this is the last time I'll help you. You can't come here any more. We have neighbours and servants. We have standing. You're not welcome here. Do you understand? Don't come back.'

'You're my sister, Jane.'

'It's your own fault, *Leo*, so don't blame me. I loved Lottie and I always will. I miss my sister every day.'

For a moment I said nothing, standing on her doorstep like a stranger. I was determined not to cry. 'If that's what you want, then all right. Send me a telegram. I'll meet him anywhere he wishes, and at any time.'

She nodded and stepped back inside the house. 'Goodbye,' she said, and closed the door.

———

I had grown accustomed to not seeing Jane or thinking about her from day to day or week to week, but once upon a time I'd been more familiar with her voice than my own, and to know that it was lost to me, to know for certain, was hard to bear.

I felt empty, as if I was craving food but unable to tolerate it. After a day, my craving turned to resentment and then to anger. I'd been her ally when she'd confided how much she loathed our father and despised his endless pedagogy; everything we saw and every place we visited turned into a lesson complete with Bible quotes and a test, as though our lives were a metaphor for his Protestant religion rather than the other way round. But the truth was clear now. What went bone-deep for me was just the ink on her fingers, easily washed off.

In the end, she'd sided with him.

But still, when I lay on my bed unable to sleep, I couldn't help but remember those summers in the vicarage, dancing around the garden flapping our arms, blessing the rhododendrons and peonies and the baby thrushes in our father's nesting boxes. We'd held them in our hands and watched their tiny, pink beaks open and close. It was as if we'd given them life.

I took to hanging around the pharmacy before I left for the hospital. Business was, as Alfie called it, slack, meaning slack like a rope that would soon pull tight, but there wasn't so much as a twitch as far as I could see. By late on Friday afternoon I'd only served three customers: an elderly woman buying arsenic for the rats, a tanner who bought the last box of salt and Miss Horner from the brewery, who came in for some carbolic after a drayman dropped a barrel on his foot and split the skin, she said, from small to big toe.

Meanwhile, Alfie was learning how to use his new contraption. It was a hideous thing – a chair, a footpump and various attached apparatus that he'd installed right in the centre of the shop – which was far too small for such a beast to be overlooked. He was practising his new craft on a pickled pig's head. It was awful; the stink of pork and vinegar, the squeak of the pedal, the whirring of the gears and, worst of all, the insistent grinding of the drill on tooth enamel.

'Dentistry is just engineering,' he explained, exchanging the drill for a pair of pliers. 'The machine does all the work. You just have to be careful not to slip and go into the soft parts of the mouth.'

He was hoping his new venture would attract more wealthy patrons to the pharmacy. I feared it would have the opposite effect, and that any customer seeking medicines would be discouraged by the sight of a man torturing a pig's head clamped to a chair.

I was about to get my coat and go to work when the bell on the door rang.

I recognised the gentleman instantly. This was the man who'd been waiting outside the house of Madame Moreau, the man who'd sent in the little girl; too scared to go in himself. Close up, he was perhaps thirty years old, straight-backed, unmistakeably military though not in uniform. He blanched at the sight of the pig, but gathered himself.

Constance came in, and he examined her. 'Are you Miss Pritchard? I was asked to come to this address.'

I knew immediately who he was. I could hear his voice in the letter: *Your circumstances make it impossible.* The pompous ass. I could hardly imagine he'd ever known Maria, let alone cared for her.

He sniffed and cast a look around the pharmacy, apparently not liking what he saw. No doubt he patronised bigger places on Regent Street or Park Lane, or had the pharmacist come to him with a case full of remedies and the respect he was due.

But Constance wasn't made that way. She reminded me of me.

'You must have made a mistake. We don't have any Miss Pritchard here.'

He raised his eyebrows. 'Captain Pritchard gave me this address for his sister. I believe her Christian name is Lottie, short for Charlotte, I suppose.'

'Are you sure it was his sister?' I blurted. 'Not a man?'

He stared at me, clearly wondering why I'd spoken. I suppose he'd taken me for a customer or, more likely, hadn't noticed me at all. 'What are you babbling about? I know what I was told. Is Miss Pritchard here or not?'

No, I thought. She really isn't.

Alfie continued tugging away at the pig's mouth. 'Do you know anyone by that name, Leo?'

'Possibly,' I said. 'What's it in connection with? Perhaps you could tell *me* about it?'

The fellow shook his head. 'Captain Pritchard said to speak to no one else. He was explicit on the point. It's a delicate matter.'

'Delicate?' said Constance, ever curious, and he studied her again. If he does it once more, I thought, I'll clamp him to that chair and see how he enjoys the drill.

'Thank you, Constance,' I said. 'I'll let you know if I need any help.'

She pressed her lips together and absolutely flounced out.

I turned to Thorpe. 'I can pass a message to Miss Pritchard for you.'

'Where can I find her?'

'I'm sorry, but I'd prefer not to give her address to anyone without her consent. What message should I pass on to her?'

He thought for a second. 'Tell her that she and I should meet. But not here.' He glanced at the chair with distaste. 'Let's say St James's Park on Sunday, on the bridge over the lake. Noon will be fine. My name's Thorpe. Major Thorpe.'

There was a sudden, wrenching crack and Alfie staggered backwards, grinning like a loon, holding up his pliers with a tooth clutched between the jaws.

'Got it!' he shouted.

Thorpe leapt towards the door, a sudden expression of shock on his face. Realising how panicked he must look, he took a breath and regained his composure.

'Make sure you pass on the message. Noon on Sunday.'

As soon as he'd gone I went upstairs and lay down on my bed, staring at the ceiling.

What have I done? How can he meet Lottie when she doesn't exist?

15

IT WAS SUNDAY MORNING, and Alfie and Constance had gone to church. Helena had always been rigid with regards to attendance, every week no matter what, and Alfie was continuing the custom. He never said so, but I sensed he was no more devout than I was, and only went to honour his late wife's wish. Like me, he had good reason to shun the Almighty.

I was sitting in my room, holding a new wig.

My first idea had been to meet with Thorpe myself and convince him to talk to me. But he'd asked so specifically for Lottie. Would he talk to anyone else?

I considered that someone might *impersonate* Lottie. Thorpe wouldn't know the difference, never having met her. But who?

I thought of Audrey. She might be excited to do it, and would welcome a small payment. We could rehearse in advance what she should ask. But Audrey was a street sparrow and Lottie was a turtle dove, a vicar's daughter, and no army major would be fooled.

I surprised myself by thinking of Mrs Flowers, whom I'd largely cast out of my mind. But I dismissed the idea – her accent was little better than Audrey's, and besides, there was something else about her: she didn't dissemble. She was direct, even rude. I didn't believe she could be convincing as someone else.

Which left only one person I could think of who was well-spoken and convincing enough to pass as Lottie. And that was why I had bought myself a wig.

The shop on Floral Street had been overwhelming, with row upon row of wooden heads wearing ladies' wigs of all styles. They had an unsettling, vaguely taxidermical quality. I couldn't decide what kind of wig I should get. Should it be something similar to the hair I used to have, nondescript brown and mildly wavy? I kept telling myself the wig was just a tool, a disguise for a purpose, and that the aesthetics of the thing weren't important. Thorpe was hardly going to confess to the crime, or not, depending on my choice of hair. I should just buy the cheapest one and leave. But still I stood there, frozen by indecision.

I wasn't helped by the obsequious assistant, his own hair contrarily full and lush. 'Perhaps this one, sir?' He picked out a stiff lump of a wig in the style one imagines the Queen might wear. 'It's long-lasting and very reasonably priced.'

My mistake had been to make up a lie on the spot, that I was buying one for my aged aunt to cover up her creeping baldness.

Eventually I chose something akin to my old hair. I didn't know why, and regretted it almost as soon as I left the shop. The assistant plainly found my choice inappropriate, and kept suggesting alternatives even as I was walking out of the door. 'Sir's aunt will wish to look her best for her age, and his choice is far too youthful. Sir should reconsider. We don't accept returns once the item's been worn.'

Now, sitting in my room, alone in the house, I loathed the thing. It felt as if I was holding someone's scalp in my hands, and that someone might be me. I was transfixed by my pounding resentment of Jane for putting me in this position. I was certain it was her doing, an act of spite. My brother wouldn't have the wit or inclination for such a scheme; his nature had always been to set his eyes on the horizon and stride straight forward. I doubted he'd changed all that much.

But I could afford no more delays. I had already scrubbed my cilices and hung them up to dry, tidied my few possessions and scraped a dried pool of wax off my shelf. Alfie and Constance would be back soon.

I put the wig over my head and pulled it tight. It was uncomfortable, clinging to my skin. When I shook my head vigorously, the hair swished from side to side, and when I bent forward, it fell around my face in a way I could vaguely recall.

I had bought some powder from the pharmacy, unbeknown to Alfie. He wouldn't care that he had one less pot and one extra sixpence. It was cold and itchy, but it covered up what was left of my bruise. I removed all my clothes and stood naked in the centre of the room, a woman to anyone who could have seen me.

I had already decided to wear Maria's clothes, and had sponged them clean, or some approximation of clean. I laid them out on the bed: petticoats, a bonnet, the dress and a pair of combination drawers of a type I'd never worn before.

I started by pulling on the combination, doing up the buttons over my breasts without a cilice for the first time in ten years. It was a plain, practical garment, and comfortable enough. I didn't hate it – how could I when it had been Maria's? But I hated me in it: my narrow waist and the bare white of my breastbone, my slender shoulders and skinny neck. Everything.

I had a sudden urge to rip it off and give up the plan entirely – let no one meet Thorpe, let me forget that I had ever wanted to know why Maria had died. For a while I just sat on the bed. Then it came to me; how I could do this. I took a cilice and rolled it up into a sausage, and pinned it into the crotch of the combination. It was a ludicrous thing to do; a pretend cock for a cockless man pretending to be a woman. It made no sense. But as long as I could feel it there, that pressure against my thigh, it would remind me who I truly was.

I breathed deeply and picked up the dress. It was cream-coloured, simple and pretty, with lace around the neckline and pleats and a bow at the back. It wasn't elegant enough, but it was all I had. It was designed for some kind of bustle, but I didn't have one. Maria must've still been wearing it when she left Madame Moreau's house. She was probably wearing it when she died, and it might even be in the grave with her. That thought chewed at me until I had to pinch my palm between my nails.

I cast around my room for a reasonable facsimile, spending some minutes experimenting with clothes hangers before settling on a folded towel, held up by a belt over Maria's petticoats. It was uncomfortable and apt to come undone. Why on earth did women tolerate such paraphernalia?

The dress didn't truly fit. The material hung from my shoulders, gaping loose across my chest and drooping at the back over my towel bustle. It was also a fraction short. My mother would have let down the hem and refashioned the bodice completely, but my sewing skills were limited to buttons and corpses, so I tugged down the petticoats and hoped that would be sufficient to appear proper.

The fact that the dress was Maria's made it easier, as if she and I were colluding. It smelled sweet, of her. I wrapped my arms around myself, hugging the dress to me, and could almost imagine she was hugging me back.

I straightened the waistband and smoothed the neckline with practised fingers, these rituals returning more easily than I would have thought possible. I searched through my drawer and found the only thing, aside from a few books, that I'd kept from my time as Lottie: a brooch my mother had given me on my eleventh birthday, a silver rose with a curved stalk and just a hint of a thorn. I pinned it to my dress.

I disliked looking in mirrors, but I wanted to check I had everything right, so I went into Alfie's room and stood in front of his with my eyes shut. I counted down from ten, and when I got to three, I opened them.

There was Lottie, in the flesh, with her long chin and awkward stance, and her fidgeting fingers that never knew what to do with themselves. I almost felt sorry for her. She put her hands on her hips, accentuating her waistline. I glared at her, and she glared straight back.

If my mother could've seen me now, she would believe her little girl had returned to her. It was an uncomfortable thought. Would it have killed me to continue wearing a dress for a few more years, for her sake? Was my sex such a fragile thing that I couldn't hide it for a little longer beneath powder and petticoats?

'Why should I?' I said out loud. 'Why should I seem other than what I am?'

I was right, but it didn't make me feel better. No matter how I justified it, I hadn't been there when my mother died.

I gathered up my own clothes and shovelled them into the carpet bag, and then went into the kitchen and took the biggest knife from the drawer, wrapped it up in a cloth and dropped it in as well. I'd spent an hour the previous day honing it to a glistening sharpness.

I arrived at St James's Park before eleven, shivering despite the navy riding jacket I'd purchased from a pawnbroker on Drury Lane for five shillings and sixpence – half a week's rent. The man insisted it was of the highest-quality wool and I didn't have time to argue with him, and it at least covered up my ill-fitting bodice and some of the makeshift bustle, which had a tendency to migrate around my waist and slip down. I'd already had to rearrange it twice on the short walk from the pharmacy, and I hoped it was now under control. I'd also purchased a wide-brimmed hat, which was more in keeping than Maria's flimsy bonnet.

I had an hour to practise being a woman.

The park was wonderfully elegant, and I was quite the clumsiest thing in it. I attempted to promenade along the shore of the lake, but kept tripping over Maria's petticoats. I realised I was walking far too briskly, fairly rushing round compared with the ladies I passed, whose pace was little more than an amble. Once I had slowed down, considerably, I was better able to stay upright.

The lake slunk along the park with black railings all around, and people with parasols strung along it like beads on a necklace. At one end there was a little island, and on it was a cottage and some net enclosures where stately storks and pelicans were picking their way between chuckling mallards and geese. I had wanted to bring Maria here after the Opera Comique in the hope it might become a regular arrangement. I had wanted us to walk arm in arm, stopping from time to time to sit on a bench and talk about our life together, and what we might become. I had wanted us to be just like other people. What a foolish fantasy.

Halfway along, the lake narrowed, girded by a bridge, too low for anything larger than a rowing boat to pass underneath. This was where I was due to meet Thorpe at noon. If I was honest, I was surprised he'd responded to Oliver's request. He was a major from a good family and Maria was a dead prostitute born in a theatre, so she'd said. I wondered what his reasons were.

On the bridge I practised my perambulation, taking care on the greasy wood underfoot. Many gentlemen met my eye, and more than my eye. Even if they were with a lady they still cast a glance, as if I was part of an exhibition they were viewing. I wondered if I ever behaved that way. I didn't think so. I certainly never called out to passing women or put a hand on their forearm while pointing out a moorhen floating by, as one fellow had done. Such confidence he had! I wondered how one develops it. And he'd been wrong about the bird, which was a coot. I didn't correct him because, I supposed, a lady has to be *demure*, even to the extent of allowing such heinous ignorance to go unchallenged.

After an hour I was exhausted and anxious, and decided to take some refreshment. I hurried over Birdcage Walk to an Aerated Bread Company tea shop, which was crowded even on a Sunday. I sat in their privy with my head in my hands, and after five minutes I did indeed require the use of the facility, and had to disrobe completely, having no idea how to cope with the arcane mechanics of Maria's combination drawers. Afterwards, I tightened the belt around my waist so the bustle wouldn't slip, although I could barely breathe.

Passing as a lady was queerly hard, especially in view of the difficulty I usually had passing as a man. It seemed absurd not to be able to do either.

When I returned to the tea-shop lounge it was almost entirely full of men. A young fellow clicked his fingers and pointed to a sign saying that the Ladies' Tea Room was downstairs, grinning and adding that he'd be delighted if I would prefer to join him and his party at their table. He seemed quite taken aback when I declined.

By the time I actually had a cup of tea in my hand, downstairs in a dim corner where no one could see me, I was shaking so badly I could scarcely hold it. When I closed my eyes I was still the same as ever, but when I opened them again I couldn't ignore the hair around my face and the lace trim on my dress.

I studied my hands. They were the same hands I'd always had, the same fingers, the same rosy, prominent knuckles. I still had the same soreness in my wrist from punching the weasel-faced man, and I could still feel the pressure of my fake cock pinned inside my drawers. I was still me.

I checked the bag, touching my thumb to the fine point of the knife through the cloth I'd wrapped it in. It was reassuringly sharp. I shook myself, feeling silly for having allowed Jane's little ploy to unman me.

I drew a deep breath and brought my knees back together. I was determined, for Maria's sake, to be the best woman I could.

At five to twelve, I was waiting on the bridge. On the dot of the hour, Thorpe came striding towards me from the north side of the park in full military uniform: red jacket and epaulettes, white belt, black trousers with sharp creases, black boots and an imposing black hat. The path was crowded with children and their parents watching the birds on the lake, but still they parted for him. His gait seemed to demand it: head up, shoulders back, forward march.

'You must be Miss Pritchard.'

'Yes. It's very nice to meet you, Major Thorpe.' I was conscious of the modulation of my voice. I'd been practising by humming in a higher register.

He removed his hat and gave me a minimal bow. He didn't appear to recognise me or Maria's dress, although the latter was hardly surprising. I wouldn't have recognised it either.

'Please, call me Augustus. I know your brother, after all. And may I call you Lottie?' He smiled and offered his arm without waiting for a reply.

The last time I'd appeared female I'd been fifteen years old, and even then no boy had ever offered me his arm. There was something about me that repelled them, perhaps my tallness for a girl or my tendency to pull faces at the hogwash they spouted. Yet here I was, walking with this gentleman as if it was the most natural thing in the world, being led by him down from the bridge towards the Queen's palace like the lady my mother had always hoped I'd become.

Beneath his uniform, I could feel the cadence of his walk, an intimate contact that made me shudder. That hand might have held the weapon that killed Maria. That bland face might have watched her die, teeth clenched, brow dripping with the effort of the kill.

The bag tugged on my hand, heavy with the kitchen knife.

'He's a good chap, your brother,' Thorpe was saying. 'And the finest shot in the regiment. He made a bet with one of the other chaps he could hit a china jug from forty yards. And he did it too. Second shot, clipped it as neatly as you like. The chap had to pay up a guinea in the mess while your brother drank from the self-same jug, with a great piece of it shot away. Can you believe that?'

'He always did love to shoot things.'

'And another time, in India, he hit a coolie who was hiding behind some bushes from as far as, well, do you see those trees over there? As far away as that. Pop, and down he goes, with a surprised look on his face. Never seen anything like it.' Thorpe briefly clutched his elbow to himself, squashing my hand against his jacket, but it didn't seem to be an overture, more a memory, an involuntary flinch. 'We did two years together in Bombay and Peshawar. You get to know a chap. Brothers in arms and all that. I must say he's never spoken of you before. You're not his twin, are you?'

'No. That's Jane. I'm younger.'

'Yes, quite right. And that other chap I met, who passed on the message?'

I shrugged. 'Someone I know. Oliver must have made a mistake with the address.'

'So the two of you aren't …?'

'Oh no.' I laughed, and part of it was genuine. 'Nothing like that. We're almost strangers.'

We were making slow progress alongside the lake, our shoes crunching on the gravel path. I was impatient to get to the point, but Thorpe seemed determined to make small talk.

'And how do you occupy your time, Lottie?'

'Well, I'm taking an interest in the murder that occurred, the girl, Miss Milanes. A purely amateur curiosity. I know it sounds macabre.'

'Certainly unusual.' He had the kind of politeness my mother would have called 'well brought up', meaning he always knew the right thing to say but never said anything interesting.

'I believe you knew Miss Milanes, Major Thorpe?'

'Augustus, please.' He looked away and I had the feeling he was mentally rehearsing his response. 'I was wondering how you got my name, actually.'

'Madame Moreau told me,' I lied. 'The woman who's been accused of the crime.'

'You met her? Gosh. Well, even so, it doesn't mean anything, does it? She might have picked my name at random.'

I smiled benignly, feeling his tension through his sleeve. 'There was a letter. From you to Miss Milanes.'

He let go of my arm and leaned on the railing, looking out across the lake towards Trafalgar Square and his barracks. I could see the strain in his jaw. He was drawn tight. 'And you've seen this supposed letter, have you?'

I knew I had to be very careful. That letter was all the leverage I had. If I denied having seen it there would be nothing to connect him to Maria and he would shut up like a cockle. But if I told him I had possession of it, he would certainly demand we went and fetched it this instant.

'I saw it briefly,' I said.

He put his head in his hands. 'You must think me such an idiot.' He was silent for a while and I thought he might have become exercised, but when he did finally speak, his voice was quite calm. 'None of this has anything to do with me. I didn't ... you know ... I didn't realise what she was. She seemed like such a lovely girl, truly lovely. We met here a few times, that's all. I had no reason to suspect her.'

The gravel path stretched out ahead of us. Maria had walked on that path, arm in arm with this same gentleman. I was wearing her clothes and literally following in her footsteps. It was almost too much to bear. The urge to run away was so strong the soles of my feet started to ache. But I had to stay to discover the truth.

'You were betrayed,' I suggested.

'Yes, exactly.' The memory still seemed painful to him. 'She told me her father had been a banker until he'd fallen on hard times, and her mother had died quite recently.

She wept on my shoulder just thinking of it. But it was all a lie. She was not at all as she appeared. I cut ties with her as soon as I found out, but, well, writing to her was an unwise thing to have done. I know that now. The thing is, I'd dearly love to get that letter back. I've tried, but so far … I say, are you all right?'

'Yes, thank you. It's just the grass making my eyes itch.'

'We could go to a tea shop if you prefer,' he offered, suddenly solicitous. 'There are some nice places nearby.'

'No, thank you, I'm quite all right. So you hadn't known her for long?'

'Barely at all. I was with the chaps over in India and we only came home, what, five months ago. I'd been wounded, not badly, some coolie with a rifle. An inch to the left and all that, but British officers aren't so easy to kill.' He smiled but it was artificial, automatic. 'That was the one your brother shot, actually. If he'd hit him with his first effort, things might've been different.'

So Thorpe had come home wounded and fearful, and Maria had comforted him. I suffered a sharp twinge of empathy.

'And how did you find out the truth?'

He looked askance at me. 'You're frightfully blunt.'

'I'm sorry.' I could feel myself reddening. I took a breath and smiled at him. My mother used to tell me: if you wish to say something, always smile, and phrase it as a question so no one thinks you're pushy. 'As I said, I have an interest. Don't you agree these girls need more protection than the police provide?'

'You'll forgive me if I don't. That sort of thing's all very well, but she was a liar and a fraud. She wanted to get married, and I, well, I suppose I was thinking along the same lines at the time. The whole idea seems inconceivable now.'

The poor fool. He probably thought *he* had seduced *her*. I wished I could know for certain, but that wasn't the sort of thing ladies were supposed to ask. I bit down hard on the inside of my mouth. Thorpe didn't notice, he was too immersed in his own tragedy to see anything else.

'You have to understand; she was so *convincing*. Well, naturally I mentioned her to my father. He's a judge. He did some investigating and that was the end of it.'

'Until she was murdered.'

He turned to face me, standing a little too close. I lifted my chin and slipped my hand into the bag. The cloth around the knife had come loose, and I could feel the hard, cold blade. It would slip in and out of him, open and shut like a fish's mouth. My fingers worked along to the handle and gripped it.

He took a deep breath. 'Yes, quite. And now that woman has my name and perhaps that letter. I did hope that you might have it, or know where it is.'

'I'm sorry, no. But if Madame Moreau is found guilty quickly, your name may never come up at the trial. You may be kept out of it completely.'

He wrapped his arms around himself and nodded. 'I can only hope so. In India we'd have hanged her and been done with it. Still, at least they've got the right person now. Second time lucky.'

'What do you mean?' My thumbs prickled with anticipation, but he hesitated, and I realised I'd been too abrupt again. 'I mean, if you wouldn't mind explaining?'

'Not at all.' He stood up straight, glad to be back on more agreeable territory. 'The police are incompetent. They don't *think*. They had someone else in custody to start with, a harmless dolt who works at the Westminster hospital and was besotted with her, apparently. The trial would've been all over the press. You can imagine the scandal; a reputable hospital, a crime of passion and all that – it would all have come out, including me. Father told them to let the idiot go and arrest this dreadful woman instead. Keep like with like, if you see what I mean.'

I felt a cold clutch around my kidneys. *Keep like with like*. That was how close I'd come: freed from gaol by Thorpe's father to keep his son's name out of the newspapers. He was probably right too; a surgeon's assistant killing his lover might be considered romantic, whereas an abortionist killing a whore was unremarkable. The trial would be over in a couple of days at most, and the story might not even make the press.

Thorpe took my arm again, guiding me once more down the path. We passed a couple coming in the other direction, and the woman, pretty and young, in her best frock, nodded to me. It was a knowing, collegiate gesture, an acknowledgement that we'd both done well, courting men of standing who were happy to promenade with us in the park. I felt sick.

Thorpe patted my hand. 'You've seen that Moreau woman, so you know what she is. She's been packed off to Newgate Prison, and it's no more than she deserves.'

'Newgate?' I felt my face blanch. But I couldn't dwell on it, not now. 'Major Thorpe –'

'Augustus, please.'

'Augustus. How did you even meet Miss Milanes?'

He took several seconds to respond, staring straight ahead at a willow tree trailing its limp fingers in the water. 'A beastly fellow I met at the club suggested it. He said she was a decent, respectable girl, but he knew she wasn't.'

There was no one else it could be. 'Was his name James Bentinck, by any chance?'

He nodded slowly. 'You're well informed. I should've known he wasn't to be trusted. He claims to be related to the Cavendish Bentincks but it's all nonsense. He's not a gentleman, he's a jumped-up nobody who made his money in the worst way and is mixing with his betters. It turned out he owned the place where she was ... *employed*, if you can believe it. The man's beneath contempt.'

We were back at the bridge, and I'd exhausted my questions and my spirit. I didn't know what I'd expected. I suppose I'd imagined him breaking down in a fit of remorse or giving away some vital clue that would confirm his guilt beyond doubt: a careless word, a speck of blood or an intimate knowledge of her lifeless body. But reality wasn't like that.

He wanted his letter back, and there might be other letters, acknowledging her pregnancy or proposing marriage. He might have confronted her – a burst of anger, shouting, pleading, and then a blow to her head, and him on his knees with blood soaking his hands, telling her he's sorry, praying for her to open her eyes, shaking as he wraps her up and carries her down to the river.

The bag was still tugging on my fingers. I could ask him to walk me home through the back streets. I could suffer a little cough, and when he stopped to see that I was all right, I could stick my knife into his neck. He would never expect it, not from a lady. It was the only way he would ever be punished, if he was guilty. If … if … if. But I couldn't be sure. I wanted it to be true, but I couldn't be *sure*.

I almost felt sorry for him. The girl he'd sent his letter to was a prostitute, and the girl he was hoping would find it would never return it to him. And she wasn't a girl.

I was chilly suddenly and missed my greatcoat. And my hat; not this silly, floppy thing with no warmth in it, but my solid bowler, shaped to my head by years of wear, more a part of me than this wig could ever be.

'I should be going,' I said. 'I can see myself home.'

'Of course. But would you be agreeable to taking another walk with me? Perhaps tomorrow?'

I opened my mouth, but the words were congesting in my throat. It took me a moment to assemble them into some kind of order. 'You mean you've *enjoyed* this conversation?'

'Well, it's been … interesting to meet you, certainly. And I should like to stay in touch in case, you know, you find out anything concerning my letter. I should very much like it back.'

It wouldn't do to turn him down. I might have more questions for him, or want to bring the police to have him arrested. Or, who knows, stab him after all.

'Not tomorrow, Augustus,' I forced myself to say, 'but perhaps on Wednesday? At noon in the same place.'

He nodded. 'Very well. Until then.'

I was about to leave when he grabbed my hand and kissed it, a formality I'd forgotten about. It was all I could do not to wipe off his vile moisture on the grass. He let go of me and hugged himself again, without apparently realising he was doing it, and strode off towards the barracks, his red jacket visible even as he disappeared into the distance.

Wearily, I trudged back over the park to the Aerated Bread Company tea shop, and once again located myself in their privy. I pulled off my hat and wig, unhooked the brooch, stepped out of Maria's dress and petticoats, and blissfully removed the towel bustle, relishing my ability to inhale fully. I felt like a snake shedding its skin. Naked, I wiped the powder from my face.

Then I took a long and satisfying piss.

Upstairs, the finger-clicker who'd invited me to his table was still there with his friends, but he didn't notice me. As I was leaving I jogged his cup with my hip so it spilled tea on to his trousers. He leapt up from his chair.

'I'm so sorry,' I said, and hurried outside before he could call me back to pay for it.

People were everywhere, milling around on the pavement and the streets, enjoying the air of London, as fresh as it ever was. I looked up and around, at the tall buildings and long, straight roads, the carriages and carts, the mess of the city. I stretched out my arms, stood with my feet apart and loudly cleared my throat. Everyone just walked around me. No one gave me a second glance.

I fixed my cap on my head and set off for home, the most thankful man in the world.

16

AS SOON AS I got home I fell into bed, but couldn't get Thorpe's face out of my mind. I could still feel the roughness of his beard on my hand where he'd kissed it. I almost retched.

I tried to think about something else, about Madame Moreau, locked up in Newgate Prison.

A man I had known, Angus McCoy, once spent three months in Newgate accused of fraud. The two of us had agreed to sell cookery books on commission among the wealthy houses in Knightsbridge and Kensington, but his basement flooded and we lost the entire stock. The publisher didn't believe our tale, or claimed he didn't, and I was forced to beg that loan from Jane to pay back my share. McCoy didn't have a wealthy sister, and was sent to Newgate to await trial. When he came out he was half the man he had been.

If Madame Moreau truly was the murderer, I was glad she'd been sent there. She deserved it. But still, I found it hard to accept. I couldn't imagine her hurting a woman.

I toyed with my chess set for a while, playing both sides, trying to pretend I didn't know my opponent's next, devastatingly clever move. But I found myself forgetting whose turn it was, staring at the wine cork that stood in for the white queen, whose banishment had brought the chess set within my budget. I found myself thinking about Elizabeth Brafton, who considered herself the queen of the brothel, but owned no part of it. Might she have killed Maria? I couldn't think why she would, but perhaps there *was* no why. Perhaps she just lost her temper one day. She had never liked Maria, or so Maria believed.

What about James Bentinck? He was surely capable of the crime, and it was an odd coincidence that Jack Flowers, who had worked for him, had died too. Maybe Bentinck had killed Jack, and maybe Maria found about it, and maybe the break-in at the mortuary was somehow connected, and … it was a lot of 'maybe'. There was no evidence. Even if Bentinck had wanted Maria murdered, I doubted he would do it himself. He would instruct Hugo, a boxer in his younger days and still dangerous now. Maria had treated him as one might an elderly dog, so safe and familiar it was hardly noticed. But he was Bentinck's man, through and through. If Bentinck had told him to kill her, he would have.

Hugo wasn't my top suspect, though. Thorpe, I judged, had been furious with Maria when he realised he'd been deceived. That letter gave him a strong motive, and he was in the army, so he knew how to kill. A crime of passion or simple self-interest, either way he headed my list.

But I couldn't go to the police with suspicions. I needed proof.

I lay down again and closed my eyes, and finally slept, with questions crowding into my mind, begging for answers I didn't have.

I awoke sweating, jolted from a nightmare in which I'd been wearing powder and a bonnet.

I knew I wouldn't get back to sleep, so I picked up *Oliver Twist*, but even though my eyes were following the words, I wasn't reading them. Eventually, I dragged myself downstairs and ate a cheese bun in the shop.

'Someone's waving at you,' Constance said, nudging me with her elbow and raising her eyebrows, clearly thinking my social life had taken a turn for the better.

I was surprised to see Mrs Flowers peering in through the glass with cupped hands, wearing a blue coat, all done up, and a dark purple hat. The young widow had already given up wearing mourning garb.

I unlocked the door and she came in, casting a brief, dubious look at the dentist's chair, which stood in glorious isolation, unused and unavoidable. Alfie had removed the pig's head once it had surrendered all its teeth and much of the pickled flesh along its jawline, and only after it had gone would Constance agree to hold her nose and clean the chair and tools. Now, they gleamed, and the odour had been reduced to a lingering, putrescent stink.

'Good afternoon, Mr Stanhope,' said Mrs Flowers. 'I hope you don't mind me calling on you. I have some questions.'

I realised I'd never seen her at her best, or anywhere close to it. When neither recently bereaved nor recently attacked, she was unexpectedly comely, with sharp eyes behind her spectacles and an expressive mouth that drew attention.

'Of course,' I said, thinking that I didn't want to talk to her *here*, with Constance in earshot. Better to go out, although I would be frightfully early to work. It wasn't yet half past four. 'I'm just leaving, but you can accompany me on my way if you'd like?'

Outside it was cold and dry, but a yellow fog had descended. It was the type the newspapers condemned daily and yet seemed oddly proud of, our city exhaling such potent vapours that its inhabitants appeared jaundiced and sickly, emerging from the dimness, muttering apologies and disappearing again as if they'd never been.

'Is your injury healing well?' I asked politely, as we walked through the patchwork of alleyways that led south to the hospital.

She adjusted her hat. 'It's not pretty under here, I can tell you. I've a bald patch and there'll be a scar. I suppose I shouldn't complain.' We were crossing over Coventry Street between the near-stationary traffic before she spoke again. 'What I wanted to talk to you about. The police have arrested someone, some woman, for killing the whore. Did you know that?'

'Yes. She's been sent to Newgate Prison.'

Mrs Flowers frowned. 'Well, whatever she's done, I don't envy her that. There's no justice to be found in there.'

'It won't be for long. They'll probably hang her soon enough.'

'So you think she's guilty, then?'

'I don't know.' I was so used to keeping secrets it had become my default position, an instinct, and only with an effort of will could I overcome it. 'Mrs Flowers, did you know your husband worked for James Bentinck, and ... what kind of business he's in?'

She looked down at her hands, and I immediately regretted asking. I was so absorbed in my own concerns I hadn't thought about the shame she must be feeling. What a terrible thing to have to admit.

'I found out. I didn't know the details. I didn't want to.' She looked up at me. Until that moment, I could never have imagined her weeping. 'I see what you're getting at though, and I've thought the same. He knew the whore.'

I didn't like her referring to Maria in that way, but I couldn't blame her. She was telling me about her husband and, by implication, her marriage.

'They probably met, yes.'

'You've no need to be so delicate. I knew what he was well enough. He never met a woman he didn't like, and he never liked a woman he didn't want to lift up her skirt. He wasn't above spending some chink too, if that's what it took, and that was mostly my money by the way, earned with my two hands baking pies.'

Having said her piece, she walked beside me in silence. I contemplated taking her arm, but her expression made me think better of the idea.

'I believe a major in the army may be involved in some way,' I said eventually. 'He knew Maria Milanes. I think he was in love with her, but his father put a stop to it. He sent a letter breaking off their friendship, and he's desperate to get it back. His name is Thorpe. Did your husband ever mention him?'

She shook her head. 'No. He was friendly with a good many people, but I doubt any of them were *majors*. Moneylenders and bookies were more his type.'

She took a deep breath, and looked at me sidelong again. I realised she was assessing me. Her conversation up to this point had been akin to kneading the dough, and now she wanted to roll it out and bake it.

'What I wanted to ask you, Mr Stanhope, is for a favour. I need to visit that brothel.'

'What?' I was certain I must have misheard her, or else the knock on her head had addled her mind. 'You can't possibly go to a brothel, Mrs Flowers.'

'I'll do as I please, Mr Stanhope.'

'But why? It's complete madness.'

She paused, clutching her hands together. 'I have to speak to them. I think maybe Jack did something foolish, and took some money that wasn't his. That'd be just like him.'

'And do you think … forgive me, but is it possible he was murdered for it?'

She bit her lip and nodded. 'More than likely, I reckon. And now they think I have their money. But I don't.'

'Is that why you were injured? The woman at your shop said you were taken to Puddle Dock, to a ship.'

Her hand unconsciously went to her head. 'Alice had no business saying such things, and anyway it wasn't a ship, just one of those boats that goes up and down the river.'

'I went to Puddle Dock. The dock-master had taken a bribe and couldn't tell me anything useful. Did you recognise the man who captured you?'

'Never seen him before. Thin. Nasty. About your height.'

The weasel. 'I think I've met him.'

'He came in polite enough but then starts asking questions about Jack, wanting to know if he'd told me something, and if I had their money. I had no idea what he was talking about. Jack never gave me a brass farthing. Drinking with his mates most of the time, and when he came back he was in no mood for conversation. But the fellow wouldn't take no for an answer, and kept asking over and over, where's the money, where's the money. I told him I didn't know anything about it, and he said there was important people who wanted it back. He said if I didn't tell him it'd be the worst for my kids.' Her face set as hard and cold as ceramic. 'He dragged me out to his carriage and still he kept asking, where's the money. When he tied me up on that boat I was worried, I can tell you.'

'That's awful. How did you escape?'

'I was yelling for help, and he kept telling me to stop, but I wouldn't. I wasn't going to make it easy for him. He got annoyed and clobbered me over the head, and then probably thought I was a goner. He was trying to shove me overboard. So I kicked him in the tallywags and ran off up to the street. Some people found me and took me to the infirmary.'

'Did you see anything unusual on the boat? The dock-master said there were coffins onboard.'

'Coffins? Mother of God.' She shivered and wrapped her arms around herself. 'No, I didn't see anything like that.'

'And you really don't know where their money is?'

She gave me a look that would have kindled stone. 'Do you think I would've endangered my children? My God, I'd have told him in a second. That's the point! He could come back, just walk into the shop, any time he likes. I worry every minute. I don't care what they do to me, but leave my children alone. That's why I need to go to the brothel, so I can tell those people I don't know anything about their money.'

There were still some things I didn't understand. 'But if your husband stole their money, why did they kill him? It doesn't make sense. Surely they'd leave him alive so he could tell them where it was.'

'I have no idea.'

I stopped and faced her as people passed by either side of us. In the fog, they were vague and faded, and we were alone in the world.

'You can't possibly go there, Mrs Flowers. You're a respectable lady.'

She snorted. 'Respectable! I'm sleeping with a cudgel by my bed. I held a skewer to some lad's throat yesterday, and he'd only come in for a pork pie. Don't tell me what I can and can't do. I've had enough of that.'

'Very well then, if you're not interested in my opinion, what *do* you want?'

'I want the address of the place. I went to the police to ask them and they fetched some priggish detective who refused to tell me. For my own good, he said.'

Unexpected wisdom from Ripley; I wished I'd been there to see it. 'I won't tell you either.'

She snorted again. 'You men. You always think you know best. I'll find out another way then. Good day, Mr Stanhope.'

She turned and walked away, vanishing into the murk. I stood there, feeling the tide of pedestrians flowing against me, pushing me south towards the hospital.

I looked back. Even if I could find her in the fog, Mrs Brafton would never let us in, not while she still blamed me for Maria's death.

I strode south down Whitehall. It wasn't my fault Mrs Flowers was so aggravatingly stubborn.

I slowed down.

I looked back again.

Damn it.

I set off after her, and hadn't gone more than thirty or forty yards before I found her sitting on a low wall.

'Mrs Flowers! I thought you'd gone.'

She looked away. 'I don't know where to go is the truth. Now, will you tell me or not?'

'I think you're being very unwise, Mrs Flowers. If Jack did steal the money from the brothel then you'll be walking into grave danger. How will it help your children if their mother's dead?'

'Either I'll be gone and they'll be brought up by Alice and Albert, or I'll make peace and so much the better. Either way, it'll be over, and that's what matters. They've been through enough.' She took off her spectacles and wiped her eyes. 'You don't have children, do you? You don't know how it is. In truth, I'm glad Jack's dead. Isn't that terrible?' She looked down at the pavement and gathered herself. 'He was sweet once, with his smile and his manners. He wooed me. We used to go dancing.' She smiled at the memory, swaying a little from side to side. 'He was so friendly to everyone, always joking. Life and soul when he'd had a few, singing in the pub, and then home to me. But I'm a bit of a harpy, and he used to get angry. He said I was the worst gamble he ever lost, and was free with his fists when the mood took him.'

'I'm sorry.'

She gave a little shrug. 'Don't be. It's normal. It was only when he started on the kids I minded.' Her voice cracked. 'Robbie's only five, poor little man, and Lillian's not even four. He knocked her out clean once, and she only woke up while I was carrying her to the doctor. When she opened her eyes I thought I would burst with relief. I just want them to be safe now.'

The church bells were tolling. Somewhere in my head there was a voice saying that I didn't have the time and it might not be safe. But the reckless part of me said I had a whole hour to get there and back, and a proud history of idiocy.

'Very well, Mrs Flowers, if you insist on going, I'll take you there myself.'

'Rosie, if you want,' she offered, apparently against her better judgement. 'I don't feel like a Flowers any more, if I ever did. Silly name anyway, Rosie Flowers. Everyone calls me Rosie.'

17

ONCE AGAIN, I WANTED to take a hansom cab, but Rosie pursed her lips and was having none of it.

'Half Moon Street?' she scoffed. 'What's wrong with your legs?'

It was properly dark and raining by the time we got there. A cab would have knocked ten minutes off the time and kept us dry besides, but it didn't seem worth raising the point.

'You realise they'll probably turn us away?' I said. 'Last time I saw Elizabeth Brafton we had words. She won't have forgiven me.'

'You poor thing,' said Rosie. 'Must be terrible to have the mistress of whores thinking ill of you.'

'You don't understand. She's an intelligent woman, educated and experienced. Don't underestimate her.'

Rosie sniffed. 'Can't be easy for her, with so little demand for the goods.'

'Will you be dismissing everything I say?'

'Quite likely, if you keep talking such nonsense.'

As we approached the house, a brief, habitual excitement erupted within me, quickly stifled by a kind of torpor. Another girl would be in Maria's room now, sitting at Maria's dressing table, brushing her hair with Maria's brush, probably even wearing her clothes. It didn't make me angry, it made me feel dislocated, as though time was going more slowly for me than for everyone else.

'I don't think we should do this.'

'Then go home,' said Rosie. 'I'm not stopping you. But I need to have peace. I can't live in fear for my children.'

She paused to raise the collar of her coat, obscuring her face somewhat from passers-by, and then marched up the steps and knocked on the door of the brothel as if she did this sort of thing every day.

Hugo opened the door, his vastness blocking out the light. The first time I met him I expected the room to tip up and all the furniture to slide in his direction.

'Oh, it's you, Mr Stanhope,' he said, and cast a brief, assessing glance at Rosie. 'No vacancies.'

'Now you listen —' she began, but I interrupted her.

'This is Mrs Flowers, a respectable widow. We're here on important business with Mrs Brafton. It's to do with Maria Milanes.'

He stroked his jaw, sending ripples across his bulbous neck, and glanced back inside. 'You're best off going home if you know what's good for you.'

There was a movement behind him, and Mrs Brafton's face peered round his massive frame.

'It's all right,' she said. 'I'll make an exception for Mr Stanhope.'

'Madam —' started Hugo, but she brushed him aside.

'And you are?'

'Rosie Flowers,' said Rosie with a shallow smile. 'I think you knew my husband, Jack.'

Mrs Brafton nodded, with a hint of puzzlement, and led us to the drawing room, indicating we should sit.

Rosie perched on an armchair, her hat remaining firmly in place. The room was exactly as I'd last seen it, oppressive and somehow *too much*; too much red in the wallpaper, too many candles on the mantelpiece, too strong a smell of rosewater and too much furniture as well. I eyed the willow-pattern bowl on the sideboard, imagining that Maria was upstairs right now, waiting for me. I could almost hear her laugh.

Mrs Brafton was as immaculate as ever. Maria had told me there were some customers who, upon setting eyes on her, decided she would be preferable to any of the girls, even though she was well over forty years old. But I'd never known her to go upstairs with anyone, except for the Colonel of course.

Hugo reappeared, but she shushed him away and sent the maid to bring us a much-needed tray of tea.

'Well, isn't this nice,' she said, smiling at us both, making some effort at warmth. I was surprised, expecting a repeat of her previous hostility.

She sat briefly on the sofa and then got up again, eventually choosing to stand with one arm on the mantelpiece as my father used to of an evening while Jane played the piano. Thank goodness no one had tried to squeeze a piano into this small room, though I sensed it was a close-run thing.

'It may be that I owe you an apology, Mr Stanhope,' she continued, talking to the rug as far as I could see. 'About before, at the funeral. Please understand, I was distraught and not really myself. It was such a blow.' She turned to Rosie. 'One of our girls was murdered, as you may know, and we're inconsolable. Who would have thought it?

Louisa Moreau. I was *shocked* when I heard. None of us ever dreamt of such a thing.'

'That's why we've come,' said Rosie. 'My Jack is dead too, but it's in the past now. What's done is done, is what I'm saying. I know nothing of his business and he left nothing behind. No money or anything.'

Mrs Brafton didn't flinch. 'That's a shame. You must be *very* concerned.' She angled her head sympathetically. 'I was sorry to hear of your bereavement. But it's important that we remain resilient in the face of such things, isn't it? Life must go on.'

'You're quite right,' Rosie continued gamely. 'I know Jack saw whores and came to brothels. And perhaps he did something stupid and took something that didn't belong to him. But I know nothing about it. Nor do I care how he died. I've three children and a pie shop to run, and I'm content to continue with that and leave well alone. He wasn't much of a husband anyway, if the truth be told. Drunk most of the time, with a rotten temper. Not much to look at neither and not the brightest.' And then, as an afterthought: 'God rest his soul.'

Mrs Brafton's eyes flicked up to Rosie's hat, purple and not black, lacking a veil. 'I'm afraid I hardly knew your husband, Mrs Flowers.' She stared pointedly at me. 'But men will have their secrets, won't they?'

I exchanged a glance with Rosie. She had wanted to make peace, but wasn't getting a foothold here.

The maid arrived with the tea, and Mrs Brafton deftly arranged the saucers and cups. Her hand was steady as she poured. There was a sound of footsteps in the hall, and the head of a young fellow appeared around the doorway, followed by the rest of him. If I'd ever wondered what kind of person visits a brothel on a Sunday afternoon then here was my answer: he was fourteen at most, dressed in trousers that showed his ankles and a shirt that showed his wrists, grinning from ear to ear.

'Same time next week,' he called out to Mrs Brafton with a kind of buoyancy, and then we heard the front door slam and Hugo grumbling that the lad had tipped him a farthing on his way out.

How does it feel, to be like him? How did he get to be so cocky?

Rosie sat quietly, nursing her cup between her hands. I could tell the lad had done nothing to revise her opinion of the male sex. 'I just want to be left in peace to run my shop,' she said eventually. 'No one wants to see black crape on the door, do they?'

'No indeed,' agreed Mrs Brafton. 'Our customers come first.'

I wasn't sure how this exchange was helping. I cleared my throat, but Rosie narrowed her eyes at me and turned back to Mrs Brafton, intent on making conversation.

'So tell me, how did you start this concern of yours? What's the story behind it?'

The older woman seemed pleased to be asked. Despite being surrounded by her girls and her customers, I realised how isolated she was.

'I started here eight years ago. We had just this floor and the next one in those days, and we let all the top rooms to students. There were a few girls here then, but I remember two in particular, Ada and Ethel, who had worked at every place between here and Portsmouth, some of them twice.

Their customers used to queue outside their doors if you can believe it, and when each man came out he would doff his cap to the next in line. Paupers, the lot of them. All these wealthy houses in Mayfair, full of thick wallets and cold beds, and our customers were vermin from the docks and factories.'

'So what did you do?' asked Rosie.

'There was nothing I could do, at first. It was Mrs O'Leary who was in charge of the place in those days, a big Irishwoman with a ruddy face. Nancy Gainsford knew her from before. I was just cooking and washing and so forth. Of course, Mr Bentinck owns it all and we're all in his employ.' She nodded in my direction. 'You've seen Mr Bentinck, Mr Stanhope. He was kind enough to speak at Maria's funeral, and a great honour it was for her that he came. He's related to the Cavendish Bentincks, you know. A very important family. Very important.'

'So I've been told.'

'Mrs O'Leary was used to running things in a certain way, with the men paying a few pence each. It was what she knew, and there was nothing wrong with it, I suppose, but there was no *order*. No *quality*. And then one day she brought in a new girl, a pitiful, mule-faced creature with no teeth and no bosom, and she announced that this girl, I can't remember her name, Binty or Bunty or something like that, would be perfect for the *lower classes*. As if we weren't already catering for the lowest possible! Well, I'd had enough.

'I went to Mr Bentinck and told him I could make more money with a better class of customer. Nancy Gainsford didn't like *that*, I can tell you. She's always been so *common* at heart. She's not really even a bookkeeper, just a secretary, and lucky to be that. But James, Mr Bentinck that is, he's a man of vision. And he has contacts everywhere: he knows judges and people in the police, here and even in Brussels!' She lowered her voice to a whisper. 'Even the Belgian royal family, so I heard.'

'What happened then?' asked Rosie, visibly discounting the rumour.

Mrs Brafton didn't notice and paused dramatically, enjoying her tale. 'He said I had a month to prove my case. So I got rid of Bunty or whatever her name was, and Ada and Ethel and the rest, and brought in better girls, nice girls. And I raised the prices. Well, you can't even imagine. There was a riot, near enough. Some of these men had been coming here for years, and treated Mrs O'Leary like their mother. She gave them discounts if you can believe it. Suddenly they had to pay two shillings for what they used to get for sixpence, and they weren't best pleased about it. They soon stopped coming, and after a month we had no customers at all. Not one. Mr Bentinck visited here with Hugo, and I thought … well, Mr Bentinck and I were of like mind, but still, my plan had failed completely. I was perturbed. But he told Hugo to fetch some carpenters and painters and what have you, and make the place like new. "Elizabeth my dear," he said to me, "if we're going to bring in a better class of customer, we need a better class of house." As I say, a true man of vision.

'And then, one by one, we got new customers, proper gentlemen from the local area, who valued what we offered and were willing to pay for discretion. And so I built the place up to what it is today.' She bloomed with pride. 'And do you know what, Mr Stanhope? The Colonel, he was the first through the door. His wife had recently passed away and, well, you know how it is.' She faltered a little, remembering who she was speaking to, and then recovered. 'Those days are long gone for him now of course, poor dear.'

'And what happened to Mrs O'Leary?' I asked.

Mrs Brafton flexed her jaw as if she'd found some gristle between her teeth and was trying to prise it loose with her tongue. 'She crawled off to Nancy Gainsford and begged to be reinstated. She told her what an evil woman I was, with my modern schemes and what she called snobbishness. But Nancy couldn't persuade Mr Bentinck of course, so Mrs O'Leary had to go. She drank herself to death and was found in a gutter down by Stepney Way. A merry enough soul, but no *ambition*.'

We had finished our tea and it seemed like time to go. I nodded to Rosie, who shrugged and pursed her lips. She had wanted to appeal to whoever had killed Jack to leave her and her children alone, but she'd made no progress. Mrs Brafton had adroitly played the part of the grieving employer, and it was impossible to tell whether she knew more than she was saying.

I could only think of one more question, though I very much doubted she would answer it.

'Mrs Brafton, does the name Augustus Thorpe mean anything to you?'

She folded her arms. 'Discretion above all things is my golden rule here. I'm sure *you* appreciate that.' She glanced briefly at the sideboard and then, more overtly, at the clock on the mantelpiece, lost among the candlesticks. 'Well, I mustn't keep you.'

As we stood up, my mind was turning fast. The last time I'd been in this room she had castigated me for missing the end of my appointment. It had been my last evening with Maria. I'd come here with those theatre tickets in my pocket and my heart in my mouth, and had walked away without even looking up at Maria's window, fearful of seeing another man's shadow against her curtain. How petty that seemed now. I'd assumed we'd have all the time in the world, and never dreamt that I wouldn't be seeing her the following week.

The appointment book, I thought. *The appointment book!* It was Mrs Brafton's lodestone, her way of keeping order in a chaotic world. That was why she'd been so annoyed with me that day. The appointment book maintained the pretence that this was some kind of gentlemen's club, rather than a market-stall for the lusty, lonely and desperate. Lord knows, I was all three.

I had to think of a way of coaxing Mrs Brafton to leave the room.

'Last time I was here I think I left a book behind. *Barnaby Rudge*. I'd love to have it back, if you wouldn't mind.'

'A book? I'm sorry, everything of Maria's ... well, the girls divided up her clothes and things. I don't remember any book.'

'It has sentimental value.'

She smiled and indicated the door. 'If it turns up I can let you know.' It was obvious she wanted us to leave.

'I'm sorry,' I said, not taking the hint. 'But I'd dearly love to have it back now. It's a bit tatty, and might be taken for rubbish. I would so hate to lose it.'

She sighed and scratched her head. 'I could ask.'

When she'd gone, Rosie sat down again with a sigh. I put my finger to my lips, and opened the drawer of the sideboard. Blotters, pens, ink and loose sheets of paper covered in fast, flowing handwriting. I scanned them briefly, but none meant more to me than the daily minutiae of life: shopping lists ('ham, cheese, small cabbage') and reminders ('sink leaking').

'What are you doing?' hissed Rosie.

There was a locked wooden box with something inside that rustled and rattled like money. Underneath that was the black leather appointment book. I slipped it out and opened it up.

'All the names are here,' I whispered. 'Every day going back months. Every girl and every customer, all in order. It's even got the daily take at the bottom of each page. Three pounds, twelve and ten, yesterday.'

'Put it back.' She was glowering at me. 'What if she finds out? She'll know it was us. I came here to make peace. Put it back right now or I'll shout the place down.'

Maria's name was in the same place on every page, right at the top. Her days were always full. Every Wednesday at seven o'clock, what had meant everything to me was reduced to: 'L. Stanhope, five shillings'.

On other days there were, of course, other names. I found Jack Flowers twice, the first with his full name and the next with just 'Jack', at four o'clock on a Monday afternoon, marked in capitals with the word 'GRATIS'.

'Look here.' I showed Rosie. 'She did know your husband. I'm sorry.'

'Don't be. Put it back this instant or I'll start hollering, I swear I will.'

'And he was *gratis*. It means free,' I said. 'He didn't have to pay.'

'That sounds like him, the skinflint. You have ten seconds.'

I could hear a sound from upstairs, heavy footsteps on the landing above us. I continued turning pages, going backwards in time. On the next page, on a Sunday afternoon, I found a name: *A. Thorpe, walk in park.*

'My goodness! Augustus Thorpe! His name's here. She booked him in!'

'Eight.'

'I wonder if he owns a boat.'

'Why would he? Seven.'

I turned the page. On a Tuesday afternoon, Maria's name was circled with an arrow down to another girl, Tilly. Written in capitals next to it was: 'MR BENTINCK, HOUSE CALL, BURTON STREET, BELGRAVIA'.

'See here,' I whispered to Rosie. 'Bentinck. He had the girls sent round to his house!'

'Five,' she said.

I turned over a few more pages, going back several weeks. There were more of the same names repeated, meaning nothing to me, until I came across one that I couldn't believe. I had to read it twice just to check I wasn't going mad. December 29th, at seven in the evening, for one hour with Maria. And again the Monday before and the one before that.

'Two,' said Rosie, standing up.

I could hear someone coming down the stairs. I shoved the appointment book back into the drawer, but it jammed. I yanked the drawer out and tried to push it home, but the book lodged against something and it wouldn't completely close.

'Quick!' hissed Rosie.

I spun round as Hugo entered the room, and finally, with a bang that must have been heard all over the house, forced the drawer shut with my behind.

He looked from me to the drawer, and seemed about to say something when Mrs Brafton came in.

'I'm sorry, I couldn't find your book. You must've left it somewhere else. Thank you both so much for coming, and again, Mrs Flowers, my sincere condolences.'

We hurried out before anyone could stop us.

———

Rosie was prattling on as we walked up Long Acre, but my mind was spinning. I still couldn't believe the last name I'd read.

She grabbed my arm. 'Are you even listening to me? You're a bloody fool. You could've cost me everything. You had no business searching through her private possessions.'

'I know, but the book contained names and places. It might help me learn who killed Maria.'

I thought this would calm her down, but it seemed to have the opposite effect.

'And my children and me count for nothing? You put us at risk, do you know that? You only care about yourself. You men are all the same, aren't you?'

I considered the question, feeling light-headed. 'I honestly wouldn't say so.'

'God, if women were in charge the world would be a better place, and it would smell sweeter and all.'

'But Mrs Brafton accidentally gave us some interesting information,' I explained. 'She told us Bentinck knows people in Brussels. Royalty, if we can believe her. Maria was found by the river, and Jack drowned, and you were held on a boat. I think the boat must belong to Bentinck. My guess is he's involved in some kind of illegal trade in Belgium.'

'The woman's a fool, is what she is. She's done everything and she's giving this Bentinck fellow all the credit. She's sweet on him is the truth. You could fill an ocean with women's tears over men.' Rosie folded her arms. 'And she wasn't friendly about that other woman, was she? Miss Gainsford, was it? Who's she?'

'She's Bentinck's bookkeeper.'

'Pretty lady, I suppose?'

'Oh yes, very.'

I thought back to my conversation with Nancy Gainsford after the funeral. There was certainly tension between the two women, Mrs Brafton believing the brothel was hers, and occupying her position rather as if she was the headmistress of an exclusive school, while Miss Gainsford treated her as little more than a housekeeper.

'We have to go to the police,' I said. 'We need them to investigate the boat and look at Bentinck's accounts for a connection to Belgium.'

She laughed, actually laughed, and wiped her eyes behind her spectacles. 'Such faith! A *gentleman* with all his wealth and connections. They'll spit in your face.'

'We have to try.'

'There's no "we".'

'Please. It'll mean more if we both go. They can't ignore us both.'

'They can and they will.'

I took a deep breath. Bentinck was a dangerous man, no doubt: *beatings and stabbings, fires, even a drowning. And at the end, there was just James Bentinck.* But I'd come this far, and I wouldn't do what Thorpe had done. Despite all the lies she had told me, and the truths she had hidden from me, I wouldn't abandon Maria.

'I have to go,' I said. 'If you change your mind, meet me at the pharmacy at seven.'

I watched her walk away, quickly lost among the crowds. I was heading in a different direction, north-east, half-running past Lincoln's Inn Fields just as the distant clocks struck the hour. It occurred to me that I'd completely forgotten to go to work, but it was too late now. I'd have to miss my shift. I knew I should care more about that, and some part of me did, but that voice was drowned out by a far bigger noise: a shout, a roar of rage.

The name in the book, who'd been with Maria every Monday for weeks – I couldn't believe it was true, but it had been written there in black and white: *Jacob Kleiner.*

18

I HAD FIRST MET Jacob at the chess club. He was playing Durant, who was the sweetest fellow before a game,
but became aggressive if he started losing, swearing and
slamming his pieces down on the board. Their match was
swinging to and fro, each having the upper hand for a
while, until Jacob closed in on the win, and Durant bit his
nails down to the quick.

'You toyed with him,' I said, when the game was finished
and Durant had stormed off home.

Jacob puffed on his cigar in a manner with which I
would become familiar, and indicated the seat opposite.

'It's educational,' he said. 'I'm teaching him not to lose
his temper.'

'By driving him mad?'

'A little madness is no bad thing. Do you want to play?'
He held out his hand for me to shake. 'Keep in mind it's
impolite to beat an old man first time out.'

The following Thursday we played again, and the one
after that, and over the weeks and months he became
something I'd never had before: a friend. When I was a
child, I'd wanted to keep company with the boys, but they
weren't interested in a girl who would either ruin their
game or show them up, and all my female friendships had

been forced upon me or, later, laced with unrequited love and lust. I had been inseparable from pretty, blonde Sylvia before she got spoony on some boy. When I stopped calling on her, she said I was jealous, and she was right and wrong at the same time.

But Jacob accepted me as a man and liked me anyway. He invited me to dinner and so I met Lilya, and after drinking too much of the dangerously sweet spirit his brother brewed, I stayed one night in the room that had been spare since their son Michael had left home to make scientific instruments in Norwood. Jacob blundered in drunk, just as I was unwrapping my cilice, and he stood there with his mouth hanging open. I hadn't realised this was the room he slept in whenever Lilya booted him out of their marital bed for snoring too loudly, and he was a creature of habit. The following morning I hoped the alcohol might have voided his memory along with his stomach, but he was gone before I awoke and I didn't see him for three long weeks. I assumed he was lost to me, until one day he dropped into step alongside me on my way to work.

'Ladies can't play chess,' he declared, and even though he was misguided, I didn't argue. I ended up telling him everything about myself, and I suppose it made us closer friends, as only the very lonely can be.

But all of that was finished now. As the hansom cab dropped me outside Jacob's shop, I was thinking: this will be my last ever visit.

I clenched my teeth and hammered on the door, sending their little dog into a frenzy of barking. I was relieved when Lilya's face appeared at the window.

'Who is it?' she called.

'It's Leo.'

She rushed for the lock and fumbled with it, finally throwing open the door with a smile. I was always surprised how lovely she was, ten years younger than Jacob at the least, with a round, friendly face and a wise mouth.

'It's good to see you, Lilya.'

She reached out and put her hand on my shoulder, feeling the bones under my skin, and then up to my cheek.

'You're so thin,' she said. 'Always so thin. You must come around here more often and I will feed you sausages and pancakes until you are fat as a pig.'

She led me through the little room, feeling her way Jacob's shop was more of a workshop, no bigger than ten feet by twelve, with a bench covered in tools, and walls lined with boxes containing all manner of tiny cogs and links and springs. She knew every inch of it, but he was not a tidy worker and was apt to leave things lying around that she might tread on.

Lilya was almost blind. She could still see a hazy circle in the centre of her vision, but outside of that little tube of light, everything was shadow. She could tell night from day and people from horses, but was unable to read a book, although she loved Jacob to read to her, in German or Russian, depending on her mood. She could still play her gypsy guitar well enough, and sing folk songs that moved me terribly, though I didn't understand a word of them. And she could still cook, moving around the stove with a musician's fingers, measuring and slicing and mixing.

'He's upstairs,' she said. 'Napping. He'll wake up when he smells the food. You'll stay and eat with us, yes?'

Jacob's place was laid out quite differently from Alfie's. A narrow stair led up to the first floor, which was far larger, sprawling across his own shop and the ones on either side, and above that was another floor with bedrooms that seemed cut from a different template entirely, as if the architect had got drunk and drawn in walls haphazardly. I loved to curl up on the window seat there and gaze out over the roofs.

Lilya was cooking and singing while her little dog scurried between her feet, hoping she would drop some chicken.

'You're so quiet,' she said eventually. 'I don't know if you're still there.'

'Still here.'

When the smell became so strong that it was almost edible itself, Jacob stamped down the stairs barefoot, wearing baggy trousers and a shirt untucked around his braces. Seeing me sitting at their little table, his face lit up.

'Leo!' he said. 'Where have you been? On Thursday I had to play some solicitor who was so useless I started giving him tips. And he was teetotal! Can you believe it? He lectured me on the evils of drink.'

He poured two small glasses of whisky and handed one to me. I pulled out my notebook and pencil from my pocket, and wrote down I KNOW YOU KNEW MARIA and turned it round so he could see it.

'What are you doing?' He read it and blanched, pushing his fingers through his hair, what was left of it. He glanced at Lilya and whispered: 'Leo ...' I gave him my pencil and he wrote briefly in the notebook: I'M SORRY.

Lilya noticed the silence and tapped on a saucepan with a spoon, clang, clang, clang. 'No! You speak out loud so I can hear you. No whispering like little girls.'

'Of course, Lilya,' I said, and then, loudly, to Jacob: 'I might be at chess next week.'

I wrote down: WHY?

'Good,' he said, scribbling on the paper: I WANTED TO KNOW HER. YOU TALKED ABOUT HER. I WAS WEAK.

'And Lilya?' I said, looking at Jacob.

'Yes?' she said.

'That smells simply delicious.'

She nodded with satisfaction. This was an old game. She always complained that her cantankerous husband never offered her any appreciation, so I overdid my praise to show him up, though I wasn't lying.

Jacob turned the paper round again: I WILL ALWAYS BE HUSBAND TO LILYA. ALWAYS. MARIA WAS TEMPTATION. I AM OLD MAN.

'And how is business?' I said.

WHEN DID YOU LAST SEE HER? I wrote.

'Never enough customers, and always they want cheap, cheap. No one values quality any more.'

He took the notebook and wrote for several seconds, slowly and precisely. A MONTH AGO. I'M SORRY. STOPPED FOR YOUR SAKE.

I wrote my reply and turned it round: GOODBYE.

'No,' he said. 'Stay, Leo, please. Have dinner with us.'

'What?' said Lilya. 'Is this why all the scratching and whispering?'

'I have to leave, Lilya. Thank you for your hospitality.'
I kissed her on the cheek and she held my shoulders, a
dusting of flour still on her hands. I looked into her blank
eyes. One day, she had told me, even that dim circle of light
would be gone.

'Why you run away?' she said. 'I never see you no more.'

'I have to meet someone.'

'A woman, yes? Yes. I can tell.'

'You're very clever, Lilya. He doesn't deserve you.'

She smiled a thin, sad smile. 'Maybe he does, maybe he
doesn't. But whatever you argue about, you must forgive
each other. Always forgive. Sins on both sides. You have a
friend and it's more than gold, but you cannot melt him
down and make him into something else. He is what he is.'

'I'm sure you're right.'

'And you are his only friend, so ...'

Jacob followed me down the stairs and let me out of
the door. We stood on the pavement, me in my coat and
bowler hat, him shoeless and shivering. I'd forgotten how
much shorter than me he was. Was he more stooped now
than when I first met him?

He put his hand on my arm but I brushed him off.

'You're angry with me,' he said. 'But you knew I went
there. I introduced you to it, remember?'

'Not with Maria.'

'I wasn't her only customer, was I? Dozens, hundreds,
I don't know. Just pay and she was yours. I tried to warn
you. I tried. You were stubborn, and wouldn't believe me.
Anyone could have her, even me.'

'Even you?' The thought of the two of them together
was sickening. 'Then why not tell me?'

'She wasn't what I thought.' He hopped from foot to foot to keep warm. 'I thought she was just another doxie, but she wasn't. Her mother was Jewish, did you know that? Rachel, her name was, from Portugal.'

'Oh for God's sake!' I actually laughed, and almost clapped too, because she was magnificent. Oh bravo! What a performance! What an actress! She had us all entranced, even after the final curtain. 'And that's it, is it? That's all you have to say?'

He hesitated, and seemed about to add something more, but then thought better of it. 'You're taking this too much to heart. She wasn't yours. She was everyone's, anyone's, for half a crown. That's the *point*, Leo. Don't you understand?'

'No, I don't. I truly don't.'

'After all this time, don't be such a woman.'

'Goodbye, Jacob.'

I left him standing there, believing whatever nonsense he chose to. Did he think I didn't know that any man could pay for Maria? Did he think I wasn't fully aware that each time I was with her, I wasn't the first that day and might not be the last? I wasn't an idiot, at least not in that way. I may not have known her as well as I'd thought, but I knew how she earned her living.

By the time I reached home, my anger had hardened into a cold suspicion. I should have asked Jacob whether he knew Augustus Thorpe or Jack Flowers. Was it possible he was involved in some way? For all his bellicosity he'd never struck me as a cruel or violent man.

But now I realised: I had no idea what he was capable of.

———

I was surprised to see Rosie waiting on the pavement by the pharmacy. From her folded arms and vexed stance, I had the impression she considered me to be late.

'Good of you to come,' she said. 'Thank goodness it isn't cold or I might have caught my death out here.' She peered at me from under her hat. 'Are you all right? You're all red about the face.'

'I'm perfectly well, thank you. I'm glad you changed your mind.'

'I haven't. I'm not going to the police with you. I came to persuade you not to. You're putting yourself in danger, and probably me and my children as well. The police can't be trusted.'

'Wait here. I'll be back shortly.' I could hear her loud tut as the door closed.

I ran upstairs and changed my cilice, which was wet with sweat. As I left, Constance called after me: 'Who's that lady, Mr Stanhope? A friend of yours?'

I ignored her.

When I got outside again, Rosie was nowhere to be seen. I looked up and down the street, but there was only a black growler carriage with its door open and lamps lit, creaking back on its wheels. The carriage lurched as Hugo climbed out. Behind him, I could see Rosie's face, white with fear.

'Mr Stanhope,' said Hugo. 'Best come with us. Mr Bentinck wants to see you.'

'You have to let Mrs Flowers go,' I said. 'I'll come with you willingly, but you have to let her go.' I stood up as straight as I could. 'I insist.'

'I was told to fetch you both.'

There was a part of me that wanted to run. The balls of my feet yearned for it – I could feel the pavement sliding away as I pounded towards Whitehall, shouting for help, skidding into Great Scotland Yard. *'They've taken her. You have to come now. We can rescue her if you act quickly!'*

It sounded almost noble, but it was still fleeing.

I took a deep breath and climbed inside the carriage. No one said anything. The driver flicked the reins and we pulled away.

19

THE CARRIAGE WAS NARROW for three, and I shifted as far from Hugo as I could, pressing my hip uncomfortably against the doorframe. Rosie was on his other side, her face turned away from me. I clasped my hands in my lap but still they shook. I couldn't stop them.

'Where are we going?'

Hugo forced his mouth into a smile. 'Mr Bentinck's house. And mind your manners when you get there, he's a proper gentleman.'

Rosie glanced towards me and I tried to look reassuring, but her expression was blank.

The traffic was dense along Piccadilly, and we made slow progress. The pavements were thronged with people, spilling into the gutters, passing so close I could've reached out and touched them. At Green Park, a man with a placard on his back was standing under a streetlamp, handing out pamphlets to passers-by. A young policeman was talking to him, grinning, his hands pushed deep into his pockets. He was no more than two dozen feet away and caught my eye as I was staring at him.

I could call out, I thought. I could beckon him over and ask for help. But would he believe me? And anyway, Hugo knows where I live. And worse, he knows where Rosie lives.

We sped up, heading south-west towards Belgravia, rumbling over the wooden paving. I stared at the wealthy houses, so formal, so clean, so symmetrical, with their massive stone walls and heavy doors, their leaded windows and shadowy basement steps. Who knew what went on inside?

Hugo had told me to mind my manners, which suggested a conversation, didn't it? Not violence. I didn't want more violence. I closed my eyes, wishing I was back at home, in bed, and that I had never sought to know how Maria had died. Perhaps if I said that to Bentinck, he would believe me, and let us go. Perhaps.

The driver pulled on the reins, and I felt my stomach churn.

Burton Street was a well-scrubbed row of identical four-storey houses set back behind black railings and aspirant columned porches, thin limbs compared with the great, gouty houses on Grosvenor Square and Mount Street, but still a world away from the gaunt alleys and thunderous factories of the slums.

The maid who opened the door considered us with a kind of bored frankness, quite lacking the usual deference of her profession.

'This way,' she said, and we followed her, with Hugo wheezing behind us.

The hallway was narrow but finely furnished, with a mirror along one side and refulgent pictures of muscular horses and hunting dogs on the other. Lamps cast icicles of light down the walls.

Miss Gainsford appeared from the stairway, her hand resting gently on the pommel. She was wearing a delectation of a dress; laced, pleated and pinched in at her tiny waist.

'Mr Stanhope,' she said, smiling. 'It's so nice to meet you again.' She turned to Rosie and introduced herself as though we had all met by chance in the street. 'Nancy Gainsford. I'm Mr Bentinck's bookkeeper and general manager. I was sorry to hear of your loss.' Her eyes flicked down to Rosie's clothing: no black gloves, no veil, and a purple hat with a black bow at the side that had the air of an afterthought.

'Charmed,' replied Rosie sourly.

'James is in the garden, but it's freezing out there. Why don't we talk in the library first?'

She led us to a small room covered on every wall by row upon row of books. It was a lifetime's reading: Pope, Dickens, Carroll and Collins, Samuel Smiles, Gerard Manley Hopkins and all the works of Shakespeare *in order*. I wondered if they were just for show. Bentinck didn't seem the reading type. I'd never been in a room quite like it, and for a pinprick moment I couldn't wait to tell Maria how marvellous it was.

'You can leave us now,' Miss Gainsford said to Hugo.

He frowned and folded his arms. Any tenderness he had was reserved for his bees. 'Mr Bentinck told me to take 'em to him.'

'I'll call you presently.' She waved a hand towards the door. 'Now shoo!'

As before, she stood just a little too close and looked me straight in the eyes, chin tilted up. I had the same urge that every man must have, that no man could entirely deny, to wrap her up in my arms and kiss her.

'Why did you bring us here?'

'I'm sorry for the manner of your arrival. We really just wanted to speak with you. James tries so hard to be a gentleman, but in our business we mix with all sorts. Please do sit down.' She perched on a little armchair, while Rosie and I squeezed on to the sofa. 'We've been branching out recently, a new venture, doing trade on the Continent.' She smiled warmly at Rosie. 'Your husband worked for us occasionally, Mrs Flowers. Anyway, you've been asking a lot of questions and it makes us ... well, uneasy. It's a delicate time. I'm sure you understand.'

'I'm not interested in your business,' I said. 'I just want to know what happened to Maria.'

'Yes, and you spoke to Elizabeth Brafton about that, I believe. I was wondering what she told you.'

I wasn't sure what to say. Miss Gainsford was treating us like honoured guests, but what would happen if I refused to answer?

'Nothing of note,' I said slowly. 'She believes Madame Moreau committed the murder.'

'Ah yes, quite right. That awful woman. She deserves to be hanged, don't you think?'

'If she's guilty.'

'Can there be any doubt? Maria was with child, as I suppose you know. She went to see Mrs Moreau to get rid of it. Something must've gone wrong. The butcher.' She took a minute to compose herself, her hand to her chest, but she was eyeing me keenly. 'Did Elizabeth say anything else about Maria? Anything at all?'

'No. We talked about the early days of the brothel. She said she'd brought in a better class of gentleman.'

Miss Gainsford's face hardened. 'Yes, well, that's true, but hardly the whole story. We don't agree on the point. I've told her again and again that she needs more customers, many more, even if they pay a little less each. A hundred men paying a shilling each is better than a dozen paying half a crown, do you see?'

'I suppose so.'

I glanced at Rosie, who widened her eyes, but I had no more idea about the purpose of this conversation than she did.

Miss Gainsford shot a look towards the window. There was an arc of lamplight on the grass, and we could hear a grunting sound and the wallop of a ball being punted.

'Well, James is expecting you outside,' she said.

She rang a little bell on the table, next to an oval bas-relief portrait of a lady. It was chipped and mottled where the glaze had cracked, but I could still make out the expression on her sweet, plump face. Miss Gainsford saw me looking at it, and touched the lady's cheek with her fingers, almost a caress.

'It's lovely, don't you think? James's late wife. They were childhood sweethearts. She died years ago, before I knew him.'

'What killed her?' asked Rosie, and I could see the suspicion in her eyes.

'Childbirth. She was weak and wasn't ready for it.'

Rosie raised her eyebrows. 'Who is?'

I picked up the portrait. She was so limpid and gentle, I felt she might almost speak to me. On the underside was a name, and I squinted at it, trying to make out the letters. When I finally read it, I knew it had to be a coincidence.

'Her name was Mercy,' I said. 'Mercy Bentinck.'

'Yes, Mercy. I suppose her parents were religious. James had this made to remember her.'

Surely there was no link between this long-dead woman and a word written on a drowned man's bottle of ale? It wasn't possible. And yet ... that bottle had been smashed in the mortuary break-in. Was that a coincidence too?

'James doesn't talk about her any more,' continued Miss Gainsford. 'It was a long time ago, and he was a different man.'

'Is he really related to the Cavendish Bentincks?'

She looked away, her eyes scanning the shelves of leather-bound books, and I caught a glimpse of something I couldn't name. Something peevish. 'I don't know about such things,' she said. 'He likes to tell people so. When I first met him he used to say he *might* be related, and then he *must* be, and now he *is*. The truth is like clay: you mould it to what you want, and then it hardens.'

Hugo loomed in the doorway. 'Come with me,' he said, and stepped back to follow us outside.

James Bentinck was on the lawn in his undershirt, splattered with mud. He had rigged up a lamp, and was placing a rugby ball on the ground, preparing to kick it at a large wooden panel he'd erected to stop it shooting off into the neighbouring gardens. Above us, the stars were emerging from the gloom, more numerous than I could count, as if someone had taken a shotgun to the sky.

He held up a finger for us to be quiet, took a run-up and then blasted the ball into the panel. It made a cracking sound like a pistol going off, and the ball ricocheted upwards, spinning end over end. He leapt forward and tried to catch it, but it slipped out of his hands and bounced away into a bush.

'Damn it!' He turned to us, embarrassed. 'Stanhope, isn't it? I won't shake your hand.' He held up his own to show they were thick with dirt. 'And the fragrant Mrs Flowers, I presume. Do you play rugger, Stanhope?'

'Not since school.' A lie, needless to say, though I had some small knowledge of the rudiments.

'Cricket then?' He bowled an imaginary ball at an imaginary wicket, and even I could see that his action was poor. 'Not really the weather for it, eh?' He grinned and clapped me on the shoulder with his grubby hands, and then made the motion of striking a six. 'I used to play for the civil service, once upon a time, did you know that?'

I shook my head. What an absurd question.

He swept another invisible ball to the boundary while we shivered.

'So!' he barked eventually, breaking off to wipe his hands on a towel. 'I hope he didn't make life unpleasant for you.' He nodded towards Hugo, who seemed about to reply, but Bentinck wasn't paying attention. 'You've been asking about that young pinchcock, what's-her-name?'

'Maria Milanes,' I replied, certain he hadn't truly forgotten.

'Of course. She had a good head on her, that one. Used to listen to my plans for hours. And full of ideas. She had the notion that men might go to the place and not even tup the girls, just watch entertainments. Dancing and singing and so forth. Would you go somewhere like that?'

He was speaking in the manner I imagined a general might, inviting a lower-ranking officer to discuss tactics.

'No.'

'Me neither.' He laughed loudly. 'Women don't understand, do they? Anyway, the wagtail's dead now, murdered by what's-her-name, the Frenchwoman, and … ah!' He looked towards the house, where Miss Gainsford was standing at the back door, a strange expression on her face. 'Nancy, what is it?'

'James, I wish –'

He shook his head. 'No, we've had this discussion. Go back to your accounts, this doesn't concern you. It has to be done.'

I looked at Rosie, and with one accord we bolted into the house, pushing past Miss Gainsford. We ran down the hallway, and I tried the front door, but it was locked. Rosie tried too, tugging on the handle, but it wouldn't open. I dived through another door, dragging Rosie behind me, but we found ourselves in a small room containing only a desk, a chair and a strongbox with a strange-looking barrel padlock.

We turned as Hugo came in, followed by Bentinck.

I took a step towards him but Hugo slapped me and dragged me back into the hallway, his forearm around my neck. I tried to twist away, but he tightened his grip.

'Stop it,' he said and pushed me down on to my knees, forcing something into my mouth, a bottle, stinking of cat piss. Rosie shouted something, but I couldn't look round because he had yanked my head back by my hair. He tipped up the bottle, and all the time I was thinking, over and over, *don't swallow, don't swallow*, and while I was thinking that I swallowed, and there was an ugly taste in my throat. For a moment I was staring at the tinted glass in their front door, an umbrella hanging on a hook, a pair of brown boots on the mat.

And then I was dropping.

Black water closed over me and I sank into it, my arms floating upwards as I descended. I could have kicked, but I didn't. I welcomed it. My lungs filled and I felt the heaviness inside me, the crushing cold, and would have laughed if I could. I closed my eyes and let go of all that I was, drifting away from the shore.

A last thought came to me before my mind dissipated like a drop of blood in the water: *Thank goodness. Now I can stop.*

20

THE NOISE WAS CEASELESS: jangle, thump, jangle, thump, jangle, thump. It was a faulty clock forever trying to tick to the next second. Thump, jangle, thump, jangle. It was a dinghy bumping against the pier, its ropes ringing on its mast. Jangle, thump, jangle, thump. It was a beggar with one good leg, hauling his possessions on a trolley behind him.

The noise wouldn't stop. I put my hands over my ears, and it got louder.

I was sitting on a hard chair, the backs of my legs sore against the wood, but it tipped up and I rolled on to the floor, staring at the rosette on the ceiling, disused, cracked and grey with dust. I was still falling. I put out my hands to break the impact, but the rug fell away and I was floating, and then it surged back, looming over me, and I swore loudly at the sudden jerk on my wrist as I dangled. Something hit me in the ribs and I hung there, swinging like a string puppet. I could hear music. Someone was singing a lullaby I knew from when I was a child, singing and sometimes weeping, in time to the thump, jangle, thump, jangle. I found myself humming along with her.

Something came into the room, and then another something. They were making noises but I couldn't hear them clearly. I was sure they were wolves, standing on their hind legs. One of them crouched down and sniffed me, and I could see his black lips and snout, and a fly creeping across his fur. I squirmed backwards and the fly flew up and landed in the corner of my eye, sucking at me with its puckered mouth. I tried to swat it away but it held on. I could feel the tickle of its tiny feet on my eyeball.

Water splashed on to my face. It was cold on my skin, seeping into my hair, running up my nose and making me cough. I wiped my forehead and rolled over, but they poured more over me, another cupful, so it puddled on the floorboards and dripped down between the gaps. It was leaking on to the ceiling below and would cause a stain, and then they'd regret their thoughtlessness. That would show them, if it made a stain. *Thoughtless, thoughtless, thoughtless.*

The wolves growled at each other and then they were gone, and the flies trailed out after them. For a while all was quiet except for the jangle, thump.

My back was aching and my wrist was agony, and I wanted to sleep. Just let me sleep. My shoulder hurt and I realised a boot was prodding me, trying to rouse me. Against my will, I drifted upwards. There were ripples on the surface and the glow of a lamp, and faces looking down; the wolves again, long jaws and pointy ears.

One of them spoke: 'Jesus. Make sure he lives, will you? We need him.'

The other, shorter and fatter, with fewer flies, nodded. 'He'll be right as rain in an hour, sir.'

The first wolf prodded me again. 'Tell me when he wakes up.'

The fat wolf grunted. 'What about her?'

'She'll go on the boat tomorrow. And shut her up, for God's sake.'

I was awake already, but I didn't show it. If you stay still, they leave you alone. A wolf is just an untrained dog, and they chase movement. I sank down into the black water again, listening to the thump, jangle, sometimes fainter, sometimes louder, and that awful, tender singing. For a while the black water carried me, until her voice grew quiet.

When I opened my eyes, the wolves had gone. I was in an attic room, right at the top of the house, the dim light from the window throwing oblique shapes across the walls. My head was bursting. Something had risen up from within me and was pushing against my skull to get out. I had to shut my mouth and block my ears to keep it inside. Nausea filled my throat, and I flopped over on to my stomach and puked.

'It passes,' said a voice. 'They gave me the same stuff. You'll feel better soon.'

The wolves had taken my shoes. I tried to get up, but I was caught by my wrist, which was cuffed in an iron manacle. I explored along the chain, and found it was padlocked to a metal frame, the wrought-iron curlicues of a bedstead. I pulled and pulled until my skin grazed, even spitting on to the metal to lubricate it, but the thing wouldn't budge.

'You'll hurt yourself,' said the voice, and I realised it was Rosie, sitting up on the bed, manacled to it, the same as me. 'I tried, and it isn't worth it.'

The only other furniture in the room was a wardrobe with a mirrored door and an upturned chair on the floor next to me. I wanted to right it, but my arms were too weak, so I just lay there, wishing the black water would come again. Slowly, the noise from before returned.

Rosie was rocking. She was sitting on the bed, rocking backwards and forwards, her arms wrapped around her knees, and each time she rocked, the bedstead thumped against the wall and the chain around her ankle jangled, to and fro, to and fro, thump and jangle, thump and jangle. And while she rocked, she sang. It seemed to comfort her.

'I'm sorry,' I said. 'I'm sorry you're here. This is all my fault. But I needed to know what happened to Maria.'

'That's not an excuse, it just means you don't care about anyone else.'

'I'm sorry. I truly am.'

She turned away, facing the wall, and wouldn't say anything more. I lay on my back on the floor, and all I could hear was her breathing, and the occasional carriage outside, so distant and disconnected it might as well have been in another country.

I prayed. I couldn't get the words out fast enough. I prayed in my mind, so hard I thought I would burst: Oh God, please save Rosie. Please save Rosie. This is my fault. Let her go back to her children. If you care for us at all, please save Rosie.

There was a sound from outside the room, and my shivering returned. I pulled my jacket around me.

'Someone's coming,' she whispered, and we both lay still.

The door opened and someone lit the wall-lamp. The glare burned through my eyelids.

'They're awake, sir.' It was Hugo's voice. 'I heard 'em talking.'

He jabbed my leg with his foot and I opened my eyes, sparks flickering on the edge of my vision like fireworks on the horizon.

'It stinks in here,' said Bentinck. He nodded to Hugo, who sighed deeply and left the room.

Bentinck opened the window and righted the chair. 'Sit down, Stanhope.'

'You have to let me leave,' said Rosie. She crawled to the edge of the mattress and sat with her hands resting on her lap and her shoeless feet dangling. 'I don't want to be here.'

He rummaged in his pocket, producing a fold of tobacco and a pipe, which he attempted to light. 'Damn thing,' he muttered. 'Must've got wet.'

'Please, let me go home. I have children who need a mother. I just want to go back to them, and I'll say nothing about anything. No one will ever know. Who'd believe me anyway? Just let me go, *please*.'

He gave her an avuncular smile. 'I'm sorry, my dear, I truly am, but I have responsibilities. I can't let anything disrupt our new venture.'

Miss Gainsford had mentioned their new venture too. She'd said they were doing trade on the Continent. I wondered what it was they were trading.

'It *was* your boat,' I said slowly. 'At Puddle Dock, where Mrs Flowers was held.'

Bentinck looked impressed. 'Yes, very good, Stanhope. And we don't want anyone talking about it to all and sundry and ruining the whole thing. So you'll be off to

Belgium, Mrs Flowers, all expenses paid. But it's a one-way trip, I'm afraid.'

'Belgium?' she said blankly. 'I can't go there. I have three children.'

'Any of 'em daughters? How old are they?'

Rosie went white, but her fists were clenched. With a sudden horror, I realised what Bentinck was transporting on that boat.

'It's *people*,' I said, scarcely able to force out the words. 'Your new venture is people. You're a kidnapper.'

'We buy them mostly. Workhouses, factories, orphanages, dolly-houses, scullery maids, fathers who want rid. There's a market among a certain class of gentleman in Brussels. I mean, a *very* high class of gentleman. And with *particular* tastes. They have more wealth than you or I could ever dream of: gold, jewels, palaces, even whole countries in Africa, and they don't want broken-down old whores. They want young virgins.' He looked positively proud, as though he was talking about a grand business he'd built exporting fine linens or sculptures. 'They can't get them locally without causing attention. The laws are much stricter over there, so it's supply and demand, and an excellent price for the right girls. Pretty, young and, most importantly, *innocent*.'

Rosie looked straight at Bentinck and spoke as though she was addressing a fool. 'I'm a widow with children.'

He shrugged. 'Oh, we ship over ordinary girls too, when we have space. May as well fill up the boat. Not for the best gentlemen, of course, but they have people and they have people and so on, so there's no shortage of customers down the chain, as it were. You'll fit in very well, Mrs

Flowers, don't worry about that.' He continued trying to light his pipe until eventually there was a puff of blue-grey smoke. He closed his eyes and exhaled slowly. 'Nothing finer.'

Hugo came back with a mop and bucket and started cleaning up the floor, replacing the bitter stench of bile with the bitter stench of lye. My eyes stung with it.

'I won't go,' Rosie said firmly, interlocking her fingers on her lap.

'It's not really a choice, I'm afraid. We'll dose you with chloral again, and you won't know a thing.'

I was reminded of Constance's game. *Chloral … what is it?* And then it came to me. I spoke without thinking. 'Chloral hydrate is a hypnotic. It makes you go to sleep.'

'Exactly. Nasty stuff, though. Evil dreams, I'm told.'

'I'll come back,' said Rosie.

Bentinck drew on his pipe, and made a sympathetic face. 'That's not how it works, my dear. There's no coming back.'

'Then why don't you just kill me now?'

He frowned, seeming perplexed. 'I'm a businessman, Mrs Flowers, not a murderer.'

'Detective Ripley knows we're here,' I said defiantly.

He clapped me on the shoulder. 'Ha! You really don't understand, do you, Stanhope? Even if that were true, and I have no doubt that it isn't, it doesn't matter a jot. You see, we have a plan for you too. You're to be the *accomplice*. That woman who committed the crime, the French one, what was her name? Can't trust the French, I've always said so.'

'Madame Moreau,' I said. 'But she isn't French, it's her married name.'

255

'It doesn't matter, Stanhope! Don't you understand? She gets the blame and you were her accomplice. You've already been arrested once and the police know you've spoken to her, so it should be straightforward. You'll be joining her in Newgate, or ...' He pulled at an imaginary noose around his neck and made the face of a man asphyxiating. 'You see? We don't need to kill you, the law will do it for us. So much easier that way.' He chuckled, looking around the room so we could all enjoy the joke together.

'What possible motive could I have?'

He shrugged. I had the feeling he hadn't even thought about it, so sure was he that his plan would work without anyone asking questions. He was probably right.

'I suppose you were the father of the pregnancy and took her to the Frenchwoman's place ...' He waved aside her disputed nationality. 'Maybe you wanted the whore dead to save your reputation. Or maybe things went wrong and you covered it up. The point is, you've been set free once, and you can be put back in the clink just as easily.'

'That was by Judge Thorpe. I doubt he'll be keen to help you after you tried to marry his son to a prostitute.'

Bentinck smiled unpleasantly. 'There are other judges. It won't be difficult.'

Rosie was rocking again, eyes down, to and fro, to and fro, the bedstead tapping the wall like a slow metronome. I had the urge to take her hand, but I couldn't have reached.

'I'll make a deal with you, Mr Bentinck,' I said, surprising myself by how steady my voice was. 'If you let Mrs Flowers go, right now, I'll say I'm guilty and make it easy for you. I'll accept the blame and confess everything, and you'll never hear from her again.'

He considered the idea for a moment and shook his head. 'It's very noble of you, but we'd never know for sure, would we? Once she's free you might say anything. No, our way is better. You go to prison and she goes to Belgium on the next boat, and it's all neat and tidy.'

He pushed himself away from the wall, stepping within my reach. I didn't think about it, I just lashed out at him, first with my fist and then, as he leapt backwards, kicking at his legs. In a second, Hugo was on me. He punched me in the neck, short and hard, and I felt the pain welling up from my throat and across my shoulder.

'Stop!' shouted Rosie, but he tugged my head back by my hair.

I heard Bentinck's voice. 'Leave him be, he can have that one. It's only fair, poor chap. But if he tries it again, pull out his teeth.'

Hugo released me and I doubled over, fearful I would vomit again. I forced myself to meet Bentinck's eyes.

'Why did you kill Maria?'

He looked genuinely surprised. 'I didn't. Why would I? She was a good employee. And anyway, I wasn't even here when it happened, I was at Cookham, entertaining some local bigwigs. A man has to unwind once in a while.' He moved the chair to the window, and sat on it, looking out into the darkness. 'I was quite fond of the little wagtail, actually. Sharp as a nail, and an absolute *vixen* in the sack. Well, you know all about that, don't you? I couldn't believe it. A *vixen*.'

'She wanted to leave you.'

'They all do, Stanhope! They get old and we let them go, or they move on or marry someone or, I don't know, become nuns, or whatever women do when they reach that age. We don't *murder* them! There are lots of pretty girls, or hadn't you noticed? Prettier than her, actually, with her …' He rotated his finger towards his cheek, meaning her stain. 'Though Nancy always said it was *endearing*, whatever that means. How would I keep any girl working for me if I went around murdering them?' He laughed to himself. 'I was *helping* her. She wanted to better herself, and she had the talent to do it too. That's why I introduced her to Gussie Thorpe. He's a gentleman with lots of money and very little intellect. Truly, very little indeed. It was a match made in heaven. Better still, he was due to go back to India and most likely get his head blown off. She'd have been a wealthy widow in no time, and owing me a debt of gratitude.'

My head was still fogged by the chloral. Our captor was protesting his innocence and I couldn't think of a single reason why he was wrong. It was utter madness.

'But then his father found out and broke it off.'

'Sadly, yes.' Bentinck waved his pipe around. 'And that was that, even though she'd cunny-caught him, with apologies Mrs Flowers, and persuaded him to do the decent thing. All unofficial, unfortunately. He'd have got a shock when the brat was born and most likely looked nothing like him, but by then it would've been too late, wouldn't it?'

'I don't understand,' I said, feeling desperate and utterly lost. 'If it wasn't you, then who did kill Maria?'

'Haven't a clue. Some thug on the street probably, it happens all the time. Or that Madame what's-it, who you say isn't French. Are you sure about that?' He didn't wait for a reply. 'Or it could've been you, in which case we're serving justice after all, aren't we?'

I strained against the chain so hard I was sure my bones would crack.

'Why did Jack have to die?' asked Rosie, very quietly.

Bentinck pulled a mock-serious face, as if she'd accused him of cheating at charades. 'Well, you do have to be fair, Mrs Flowers. He wasn't a very good husband, was he? A strong lad though, which we need now Hugo's getting on a bit.' Hugo shifted his position and said nothing, flexing his thumbs. 'Jack used to help us out lugging everything on and off the boat, and around the house sometimes. He was loyal, or so we thought.' He sucked on his pipe, immediately withdrawing it from his mouth and staring irritably at the bowl. 'Damn thing won't stay lit.'

'He stole from you,' I said.

'He tried. Bloody idiot. We found him downstairs with the strongbox open, piling our money into his satchel. More than two hundred pounds. Can you believe it? Like it was his own. After everything we'd done together too. I miss him visiting here, if I'm honest. We used to wrestle from time to time, and he even had the decency to lose.'

'So you murdered him.'

He shrugged, and struck another match for his pipe. 'It's not the same. He knew the punishment. I can't fetch the police in my business, and I can't have people stealing from me either. Hugo dosed him with chloral and took him out on the boat. Up and over.'

No signs of a struggle, I thought. He drowned sleeping.

'With his satchel?' asked Rosie, leaning forward. 'Was it still on him when you drowned him?'

He frowned at her, losing patience. 'His satchel? How the hell should I know? We thought we were rid of him until he washed up.' He nodded in my direction. 'And even then, Stanhope here did us a favour and told the police it was an accident. You really have been very useful, for the most part.'

'But why did you kidnap Mrs Flowers and demand to know where the money was, if you already had it back?'

Bentinck's face clouded. He clenched and unclenched his fingers. 'I suppose we do owe you an explanation for that, Mrs Flowers. A few days later I realised it had been stolen *again*. It was very strange. We'd put the money back in the strongbox, but when we went to get it out, the thing was empty. And the money hasn't been found, even now. We thought Jack must've told you something about it, Mrs Flowers. But it was obvious you didn't know anything, so … well, my man on the boat got carried away. I think he enjoys that sort of thing, unfortunately, but it wasn't my instruction, I assure you. We're not monsters.' He removed his jacket, slipping out of his braces and stretching his arms. 'Anyway, enough talking.'

Hugo left the room, clanking the mop and bucket with him, and Bentinck stood up and started unbuttoning his shirt.

'What are you doing?' I asked, with a sudden dread.

'I'm sorry, I truly am. But it has to be done.'

'What has to be done?'

He pulled his shirt over his head, revealing a plump back carpeted in hair. 'What with one thing and another, funerals and missing money and what-not, I haven't had any fun for a while.' He nodded towards Rosie. 'And Mrs Flowers here has a life of whoring ahead of her, so I have to make sure she's fully prepared, don't I?'

And with that, he removed his shoes and trousers.

21

'PLEASE,' I SAID. 'DON'T do this. What would Mercy think? What would your wife have said?'

He sighed deeply and closed his eyes. 'She would hate it, and me as well, more than likely. She had a soft heart.'

He unlocked Rosie's manacle. She watched while he fiddled with the key, no expression on her face. As soon as it was off, she sprang towards the door and almost made it, but he caught her ankle, dragging her to the floor. She clung to anything she could, hauling the blankets after her.

All this without saying a word. No wailing or shouting or screaming. It was happening almost in silence.

'If you touch her, I will kill you,' I said, and meant it.

She kicked out, but he caught her other ankle and pulled her legs apart so he could kneel between them. He did this without any ferocity or anger, more as if it were a task he felt compelled to perform.

Anchored to the bed, I couldn't reach them. I heaved on the chain, jerked on it, tried to push my fingernails into the cracks between the floorboards, but I couldn't get enough traction. The bed was too heavy and I was too light, too weak. I threw myself backwards and it moved perhaps half an inch. Then another. I had at least five feet to go.

Rosie was struggling, trying to punch Bentinck and spit at him, but he seized her wrists and forced her down by his sheer weight. She let out a noise, a formless lament.

I dragged the bed another half-inch with a kind of berserk anger, ignoring the burning pain. I would have sawn through my own arm and beaten him to death with it, joyfully, if I had only had the means.

'Please lie still, Mrs Flowers,' he said. 'It's better this way, honestly. This'll be much pleasanter for both of us if you just let it happen.'

He fumbled in his drawers with his free hand and pulled out his cock.

And that was when I stopped.

All was quiet.

In that single second, between one tick and the next, between heartbeats, between her eyes being open and clos-ing again, I was still. The last remnant of the chloral in my blood was making me fuzzy, but the black water wouldn't come. I couldn't sink and lose myself. I was here, now, in this room, as one second ticked on to the next. And the next.

'Bentinck,' I said, calmly enough to get his attention. 'Listen to me. I'm not what I appear to be, not entirely. Underneath these clothes, I am female. A maiden. Leave her alone and take me instead.'

He stared at me.

'What are you talking about?'

'I was born as a girl. I have a woman's body.'

Rosie squirmed away from him towards the door, staring at me.

Run. Run, Rosie. You're unchained! Run, run, run far from this place.

'A woman's body?' he said. 'I don't believe you.'

I set back my shoulders and took a deep breath. My mind was empty. Consequences no longer mattered.

'It's the truth.'

He put his head on one side, as if he might know, just by looking, whether I was lying.

'Prove it.'

'First, let Mrs Flowers go.'

'You're in no position to bargain with me.'

I shuffled backwards, my wrist still chained, and he followed me, putting a hand against my chest, looking straight into my eyes. His mouth was just inches from mine. I didn't even shiver.

Run, Rosie.

He very slowly pulled up my shirt and slid his hand inside. I could feel his fingers against my skin, reaching up. When he touched my cilice he frowned and licked his lips, and pushed his fingers underneath. He pinched my nipple hard and I bared my teeth. But I would not cry out.

He raised his eyebrows, and I crashed my forehead into his face.

'Jesus!' he shouted, covering his eyes with his hands. 'Jesus! You've broken my blasted nose!' He felt it gingerly, blinking as his eyes watered.

I tried to crawl away, under the bedstead where it was dark, thinking I could turn and claw at him, but he grabbed me and slapped me across the temple. The world went black, and I could feel his weight on me, my shirt being torn open. As my vision returned I noticed a button lying on the floorboard, a stub of cotton still attached. I reached for it, holding it tightly in my fist, thinking: *I mustn't lose this. I can sew it on again, even though I hate sewing buttons.*

No matter what, I kept hold of that button.

He pulled my trousers open and tugged them down with my drawers, ripping out the roll of cloth sewn into them and flinging it away. I tried to kick him, but he was too strong, and pinned me to the floor, his nails digging into my breast.

He stared down at my body and wiped his face with his hand, plastering his wet fringe across his brow. The veins on his neck were standing out.

'Look at that. A maiden who thinks she's a man. And I thought I'd seen everything.'

I held my button so tightly it hurt my fingers. I thought I might break it and then I'd have to buy another, and it wouldn't be the same. *They all have to be the same. Mummy insisted on replacing every single button on my pinafore dress even though I'd only lost one of them.*

He wriggled his knees between mine, and reached down between his legs and pumped himself a few times, his lower jaw extended with the tension of it. A drop of his sweat dripped into my mouth and I tasted the salt. He took hold of his cock again and lunged forward into me, and lunged again, and again, and as he pushed in, all my insides were pushed out, until only my clothes and skin were left, lying beneath him on the floor, and nothing within. It was no longer me. It was no longer anyone.

And then there was another sound, a thump and jangle, and a final thump, and he collapsed on to me. I couldn't breathe, but I twisted and wrenched myself away, and he rolled off me on to his back, gaping at me with wide eyes, blinking once and then ceasing.

Blood was pooling around him, soaking into the rug, dripping down the gaps between the floorboards.

And then I heard it again, that thump and jangle as Rosie swung her manacle over her head and crashed it down on him, and again, and again. His head was pouring blood.

She dropped the chain, panting, and tossed the keys towards me. 'Get that thing off your wrist. We have to get out of here.'

I pulled my drawers and trousers back up and repositioned the cilice over my breasts with trembling fingers. In a daze, I struggled with the lock. It wouldn't turn. Rosie snatched the keys and tried each one, but none of them worked. We stared at each other – if we couldn't remove the manacle, I would have to remain here, to be found with Bentinck lying in a puddle of blood. I was shaking uncontrollably, but she took my hand.

'I won't leave you,' she said. 'I won't. Wait, what about the other end?'

The other end of the chain was looped round the bedstead and fixed with a padlock. The first key I tried turned smoothly. I was free, although I would have to take the chain with me, still manacled to my wrist.

Rosie listened at the door. 'It's quiet,' she whispered. 'Are you ready?'

When I didn't reply, she looked over at me and my ripped, bloody shirt, and sighed. She opened the wardrobe, and inside there were clothes hanging, women's clothes. She fingered through them and tossed a white camisole over to me. 'Put this on. You can do up your jacket over the top.'

I sat down on the bed, and couldn't speak, couldn't move.

Rosie pushed her fingers through her hair. 'It's all right,' she said gently. 'I'll do it.'

She helped me take off my jacket and peel away my shirt, threading the chain out through the armholes. My skin was stained red and I was shivering in the cold. She eased the camisole on to me, covering my cilice, and lastly buttoned up my jacket.

'There,' she said, pulling the lapels tightly together. 'No one will be any the wiser.'

For a moment, our hands touched.

Bentinck was sprawled on the floor in front of us. He wasn't breathing. There was a lot of blood. We'd trodden it into the rug and it was soaking into the hem of Rosie's skirt. The button I'd been holding was lying in a pool of it.

There was a sound on the stairs.

We were trapped.

'We'll have to go out over the roofs,' she said.

She heaved open the window sash and we looked out into the night. There was a pitch of tiles and a valley where the house met the one next door. Rosie climbed out on to the sill, holding on tightly. Her fingers were white.

The door opened and Hugo's face appeared. He gaped in mute disbelief. Rosie let go and slid away into the darkness as he lurched forward, but he slipped on Bentinck's blood and fell. I climbed out after Rosie, skittering down the wet tiles, grateful to feel the lead flashing under my feet where the two roofs joined.

Hugo was yelling from the window and I could hear the grief and fury in his voice. I recognised it. He seemed as if he might try to follow us, heaving his bulk on to the sill and glaring down, but then he ducked back inside, and we were alone.

I crept along to the edge, where Rosie was peering over at the balcony of the house next door. The ground was a long way down. We were above the height of the tallest trees in the gardens.

'We have to,' she said. 'We'll be dead anyway if we don't.'

She went first, holding on to the drainpipe and clambering over the side. She slithered down and found the railing with her feet, steadied herself and dropped neatly on to the flat of the balcony.

'Come on,' she called, reaching up to me.

The drainpipe was cold and slippery in the drizzle. I clung on, not looking down, grazing my knuckles on the bricks, and then felt Rosie's hand on my ankle, guiding my foot on to the railing. I let go of the drainpipe and pushed away from it, and for one moment I was precisely balanced, standing on the railing. Then I felt my weight tip forward and was able to jump down on to the balcony next to Rosie.

'Mother of God,' she muttered, blowing out her cheeks.

She tried the glass door and it was unlocked. We slipped into the house as quietly as shadows, creeping through an empty bedroom and on to the landing, down two flights of stairs and along the hallway just as faces appeared from the lounge, a woman and an aged fellow in a dressing gown, mouths open. But we were out of the front door and running along the pavement, and we didn't stop running until we reached the junction with the main road. Rosie pulled me across by the hand, dodging between angry carts and carriages in the rain, and we ran on until we reached a little park and threw ourselves down on to the grass.

We lay there for some minutes, gasping for breath. I began to claw at my belly, trying to tear off my skin. I didn't want it any more. I wanted to take it off like my cilice, and leave it behind.

'Stop,' said Rosie. 'Please, Leo, you have to stop.' Her hat and spectacles were gone and her wet hair was plastered to her head. She was shivering. 'What you did, it was ... Leo? Are you listening to me? Leo?'

I stood up. All around me the traffic was deafening, wheels and hooves, voices calling and the rattling of a train. Despite the damp grass under my feet, this was a city, swollen with sounds and people.

Rosie put out her hand as if to grasp me, but I flinched away, and having started moving, I couldn't stop. I was running again, carrying the chain in my two hands, and for a few seconds I thought Rosie was running after me, calling my name. But her voice got fainter and then I couldn't hear her at all.

I slowed to a walk, breathing hard, and stumbled into St James's Park where I'd once met with Augustus Thorpe. I skirted along the south side, past the tea shop, just another man lost amongst all the other men, on their way somewhere, going home or walking the dog, men in hats and raincoats, carrying canes, men with beards and moustaches and holly-bush eyebrows.

I passed the hospital without a glance, and then I could smell it: a rank, oily stink, the unmistakeable sewer of London, the Thames, long and dark, a wound across the city. It filled my nostrils as the bridge came into view.

The water was calling.

22

THE SLATS OF THE bridge were wet and slippery, so I held on to the railing as I looked out at the fields stretching away on either side, tall grass and yellow crops made liquid by the wind flowing over them. It was a rare rainy day after a long, dry August, and the clouds were boiling across the sky, storing up more bad weather.

It was our first day back from holiday and we still had sand between our toes. Oliver was already in the army, but the rest of the family had had three unforgettable days in Margate, walking on the beach in bare feet and writing our names with stones. We bought ice creams from a stall, and my father took us to a cavern covered in seashells while Mummy rested in their room. We stayed at the Ship Hotel, which had a picture of a sailing boat on the sign and flower baskets on the porch. It was so warm that Jane and I kept our bedroom window open all night, and fell asleep to the weeping of the seagulls and the music of the bandstand by the pier.

It was Sunday tomorrow. My father had insisted on being back home in time to prepare his sermon, as he hated the thought of anyone else doing it. Who knew how his flock might be led astray, without his weekly guidance? While Mummy and Jane were unpacking, I put on my pinafore dress and my stoutest shoes, and took my old schoolbag with four heavy stones from the beach, a rope and my copy of *Barnaby Rudge*, and walked through the town and across the farmland to the bridge over the New River. I stood upon it with the wind in my hair and the frayed handle of the bag cutting into my fingers.

I'd been here before. Jane and I had stolen away a couple of times on hot days, cooling our toes in the water and watching the silvery fish dart to and fro. We'd never dared go deeper, although we were both competent swimmers.

I knew my instinct would be to struggle, so I cinched the bag of stones tightly around my waist with the rope, and climbed up on to the wall, my back to the water. No time to waste, no pause for second thoughts.

Eyes open, I thought. I want to see.

For some reason, I clutched the rope as I tipped backwards. I was in the air for a heartbeat before the freezing water closed over me, so shockingly cold I almost gasped it in. Weed reached out for my limbs and I tried to swim, as I'd known I would, my hands shoving the water downwards, increasingly frantic. But the stones and my saturated dress were dragging me down. My fingers touched the soft mud at the bottom, and my hand sank into it.

The light above me was growing dim and my lungs were starting to ache. I clawed at the weeds and the mud, kicking out, tearing at the cloth of the bag and digging my nails into the knot in the rope. No matter that I had done this to myself, no matter my reasons and justifications, my whole world had become my lungs. They were shouting at me, and then screaming, to reach the air and take a precious breath. Please, God, just one last breath before dying. But I could not.

And then there was a hand. Strong fingers tugged me upwards, and as I broke the surface I inhaled deeply, and was shamefully grateful. He pulled me to the side while his dog ran up and down on the bank, barking madly.

I crawled on to the grass and lay there, curled up, shaking and coughing. My rescuer, a farm labourer, not even twenty years old, swore at me richly and threatened, his eyes pink from the water, to drag me by my collar to the police station unless I promised never to try such a stupid thing again. I promised, covering my face. He probably thought I was weeping, but I simply wanted him to go away. He hurled my stones into the river and stuffed my rope into his pocket, and made me repeat my promise, hand on heart, before he would leave me.

I had lost the courage anyway. Drowning had hurt more than I'd thought it would, and I was frightened of the water, the first inhalation of it, that bitter penetration. I started walking home when the rain set in, ashamed of my failure.

But that night, when the bedroom was dark and all I could hear was Jane's breathing, I knew that my life could not continue as it had been. I couldn't keep performing the part of a girl, giggling at my father's jokes and lifting up my sheepish skirts to paddle in the sea. I couldn't keep pretending I was normal when I knew to my very core that I wasn't. And I couldn't carry on living in a state of utter hopelessness, looking in the mirror every morning at someone who wasn't me. Not any more.

I'd rather be dead than be Lottie Pritchard.

———

The wind was whistling across Westminster Bridge, blowing through my hair, flapping around my clothing, driving the rain against my cheeks. I could barely stand against it, and without shoes I was losing all feeling in my feet. In this weather even the occasional late-night cart and carriage seemed anxious and harried, impatient to get home.

The manacle was still locked to my wrist, and I was holding the chain in my hand. I stopped next to one of the trident streetlamps and leaned on the stone plinth, facing Lambeth Bridge, almost due south as the bends of the Thames wormed through London. Underneath me, a drop of forty or more feet, a chugging tugboat crept through the arch, its smoke billowing up and stinging my eyes.

I climbed up on the stone plinth and sat with my back to the streetlamp, the pavement on my left and the drop on my right, the chain hanging down. If I moved just a little, I would fall. My body might be caught against the stanchion of the bridge, turned over and over by the force of the flow, grinding against the brickwork until all my features were worn away: my clothes, my face, my skin. But more likely I would survive the drop, and bump through the arch as hypothermia took hold, sliding away downstream to be washed up near Blackfriars or Limehouse, bloated and grey. I would be wearing a manacle and whatever of my clothes had withstood the water. Back at the pharmacy, Alfie and Constance would wonder where I was. Eventually they would tell the police, and search through my possessions, finding my cilices and sanitary cloths, and wonder what kind of person they had welcomed into their home.

I sought inside myself for the guilt I must surely owe them for such deception, but found nothing. I had been emptied out.

'Careful, m–m–mister.' A young fellow in mismatched boots and a knitted sweater was passing. He was carrying a tankard and pointed it at me, swaying a little. 'You'll f–f–fall.' He noticed the tankard was empty, and tossed it over the side. I watched it go. It was in the air for a second, spinning end over end, and then hit the water, making a meagre splash among the white horses streaking along the river. 'Are you g–going to j–j–jump, m–mister?'

I didn't move and he dug into his pocket, pulling out a piece of paper.

'There's a p–p–place on Old K–Kent Road that's still open if you'll b–b–buy me a drink. I h–have the address.'

I started twisting the chain around my hand, out of his sight, leaving a few inches loose so I could swing it with force. He wouldn't know what had hit him. *Take a step forwards and you'll be bleeding from the head, my friend, and I will flay you where you lie. Take one step forwards.*

He gave an exaggerated shrug. 'Your choice, m–mister. Jump for all I c–care.'

I watched him go and released the chain again, feeling it unwind and tug on my wrist as it reached its limit.

More people noticed me but none stopped. I was shivering, saturated by the rain and the dampness of the stone. I shifted my position, lying for a while on my back, gazing up at the blackness. I wasn't angry, not in any recognisable way. I'd been angry with my father, and with Jane and with myself, and more lately with Jacob and Thorpe and Lord knows who else, but this was a colder kind of fury that was not *righteous* or *just*, but simply *was*.

The rolled-up cloth in my trousers had gone, left behind in that room. Had I ever truly wanted a real one? Surely a fake was better than that vicious, tumescent shaft. He had invaded me, forced me to be what he wanted me to be; not a man or a woman, but a *thing*, not even alive. He had used my body as one might a flannel or a comb, and when he was finished he would doubtless have disposed of it with the same disregard.

If that was a man, then I wasn't one.

I'd rather be dead than be that.

My heartbeat slowed and I willed it to stop, finding it curious that I couldn't. Is this still my body? Can't I control when it breathes, when its eyes blink, when its heart beats? If not me, then who? Surely not God, who has never shown any sign of caring for me. He doesn't impel my heart any more than He moved my limbs to kick when I would have preferred to drown. These things happen with no grand design, they are the products of an instinct for survival imbued in the smallest mouse, even in ants and slugs, in all His creatures, proof that we are nothing better than insects. Living or dying, it's all the same to Him.

I climbed down on to the pavement, tilting my face up to the rain. My feet were icy and wet and my skin was sore along the line of my cilice. There was blood on the white cotton camisole, and my teeth were chattering so hard from the cold I thought they would fall out.

Between the streetlamps there was an iron balustrade. I crouched down and took a link of the chain in my hand and scratched it against the grey paint, making an inch-long vertical line beneath the handrail where no one would notice it. I thickened it and scraped another line perpendicular, and then another parallel to the first. Then three horizontals and a circle, to mark the name 'LEO' in the paint. I continued, scraping and scratching, until the word 'STANHOPE' was written next to it, and so my name was complete.

That was my name: Leo Stanhope. Not Lottie Pritchard. Not *Charlotte*, which I'd always hated, even back then. No man could make me something I wasn't, no matter how they used me. Someone really had been reborn in the New River all those years ago, just like the Baptists say, although in their cant they make little allowance for the newly made to ruin his dress and be told by his father to sweep all the leaves from the churchyard as punishment.

I was what I was, a boy who'd been named Lottie and was now Leo, and like it or not, all my burdens were mine. I had loved Maria, and my most precious burden was to discover who had killed her.

I traced my finger around each letter of my name in turn, feeling the hard edge of the paint, and made a promise to myself: I could return to this spot at any time. I had no fear of it. But not until I knew.

I stood up and looked back the way I'd come.

One last breath.

By the time I reached the pharmacy, night was turning into morning. It was raining hard, and the yard was awash. Streams were pouring over the stones, wicking into the mud, forming deltas, tributaries and teardrop islands.

Inside, I steamed in the warmth, slopping footprints across the back room, which was unusually empty. There were no boxes of stock piled up, not even discarded cartons and bags. It was bare, with just the table and chairs, and one of Constance's drawings exposed on the wood panelling. Like so many of her pictures, it was of a prim cat, a hint her father resolutely refused to take. We had sat side by side at the table one lazy afternoon, with sheets of paper and coloured pencils. She had no natural gift, but diligently copied my large oval for a body, a smaller one for a head, with two triangular ears, circular eyes and little lines for whiskers. Had that really been me, or was that another man altogether?

I found Alfie's hammer and spent ten minutes in the yard breaking the lock of the manacle. Once it was off, I hurled the thing over the fence as far as I could.

The pan on the stove contained an inch of water. Barely enough to wash, but I dared not turn on the tap as it would clonk and gush, and wake Alfie up. So I carried the pan to my room, took off my clothes and cleaned every part of my skin, slowly and methodically, exactly as I would a dead body in Mr Hurst's examination room.

I wasn't clean, but I'd run out of water, so I put on a nightshirt and crawled into bed, wrapping myself up in the blankets. I was paralytic with tiredness, yet I couldn't sleep. I lay awake until the glow of the sun seeped through the darkness outside.

The camisole was on the floor where I'd dropped it. I wondered whose it had been. Perhaps some girl had been kept in that room before Rosie and me, and someone was out there looking high and low for *her*. Had she been sent to a wealthy aristocrat in Brussels, or discarded in a whore-house, or killed?

The shadows inched along the floor. Outside, carts were clattering as the first deliveries of the day arrived. I could hear Ted Boyd next door opening the shutters of his grocery, and imagine him scratching his beard and stamping his feet in the morning chill. Alfie and Constance would be getting up soon.

There was nothing else to be done.

I silently opened the door and crept down the stairs and into the shop. In the centre of the room, the dentist's chair was still gleaming.

The shelves were half-full at most. Where normally they would have been crammed with packets and pots of all sizes, shapes and colours, lined up three or four deep, there were great gaps, single remedies standing on their own like little sentries. Even the window display was depleted. Constance was usually so careful about it, arranging the bottles so that, with the light behind them, they cast a mosaic of colour across the floor. But today they were sparsely spread and I could see beyond them to the street outside.

With no bank loan and no takers for his dentistry, Alfie must have been forced to sell his stock wholesale, which meant a heavy loss. I knew I should care more about that, but I was distracted. There was something I needed to find.

I scanned along the racks, uncertain whether it would be there or not. I'd almost given up hope when I saw it, a tall, dusty vial, mostly full. The label was faded, but easily readable: *chloral hydrate*.

I swigged a tiny amount, not even a spoonful, re-stoppered the vial and put it back. No one would ever know.

It acted fast. I had barely made it back to my room and lain down before the walls started to swing away from me and I was descending. The sky opened up above my head. I shut my eyes and drifted down as my breathing slowed and the black water closed over me.

23

THERE WERE THREE HOOKS on my wall, for my coat, my jacket and my bowler, and now one of them was empty. They'd taken my bowler hat. I'd gone to that house with it on, and when I'd awoken on the floor, my head was bare. That hat had been my favourite and fitted as if it was made for me specially, in a small size but with a tall bowl and a wide brim.

I tried to find my flat cap to put on the hook, to cover it up, but it wasn't where I thought I'd left it and wouldn't come to hand no matter how frantically I searched. And when I woke up again, sitting in front of my wardrobe, I was certain I was back in that house, and my heart raced so fast I thought it would burst out of my chest.

I opened the window to breathe in some air. Dawn seemed to be rising, except the shutters on the shops were already open and there was a weariness in the people that spoke of the late afternoon rather than early morning. I'd slept most of the day, and still I was exhausted.

I heard a knock at the door and opened it a crack. Alfie frowned at my nightshirt. I put my foot against the door.

'Someone came here today,' he said. 'Looking for you. Didn't leave a name.'

'What was he like?'

'Dangerous. I wouldn't turn my back on him. Smelled like a tar from the docks.' *The weasel.* They knew where I lived. I should have thought of that. 'He was very keen to see you. I told him you weren't here. What's going on?'

'Nothing. Just don't let him in. And keep a knife handy just in case.'

'In case what? Constance lives here too, you know.'

'Hence the knife.'

He looked at me quizzically. I tried to close the door, but he hadn't finished. He cleared his throat. 'Leo, come downstairs. We need to talk.'

'What about?'

'It's the shop. You must've noticed it hasn't been doing well. We need to discuss things.'

'All right.'

From the look on his face I knew I should say something more, or show greater sympathy, but my head was aching too much, and I was so angry about my hat that I couldn't concentrate on anything else. When I shut the door I could hear that he was still standing there.

I lay on the bed again and listened to the rush of blood in my ears, the sound of my own heart pumping. I dreamt of a lake I had heard of once, in Scotland, which was so deep that no one could find the bottom. Even if you were able to swim down that far, hold your breath for all that time, it was so dark and dense you would be crushed by the weight of it. What kind of fish might live in such a place? Small and strong and enclosed in a carapace of pearl, with owlish eyes and teeth like razor blades.

When I finally came downstairs, Alfie was eating bread and cheese at the table, and Constance was resting her head on her folded arms opposite him. She looked up at me with red eyes.

'There's a letter for you.'

Alfie held out a brown paper envelope. 'A fellow dropped it off this afternoon. He didn't seem all that happy.'

I ripped it open. It was written on headed notepaper.

February 18th 1880
Dear Mr Stanhope,
You are hereby dismissed from your position as Porter due
    to persistent absence.
Your truly,
Lloyd Greatorex (Senior Porter)

I screwed up the letter and thrust it into my pocket. Alfie sat back in his chair.

'What's got into you? Did you hear what I said before, about the shop? We've almost run out of money. We have to get out while there's still some capital left. I'm sorry, Leo, but you'll have to find another room.'

'Very well.'

'Very well? Is that all you have to say? You're out all night, you sleep for days, some ruffian turns up here looking for you, this letter, and the state of you! What the … what's going on?'

I was sick of his questions. 'I'm quite fine, thank you.'

Constance shook her head. 'No, you're not. Have you been given the sack?'

I looked at her squarely, without expression. She was always so precocious. If she acted like an adult she deserved to be treated like one. 'It's not your business.'

Alfie slammed his fist down on the table. I'd never real-ised before how snappish he could be. 'No, you're right, it isn't! Not any more. Very well then, you have two weeks, and then we all have to leave. All of us! We'll be going to my sister's family in Chelmsford. She has a mattress, and Constance can share with her cousins. You do whatever you want. Pack up your possessions and go.'

'All right,' I said. 'I shall.'

Constance leapt to her feet and glared at me, and I thought she was going to shout, but she remembered herself and fled the room, slamming the door behind her and running up the stairs.

Alfie began packing the following day. He started with his own possessions, lugging boxes of clothes and other things into the back room. I noticed his old army uniform in one, neatly folded, and another contained his medals and bundles of letters bound with string. Constance refused to join in, and spent the morning sulking, only emerging to tear down her cat picture from the wall and throw it in the rubbish.

By lunchtime, there was a thick fog outside and pedes-trians were groping along the pavement, blundering into each other. I was standing in the shop watching them, and waiting for someone to come. The police or Hugo Cooper, I didn't know which I dreaded more.

We had killed a man, Rosie and I, and you can't do that without consequences. I had considered running, but it would only confirm my guilt, and they would chase me anyway. I could call myself Lottie again to hide from them, but I wouldn't do that. Come what may, I would remain Leo Stanhope.

I wasn't sorry Bentinck was dead. For what he'd done to me and many others, I could see him die a thousand times and still not be sated. It was justice.

And surely he had murdered Maria too. Surely he had. And yet ... there was still a quibble, a hateful quibble, a small part of me that wouldn't make it true simply because it *should* be so. The part that reminded me that he'd told us he was away at the time, and anyway, *why* would he kill her? I had objected when the police had jumped to the easiest conclusion, and I refused to do the same now. He was guilty of so many things, of murder, kidnapping, procuring and ... and other crimes I wouldn't name, but I couldn't be certain he was guilty of *this* thing.

I needed some more chloral, but I wouldn't take it, not yet. Not while I was waiting for someone to come.

The police might have gone to arrest Rosie first. If so, she would explain that she killed Bentinck to save me, and then I would be exposed and she would be hanged. After all, he was a man of means and she was nothing but a butcher's daughter. It would be the end of both of us.

But then an idea came to me, the exact opposite of my usual method. Why not be honest? Or almost honest. Instead of waiting for the police to come and arrest us, what if we went to them instead? We could tell them how we were captured, and about the boat and the young girls being sent to Belgium to satisfy the cravings of those *very high-class gentlemen*.

And to avoid difficult questions, we could bend the truth, just a little. A simple transposition. It would be *Rosie* who was rescued and *me* who had brought down the manacle on Bentinck's head. It was a more plausible explanation anyway, and there was no one alive who could argue with it. I wished it *had* been me. It *should've* been me.

I just needed Rosie to come too, and tell the same story.

I put on my jacket, wrapped up the poker in a towel again, and set out, grateful for the fog. Whoever came for me, they would struggle to find me in this.

———

I couldn't see more than a few yards along the pavement. At first I walked slowly to avoid other pedestrians as they coalesced and dissolved, but then I experimented with closing my eyes and striding forward, letting chance decide whether I collided with someone or wandered into the road. It was strangely peaceful, that world of sounds and smells, feeling my feet, untethered from my purpose, carrying me wherever they chose. But my head began to daze, and unwelcome thoughts crowded in: a wolf's face, straining red, bristling hair on his shoulders and chest, his thighs hard under my fists as I beat against them.

On the edge of my hearing there was a voice I knew I should be listening to. It sounded like Madame Moreau.

I opened my eyes. I was alone.

By the time I reached Rosie's shop, the temperature had dropped and my teeth were chattering. I was about to knock when something made me pause.

It was starting to get dark, and the view through the window was like looking at a stage. Rosie was sitting solemnly on a stool with her little girl on her lap, next to the leather-faced woman whose name I couldn't recall, and a genial older man who I took to be the woman's husband from the way she fussed over him. From where I was standing I could just about hear the sound of their voices, but no words. There was another man there as well, younger, my age perhaps. He was leaning in towards Rosie and tweaking her daughter's nose to make her giggle. Rosie batted her hand at him and he caught it briefly before letting it go.

For the first time in a long time I didn't feel jealous of such easy, masculine flirtation. I felt a coil of revulsion and a rising, venomous anger, not just for this fellow but for all of them, all the charmers, persuaders, cajolers, seducers, kidnappers and molesters. All of them.

He looked out of the window, squinting at the gloom outside. I wasn't sure if he could see me. He turned away again, giving Rosie his full attention. He had an open face and dark hair, unshaven but not properly bearded.

I remembered Jack, lying on the slab at the hospital. He was a hairy man, Jack Flowers, much like this fellow, about the same height, and the same weight, more or less. They were eerily similar.

Now I came to think of it, I had seen nothing to identify Jack. Rosie had told the police her husband was missing, and had named the body on the slab as him, but we only had her word for it. No other member of his family had come in. There had been no reason to be suspicious; she was the grieving widow, and anyway, Mr Hurst had determined it was an accident.

But what if Jack had survived his drowning after all, and had swum to the shore? And what if he had snatched another man who looked similar, and drowned him in his place? It would be easy enough to do. What if I was looking at Jack Flowers right now, alive and well?

I tried to remember what Bentinck had said, back in that room. My mind wanted to sink down into the black water again, and I had to paddle hard to stay afloat. Bentinck had said that the money had been stolen a second time, and was still lost.

If Jack Flowers had indeed survived the Thames, then he might have gone back to the house and stolen the money again. And if Maria had found out that he was still alive then he might have silenced her in the most permanent way possible. He'd already killed whoever ended up in the mortuary, so I knew he was capable of it.

All the pieces fitted. Everyone thought Jack was dead, so no one would suspect him. And now he was rich and free.

No, not *he*. Both of them. Rosie must have been part of the plan too. She had fooled me completely, following me and berating me and steering me on the wrong path, and all the time covering for her husband.

No wonder she hadn't worn weeds.

I thought I was going to be sick. I remembered how she had tried to stop me looking at Elizabeth Brafton's appointment book, where Jack's name had been written, and how she had begged me not to talk to the police. Yes, she had saved me at Bentinck's house, but in doing so, she had saved herself as well.

The fog had cleared the streets, too dense even for the costermongers and beggars. I was alone on the pavement, unable to move. I had come here to convince Rosie to let me save her, but all this time, she had been lying to me, distracting me from finding the truth. It was almost too much to bear.

How could I have been so blind?

And now I had no plan, and could only go home and wait for the police or Hugo to come for me. There was nothing else to be done.

As I turned to go, I noticed a movement over the road, a shape in the fog that seemed to be a man. I couldn't be sure, and was about to step closer when a carriage came between us, and when it had passed, the figure had disappeared. Perhaps he wasn't real. Perhaps my mind was making shapes from the angles of the doorway and shadows on the pillar, piecing together something that wasn't truly there: a man in a long coat, watching me.

I rushed home through the market. The traders were packing up, buckling their money belts while their boys sorted through the leftover onions and cabbages, picking out the good ones for tomorrow and tossing the rest on the pavement. I nearly wept as I squashed the mouldy vegetables under my shoes.

By the time I reached Soho Square, almost all the way home, the fog was lifting, and the people of London were emerging like moles in springtime. There was a queue of traffic at the corner, and the drivers were yelling insults at the poor fellow at the front who had lost a wheel to a pothole.

I had the sense of someone behind me, and then heard a man's voice.

'I say!' I turned, and there was Augustus Thorpe waggling his finger. 'I say! You there! You're the chap from that pharmacy, aren't you?'

He was the last person I'd expected to see. My mind was so full of Rosie's treachery I had trouble fitting him into it, as though he was someone I had met years before in a different city.

'What? Were you following me?'

'No, don't be ridiculous.' He was wearing a tight military jacket, rather than a long coat. 'I was just coming to see you about Miss Pritchard. We agreed to meet in the park yesterday and … I suppose she had to make another arrangement. I'd appreciate it if you'd give me her address so I can call on her. Would you mind?'

'No, I'm sorry.'

'You don't understand. She said … I mean, we *agreed* to meet. We're friends. She said you could give me her address and it would be all right.'

'Leave me alone.'

I turned away from him, but he put his hand on my arm. I was utterly repulsed by his touch. I, who had weighed the cancerous liver of a navvy crushed by a fallen wall, who had held together the torso of a man pulled apart by dogs so Mr Hurst could count his remaining ribs, could not abide Thorpe's hand on my arm. Not even for a second.

I slapped his hand away, but he grabbed my lapel. 'How dare you!' he shouted. 'I'm an officer in Her Majesty's army and you *will* do as I say!'

I can't explain what happened next, not fully. It seemed to me that Thorpe and Bentinck had become the same person. I knew they weren't, but even so I had to get his hand off me, no matter the cost. I lashed out with my poker and he ducked. He shouted something I didn't hear, and I swung again, this time making contact with his shoulder. He swore and groped at his side for a weapon, finding only air.

'You'll pay for this!' he bellowed.

People were gathering, out of reach, watching the fray. One of them was yelling encouragement to Thorpe, and when he looked at me with those small, round eyes, I realised he was the weasel. He seemed to have found himself a new coat since I'd last seen him, a sleek black greatcoat with a velvet collar, much too large for him. It flapped open like an awning adrift from its frame.

He raised his eyebrows and flashed me a grin.

'Hello again, Stanhope.'

I flailed at him but he sprang backwards, reaching into his pocket and pulling out a short, narrow knife. I thought he would rush at me, but he glanced at the crowd and thought better of it.

'I'll see you soon,' he said, and was gone.

I was surrounded by faces I didn't know. They parted as I ran.

24

THE BELLS WERE RINGING for six o'clock when I got home, utterly exhausted. I wanted to sleep, but I couldn't, so I sat on the bed and absent-mindedly pushed chess pieces around the board.

Rosie and I, we had protected each other in the frenzy of that attic room. She had looked me in the eyes and told me: *I won't leave you.* And I had trusted her. And perhaps she wasn't deceiving me, at the time. Perhaps we *had* been bonded together, truly together, because otherwise we wouldn't have survived.

But afterwards … well, Jack was alive and Bentinck was dead, so it had all worked out quite well for her, hadn't it?

I knew I should tell the police, but Ripley had treated me like a bumbling idiot; admittedly, with some justification. Before I could go to him again, I needed to be sure.

I took my opponent's knight, and held it up, thinking about Thorpe. On impulse, I poked it into the candle flame, watching the dark-brown paint blacken and start to smoke. I'd seen another side to him that day, not just puerile but bullying and self-serving as well. I could easily believe he would commit murder to retrieve his letter. But was he a better suspect than Jack?

When the knight caught fire, I blew it out and set it on my chest of drawers, and picked up the cork that substituted for the white queen. Might Elizabeth Brafton have been overwhelmed by jealousy, resenting Bentinck's liking for her young employee? It didn't seem likely. She was too proud to allow herself such rage, such indulgence.

A rook and a king for Hugo and Bentinck. They were capable of killing, but they had no motive I could think of. I laid the king on its side, resigned.

What about Jacob? Might he have killed her? He had been with Maria and had lied to me about it. I wanted to believe he was a suspect, but I was so angry with him I couldn't think clearly. Still, it gave me some satisfaction to represent the impious Jew with a white bishop, and line him up beside the others. He deserved no better.

And finally, a pawn to represent Jack Flowers.

I lay back and examined my little assembly: knight, cork, rook, king, bishop and pawn.

'Confess,' I whispered to them, but they didn't.

No matter which way I looked at it, if Jack was alive, he was the most likely killer. He had the best motives – money and freedom – and he was already a murderer.

And that meant Rosie too.

Why was I always so tender? Other people seemed to have such resilience, while I hurtled around like a sparrow shut in a room, banging against every wall until my wings were broken.

Damn you, Rosie. I really believed you were my friend.

In the morning, I thought I heard a familiar voice talking to Alfie in the pharmacy, but couldn't be sure. The previous night I'd taken another teaspoonful of chloral, and now the world seemed warped and wavering, as if I was looking at it through an uneven windowpane.

I went downstairs and was surprised to find Lilya seated regally in the dentist's chair, with her little dog twitching on her lap.

'Is that Leo? Come here, let me touch you.'

She couldn't see my shudder as she reached out and pinched my cheek. 'Ah, Leo. I'm very cross with you. I have to come here because you never visit no more. Jacob is so *sad*, and he says nothing's wrong but I know him. Twenty years married. Before you were born.'

'I'm twenty-five.'

She dismissed the mathematics with a wave of her hand. 'So I says to go to the club and he says no I don't want to. So I says it's Leo isn't it? And he goes upstairs and he don't come down until it's time to light the lamps. What happened, Leo? You must talk to him.'

'There's nothing to talk about.'

'Always things. Talking is the water that flows in the river. Always different water, but without it there's no river.'

'How did you get here, Lilya?'

She sucked her teeth. 'I walked. My eyes don't work so good but my feet work quite well. This I how much I care about you, and that daft old man, my husband.' She sniffed. 'This room smells funny. You smell funny too.'

'I don't believe you. You never leave the house on your own. Is Jacob with you?'

'This is for fixing teeth, yes?' She groped around the metal base of the chair, fingering the mechanism that tipped it backwards. 'I have a toothache. Here.' She pointed at her jaw. 'Maybe your friend here could pull it out? How much?'

'One and six up-front,' said Alfie, rolling up his shirt-sleeves and glancing down at her dog, which was avidly chewing on her purse. 'Then it all depends.'

'I don't see very good,' she said. 'You must tell me what you're going to do.'

'Of course.' He fetched the little mirror he'd soldered on to a stick. 'Open your mouth please, and relax.'

He was barely able to keep the tremor out of his voice; she was the first living customer he'd ever had.

I went outside. It was gloomy and bitter to the bone, and the people were shrunken into their coats and muffs, with scarves wrapped around their necks. On the other side of the road, a man was shivering in a doorway, his hat pulled down over his forehead and his hands in his pockets. I couldn't see much of him, but I could see that he was throwing furtive glances in my direction.

I crossed over.

'What kind of coward sends his wife to plead for him?'

Jacob stamped his feet, trying to get warm. 'It was her idea. I'm just here to make sure she doesn't bump into things, though goodness knows she's better in this bloody fog than I am. She ended up leading me.'

'She says she has a toothache.'

'Maybe she does. She would have them all pulled out just to annoy me.' I turned to leave and he held up his hands. 'Wait, wait. Don't go, Leo. It was her idea to come but I was glad of it too. There are things I want to say.'

'Such as? Say them fast, it's freezing out here.'

Even if he told me the truth, how would I know? Once a liar's been caught out, nothing he says can be trusted.

'You're young, Leo, and you don't understand. You toy with life. It seems like for ever, but soon you'll find out that your life is a day and it's evening already. For me it's getting dark and I can hear the clockwork ticking. Maria was young and lovely, and I wanted to have her, but I couldn't. She just *listened* to me, to my stories of when I was a boy. No one else wants to hear them, the stories of an old man, far from home, whose children have all grown up.'

'What nonsense. Three of them still live with you.'

'Millicent is eight and the others are boys. Boys don't want to listen. They run around shouting and hitting things with sticks. Maria was *interested*. Her mother was Jewish, she said. I know, I know, but I'm an old fool and I believe what I choose. Bah! I want to believe she was Jewish and I'm a young stallion who can cover any filly. I want to believe you're a man too, if you say it's so.'

'Are you claiming you never shared a bed with her?'

'I'm barely more of a man than you are.' He coughed coarsely, blowing steam out through his scarf. 'Bloody weather. Bloody England.'

I wasn't comforted. 'Very well,' I said, sourly. 'You've told me.'

'I think she loved you, in her way.'

'What are you talking about?'

'These girls, they don't discuss their other customers, of course not. But one time she was sick, bad sick, like a cat. Lilya was the same, many times. It was obvious why.'

'I already know she was pregnant.'

'So she says I mustn't tell that Brafton woman and I ask her if she knows anyone who could get rid of it for her. It was a thoughtless question, but she says she will have the baby, and there's some fellow who will marry her. A soldier. An officer. But then she starts weeping and I've got my arm around her and wondering why I'm paying for this.'

'What a touching story.'

'Ha! A little of the old Leo back again. Good! Yes, a touching story. So I'm there and she's weeping, my God, so much weeping. So I say, if there's a soldier she can marry, that seems like good news, doesn't it? But still she weeps, more and more, like a torrent.'

'Why are you telling me this?'

'She was sad because of *you*, Leo. Because she cared about you. It's obvious.'

I took a step forward and had to clutch my hands together to stop myself from punching him, right there in the street, an old man who couldn't even walk up a flight of steps without wheezing. What right did he have to tell me these things, and tell me *now*, when she was dead and buried?

'That doesn't mean anything.'

'Didn't you tell me she used to blow you kisses from her window as you were leaving? That means something.'

She hadn't blown me any kisses on that last day. By the time I had left, another man was in her room. He got all the kisses.

'Is that it?'

'I was jealous of you. What foolishness we find in our old age, becoming moonful boys again.' He waved his arms around, remonstrating against the world. 'I was jealous and angry, so I stopped comforting her. I told her a story about a dock whore I knew back in Nikolaev who was pleasuring the ship's captain when a rope slipped and sliced her in half.'

'Is that even true?'

'How would I know? I heard it. Anyway, I felt guilty and the next time I brought her a doll. I got it for Milli but she doesn't care about such things any more, and with Maria, I don't know, it might have been a girl. That was the last time I was with her, and that's everything, Leo. Everything.' He peered at me from under his hat. 'What have you done to your face? Are you hurt? What happened to you?' He pointed at his forehead and I put a finger to my own. It was sore, a sharp pain where the skin was broken. I couldn't remember how I'd got it.

'I'm going now. Goodbye, Jacob.'

As I crossed back over the road, I heard him call after me: 'She cared for you in her own way, Leo. You mustn't forget that!'

Inside the pharmacy, Lilya was tipped back in the chair while Alfie pored over her. She pushed him aside.

'Is that Leo? You talked to Jacob, yes?'

'He had advice for me, as ever.'

'Good, good. You talk and agree to be friends again. And follow his advice. He's the wisest old fool in the Queen's empire. He gives the best advice and never follows it himself.' Alfie bent to his work again, pliers in hand, but she hadn't finished. 'And what about the lady you were rushing off to last time? What of her?'

'She ... has someone else.'

'Ah, but you mustn't let that stop you. It was the same with Jacob when I met him first time, and here we are. Twenty years married. Before you were born.'

It wasn't worth correcting her again. Once she had an idea in her head there was no shifting it.

'You're very lucky, Lilya.'

She closed her unseeing eyes and hugged her little dog closer. 'Lucky? Perhaps. I have a husband, but I know what he is, where he goes. I'm blind, but I'm not *blind*. Maybe you have better luck than me.'

'But I thought …'

She snorted. 'Yes, you thought, I thought, he thought. We all *think*, Leo, but none of us *know*. Matters of the heart are like the river. They bend this way and then that way, and sometimes there are rocks around the corner. Sometimes. But sometimes not. You never *know*.'

———

'Mr Stanhope!' Constance's shrill voice cut through my non-dream. I wasn't sure what time it was, or even what day. 'Mr Stanhope! The police are here again!'

Finally. At least it would soon be over with.

Downstairs, Detective Ripley was waiting for me. Pallett was with him, taking up more space in the room than was strictly natural. He nodded to me in that formal manner he had, somewhere between a senior servant and a hangman about to release the trap.

Seated at the table was Thorpe.

Ripley indicated the empty chair. 'Sit down, Stanhope. You look bloody awful.'

'Thank you.'

'I gather you've met the major.' He waggled a hand at Thorpe without looking in his direction. 'He gave me this address and a description of you. Hang on, I've got it written down here: unpleasant type, slim, dark hair, beardless, shifty, bad temper. Sounds like you, doesn't it?'

'What do you want?'

Ripley pulled out a cigarette and lit it, taking his time. 'I have some questions about a young lady who's gone missing. Seems you're connected to this one too.'

'Another one like Maria?'

He stretched his back, wincing. 'What's wrong with your face?'

'It's just a bruise. What young lady?'

He leafed through his notebook. 'Here we are: Miss Charlotte Pritchard, known as Lottie apparently. Do you know her?'

'What?'

'You know damn well what,' blurted out Thorpe. 'I met with Miss Pritchard in the park. We made another arrangement, but she didn't arrive. When I asked you about it you were insolent and barbarous. Like a wild beast.'

Ripley sighed, and held up his hand. 'All right, Major, that's enough. Now, Stanhope, a simple question: do you know Miss Pritchard or not?'

My mind went completely blank while Ripley examined me through the smoke. Eventually, I managed to say: 'Yes, I know her.'

'And did you arrange for Major Thorpe here to meet her?'

'Yes.'

He had his pen at the ready. 'Good, then we can clear this up. How can I get in touch with her?'

I couldn't form words. I was returned to that attic room, shoeless and hatless, my wrist burning with the pain of the manacle. *Underneath these clothes, I am female. Leave her alone and take me instead.*

No matter the consequences, I vowed I would never be Lottie again.

There was a sound from the little hallway at the bottom of the stairs, and Constance came into the room.

'Shall I make some tea for you gentlemen?'

Ripley looked surprised. Perhaps he wasn't used to such hospitality. 'We're just asking Mr Stanhope here some questions about a young lady he knows who's gone missing.'

Constance glanced at me. She was still angry, but she was a pig-headed girl and I feared she might make up some lie for my sake. 'Constance …' I began, but she interrupted.

'I'm sure Mr Stanhope has ever so many friends, and he can't possibly keep track of them all.'

Pallett smiled, but Thorpe shifted his position irritably. 'Get out, girl.'

'That's enough, Major,' said Ripley. It wasn't a request.

But Constance wasn't daunted. 'Major?' she said. 'Are you Major Thorpe, who sent the letter? You broke that poor lady's heart.' She gave him a hard look, and turned to me. 'Is *she* the one who's missing?'

'No, but please leave us alone now, Constance. I'm sure your father must need some help.'

For once, she did as she was told.

Thorpe was on his feet. 'You have my letter?'

Ripley stood also, with no sign of his stiff back. 'Sit down, Major. Now.' He turned to me. 'What bloody letter?'

I considered denying all knowledge of it, but what good would that do me now? I already knew what it said. I fetched it from my room and handed it to Ripley, who read it carefully and passed it to Pallett. Thorpe watched the piece of paper travel from hand to hand with the look of a spoiled child ogling the last biscuit on the plate.

'That's mine,' he said, his fingers twitching towards it, but Ripley put it into his jacket pocket.

'It's evidence. The regiment haven't been much help so far, but maybe when I show them this, they'll be more accommodating.'

'They'll do what any right-thinking gentleman would do, and send you on your way. Who are you to be asking questions about me?' He was going red in the face. 'I'm an officer in the British Army, and the son of a judge. You're just a ...' he searched for the right word, his mouth twisted in disgust '... a blasted lackey!'

Pallett got to his feet, but the major was already leaving. He slammed the door so hard behind him I thought it would fall off its hinges. In the silence that followed, Ripley lit another cigarette, utterly unbothered by Thorpe's exit.

'I've done some investigating of my own,' I said. 'I may know who ... that is, I believe I know who killed Maria Milanes.'

'Good for you. Now, about this Miss Pritchard. What's her address?'

'Did you hear what I said? I believe –'

'Yes, yes, I heard you, but one thing at a time. Now, the address?'

I had to tell him *something*. 'I don't have it, but I have her sister's, Jane Hemmings.' I gave him the address on Maida Vale. 'I believe, Jane and Lottie are ... they're estranged.'

Saying it out loud made it true.

I wondered what Jane would tell Ripley. Very little, I suspected. She didn't want the police asking questions any more than I did.

Ripley sniffed. 'I wish I was estranged from my sister sometimes, and her feckless husband more so.' He took a pull on his cigarette. 'Look. Thorpe's not the brightest star in the firmament, and I wouldn't normally bother with him. Except that rather a lot of women go missing, or turn up dead, around *you*, Mr Stanhope.'

'Are you accusing me of something?'

He watched me for a long moment. 'I'm wondering if you're starting a business of your own.'

'What do you mean?'

'You wouldn't be the first to earn a little extra running girls on the side. It starts with walks in the park and ends with ... well, you know where it ends.'

'Absolutely not.'

'Good. It's a dirty game, and you're not cut out for it. Either way, I'll get to the bottom of this in the end. I usually do.' He brushed a speck of talcum dust off his lapel, as if it was the single blemish on otherwise perfect tailoring. 'Now, do you know someone named Hugo Cooper? Used to be a boxer, apparently.'

'What?' I was struggling to keep up. 'Why do you want to know?'

'Do you or don't you?'

302

I swallowed hard. 'Yes. I mean, I've met him. He works at the brothel on Half Moon Street. He's the doorman.'

'He murdered his employer, it seems. There's a lot of it about.'

'Hugo?' For a moment I didn't understand. 'You mean … you're saying *Hugo* killed James Bentinck?'

'Smashed his head in with a metal chain. The poor bastard was stark naked in his own home. Bloody mess, it was.'

I couldn't think of anything to say. My mind was too clogged and my heart was beating too fast. Was he trying to trick me? I searched for signs of artifice on his face, but he was unreadable.

'Why are you telling me this?' I asked eventually.

'Two reasons. One is because Bentinck's the second person from that place who's been murdered, and that's a bit suspicious, even by the standards of a whorehouse.' He blew a smoke ring, and watched me through it. 'Of course, Hugo Cooper could've done for the girl as well, but why would he? The others said he never showed any interest in 'em. I s'pose it's like working in a chocolate factory, after a while you stop craving the merchandise.'

'But you're sure he killed Bentinck?' I was aware I was sitting forward in my chair.

'He was the only one in the house, and Bentinck's book-keeper told us it was him. She pointed the finger right away, and he doesn't seem to have a better explanation.'

'What *was* his explanation?'

'Well, that's the other reason. Doesn't really hold water, but he insists it's true, and he's not blessed with a potent imagination. He says you did it.'

'Me?' I took a breath, trying to steady my voice.

'You.' He seemed relaxed, almost somnolent, but he was studying me keenly. I had the impression he was hoping I would fill the silence with a confession, but I'd spent my childhood in church, where oppressive quietude was the norm, and I wouldn't rush to redemption from my sins now any more than I had then. Eventually, he continued: 'He said you were there with the widow of Jack Flowers. I take it you know her?'

'Yes, but that's absurd.'

'I agree. Mrs Flowers seems like a fine woman. She's got spirit. Gave me what-for about her husband and she didn't even like him much. Reminds me of a girl I knew years ago, before I was married. We used to call her "The Charity Box" on account of … well, I'm sure I don't need to explain, but those were good days.'

Pallett cleared his throat, and Ripley gave him a look. 'What is it? Out with it, Constable.'

'The chloral hydrate, sir.'

'Ah, yes. That bookkeeper …' He paused, as I would imagine most men do when contemplating Miss Gainsford. 'She pointed out that Hugo Cooper had a bottle of chloral hydrate on him. That's very strong stuff. Makes you hallucinate, if that's the right word.'

He knew full well that it was. His simple-policeman act was paper-thin.

'Then I suppose that answers that,' I said. 'Hugo was insensible with the narcotic. He doesn't know what he saw.'

Ripley worked his mouth as if he had a fish-bone stuck in his teeth. 'Quite. But it does seem all very … tidy to me.' Pallett cleared his throat again, and Ripley rolled his eyes. 'Go ahead, Constable. You don't have to make a sound like an embarrassed vicar every time you want to say something.'

'I was thinking we should visit Mrs Flowers too, sir. Maybe she can shed some light.'

'A fine idea. A nice pie for our lunch tomorrow, and maybe a glass of beer too. We'll see what's what.'

'It's Sunday tomorrow, sir.'

Ripley stared at Pallett for a full ten seconds while the constable grew more and more red, and then turned to me. 'Right, Stanhope, you were saying you had an idea who murdered the girl?'

'I misspoke,' I said, clinging to what little lucidity I had left. I could hardly accuse Rosie of killing Maria having just dismissed Hugo's accusation that she and I had killed Bentinck. Things were moving too quickly; I needed time to make sense of it all. 'What I meant was, I don't think Madame Moreau did it. You believe that her profession is enough to condemn her, but –'

'What Mrs Moreau does is inexcusable and, more to the point, it's against the law.' He dropped his spent cigarette on to the table, where it smouldered.

'You have no idea what she does. You think that just because –'

He held up his hand. 'I let her go. All right? There was nothing to incriminate her for the murder, so I let her go, despite what she does.' He paused, apparently reliving an unpleasant memory. 'It didn't make me very popular with the higher-ups, as you might imagine.'

'So she's at home again?'

'I suppose so. I had Pallett here make sure she got back safely. I regretted what happened with Sergeant Cloake, before. He's too much whip and not enough oats, if you get my meaning. She'd suffered enough.'

'She shouldn't have suffered at all.'

'It's imperfect justice, but then it's an imperfect world. Leave it to us now, all right?'

'Of course.'

But that was a lie.

'No more asking questions. You understand?'

'Yes, absolutely.'

But that was an even bigger lie.

After they'd gone I sat in the back room, watching the shadow of the window frame sharpen and soften as clouds blew across the sun. The floor needed a sweep. Constance had been remiss, what with one thing and another, and Alfie rarely remembered to remind her. It was probably just as well, as she was apt to try out different formulas of polish, and had once made it so slippery the three of us had spent a hilarious half hour skating from one end of the room to the other. I smiled at the memory of it. This room was my favourite in the house, my favourite in the world. Here, I could just sit quietly and think.

Why had Miss Gainsford accused Hugo of killing Bentinck? He was their most loyal servant, and she must know it wasn't true.

And now that Ripley and Pallett were going to question Rosie at the pie shop, would they see Jack Flowers for themselves? Would they arrest the two of them?

And that was another thing I didn't understand: I should feel *glad* they were going there and might arrest Rosie, and yet I didn't. Despite everything, I felt worried for her.

———

As evening fell, I hung around in the pharmacy, waiting for Alfie to finish so I could get a teaspoonful of chloral. He opened up the metal box where he kept his money and scooped the few coins into it, his takings for the day. They made a dismal clang. He closed it up and lowered his head on to the lid as if in supplication.

There was something about the box that scratched at me; something I ought to remember. A part of me recognised what it was, but my mind wouldn't surface.

'How does that work?' I asked eventually.

'Why do you care?'

'I might've seen one like it before.'

'It's a padlock.'

'I can see that. But there's no key.'

The padlock appeared quite normal at first glance, but instead of a hole for a key, there were five rings, like rings on a finger. When I looked closely, I could see letters engraved on the circumference of each one.

'What do those do?'

Alfie shook his head. 'Are we truly going to talk about padlocks, Leo? What's next? We can discuss the principles of crop rotation if you like, or the exact chemistry of paraffin. Or astronomy. I've always wanted to know about the planets.'

'Just this padlock, thank you.'

He threw up his hands. 'Very well, if that's what you want. You see these bezels? You turn them to a particular combination of letters, and the lock opens. Unless you know the right letters, you can't open it. Keys can be lost or copied, but this is safer because only I know the right letters.'

'If you can remember them.'

'That's the clever thing.' He was warming to the topic despite himself. He was a man of enthusiasms. 'The locksmith can set them to anything you want. So you choose a combination you won't forget.'

And that was it. It truly was as simple as that: *you choose a combination you won't forget.*

Mercy, I thought. Five letters: M–E–R–C–Y. Bentinck had put a padlock like this one on his strongbox, and he had chosen the letters to spell his late wife's name, because he knew he would never forget it.

But this type of lock had a flaw that keys did not. Jack Flowers had worked for Bentinck, loading and unloading, and must have spied on him opening the box. He had probably watched him for days, getting one letter at a time. But Jack wouldn't know the letters spelled 'Mercy' because he couldn't read or write. They would just be five individual shapes to him. So he had copied them on to a bottle of ale, one by one until he had them all. No one would question him carrying the bottle because everyone knew he liked a drink. And when the opportunity came, he broke into Bentinck's house, opened up the box and stole the money.

Of course, Bentinck had caught him and Hugo had drugged and tried to drown him. But Jack had lived, and had gone back to the house and stolen the money for a second time.

Except ... except that couldn't be right, could it? I was missing something. Why would the word 'Mercy', the exact combination of letters for the strongbox lock, be written on a bottle in a drowned man's pocket, if the drowned man wasn't Jack?

I felt as if I was halfway through a game of chess and had discovered that both my bishops were on white squares. At some earlier point I must've made an illegal move, but I didn't know when.

Suddenly, my theory about Rosie and Jack seemed less certain. I'd seen someone who looked like Jack, but there was no other evidence he *was* Jack. He could've been anybody. And if Jack really did drown in the Thames, and it really was his corpse in the mortuary, then I didn't have any idea who had stolen the money for a second time. Or who had killed Maria.

In fact, I didn't know anything at all.

What a waste. Everything I had done was for nothing. No income, no home, no friends, no family, no Maria, no idea. All I had to cling to was my name scraped into the paint on Westminster Bridge, but I wasn't sure I had the nerve to go back there. It's no easy thing to jump.

After an hour, I heard Alfie light his candle and head up to bed. I crept into the shop, which was dark and quiet but for a drunkard singing in the doorway opposite.

I found the vial of chloral, pulled out the stopper and upended the entire contents into my mouth.

25

I AWOKE IN A sweat. Or I thought I did. I couldn't be sure whether I was truly conscious or was only dreaming of waking. I reached for my box of matches in the pitch darkness, but it wasn't there, so I lay on my bed, unable to see my hand in front of my face.

The weasel had been outside Rosie's shop in the fog, a shadowy figure in a long coat. Had that really happened or had I dreamt it? I couldn't be sure. I wasn't even sure I was in my own bed or my own room. I got up and fumbled around, feeling for a door or a window frame, finding the hooks in the wall and holding on. The floor was tipping and sliding, so I crouched down, and then lay down. Nothing would stay still. I curled around the leg of my bed as the furniture spun around me.

Jack Flowers had been dead, and then alive, and now he was dead once more. And if he truly *was* dead this time, then Rosie couldn't be in cahoots with him. And that meant she was in danger. I needed to warn her.

I was drifting again, and falling, uncertain whether it was still night-time or whether I had simply closed my eyes.

When I awoke, the bells were ringing outside and a weak, dawn light was coming through the curtain. Was it still today?

I got dressed and stumbled downstairs, desperately thirsty. I drank straight from the tap and scooped water over my forehead and neck, relishing the sharp cold of it running down my spine and soaking into my shirt.

Everything was locked up. Alfie and Constance must still be in bed. Their boxes were mostly filled, piled around the table, tied with string and labelled A or C or a cross for the things to be thrown away. There were lots of crosses.

I left through the back door, creeping along the alley-way behind the yards. It snaked along parallel to the road, emerging at a nondescript gate on Great Windmill Street. Anyone trying to follow me would require a pretty good knowledge of the local geography.

The long walk to Rosie's shop brought me to some kind of consciousness, but even so I couldn't have recalled a single thing I'd seen on the journey.

The shop was closed. I tore a piece of paper from my notebook and wrote out a message, and was just about to push it through her letterbox when the door opened. Rosie came out in a smart coat and hat, followed by a little troupe of her three children, holding hands, and the woman with the leathern face and her husband, neither of whose names I could remember. No sign of the man I had thought was Jack.

'Leo!'

I held up my piece of paper. 'I was leaving this for you.'

'Why?'

'I came here before, the other evening. There was some-one watching your shop. I think it was the same man who kidnapped you.'

Rosie stared at me for several seconds. Her eyes flicked down, just momentarily, clearly wondering how she hadn't realised before. I was like a magic trick, obvious once you know how it's done. Finally, she turned to the older woman. 'Alice, would you take the children? I'm going to have a talk with Mr Stanhope here.'

The bells were tolling at St Paul's, and I realised it was a Sunday. 'You're going to church.'

'I was.'

'I don't want to delay you.'

She took my arm and pulled me into the little side street by her shop. 'Are you all right?' she hissed. 'You ran off without a word.'

'I'm fine.'

'What you did, in that room, for me. I just want to say –'

'I have to go. Just watch out for that man, won't you? He's dangerous.'

I would have left immediately, but she still had hold of my arm. 'I don't regret it, you know.' Her voice sounded constricted. 'I'd do it again in a heartbeat. That man, Bentinck, he deserved to die for what he did to you and me. And he's a murderer himself.'

'Yes, he is.' But the quibble wouldn't stay down. 'Although I don't think it was him who killed Maria. I don't think he was even in London. Why would he lie about that?'

'Then who?'

'I don't know.' I closed my eyes, wanting never to answer another question again. They felt like bee stings, jabbing into my skin and leaving little barbs behind. 'I did think … but it's not important.'

'What? Tell me.'

312

'A foolish thing. I went to your shop and I saw a man with you, and I thought he might be Jack, still alive. It seems silly now.'

For once, her reply wasn't sharp. 'Yes, it does. That was Billy, his brother, my brother-in-law.'

'You seemed –'

'*He seemed*, not me. It's the shop he wants, but he won't be getting it. I've had my fill of Flowers, thanks very much.'

'I see. Well, that explains it.'

'And what now, Leo?' She hesitated. 'Should I still call you "Leo"?'

She was looking at me oddly, in a way she hadn't before, her eyes searching my face and neck and hands, all of me, perceiving the shape of the body beneath my clothes. But she couldn't see inside my chest, where a man's heart was beating.

I pulled my coat more tightly around myself. 'Yes, of course.'

'It's only that … I don't understand what you are. Have you always been this way?'

'Since I was very young. Since before I knew what it meant. I'm a man, regardless of my physical nature.'

She nodded, but was frowning. 'Well, it's beyond my experience, I must say.'

'I know, but Rosie, you have to keep it a secret. From everyone.' I sounded as if I was pleading, but I had no choice. 'They'd put me in prison or an asylum and make me take medicines or worse. They'd try to change me, and it would destroy me. Do you understand?'

'How many people know?'

'Very few. And it must stay that way. Will you keep my secret?'

She took a deep breath and looked at me squarely. 'Yes, I will. I owe you at least that.' She fixed her hat and smiled, though it was forced, an attempt to put things back to how they'd been before. 'So what now, Leo Stanhope?'

I sagged against the wall. 'I don't know. It all seems so pointless. I just wanted to know who'd killed Maria, that was all. Some justice for her death. And now everything's fallen apart. I've lost my friend, my position, my lodging and almost all my money.' I rubbed my face with my palms. 'And yet I'm as much in the dark now as I was at the beginning. I don't think I'll ever find out the truth.'

She pursed her lips. 'Well, that's no good.' She peered into her bag and pulled out a pie wrapped in paper, half-sized, and handed it to me. It had an 'R' baked into the pastry. 'Eat this. Robbie can share with his brother and sister.'

'I couldn't.'

'Just eat it, you idiot.'

So I did, standing there on the pavement, and even through my despair it tasted spectacular. Spicy minced lamb with leek. It wanted for nothing, save perhaps a flask of tea to wash it down.

Rosie glanced at me from under the brim of her hat. 'That poor girl, murdered by Lord knows who.'

'You're more sympathetic than you were,' I said, through a mouthful of pie.

It was her turn to look away. 'Yes, well, experience'll do that to a person, I suppose. It's just a shame. Likely now we'll never know what happened or why, will we?'

'It's to do with the stolen money, I think. But I've no idea how that links to Maria's death, none at all. Whoever stole it the second time found the combination of letters to open the padlock written on Jack's bottle of ale. The break-in was skilfully done too; the mortuary window wasn't broken. No one even noticed it until Flossie came in on Monday morning.'

Rosie was looking at me with a perplexed expression. 'All right. So you're saying you've no idea who broke into the mortuary, is that it? Well, whoever it was, they must've known Jack. And they must've known where he was.'

'Yes.'

'And it wasn't you or me.'

'No.'

'Did you tell anyone else?'

'No. Only Maria.'

She took another deep breath and shook her head. 'I do swear that men are the blindest and stupidest creatures on God's earth, especially when it comes to women. And this proves beyond any doubt, Leo Stanhope, you truly are a man.'

We argued for at least ten minutes. I said it wasn't true, and she said it seemed to her I wasn't much of a judge of what was true and what wasn't, and I needed someone blessed with common sense to make me see what was staring me in the face. In the end, we agreed there was only one way to be sure.

I had to speak to Maria's mother.

I didn't know where the woman lived, but I knew she went to the church in Bow. I would have to go there today or wait another week, and as Rosie knew the way and I didn't, I had no choice but to accede gracefully to her insistence, and allow her come with me.

This time, she let me hail a hansom cab. The roads were almost clear and we made good pace eastwards along Whitechapel High Street, bordered on either side by shops with closed shutters. Young men were standing in groups, drinking and watching in silence. At the canal bridge, the driver pulled up his horse and told us he would go no further, so we had to get out and walk. The shops and factories gradually petered out, replaced by shadowy alleyways and looming tenements, and even those seemed the height of luxury compared with the grim shacks and doss-houses further along in Bow, their billysweet walls sagging and sweating on to the pavement.

It amazed me. Maria had been brought up in this place, and yet she had shone like a kingfisher flickering across the water. Perhaps that was why. Perhaps she looked at these streets and decided she was not part of them, and they were not part of her. She became what she chose to be, over and over again, every day. Something I could understand.

The church was a white stone building hidden behind some trees in a half-hearted graveyard where the road divided. From a distance, it resembled a fairy-tale castle, the battlements on its pale tower rendering it even more other-worldly. Close up, it was in as much disrepair as the slums surrounding it, and the faith of the congregants, singing merrily inside, might have been all that was keeping it upright.

We waited for the service to end. Our earlier conversation about my physical nature seemed to be preying on Rosie's mind, and we talked of the weather and the glut of recent fogs as if we were acquaintances who had never fought for our lives together or violently killed a man.

Finally, the reverend came out and stood near the porch, and I recognised him as the deaf old fellow who had conducted Maria's funeral. He looked like a man in need of a smoke, but I didn't have any tobacco, so we just watched from the pavement. The congregation was starting to emerge. First out was the woman who had accosted me at the wake and asked whether I'd ever been in a mental asylum.

'Is that her?' whispered Rosie.

'No. There she is.'

Mrs Mills was short in stature, with Maria's curly hair, though thinner and greyer. She had her daughter's way of holding her hands and even something of her restlessness as she glanced around at the trees and up at the sun. But she was florid where Maria had been pale, and bony where Maria had been soft, and Maria had never walked like that, limping as if each step was agony.

She found her way to a bench under a tree, and eased herself down on to it. As we approached, I could smell her, a corrosive pall of alcohol and piss that turned my stomach.

'Mrs Mills? I knew your daughter, Maria.'

She nodded, and kept nodding, shaking as if she was cold, although the weather was as mild as a spring day.

'My name's Stanhope and this is Mrs Flowers.'

'Are you him?' she asked, eventually.

'Who?'

'Her soldier. The one she's going to marry.'

She seemed crestfallen when I shook my head. 'No. I just want to ask you some questions.'

'She's here somewhere. We always come together. She'll be back soon.'

She was looking around, searching among the congregation still gathering outside the church, for her dead daughter.

'I saw you at her funeral,' I said, as gently as I could.

She clutched her hands into her lap. She was just like Maria, sitting on the bed, looking down at her fingers while she talked.

'She was my last. I buried all the others, you know. Three born dead, two never lasted a month and one made it to five years. My little boy.'

'I'm sorry. It must've been hard back then, making ends meet. How did you survive?'

She looked at me with Maria's eyes, even with some of their brightness. 'I sang at Wilton's in Graces Alley, though it's gone now, burned down. Such a shame. Maria was born under that stage, you know.'

So that much was true, at least.

'What was she like, when she was a child?'

'A performer. She could mimic anyone, accents and everything, and tell yarns that'd make you laugh and cry at the same time. Such an imagination! She persuaded old Mr Wilton she was being adopted by an earl once, who had a solid-gold rocking horse at his mansion.'

'And in those days, was she … did she ever have to steal things?'

The old woman looked up sharply. 'You a copper?'

'No.'

'All right then. I don't want no police poking around. What's mine is mine.'

'Of course. It's nothing like that.'

She sniffed, and we sat for another minute or two. It was oddly peaceful. Above our heads, a thrush was bursting out its song, sweeter even than a nightingale's. But we couldn't stay for ever. One of the fellows from the church was looking suspiciously in our direction.

Rosie crouched down in front of Mrs Mills. 'You must be very proud of Maria.'

'Oh yes.'

'We just want to know whether she used to steal things when she was much younger. Then we'll leave you in peace.'

Mrs Mills shrugged. 'She likes to help me, that's all.'

'Of course she does. You're her mother. Any daughter would do the same.'

'She's got brains, you see. Not like me. She knows all the tricks.'

'What kind of tricks?' The old woman didn't reply, and Rosie took her hand. 'Please tell us.'

'It's for Maria that we need the information,' I said. 'No harm can come to her because of it.'

'I know,' said the old woman, and there were tears on her cheeks. 'I know she ain't with us no more. She was my last.'

'I'm very sorry,' I said. 'I truly am. We're trying to find out what happened. Please tell us about her when she was young.'

She wiped her face and spoke quietly. 'She was sharp as a needle. She could jimmy a window and be in and out before they even knew she'd been there. Like a ghost. Coins if she could get 'em, or jewellery for me to sell in the market. Sometimes a ribbon or a trinket for herself. She liked pretty things.'

'And you never worried she might get caught?' I asked.

'Oh, she was nabbed a few times, but she always had a story and a winning way, and they let her go. Can you believe it? They catch some scrap of a girl in their home with her fingers on their valuables, and she talks her way out of it. One lady gave her lunch and half a crown.'

The fellow who had looked in my direction was approaching us. He was mousy and bald, in his best Sunday clothes, such as they were, and wearing a temperance medal on his jacket. 'You after something?'

'I was a friend of her daughter.'

'Right.' He frowned, disapproving, making clear that he knew what Maria's profession had been. 'Best not to upset Mrs Mills. She's a bit bewildered. She's had a long life and she can't always tell what part of it she's in.' His lips twitched. He was determined to make his point. 'Little enough of it was on God's path, her or her daughter. Works of the flesh.'

I felt myself getting irritated. He hadn't even come to Maria's funeral, but he thought his little badge gave him the right to judge her.

'It wasn't Maria's fault.'

'We've all got a choice.'

I raised myself up and was about to respond with some heat, when Rosie interrupted me.

'Well, it's good of you to look after Mrs Mills, anyway.'

'A little charity on a Sunday, nothing more. She's in the dosshouse the rest of the week.' He clearly thought that was what she deserved. 'Time we was going.'

We watched him lead her away. The poor woman could barely walk. It was a strange kind of farewell to Maria, but I'd learned more about her in that short, muddled conversation than in all the others I'd had. I could easily imagine how it had been, ten years or more ago: little Maria Mills from Bow, born under a stage, stealing and lying to keep her drunken mother and herself alive.

Rosie was right. Maria, the one-time thief, had been the intruder in the mortuary.

The parts pulled together as a length of thread pulls together a cadaver's skin.

My keys hadn't dropped accidentally from my pocket on that last evening with her. Maria had taken them while I was asleep, and then waited to wake me up until I was late, too hurried to notice their absence.

She knew I was Mr Hurst's assistant and she knew Jack Flowers couldn't read, so he must've copied down the letters to tell one from another. She went to the mortuary after Flossie, Mr Hurst and I had left for the day, and tried my keys in the lock. But they hadn't worked. They were just the keys to the pharmacy doors, front and back. She must have tried and tried, and when the door wouldn't open she'd panicked and … no, she knew exactly what to do. She went around to the window at the back of the building and forced it open, just like when she was a little girl, all the while listening out for a dreaded footstep behind her. And once it was open, she slipped inside, and found the combination of letters for Bentinck's padlock written on a bottle of ale.

My poor girl. How desperate she must have been. How she must have yearned to escape from the life she was leading.

'It was Maria who stole their money,' I said to Rosie, as we walked back towards the city. 'And they killed her for it.'

She grimaced. 'Bentinck, after all. What an evil man he was.'

'I still don't think so. He didn't get his money back, and he wouldn't have killed her unless he had. It must be someone else, someone who knew what she'd done. And my guess is, whoever it was still has that money.'

'That major you mentioned before, what was his name?'

'Thorpe. But he's the son of a judge and an army officer. Would he commit a murder for two hundred pounds?'

She didn't reply. We were almost at Aldgate before she spoke again. 'Leo, we need to talk about that night. What happened to you.'

My fingers prickled. Why did she keep raising that subject?

'There's nothing to say.'

'Yes, there is. Leo ...'

'I'm going to take the underground railway home.'

'Leo!' She grabbed my sleeve and made me face her. 'All right, you don't want my thanks, but you have to listen. This is important. When things happen, other things follow. It's nature. One thing leads to another thing, and even if the first thing is wicked, terrible, the worst thing in the world, still, the other thing can follow. Do you understand?'

'I don't know what you're talking about.'

'You don't want to think about it. It's unbearable, I know, but it's a fact of life. I've been through it. Jack was …' She broke off and cast around, looking for somewhere to sit, a bench or a step, but there was nowhere. In the end she clenched her fists and stood in front of me. 'I got little Sam, and I love him. He's as precious as the other two, more so if anything, for being my youngest. But it wasn't love that made him. Do you understand?'

I did understand. I thought she might be the bravest person I'd ever known. Part of me wanted to take her hand in mine and tell her so, but another part couldn't bear to. If I started talking about that night, I would never stop. I would be lost. There would be no line between where it ended and I began, and I would flood away into it.

Two gentlemen were coming the other way, dressed up for Sunday, coats brushed and shoes shined. I stood aside for them to pass.

'I have to get my train.'

'Damn it, Leo!'

I heard her call my name again as I walked away, but she didn't follow.

The train was blessed blankness, a barrage of sound that blocked out my thoughts.

There was no more chloral at the pharmacy, but still I was wracked by fearful dreams. Mrs Heppelthwaite, as kind a woman as you could hope to meet, was singing high C while I warbled in response, and my father, red-faced, his veins standing out like wormcasts on his forehead, was yelling himself hoarse at me for not even trying. My sister and brother are both in the choir, why can't I be more like them?

Because I'm not like them, I keep saying. I'm not. Don't you understand? The rules that apply to everyone else don't apply to me.

My body was an error, as if I'd received the wrong parcel in the post. I had hidden my form, faked its sex, lowered my voice and starved my hips, and in all that time I never considered that it might betray me at the first opportunity, and assert beyond doubt it was female. I never imagined there might be one rule that did apply to me.

In the morning, I left the house.

26

WHEN MADAME MOREAU OPENED her door I was shocked at how she looked. She seemed to have aged a decade. Her face was pale and haggard, and her hair had been hacked short, pinned close to her scalp, pulling back the skin on her forehead. She wasn't wearing a bonnet to cover it up – she was defiant.

'Oh, it's you,' she said, stepping aside for me to enter.

I didn't want to go in, but I had to. If I didn't do it now, I feared I never would.

The mess the police had left behind had been tidied up, and the things they'd broken were swept into a pile in the corner. In the back room there were two other people sitting at the table: a squat woman with a square chin and a skinny girl, perhaps fifteen years old, but it was hard to tell. She might've been younger. She had almost transparent skin and an absent expression, and was draping herself over her larger companion.

Madame Moreau nodded in their direction. 'This here's Berthe, my neighbour, and a customer. Not herself, I mean, she runs the doxie place up the road. And this is Myrtle, one of her girls. Do you want some tea? And a slice of cake? Berthe made it, bless her heart.' Her neighbour seemed none too thrilled to be sharing it with me, but

Madame Moreau didn't seem to care. 'No need to worry, Berthe, he's a lady.'

'What?' she said.

'I know he don't look it, but underneath them clothes he's a lady. Truly.'

'Sweet Jesus on a carthorse.'

'No need for that language.'

'Please be more discreet,' I said sharply.

Madame Moreau touched her shorn hair, brushing it back behind her ear as if it was still as it had been. 'We're all friends here.'

Myrtle appeared to be half-asleep, but Berthe was examining me as if I was a specimen in a museum. 'How do you piss? Do you have a quim?'

'Stop it, Berthe,' said Madame Moreau. 'Leave us alone now, will you?'

'I wouldn't dream of staying. You should be ashamed allowing *that* into your house.'

'You owe me sixpence,' said Madame Moreau, indicating Myrtle, but Berthe just muttered something about her tab and left through the back door, the girl following her out like a dinghy caught up in the wake of a ship.

Madame Moreau smiled thinly. 'My apologies. I've known her a long time, but she can be a bit harsh. She just came round for Myrtle.'

'Why is the girl like that? Did you give her something?'

'Not me. Berthe gives her girls opium to keep them in line. Docile, you might say.'

'She's certainly docile.'

Madame Moreau folded her arms. 'Myrtle works six days a week, and they use every part of her, you know, every part. It's all I can do to keep her alive, the way they treat her, and she's just a little thing, not built for it. One day she won't come back, and it'll almost be a blessing. Such a tiny life, wouldn't you say? But I'm forgetting my manners. Have a slice of cake. Berthe brought it round to celebrate my coming home. I suppose I've you to thank for that, have I?'

'No, it was the police detective who let you go.'

'Oh. Have they found out who did for poor Maria then?'

'No. I know some of it, so ...'

But she wasn't listening. She seemed entirely detached, neatly cutting the cake and pottering around with the strainer and kettle. I felt like a child, sitting on the kitchen stool while Bridget prepared afternoon tea for my parents and gossiped with the gardener on his break, using winks and whispers to keep the really good stuff from my juvenile ears. It was years before I realised that her description of our neighbour's maid as *a very friendly girl* wasn't meant as a compliment.

'I must look a sight,' said Madame Moreau, and touched her hair again.

'Not at all.'

I excused myself to visit the privy, and when I returned she had spun her chair around to face the piano and was playing a surprisingly rambunctious tune. I wasn't familiar with it, but found my fingers drumming along, and my foot tapping, and before long I was lost in the music. One of the keys was faulty and made a thunk every time she pressed it, but she didn't seem to notice as she never skipped it, and I was certain she heard the tune perfectly in her head. Watching her sway from side to side, her hands rippling up and down the keyboard, I almost forgot why I was there.

I wasn't hungry in the slightest. In fact, I was feeling sick, and the embers of the fire were making me drowsy. But out of politeness I bit into the cake, and it was delicious, crumbly and rich with butter and strawberry jam, at least the equal of the ones in the tea shop I'd visited with Constance. *Ingrid's*, was it? I could scarcely remember being there. It seemed like a hundred years ago. *Celine's?*

When she'd finished playing, I clapped and she gave an apologetic little bow. 'I'm not very good. I only know what I know, a few ditties from over the years. But I've been playing more these last couple of days. Roselin hates it.' She pointed to the finch, which had survived her absence, flapping and hopping in its cage. 'But it helps me to not think about things.' Her face took on an odd expression, or perhaps, more accurately, no expression at all. 'What did you do to yourself, Mr Androgyne? Been in a fight, have you?'

'Stanhope,' I corrected her, with little optimism. 'And it's just a bruise. It doesn't matter.'

'Why not?' She looked at me suspiciously.

'Because ...' My voice wouldn't stay constant. I took a breath. 'Did you know James Bentinck is dead?'

'I heard. They say old Hugo Cooper did it, out of his mind. Nancy Gainsford's taken charge.' She took a sip of tea and studied me over the rim. 'Is that why you're here?'

I shook my head. The words wouldn't come. I couldn't say them, even to her, whose job it was to help women. Because I wasn't a woman. Only physically.

She spoke gently. 'Why *are* you here, Mr Androgyne?'

'I was with Bentinck before he died. At his house.' I looked down and realised I was twisting my cap in my hands. The stitching was straining and coming apart.

'Oh. I see.' She put down her cup. 'Did he find out what you was? Not one to take no for an answer, was he? I've seen it a hundred times. A thousand. Half the servant girls in London have been through here after some young master decided he wanted his sheets turned down. Or it's the land lord or her uncle or her mother's latest hankering.' She took my hand in hers. 'When did this happen? A few days ago, was it?'

I nodded slowly.

'Too soon, I'm afraid. What's done is done. You'll have to wait if you want to be certain.'

I could only mouth the word: 'Please.'

She sighed deeply, and beckoned me to follow her. 'All right, we can try. No guarantees, though.'

In the front room, the sun was streaming through the net curtains, casting a trapezium of light across the table. I climbed on to it and she guided my head back with her hand. It was disorientating, being so close to her, inhaling the sourness of her patchouli oil and sweat. I tried to keep my eyes fixed on the cracks in the ceiling plaster, but kept noticing the implements hanging on the rack and arrayed on the shelves: wooden spoons, hinged forceps, a collection of hooks and a mechanical contraption whose brutal purpose was all too obvious.

'It won't take a minute,' she said, putting a cushion under my head.

'Will you give me something for the pain?'

'A douche don't hurt, mostly. A bit of a twinge is all it'll be, honestly.'

'But you do have something?'

'If I'm using the hook, I give the ladies a little chloroform or some chloral, yes, to ease their worries. All over before they know it's happened.' She turned and frowned at me, while tying her apron strings behind her back. 'But you ain't going to need it.'

'But if I want some chloral? I've never done this before.'

'It ain't nice stuff. Look what it did to Hugo Cooper.'

'Just a little?'

She blinked several times. 'Well, all right then, if you must.'

I was so tired. To sink beneath the black water, even here, would give me peace for a short while. I was sure of it.

She drew the curtains and fiddled with a spoon, eventually pouring a miserly drop into my mouth as if I was two years old. It tasted different; still foul, but with more of a taint of liquorice than the chloral from the pharmacy. I lay back and closed my eyes.

She stood over me as if I was a feast she was about to set upon. I felt her undo my trousers and pull them down, pausing to inspect the rolled cloth I'd re-sewn into them: the weight, the bulge, the fakery. She took down my drawers as well, below my knees. I covered myself with my hands.

'No need,' she said. 'It'll be over in no time.'

She collected a thin wooden stick, a horseshoe-shaped metal implement and a little hand pump with a tin reservoir of liquid that smelled like lamp oil. She settled down to her work. It should have been a violation, and yet she was so matter-of-fact. And anyway, it was just the parts. Like Maria's remains being put into the ground, it was just the parts.

I felt a peculiar pressure between my legs and a sudden pain that made me clutch the sides of the table. Then I heard her squeezing the little hand pump, and felt a cool wetness around my thighs. She fetched a cloth and wiped me thoroughly. When she straightened up, the cloth was pink.

'All done. You can get dressed now.' She had brought her teacup through and was sipping from it, watching me. 'You owe me three shillings by the way.'

'Myrtle was only sixpence.'

'And I didn't even get that, did I?' She shrugged. 'You can afford it. And think yourself lucky, it would've been four with the chloral.'

'What do you mean?' I realised I was feeling unstable, foggy, but no more. A dark suspicion grew. 'What did you give me?'

'Absinthe. It ain't nice either, but it'll settle your nerves and at least you won't get so attached. Chloral's all right if you need it, but it ain't soothing to the soul. Makes you see all sorts of devilish things.'

I had an impulse to leap up and demand what she had promised, or tear the place apart to find it for myself. She was weakened and wouldn't be able to stop me. But I remembered her raising a hand to that thug, Micky, and the feeling passed.

'Damn you.'

'I'm already damned, aren't I, and so are you. We're just the little people. We try to get by, but the world was made for them, not us. The good book tells us we'll inherit it afterwards, but what use will it be after they've finished with it, eh? Answer me that.'

She wandered into the back room, and I was left to do up my braces and follow her. I supposed the woman had to be paid, but I was desperate to leave.

She was sitting very still at one end of the table, and I realised again how old she'd become, old and weary, with her glorious black and white hair cut short. And for what? She was guilty of nothing but curing women of the conditions men had forced upon them, and I knew exactly how that felt.

'How long since you last bled?' she asked, with a plainness I found startling. I hadn't discussed the monthly curse with anyone since Jane first gleefully explained it to me while I sat on my bed, hugging my knees, certain she must be lying and terrified she wasn't.

I found it hard to say the words. 'Two weeks ago, or thereabouts.'

Madame Moreau pushed a paper bag towards me. 'Widow Welch's pills then, just in case. You should take 'em in a few days. No extra charge.'

I gave her three shiny shillings. She put them in the pocket of her apron and poured two more cups of tea without asking.

'You loved her, didn't you?'

I nodded, feeling light-headed and hot, as if my skin was too tight on my bones. 'I don't know if she loved me back, or even if she had the ability any more, doing what she did.'

'Well, I can't say as I know if she loved *you*, and maybe she didn't know neither, but as for the question, *can* they love, well of course they can. Just because a barmaid serves you a glass of ale don't mean she's never thirsty herself. We all need love, don't we? Even girls like Maria. Course, it changes them, what they do. I see 'em when they're young and fresh with all sorts of ideas, but it don't last long. A couple of gentlemen with hasty fists or hands around their necks, and there ain't a lot of sweetness left. But they can still love all right. Often as not they love each other. I thought you of all people would understand that, being a lady underneath'

'I'm a man.'

She smiled knowingly. 'What man would come here and talk about *love*, eh? No man I know of. These girls are with men all the time and are treated like filth. After that, I daresay you need someone soft to warm the bed on a cold night, someone who knows what your life is all about, who's doing the same as you. Someone who won't lay you out for weeping, or for not weeping enough.'

I hadn't considered it before. I'd only thought about *men* as my rivals for her affection, but perhaps it wasn't a man I should have been looking for; not James Bentinck or Jack Flowers or Jacob Kleiner or Augustus bloody Thorpe. Perhaps I should have been looking for a *woman*.

I remembered Maria touching me there. I wouldn't let her put her fingers inside, but still it felt nice, what she did, and she seemed to like it too.

'Thank you,' I said. 'I have to go.'

'All right, but you should watch out. That feeling I get sometimes when something bad's about to happen, an ache in my bones? I'm getting it now, about you. It ain't good. You should go home and stay there.'

As I left her, I heard the piano start up again. Cheerful tunes seemed to be all she knew.

27

BY THE TIME I reached the brothel on Half Moon Street, the cold wind and a brief hailstorm had made me feel oddly better, as though I was finally waking up after a long fever.

I peeked in through the front window at the parlour where Mrs Brafton normally disposed herself to greet her customers. There were workmen inside. Two of them were dismantling the table, and another was removing the mirror from over the mantelpiece.

I tapped on the window and one of them looked up and called to someone. I retreated down the steps, just in case, but there was no need. It was little Audrey who opened the door. 'Oh, it's you, Mr Stanhope. We're closed, I'm afraid. But I suppose I could accommodate you, as you're a regular.' She raised her eyebrows fetchingly, but nothing could have been further from my mind.

'No, thank you.'

'Suit yourself.'

I waited to one side while a labourer passed with a paintbrush in his hand and another manoeuvred a metal bedstead around the corner of the stairs. I could hear the sound of wood being sawed in the kitchen.

'What's going on?'

'You must've heard. Poor Mr Bentinck was murdered in his own house. They say it was Hugo, but I don't believe it. He worshipped Mr Bentinck. Esther thinks he was attacked by a bear, but that can't be true, can it?'

'It seems unlikely.'

'Poor Mrs Brafton went white as a sheet when she heard, and started screaming the place down. There was a proper carry-on. All the gentlemen were running about with no trousers on. Never seen anything like it. What do you want, anyway?'

'It's about Maria.'

Audrey sighed, and a sour look crossed her face. 'Everything always is, isn't it?' She shook herself and forced a smile. 'Sorry, I know you was fond of her. It's just, everyone always made such a fuss, even when she was alive.'

I was shocked. I had thought they were friends.

'Things came easier for her, is that what you mean?'

'Golden girl, wasn't she?' She examined the palms of her hands. 'It ain't easy, doing what I do. Too gentle and they complain, too rough and they go home bleeding. Still, I suppose it's what got me here, into these fine clothes. I must sound ungrateful.'

'You've survived, even if Maria hasn't.'

I had meant it kindly, but she threw me a piercing glance. 'I'm only saying what all the girls thought. Maria was a bit high and mighty is the truth, always chattering away to Mr Bentinck and that.'

'Was she especially close to any of the other girls?'

'Like I say, she kept herself to herself.'

A fellow carrying a pot of paint in each hand picked his way down the stairs, which were covered in items from the upstairs rooms: towels, jugs and coat-hangers, even an auburn wig. The pictures were hanging crookedly; somehow that was the most distressing thing.

'Where's Mrs Brafton?'

'Weeping mostly. She was soft on Mr Bentinck, and she took the news badly. Miss Gainsford's in charge now, and she says we can make more chink if we have more rooms and use them more often. She says men will pay for half an hour or even a quarter. Bloody toshers and mudlarks, just like the old days. These lads are turning the parlour into another bedroom and the same in the back and two more upstairs. It'll be first come, first served, no more appointments.'

She indicated a roll-top bureau in the hallway, and I saw that the appointment book had been slung on some papers, along with a scattering of pencils, pens, an inkpot and a jet necklace I'd seen Mrs Brafton wear a couple of times. Next to it there was a bucket containing oddments from the parlour: candlesticks, ornaments and the willow-pattern bowl, broken in two.

'Would you be kind enough to fetch her for me?'

She shook her head. 'I could try, but she won't come out. Even with all this going on, she hasn't done a thing.' She glanced at me, a sly little look, and I thought: you're hoping Miss Gainsford will put you in charge of the place. Ambitious. 'She moved into Maria's old room. You can go up if you want.'

I stood shivering outside Maria's door. Last time I'd been there, I'd hesitated, relishing that brief delay before she threw her arms around my neck and kissed me. It would never happen again.

I knocked, rat-a-tat-tat. There was no answer, so I pushed it open and went inside.

All of Maria's possessions were gone. The bed was unmade, with blankets scattered on the floor, and Mrs Brafton was sitting at the dressing table, which had two bottles on it, not perfume but gin. One was empty and one half-full.

She turned to look at me with a face like carved stone.

'What do *you* want?' she asked, perfectly clearly. There was no sign that she was drunk.

'Are you all right, Mrs Brafton?'

'Of course. It's all just business. That's what he always said, just business.' She turned away from me, but continued talking. 'He was a great man. He believed in something, a better world through commerce. And now he's gone.'

'I want to talk about Maria. It'll only take a minute.'

Downstairs there were noises of men banging heavy furniture into the walls. I could imagine the plaster being gouged out by the corners of her precious sideboard, but Mrs Brafton didn't flinch. She poured a small shot of gin into a tiny glass, like something you'd find in a doll's house.

'I don't normally drink,' she said. 'But it's what people do, isn't it? Drown their sorrows. I don't even like the taste, and it's not working anyway. Do you drink? Does it help you forget you're a woman?'

'I don't need to forget anything. And yes, I like a whisky occasionally.'

'I don't have any.'

338

'That's quite all right, thank you.'

'What was your name, before, anyway? Elsie? Mildred? No, you're an educated person, you have breeding. It would be Anne or Victoria, something like that. Victoria Stanhope sounds about right. How old are you?'

'Why is that important?'

She downed the tiny glass and winced with disgust. 'I just can't comprehend why something like you is still alive, and a man like James Bentinck is dead.'

Her words didn't matter. Once you've taken off your skin and laid it aside, there's very little anyone can do to prick you. Still, I saw no reason not to tell her the truth.

'He was a vile man, a coward, who cared nothing for you or anyone. He deserved to die. The world is a better place without him.'

'Audrey!' Mrs Brafton shouted, and I heard footsteps coming up the stairs. Her head appeared around the door.

'What is it?' she asked, with minimal respect.

'Go and fetch the police right now. Tell them we've got a criminal in the house.'

'Police? What, here?'

'Do as I say. And tell them she's a grotesque, a woman pretending to be a man, who dresses like a man. And tell them she calls herself Leo Stanhope. Tell them everything! Go! What are you waiting for?'

Audrey scuttled away down the stairs. I thought of chasing after her, but what would I do if I caught her? I didn't fancy my chances. She'd had years of practice at beating men with sticks.

Mrs Brafton turned back to the dressing table, as though nothing had happened, and poured herself another thimbleful of gin. 'It was Nancy Gainsford, of course. She killed him.'

'The police say Hugo did it.'

'Nonsense, he would never hurt James. He's been with him for years. And even if it is true, it's because she put him up to it. Turned James's own man against him. She always resented his success and hated how close we were. I could see it. The only way to usurp him was to kill him, and that's what she's done.'

'She's taken over the business.'

'All the time I've put into this place, and James hadn't even been dead a day before she swanned in, gloating and preening, with that ghastly little docker of hers, and told me to pack up my things and be out by tomorrow.'

Mrs Brafton was a strong woman, but I feared she might be about to break down. And there were things I needed to know.

'Was Maria especially close to any of the girls?'

'Don't be jealous, Victoria, my dear. It'll drive you mad.'

'I'm trying to work out who murdered her. Was she close to any of the girls? Or a customer? Are any of them female?'

Mrs Brafton downed another gin and licked her lips. No wince this time, she was getting used to it. 'Nancy Gainsford,' she said. 'She was besotted with Maria. They had a … you know. The usual silliness.'

'Nancy Gainsford? You're saying *Miss Gainsford* was in love with Maria?'

It seemed impossible, but I remembered how Miss Gainsford had confided in me at the funeral, talking of their great friendship and asking if Maria had ever mentioned her.

Mrs Brafton poured herself another glass of gin, with no sign of a tremble in her hand. 'I used to send Maria over to James's house, but it wasn't really for him, it was Nancy she was with. The woman was forever giving her dresses and jewellery, and spending hours brushing her hair as if they were sisters. It was pathetic. Ludicrous.'

'Why would I believe you? You obviously hate her.'

'I don't care what you believe. She was infatuated with Maria and she killed James. But she's nothing without him, nothing.'

I went to the window where Maria used to stand and blow me kisses. Those kisses used to last me for days, seeping into my dreams. But perhaps she'd been thinking of someone else when she blew them.

'Mrs Brafton,' I said, despising myself for such civility. 'Please would you tell me where she lives.'

'Marylebone, but she's not there.'

'Oh? Where is she?'

'They have some sort of boat. Importing and exporting. It's down at Puddle Dock in Blackfriars. That's where she'll be.'

I ran. Straight down the stairs two at a time, almost tripping over at the bottom. Blessed, freezing air was blowing in from the yard. The back door was open for the workmen.

Audrey appeared and I almost shouted at her. 'Did you fetch the police?'

'No, I never,' she replied, eyes wide. 'I don't do what Mrs Brafton says no more.'

I dashed out through the back door and across the wet grass where Hugo's beehives stood like little castles, and through the gate.

I never saw him step out. I felt a hand on my shoulder spinning me round and I was staring into the weasel's face. He stank of the river.

'The lady's waiting for you,' he said.

There was a hard pain in my side as if I'd been punched. I put my hand there and it was wet, and I thought: *someone's thrown something at me, and it's spilled over my shirt.* I looked at the ground, but there was nothing there, just red dots. I opened up my palm, and it was red too.

The weasel pulled back his fist.

28

I WOKE UP WITH a jolt, sensing I was afloat. Above my head, a tarp was shading me from the sun, and I was sitting on the deck, propped against a metal rail.

My right side was agony, spreading around my waist and chest, sharp and dull at the same time. I was shivering, or perhaps that was the vibration of the engine, which was rumbling and belching out clouds of smoke that drifted back along the boat. I coughed and almost cried out, but at least the pain meant he'd missed my lungs.

My hands were tied together in front of me with coarse rope that bit into my wrists, and my jacket had been removed. I managed to hitch up my shirt. The wound was shallow, the size of a baby's mouth, drooling blood. How much blood could a man lose before dying? Three pints? More?

A seagull was standing on the flagpole, and it flew off as someone came into view. And there she was: Nancy Gainsford, as calm as you like, dressed in a homely brown frock with a shawl over her shoulders. Even so, she caught the eye. She couldn't help it.

She was examining something, bending over and testing the edges with her fingers. I realised what she was looking at.

It was a coffin.

There was another one beside me under the tarp, and two more at the stern, one laid on top of the other. They were made of a light wood, cheap and thin. I prodded it with my foot. There was something heavy inside and it wouldn't move, so I tried pushing harder, and the pain speared through me.

A man came up from below and I recognised the weasel even from the back. He started fiddling with the engine in a proprietorial manner, adjusting something with a spanner to make it bark and splutter. He seemed satisfied, and gave a thumbs-up, and then pointed in my direction.

Nancy Gainsford looked up. She was quite at home afloat, her poise perfect as she strolled towards me. Her throat was slender and pale. Windpipes are surprisingly narrow, barely wider than a corn stalk. It doesn't take much pressure to close them up. I could've taken it into the crook of my arm and eased the life out of her as easily as squeezing pips from a lemon, if only the weasel wasn't so close. And if only I could stand up.

'Finally, Mr Stanhope,' she called out. 'I was beginning to wonder if that idiot would ever get hold of you. I'd almost given up hope. Yet here you are. I admit I'm impressed.'

She was quite different from how she'd seemed before, much more offhand and confident.

'Who's in the coffins? More of your kidnap victims?' I could hear the quiver in my voice.

'We prefer to say *purchases*. Two sisters, very pretty, very young, and quite untouched. The daughters of a railway clerk in Surrey who couldn't pay his debts. They're mine now, and will fetch a healthy profit in Brussels. We dosed them with chloral, so they won't wake up for hours. The coffins help us get through customs. No one wants to open a coffin, do they?'

'What an evil way to make money.'

'You're a romantic, Mr Stanhope. All this for a girl who didn't care a jot about you. Not a jot. Not for any of you.'

'But Maria was in love with *you*, I suppose?'

She rolled her eyes. 'Men don't understand such things. You think it's so simple, that your manly organ is the only way to a woman's heart.'

'I've found it helps.'

I tried to push myself up, but my legs didn't have the strength, and I slid back down on to my behind on the deck. She was right there, six feet away. I couldn't believe that her wickedness didn't show somehow. It ought to seep out of the pores of her skin, burning through the hull and hissing into the water beneath. It was a travesty that she was so self-contained while I was leaking all over the deck.

The weasel was sitting on the engine hatch smoking. She beckoned to him and then clicked her fingers.

He jumped up. 'We're ready to go, ma'am, rudder and engine. We could steer through a hurricane.'

'Let's hope we don't have to,' she muttered, and then louder, to him: 'Go to that pie shop on Ludgate Hill and bring the Flowers woman down here. Be as quick as possible, but be discreet this time, for God's sake.' She turned back to me. 'On the way to Tilbury, you and Mrs Flowers will have a terrible accident. You'll drown together, lovers in a final embrace. It'll be *ravishing*. You'll make the front page of the *Pall Mall Gazette*. Women will be sobbing all over London.'

I could feel myself getting drowsy, and yet my heart was beating faster, pounding in my chest. My eyes were throbbing with it. There was something on the deck, a dark patch I thought I should recognise, staining the wooden planks. An image came to me: a trapezium of light shining across Madame Moreau's table, and the grim stigma that marked it.

'Perhaps I should thank you for killing James, by the way. I was fond of him, but it was time. He'd become distracted and self-indulgent, satisfying his own whims.'

I nodded towards the coffins. 'Isn't satisfying men's whims your business?'

'Yes, exactly; *business*. My business now.'

'Why did you tell the police that Hugo killed Bentinck? You know it isn't true.'

'It had to be *someone*, Mr Stanhope. The police were asking questions, and I could hardly tell them the truth, could I? They'd want to know why you were up there and what we'd planned to do with you. Hugo was the obvious choice. Dumb as an ox, with chloral in his pocket and a history of savagery, babbling about you and Mrs Flowers.'

'He was loyal to the two of you.'

'Yes, like I said, dumb as an ox. And don't feel too sorry for him. He did kill Jack Flowers after all.'

'Because Bentinck told him to. Aren't you worried he'll inform the police about this business of yours?'

She shrugged. 'He couldn't tell them anything without making himself just as guilty. And they think he's a chloral addict anyway.'

'So you'll just carry on kidnapping children.'

'Who are you to judge me? You know nothing of a life like mine. Do you think I've always been as you see me now?'

'Everyone used to be someone else.'

I thought she would strike me, but she brought herself under control, clenching her fingers together. 'While you were sitting in a schoolroom, I was being made a whore. Nine years old. Does that shock you? Gainsford isn't my real surname, I have no idea what that is. I was named by the Irish whores after the street I used to beg on.'

Irish whores. I put two and two together. 'Mrs O'Leary. The woman you put in charge of the brothel before Mrs Brafton. The one who drank herself to death.'

'Her name was Maggie, not that James would've remembered it. She used to give me food when I was hungry and even shared her mattress. She taught me to read and write, after a fashion, and count. Most of all, to count. I counted the money and learned how to make more of it. I did all the work and James got rich. You've seen one of his houses, and he has another in Berkshire, and what do I have? A basement in Marylebone. This is my chance now. James and Elizabeth never understood the common man. They treated the place as if they were king and queen. Not any more. It's a whorehouse, not a gentlemen's club. Men go for one thing and one thing only, and they'd bed a sheep if it was wearing a bonnet.'

She raised her chin, revealing a white scar along her jawline. Her eyes were alight, and I had a glimpse of her when she was someone else, before she became Nancy Gainsford and learned to speak like a lady.

'You loved Maria, didn't you?' I said. 'It must have hurt you to see her with all those men.'

She laughed, but it sounded empty. 'Don't be ridiculous. She fooled you all. She was a little girl for one and a scolding mother for the next, and a panting harlot for the one after. She could turn it on and off like *that*.' She snapped her fingers. 'But she always came back to me.'

Another one, I thought. Another buffoon. We blunder about in the worlds we make for ourselves. Who can ever truly understand what's going on in someone else's head?

'But you knew she was with child.'

'Oh, Mr Stanhope, you can't think it was yours?' She laughed again, throwing her head back, exposing her neck even more. 'Is that why all this? My goodness, you men are so arrogant, believing your potency can overcome all others, and whatever happens to a woman must somehow be to do with you. There isn't a better chance than one in fifty. One in a hundred!'

Less than that, I thought, if you only knew. 'I think Maria was sick of her life. She didn't want to be what she was any longer. Bentinck introduced her to Major Thorpe and she thought her chance had come. She even got herself pregnant and convinced him it was his. She thought she would marry him and become an officer's wife.'

'He's such a fool,' said Miss Gainsford, almost spitting the last word. *Because only a drivelling lunatic would fall in love with a whore.*

I put my bound hands up to my eyes, but my fingers were numb. I felt as if someone else was comforting me. 'Didn't you care that she was hoping to be married?'

'You've been to the brothel often enough. Does it seem to you that marriage has made much difference to anything? But do please continue with your story.'

'When the marriage was stopped, Maria despaired. She thought her chance of escape had gone. But she had a stroke of luck. Jack Flowers told her that he had discovered how to open Bentinck's strongbox, although he didn't tell her what the combination of letters was. It was *Mercy*, Bentinck's wife's name.'

'Is that right?' she said. 'How sentimental. And I suppose Jack thought Maria would run away with him? She must've seemed so much sweeter than his shrew of a wife. Another fool. I sometimes wonder how you men function from day to day.'

'Maria broke into the mortuary and found the combination for herself, and stole the money from Bentinck's strongbox so she could start a new life. And you killed her for it. You bludgeoned her to death.'

Rain was falling again, and that dark stain on the deck was made even darker, and shinier. But it was just the parts. Not the real Maria, with her hair tickling my face as she slept, her chest rising and falling with each breath. It was just the parts. Just her blood.

I didn't know what to feel. After all this time, surely, I should feel *something*: some anger, some hatred, some new onslaught of grief. I sought inside myself for a boiling rage, setting my eyes on the stain on the deck, fixing it in my mind. *Perhaps I should crawl to that spot and die upon it. Wouldn't that be romantic?*

But the truth was that the stain probably didn't mark the place. It might have nothing to do with Maria. This was a working boat and things got spilled all the time, and I would be dying upon a dropped pot of coffee.

Miss Gainsford was gazing out over the river, scanning along the opposite bank, her eyes resting longest on the little lanes heading south, away from the city. The wind was getting up and the chop had grown stronger, so she had to hold on to the rail.

When she spoke again it was in a small voice. 'You're wrong. What you believe doesn't matter, but ...' I could see her welling up. She took a slow breath. 'She didn't die on the river. She died back at the house.'

My own vision was blurring too. I tried to wipe my eyes, but my hand was greasy with blood.

'You mean Bentinck's house?'

'Yes. After she'd opened the strongbox, she must've heard me come in. It was morning, and James was away. I think ... I think she heard me, and ran upstairs. I had work to do, and was bustling around, and she must've been hiding up there for some time. Hours, I think.'

'So you murdered her at the house and dragged her body down to the river?'

She shook her head. 'No, you don't understand. I was in the house, and suddenly I heard her. I would know her voice anywhere. She shouted something but I couldn't make out what it was. As if she was in pain. At first I thought she must be outside, and then I realised she was upstairs. I ran into the hall just in time to see her fall from the top of the stairs. But there was no one else there, no one else in the house. She just fell. She was there and I looked up, and she just ... fell.'

I couldn't understand what she was saying. It didn't make any sense. 'You can't think that she would … no, she would never hurt herself deliberately.'

'She hit her head on the pommel of the bannister, and by the time I got to her she was quite dead. I didn't know what to do.' Miss Gainsford clenched her hands together so hard I could hear her joints crack, even over the noise of the wind. 'She was wearing a satchel with the money inside, and I took it. It was my due, but I'd pay every penny back a hundredfold to have her here now, with me. Hugo and I cleaned everything up, and he brought her body down to the river to drift off on the tide. But I couldn't bear it, the thought of it. She deserved a proper funeral. So I told someone and they fetched the police. I watched them take her away. You know the rest.'

In my mind, a vision flashed like a lamp guttering as the gas runs thin: Maria's eyes, cold and still in the mortuary. *Conjunctiva inflamed*, Mr Hurst had said, but he never thought to find out why. He was in too much of a hurry.

And then, quite suddenly, I knew everything. I knew exactly what had happened. Not suicide; Maria was far too full of life for that. Something else. It was a weight that almost crushed me.

You don't have children, do you? You don't know how it is.

I could hear distant voices shouting.

Miss Gainsford looked past me and narrowed her eyes. She went to the back and loosened the last rope, working quickly, and the boat eased and settled on the water. When she returned, she had a bottle in her hand. I could smell it and almost taste it. She clamped my nose between her thumb and forefinger and shoved my head back. She was remarkably strong.

'Enough talking,' she whispered. 'Sleep tight.'

She upended the bottle, and the black water filled my mouth. I felt no fear, clung to no hope, offered up no prayer. There would be no suffering. My last thought before I closed my eyes was: I will never wake up from this sleep.

The voices were getting louder.

'Leo! Leo! *Leo!*'

29

I ALMOST SWALLOWED IT. I was so close, savouring the bitterness in the back of my throat, my body yearning. Swallowing would be so simple. One moment and it would be done.

But I could still hear Rosie.

'Leo!' she called again.

I made as if to swallow and then swooned and sank down. Miss Gainsford had moved to the back of the boat and was standing with the tiller in her hand, her eyes fixed on the mouth of the dock where it met the river. The sound of the engine grew louder, and clouds of smoke wafted over us as the boat bobbed in anticipation of forward motion.

I sat up and spat out the chloral. My shirt was wet and I was feeling dizzy. I dug my fingers into the cut in my side to wake myself up, but there was no greater sharpness to the pain. My wound had become abstract, a dislocated agony.

On the quayside, people were running. The weasel was at the front. He was coming straight down the lane that led to the dock, so I had a good view of his red face and billowing coat. He kept looking back over his shoulder. Rosie was giving chase, lifting her skirts with one hand and holding her shoes in the other, her hair streaming behind her. But it wasn't Rosie he was afraid of. Pallett had rounded the corner and was pounding down the hill in great strides, his helmet flying off and bumping along the ground.

The weasel sprinted full pelt towards us. I could see him waving, beckoning for Miss Gainsford to come back for him, but she was gunning the engine, nosing the boat towards open water. It was slow, hindered by its own inertia, but the gap was widening. As he reached the edge of the quay he leapt, but not far enough. Our eyes met and his mouth gaped, and then he disappeared out of sight into the river.

I struggled to my feet, holding on to the rail just to stay upright. With my wrists tied together it was hard to get any balance, and the boat was rocking more than I had expected.

If I didn't do something now I would be dead for certain, and the railway clerk's daughters would be sold into slavery in Belgium. I had to act, but my arms felt like wet string. All the strength I had was going into shaking.

Am I brave? Is this what heroism is? If so, I didn't feel it. If anything, I was afraid of everything. It wasn't bravery that drove me forward, it was pure desperation.

Miss Gainsford was looking back at the shore. I launched myself forward and attempted to run at her, but misjudged the movement of the boat and fell hard against a cleat. She turned and saw me, and might have shouted something. I tried to stand but the boat was spinning, and all I could do was shuffle towards her on my knees.

She picked up a spanner, a heavy, blackened thing, and took a step towards me, holding it high. I had one last chance. One last breath.

The deck veered sideways and I ducked under the spanner, crashing into her and the tiller both. She weighed almost nothing. For one second we hung together, arms flailing in the air, and then we pitched over the side and into the water.

———

The shock of the cold squeezing my skin, and then a hand, pushing me down. I shoved her away and managed to get to the surface and steal a single, precious breath, furiously pushing the water downwards with my bound hands. She grabbed for my head again and I didn't know whether she was trying to drown me or be rescued by me.

We were still in the shadow of the boat, and the engine noise was deafening. With no one steering, it was circling in the narrow dock. I tried to kick away, into its wake, but I couldn't get a breath, and the next thing I knew was a huge blow on the back of my head.

I went straight down, under the hull, into the blackness and the throbbing, churning roar. Something solid struck against me, an unyielding force, and I clutched at it wildly as I was bumped and spun into deeper water.

And then there was almost silence, a plentiful warmth, a numb relief. I was too tired to swim, so I let myself go. The current was gentle as I sank down into it. I could feel it brushing through my hair, and then grasp me, a strong hand at my collar, hauling me upwards. I broke the surface and gasped, breathing in water. It was foul and salty, making me retch.

And then a woman's voice: 'Stop bloody struggling or I'll punch you on the nose.'

I opened my eyes, and there was Rosie, in the water with me, tugging me towards the quay where it sloped up to the street. The boat had swung away towards the shore, and there was a flash of colour, something clinging to it: Nancy Gainsford.

My eyes locked with Rosie's. We were still twenty or more yards from the shore, on the edge of the current. I could feel it pulling at us. She couldn't hold on to me and stay above water, and she slipped under. I reached down as far as I could but she came up anyway, tossing her head, stretching for my hand and clasping it, turning on to her back. Her teeth were gritted, but her strokes were getting weaker and the quay was getting further away. I knew that if we passed out of the mouth of the dock and into the main flow of the Thames, we would be lost.

I could see from her face that she knew it too. Still, she gripped my hand in hers, and kicked.

There was a metal ladder down to the water at the very corner of the dock, the last possible thing to grab before we were swept out into the river. It was close, ten feet. Ripley was there, shouting, and Pallett too, jacketless, leaning down. She kicked again, stretching out a hand for the ladder, and I held my breath. Four feet, but it was slipping past. Five feet now. Six.

She tugged on my hand, but I snatched it away.

Our eyes met.

'Leo! No!'

I shoved her feet forwards, pushing her with all my strength towards the ladder, and myself backwards into the stream. The cloth of her skirt drifted through my fingers as I was swept away.

I couldn't paddle any more. I heard her shout my name one more time as my mouth filled with water.

I woke up choking.

The ground was mercifully solid.

I was lying on my side on the quay while someone pounded on my back, sending great waves of agony from my wound through my whole body.

'Enough! Please.'

Rosie ceased, and started adjusting a bandage wrapped tightly around me. For a second I panicked that I'd been exposed, but then realised it was my cilice, slipped down. She was studiously careful, tying it under my shirt and covering my shoulders with a blanket.

I couldn't speak, but it was all right. She was doing enough for both of us.

'You're a bloody idiot,' she was saying. 'What's the point of my trying to rescue you if you won't be rescued? A fine fool I'd be looking if this handsome constable hadn't dived in after you. You'd have washed up God knows where.'

Pallett went red at the compliment. He was sitting against the wall of the dock with his foot propped idly on the weasel's back.

I heard a laugh from Ripley. He was in his shirtsleeves, already smoking, holding Nancy Gainsford by one arm. She was bedraggled and bony like a dead starling, her blouse clinging to her skin.

'How did you know I'd be here?' I asked.

He tossed his still-glowing cigarette on to the ground. He was intolerable. Was it really so hard just to step on it like everyone else?

'Mrs Flowers makes the best pies in London,' he said, nodding to Rosie, who shrugged as if that much was obvious. 'So we went back again for lunch and a glass of beer. Just as we're leaving, I spot this nasty piece of work go into the shop.' He pointed at the weasel. 'So we keep an eye.'

'He told me they were going to murder us both,' said Rosie.

'I haven't done anything wrong,' grunted the weasel. 'You can't prove anything.'

Pallett pressed his foot down a little harder.

'Next thing we know,' continued Ripley, 'he's round the counter with a knife in his hand, trying to accost Mrs Flowers. She smacks him in the chops with a cudgel, and very fine work it was too. And he legs it down here. So we give chase.' He stretched his back and winced. 'Constable Pallett was a little quicker, given my current infirmity.'

Pallett raised his eyebrows.

'Good thing you did,' said Rosie. 'For them too.'

Two young girls were lying half under Ripley's jacket, still sleeping soundly, dressed in calico frocks the colour of cheese rind. Neither looked older than eleven. They seemed unharmed by their spell in the coffins.

'Well, anyway, that's that,' said Rosie. 'It's all over now.'

'Almost over,' I said.

———

Rosie and I were sitting on our own, sharing the blanket in a patch of sunshine by the wharf gate, watching a barge manoeuvre Bentinck's boat back alongside. The railway clerk's daughters had woken up, confused and hungry, and had been taken away to the hospital, and Pallett and Ripley had left with the prisoners in a police carriage.

'What is it?' asked Rosie. 'What's wrong? We need to get you to the infirmary.'

'I need to know the truth, Rosie. About Jack.'

'What truth?'

'You said he used to hit you. And your children.'

She looked into my eyes, and then lowered her own. 'Jack was a bastard. To start with it was just me, when he was drunk or had lost at cards, but it got worse. He was an unhappy man, always around people richer than himself. He resented it. He started hitting me more often and then little Robbie and Lillian too. Back of his hand to start with, but soon it was clenched fists and then his belt. Once, he picked up a knife and I had to stand between him and them while he raged and raged, yelling all sorts. I thought he'd kill us all.'

'You'd had enough.'

'I put up with it for years. It wasn't so bad when it was just me, but the children … when he hit Sam, my youngest.' She started to sob. 'He's two years old. After that, I knew he would never stop until we were dead.'

The barge was churning up the water, trying to nudge the bigger boat towards the quay. Briefly, the noise was too loud to talk over, but it died down and we could hear the seagulls again, crying along the shoreline.

'So you decided to kill him.'

She wiped her eyes. 'How did you know?'

'When I first spoke to you, in the hospital, you were so interested in what had happened to his satchel. And again when … with Bentinck. There must've been something in it that concerned you.'

She nodded, calm again. She seemed almost relieved to be telling me. 'We keep arsenic in the shop for the rats. I mixed it in with some sugared plums so he wouldn't be able to tell. I made a beautiful plum pie. I put it in his lunch and waved him off for the day.'

'Enough arsenic to kill him?'

'Oh yes. No half measures. I thought, if I'm arrested and hanged, at least the children will be all right. Alice and Albert will look after them. When I met you and that young police-man at the hospital after Jack was dead, I thought for sure you'd found out. But then you said what had happened, and I've never felt so grateful in all my life. He was drowned before he had the chance to eat it. He never even touched that pie.'

No, but Maria did.

Mr Hurst had been in too much of a hurry to examine her properly, and the cause of death was obvious. So he ignored the inflaming of her conjunctiva – the skin on her eyes – which was a symptom of arsenic poisoning. A simple test of the stomach contents would have confirmed it, using granulated zinc and sulphuric acid. But why bother? After all, she was just a whore.

It was so appallingly simple. Rosie had made a poisoned pie for Jack and she'd put it in his satchel. When he went to steal from Bentinck, he brought the satchel to put the money in, with his lunch still inside. And when they caught him, they put the whole thing back in the strong-box: satchel and money and plum pie.

It was all there for Maria to find. She stole the money and hid upstairs from Miss Gainsford, and while she was there, she ate the pie. Agonised and delirious from the arsenic, she fell down the stairs and hit her head on the pommel of the bannister.

All this time I'd wanted to know what had happened, and now I did, I'd give anything not to know again.

I closed my eyes.

In the glorious heatwave of last summer, we had lain on her bed with the sun blazing in through the window. Maria's face was alive with the pure joy of it, and her fingers were sticky with juice as she made as if to pop a plum into my mouth but at the last moment ate it herself, and fell back giggling, and apologising through her giggles, and then doing the same thing again, giggling and apologising even more, until neither of us could eat or speak or breathe for laughing. I could see her hair and her hands and the little ramp of her nose, and her stain and all the parts of her, all one, all moving. She was always moving, my Maria.

She adored plums more than anything.

30

THE RAIN HAD STOPPED, and it was just about warm
enough for Alfie to have put a table out on the pavement
with a couple of chairs. I was resting my eyes beneath the
rim of a new bowler hat and trying to ignore the stiffness
in my side. Later, I was planning to go to chess club, and
wanted to be on form so I could give vent to my anger
with Jacob by slaughtering all his pieces.

'You're snoring.'

Rosie's green eyes were looking down at me. She helped
herself to the other seat and arranged her skirts. Since that
day at the dock I'd seen her only once, when she'd visited
me briefly, but Alfie had been there at the time and we
hadn't been able to talk.

'You're feeling better then,' she said, a statement not a
question. 'Just as well it was a shallow cut. Fuss about nothing.'

'It's healing. I'm just tired.'

She nodded and angled her face up to the sunshine. She
had a pretty profile.

We were interrupted by a young woman exiting the
pharmacy, the doorbell clanging. Alfie followed her out in
his dentist's apron.

'I can't believe it,' he said. 'We're completely booked up.
All these ladies wanting their teeth attended to, I've not got

enough hours in the day.' He glanced back into the shop to where Constance was perched on her stool, and lowered his voice. 'I'm not complaining, and I'm grateful to you, Leo, as I hope you can tell. But I know I've become the whores' dentist.'

Audrey had been so pleased. She was reopening the brothel under her own management, once again aiming for an elegant style, after Elizabeth Brafton had chosen to retire. The new proprietress had asked what she could do to repay me, cocking her hip in that way she had, and seemed genuinely shocked when I told her what I wanted. She'd spread the word to other girls from all over London, and now Alfie had been fixing teeth for a fortnight solid, and was selling them face creams, powders and all sorts of other ladies' things besides, and hoping Constance wouldn't notice the looks their neighbours were giving them.

In truth, she was too busy to notice anything, as the proud owner of a new tabby kitten with sharp teeth and a pleasing way of chasing cotton reels around the floor. She'd named it Colly after the Coleoptera beetles that cured … whatever it was. Something that wasn't ulcers.

Alfie was so grateful he'd offered me room and board at no charge, at least for now, while business was good and I was recovering. But I would soon be able to pay him rent again, with any luck. I'd received a reply to one of my letters that morning from a Mr Sweeting, the clerk to the bursar at St Thomas's Hospital, who would be delighted to interview me for the post of junior porter. Greatorex had even agreed to write me a reference, though he'd insisted on coming round to check my injury for himself, just to be sure. Alfie and I had persuaded him to share a glass of ale with us before he traipsed back to work.

Alfie went back inside to tend to his next customer, and Rosie shifted uncomfortably in her seat.

'You're ... you're welcome to come over to the shop and talk to me when you're properly recovered, you know. I'd like some company once in a while. You'll have to pay for the pie, mind.'

She looked away when I didn't immediately reply, and I could see her neck blushing pink. It would have been lovely to say yes, of course, and spend the afternoon with her at her pie shop, chatting about this and that while she kneaded pastry and sliced apples. But I could not. It would be a betrayal.

'That's very kind, but ... I'm not certain I'll be able to come and see you. I'm so tired. I'm sorry.'

She stood, seemingly on the verge of saying something but then changing her mind about what it would be. 'All right then, suit yourself. I can't sit around here wasting time. Pies don't cook themselves, you know.'

'Rosie ... maybe one day I will visit you. When I'm ready. Just not yet.'

She nodded, and gave me a tense little smile as she left. I watched her bonnet bobbing among the other pedestrians until she was lost from sight at the corner. I had decided not to tell her the truth: that it was her who had killed Maria. What would be gained by her knowing? Better she lived happily in ignorance than had to bear that burden.

Ripley had arrested Nancy Gainsford for Maria's murder. It seemed fitting somehow; she and Hugo were both guilty, just not of the crimes they would hang for. It was imperfect justice, but then, as Ripley himself had once said, it was an imperfect world.

I closed my eyes again, enjoying the warmth of the sun on my face.

The previous day I had taken a cab to the cemetery to visit Maria's grave. The church bells had been tolling, growing quieter as I headed out of the city, and then the next set had grown louder, until I passed those also, and then the next ones had taken over, and then the next, and the next, and so I was accompanied all the way by music.

I sat beside her for an hour, not saying anything, just listening to the birds in the trees and the sound of her voice, and the thump, thump, thump of her heels against the frame of the bed.

Acknowledgements

I owe so many people for so many things, and I apologise with all my heart to anyone who feels they should have been acknowledged here, but isn't. I promise to include you in the next one, subject to my exhaustive terms and conditions.

My immense and eternal thanks to Carrie Plitt, the best agent ever, for her support, encouragement and expert guidance, and for her belief in Leo and his story.

My huge gratitude to Alison Hennessey, chief of the ravens at Bloomsbury, for making it into what it is. Alison also acted as Leo's therapist, such that I had the question 'and how does he feel about that?' stuck on my wall to save time. All the team at Raven Books are simply amazing, and my massive thanks also go to Marigold Atkey, Sarah-Jane Forder, Callum Kenny and Francesca Sturiale for their professionalism, commitment and general brilliance. You couldn't find a group of people more enthusiastic about books.

Thank you to Greg Heinemann for designing the fabulous cover.

I'm immensely grateful to Dr Jane Hamlin at the Beaumont Society for her excellent feedback, insight and patience. The Beaumont Society does important work supporting the transgender community and advising on transgender issues. You can find them at www.beaumontsociety.org.uk.

Big thanks to Cath Harries for taking a photo that both looks human and is of me; a remarkable achievement.

Also Jo Unwin, who gave me such generous support and advice.

It seems redundant, even clichéd, to thanks one's mother, but she always said I should write a novel one day, and then I did, so thanks Mum. Also for, you know, creating me and all that.

My two sons, Seth and Caleb, were full of splendid ideas. Unfortunately, the zombie versus alien sub-plot didn't make the final draft this time, but I promise to consider the option of Leo becoming an android for the next one.

And finally, Michelle. No words can satisfactorily acknowledge her contribution to this novel or anything else in my life, so a squeeze of the hand and a brief nod will have to suffice, and then we'll get on with the laundry.

A Note on the Type

The text of this book is set in Bembo, which was first used in 1495 by the Venetian printer Aldus Manutius for Cardinal Bembo's *De Aetna*. The original types were cut for Manutius by Francesco Griffo. Bembo was one of the types used by Claude Garamond (1480–1561) as a model for his Romain de l'Université, and so it was a forerunner of what became the standard European type for the following two centuries. Its modern form follows the original types and was designed for Monotype in 1929.

COMING SOON...

THE ANARCHISTS' CLUB

It's been a year since Leo Stanhope lost the woman he loved, and came closing to losing his own life. Now more than ever, he is determined to keep his head down and stay safe, without risking any of those he holds dear.

But Leo's hopes are shattered when the police unexpectedly arrive at his lodgings: a woman has been found murdered at a club for anarchists, and Leo's address is in her purse. Not only that, but a member of the same club knows Leo's birth identity and will share it with the authorities if Leo does not provide him with an alibi.

If Leo is unmasked, he will be thrown into an asylum, but if he lies, will he be protecting a murderer?

B L O O M S B U R Y